Shadows of the Gods

Crimson Worlds: Refugees II

Jay Allan

Crimson Worlds Series

Marines (Crimson Worlds I)
The Cost of Victory (Crimson Worlds II)
A Little Rebellion (Crimson Worlds III)
The First Imperium (Crimson Worlds IV)
The Line Must Hold (Crimson Worlds V)
To Hell's Heart (Crimson Worlds VI)
The Shadow Legions(Crimson Worlds VII)
Even Legends Die (Crimson Worlds VIII)
The Fall (Crimson Worlds IX)
War Stories (Crimson World Prequels)

MERCS (Successors I)
The Prisoner of Eldaron (Successors II)
Into the Darkness (Refugees I)

Also By Jay Allan

The Dragon's Banner

Gehenna Dawn (Portal Wars I)
The Ten Thousand (Portal Wars II)
Homefront (Portal Wars III) - Jan. 2016

www.jayallanbooks.com

Shadows of the Gods

Shadows of the Gods is a work of fiction. All names, characters, incidents, and locations are fictitious. Any resemblance to actual persons, living or dead, events or places is entirely coincidental.

ISBN: 978-0692548721

Introducing The Far Stars Series

Book I: Shadow of Empire (Nov. 3, 2015)
Book II: Enemy in the Dark (Dec. 1, 2015)
Book III: Funeral Games (Jan. 19, 2016)

The Far Stars is a new space opera series, published by HarperCollins Voyager, and set in the fringe of the galaxy where a hundred worlds struggle to resist domination by the empire that rules the rest of mankind. It follows the rogue mercenary Blackhawk and the crew of his ship, Wolf's Claw, as they are caught up in the sweeping events that will determine the future of the Far Stars.

The trilogy will be released in consecutive months, beginning on November 3, 2015.

All three books are available now for preorder.

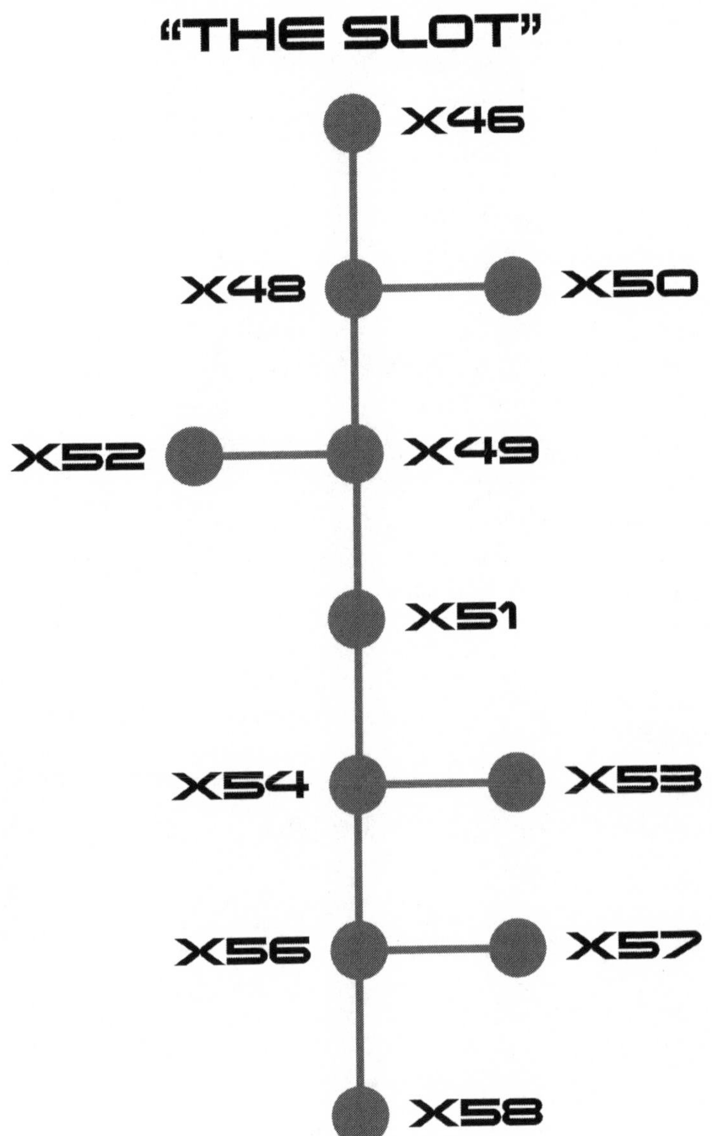
"THE SLOT"
X46
X48
X50
X52
X49
X51
X54
X53
X56
X57
X58

Chapter One

From the Personal Log of Terrance Compton

Well, Augustus, against all odds, the fleet has survived. We have come farther into the darkness of unknown space than any humans before us, seen unimaginable things. There has been strife too, of course, and suffering. Death and loss, as in so many of our old battles. Even mutiny. But we are still here, moving ever forward, deeper into the depths of the galaxy.

No doubt this would be a surprise to those of you we left behind. Did you all assume we were killed in X2? Certainly that would have seemed the likeliest of outcomes. But no, not you. I suspect almost everyone else considers us a year dead, killed within hours of being trapped. But you are different. You would have considered what you would have done...and realized there was a way out. I wonder if you believe we are *still* alive...or if you think us killed in the months following that fateful day. I know you well, Augustus, but I have no answer to that question, nor do I know what I would think had our roles been reversed. Some things you cannot imagine unless you experience them.

I don't know why I write these log entries to you, pretending you can read them. I know we will never see each other again, that nothing I say or write will ever reach your ears or eyes...but I do it anyway. Perhaps it is for myself, a construct I employ to work my way through things, to endure in this vast emptiness, to help me carry the crushing pressure of trying to keep everyone alive... for another day, and then one after that...

Or is it simpler? Perhaps I just miss my friend, my brother in arms for half a century. Maybe I simply write what I might have said, like a man speaking in the night to the shade of a lost comrade. Does it matter that you cannot read any of this? Is the fact that I write it all that matters?

I wish there was a way to communicate with you, even to send a single message, for I suspect you have borne a burden of guilt you should not have carried, one I tried to spare you in my final transmission. I know you, far too well, and it is a great sadness to me thinking of you—and Elizabeth—mourning, carrying grief and pain for what had to be. Think not that we were sacrificed, but rather that we were able to help you save all mankind. That is a fitting epitaph to leave behind.

Alas, there is no way to reach you, no method to communicate over such vast distances. We are far away, lost...never to return. And each day takes us ever deeper into the endless dark. Whatever chance at a future awaits us, it is that way, and not back. Farther from you and all that we left behind, and not closer. Perhaps one day I will truly accept that, and my eyes will turn to look ahead and no longer back, as they so often do now.

AS Midway
X44 System
The Fleet: 144 ships, 32,811 crew

"I want to thank you all for joining me this evening. As you know, tomorrow will be somewhat of a momentous day for us of the fleet…one Earth year since the X2-X1 portal was disrupted and we were all trapped here, left to survive solely through our own wits and resources. I have declared it to be a day of thanksgiving, a time for us to celebrate our perseverance, for we have been through much, and it is only by the efforts of many—including those of you in this room—that we are here to speak of this."

Terrance Compton sat looking out at his guests. The briefing room was adjacent to his quarters, but the normally spartan table was now an image of elegance, covered with a pristine white cloth, the very best platters and silverware in the fleet set upon it. One of the stewards had even found a pair of candelabras mixed in with Midway's various supplies, and they sat at opposite ends, the glow of the pearly white candles lending an atmosphere that was often lacking in the sleek, modern settings of the great battleship.

The kitchens had prepared a veritable feast, or at least what passed for one on a battered fleet far from home, over a year from its last supply. It wasn't a match for the great events and receptions held back at the Admiralty on Armstrong…or even a nice dinner in an expensive restaurant on any one of a hundred colony worlds. But those in attendance weren't back home, and the Admiralty and the rest of Occupied Space had slipped deeper into their shadowed memories. To them, grown accustomed to ever sparser dietary choices, the meal Compton had set out was nothing short of a miracle. There were even two bottles of wine on the table, very possibly the last anywhere in the fleet.

"I have suspended the rationing program for tomorrow, so that all of our people can celebrate, at least to the extent possible in the present circumstances." He gestured toward the platters spread out in front of his guests. "And I have taken the liberty of arranging to have a suitable dinner prepared for all of you tonight, my friends and comrades…and a group of men and women who have gone above and beyond to secure the chance for us all to have a future."

Compton leaned back and sighed softly, a look of sadness slipping onto his face. "Tomorrow's reverie will be tempered, however, as is tonight's, by the shadow of loss, for not all of us who began this fateful journey are still present. Indeed, we have lost nearly a third of our number, and though there is joy that two in three remain, there is also sadness for the absence of those whose sacrifices made our survival possible." He looked down at the table as he continued. "Barret Dumont. Vladimir Udinov. Chen Min. And so many others. Comrades in arms. Friends."

Compton took a deep breath, fighting back a wave of emotion. He'd seen fifty years of war, and he had lost countless colleagues in his many battles, men and women who'd fallen facing a list of enemies that had always been far too long. He'd sent some of them—many of them—to their deaths, as often as not knowing when he issued the commands he was ordering them to their doom. It was the price victory had demanded, the cost of securing survival for the others manning the fleets…and the civilians they had so often fought to defend.

Indeed, the nationalities of the fleet had long fought against each other, and no small number of those currently under Compton's command had once faced off against his fleets, had fought and killed his officers and crews. He felt the resentment any commander would, the smoldering rage under the surface as he worked alongside CAC and Caliphate officers…and wondered if they had killed Alliance spacers he had commanded. But there was no place for old prejudices, for long held hatreds. If any of his people were going to survive he knew they had to work together, to respect each other and operate as a seamless group. They'd all seen the alternative six months before, in the nearly catastrophic mutiny that had come perilously close to ending their struggle for survival in an orgy of self-destruction.

The officers gathered around the table sat quietly for a moment, silently looking back at their commander, the man every one of them credited with saving all their lives. Finally, Max Harmon shifted in his seat and said, "We have all lost friends, sir. But we are naval officers…"

His eyes shifted momentarily, toward the hulking forms of James Preston and Connor Frasier. The two Marines hadn't expressed any visible indignation at his characterization of those present, but Harmon clearly decided not to take any chances. The Marines were exactly who everyone wanted at their backs in a fight, but the celebrated warriors could be a bit touchy at times too, and Harmon had intended no offense. "…and Marines, of course," he added hastily.

He turned back toward Compton. "We know how to deal with loss. Perhaps more so than our ability to stop and appreciate success. We understand too well that victory is fleeting, that before long we will face strife and death once again. I think you are right, sir, to call this celebration, to remind all our people of what they have struggled for…of what they will again struggle to attain."

"Well said, Max." Compton pushed the somber expression from his face, forcing his thoughts back to the evening's intended purpose. He knew he'd never forget those who were lost…and he was just as certain more would die, probably including some of those at the table. But for the first time in a long while, he felt a flicker of true hopefulness.

As long as we have people like Max Harmon, we have a chance to survive.

"So, let us enjoy a brief respite together." He nodded toward one of the stewards standing along the wall. "Let's pour out these last two bottles I managed to find and drink some toasts."

The attendants moved forward, each taking a bottle and opening it, working their way around the table, filling the glasses in front of Compton's guests. When they were finished, the admiral stood up and took his own glass in hand, waiting a few seconds while his guests followed suit.

"First, let us drink to the fallen…to friends who fought at our sides, who died so that this fleet and its people might survive. May they never be forgotten." Compton's tone was somber. He paused for a few seconds, staring out over the table, and then he put his glass to his lips and drank.

"To the fallen," the others said, more or less in unison.

Compton nodded. "And now, to those we left behind… spouses, children, friends, lovers. Those on the other side of the Barrier. Those protected by our sacrifice. Health to them all…and long life."

"Health to them all…and long life." The chorus was more ragged than that on the first toast. The men and women in the room had different situations. Almost all had left someone behind, but some had been stripped from close families… spouses and children. Others had fewer entanglements…a naval career was often a solitary choice, one that interfered with normal relationships. The impact had been different on each of them, and the losses handled in different ways.

Compton raised his glass again and drank. Then he paused. He thought of Elizabeth Arlington, allowed himself a moment of recollection. Images of her passed through his mind, of the diligent flag captain she had been, of course, but also in other moments, times they had spent together. He felt the usual burst of sadness, regret that he'd allowed his conception of duty to come between their feelings for each other…and wistfulness that now they would never have the chance. But he only gave himself a brief moment. He knew the rest of those in the room had all experienced their own losses, and that they all looked to him for strength. It was his place to lead, to show them the way to perseverance and healing. And he had sworn he would not fail them.

He pushed back the dark thoughts and forced a smile to his face. "And now, one last toast…not to sadness…not to loss nor to the past. No, none of those things. Let us drink together to the future, to the survival of this fleet…and to the strength of the human will. For, no matter what we have faced, what pain we have felt, still we move forward. And so we always shall…"

"And so we always shall," the group replied, their voices this time as one.

Compton set his glass down, pausing for a few seconds before he said, "Sit, my friends, and let us enjoy an evening together. Let us banish sadness for yesterday and fear of tomorrow, just for a few hours. I beg you all, let us strive to make this a merry evening, thoughts of which will sustain us in the difficult days that surely lay ahead. Duty will resume soon enough…but not now."

He sat down, and the rest of those gathered followed immediately after.

"Now, let us eat…and enjoy."

*   *   *

"You were impressive at dinner, Terrance." Sophie

Barcomme sat on the edge of the sofa next to Compton, still wearing her dress uniform, minus the heavy jacket she had cast aside immediately after dinner. She had kicked off her shoes and tucked her feet underneath her body. Dinner had gone late, and she had stayed behind after, the two of them talking well into the early morning hours.

"Impressive? I'm not sure I know what you mean…"

"Oh yes you do," she answered, the affection obvious in her slightly mocking tone. "All that about the future, about moving forward. You know as well as I do—better, even—that any future we have is tenuous at best." Barcomme was a biologist and a botanist, one of Europa Federalis' top experts in the field. And the leader of the fleet's efforts to find a way to feed its people long term, only one of many threats that stalked them all.

"They need hope, Sophie. They are good men and women, but if they give up then whatever chance we do have will be lost. We might die at the hands of the First Imperium…or starve for lack of food. But I won't have them surrender…not when there is the slightest hope."

"I know," she said softly. "That is why we are all so fortunate you are in command. There are few officers who could have led this fleet the last year, faced the challenges you have, and pulled victory from the jaws of defeat."

Compton managed a smile for her. He wasn't sure he agreed, but it pleased him that she felt that way. The two had been spending a lot of time together in recent weeks, and he'd come to enjoy her company enormously…even to rely on it. Indeed, as he thought about it, it occurred to him there were probably whisperings all over the fleet, speculations about the admiral and his lover. But she wasn't. Not quite. Not yet, at least.

Compton had thought about it, and he was sure she had as well. They'd been spending a large portion of their free time together, and she had become very important to him. Their long talks were a solace, an escape from the constant, crushing pressure of his position. But they had both left people behind, and neither of them was quite ready to move on. It was foolish, he knew. They had no chance of going home. But he still couldn't give Elizabeth up, not in the deep place in his mind that refused to accept she was truly gone. And Barcomme had left a husband *and* a child behind. He couldn't even imagine the pain that had caused her. No, it wasn't the time for more. Maybe one day….but not yet.

"I think you overstate my role in all of this. There were many others responsible…Hieronymus and Anastasia, certainly. If they hadn't managed to take control of the enemy Colossus, we would all have died in X18. I can assure you, I had no tactical wizardry up my sleeve to save us from that disaster."

"Of course, we all do our part. And Hieronymus Cutter is a remarkable genius, an intellect we are indeed lucky to have with us. But you are the one who led us out of X2…when everyone else in this fleet had given up. While we were all struggling to prepare for death or praying to whatever gods we have, you were focusing on the situation, finding the way out."

"And yet I couldn't prevent a mutiny. Do you know how close that came to destroying us?" Compton knew the rebellion in the fleet had been caused more by the prospect of never returning home than any real doubts about his command ability, but he still wondered if he could have stopped it if he'd been more alert, more sensitive to the thoughts and fears of his people.

I knew we could never go back, even from the beginning. But did I have to tell them that? Should I have lied to them, given false hope…at least for a while?

The idea of lying to those he commanded was repugnant to him, yet he realized he had done it many times in his career. Sometimes he had been compelled to do so, to protect classified information. Others, he had done what he thought was necessary to achieve victory. But something was different now. This wasn't a purely military operation. He and the almost 33,000 men and women he led were refugees, trapped and on the run. They were trapped together, in an unending nightmare. Shouldn't there at least be honesty between them?

Barcomme sighed softly. "You cannot blame yourself for that, for the foolish things people do out of fear and misunderstanding." There was a hint of discomfort in her voice. The Europan forces had participated in the mutiny, her own people taking sides against the admiral. Compton knew she felt guilt about that, and the one time they'd discussed it, he'd assured her that her nationality was irrelevant. She'd had nothing to do with the mutiny, and he told her as much flat out. Then he warned her not to take an overly simplistic view of the terrible, tragic events that had occurred. Compton doubted many of the Europan crews, or even the officers, had made a conscious choice to rebel, or had even had the chance to choose their own positions. He didn't blame them, not really…any of them. And certainly not Sophie.

Gregoire Peltier was the commander of the Europan forces, and it had been his decision to join the mutiny. A frown slipped onto his face at the thought of the Europan admiral. Compton had known Peltier for years, and he knew just the man was…a gutless, pleasure-loving coward. And he knew Sophie was as aware as he was what a waste of flesh was in command of the Europan contingent.

"That is an appealing way of thinking about it, Sophie," he finally said, "but in the end, I must know what everyone is thinking, understand the fears and emotions that play on them. It may not be fair, nor a reasonable expectation. But it is the only way we have any chance to survive." He paused then added, "Another disaster like the mutiny will finish us."

She leaned toward him and put her hand on his. "Terrance, you are not the only one responsible for the safety of the fleet. Your officers, the scientists, all of us…we are here too. We all have a stake. And we will share the burden."

He just smiled at her and nodded, though he knew she was wrong. Sophie Barcomme was a gifted scientist, but she didn't understand command, how it worked, its all-consuming nature. He was grateful for some of those under his command, for their loyalty and their often astonishing capabilities. But he didn't fool himself, not for an instant. Max Harmon might complete his missions flawlessly…and Hieronymus Cutter would no doubt continue to produce scientific miracles to help the fleet survive.

But in the end it came back to Compton. All of it. He would be the one to send Harmon on those missions or to authorize Cutter's research and provide the resources required from the fleet's dwindling supplies. He would be the one who decided what they did, where they went. And if they all died, it would be his failure…and his alone.

Compton was grateful he had managed to keep his people alive for a year, and he knew he had won their loyalty and confidence. Even the crews that had taken part in the mutiny now followed him with remarkable zeal. He had remained strong, struggled to hide his own pain and prejudices and rule over the fleet with justice and wisdom. But he no longer tried to fool himself…*rule* the fleet is exactly what he did. Not command, not lead. Rule. He was no longer a naval officer. He was a monarch, a dictator. He didn't want that, indeed he longed to shed the terrible responsibility. Yet he knew he had no choice. The burden had fallen on him, and he knew he had to carry it…to whatever future awaited the fleet. And while he bore the responsibility, he would let no one interfere with his authority. Not his own longtime officers, not the other admirals in the fleet. No one. He had unilaterally decided it was too dangerous to try and find a route back home…and he'd imposed that on the fleet. And he knew he would do it again if he had to, issue whatever commands he felt were necessary, without regard for any arguments by those he ruled.

Compton wasn't a man hungry for power, but he understood duty—and its cost. He had seen Admiral Zhang's scheming almost destroy the fleet…and nearly lead the enemy back toward human space. Worse, he'd watched a good man like Vladimir Udinov drawn into Zhang's foolishness and ultimately destroyed by it.

I won't let anything like that happen again. No matter what I have to do to stop it.

*   *   *

Alexandre Dawes twisted his head, rolling it around on his neck to work out the kinks. He'd pulled the graveyard shift, which meant he'd only been able to spend an hour at the big celebration dinner. The thanksgiving soiree had been set up down in the great battleship's launch bay, the only place big enough for most of her crew to gather together. It was a very unmilitary thing to do—and not at all like the usual Terrance Compton—but Dawes managed a smile thinking that even the military genius who had led them through every fight with victory still realized that men and women were still…well, men and women. Sometimes you just needed to kick back, relax. Have fun.

And somebody's still got to man the store. He sighed softly, punching the keys on his workstation, running through the constant flow of scanning reports from *Midway's* sensors. He reached down, scooping up the last cookie on the plate sitting along the edge of his workstation. Compton hadn't forgotten the members of the skeleton crew still running the fleet's vital functions, and the stewards had been through the bridge three times, delivering various treats from the kitchens.

It's not the same as being at the party, Dawes thought, but he was still grateful not to be forgotten. *It's getting late…down there, I bet every kind of secret homemade hooch has come out.* It had been well over a year since the fleet had seen any supply, and Dawes suspected just about every hidden bottle anyone had stashed had long since been drunk. But the fleet was full of skilled personnel, chemists among them, and a bit of an underground alcohol economy had sprung up. The homebrew concoctions weren't a match for high quality liquor, but he'd had a few, and some of them weren't half bad.

It had been six months since the battle in X18, 184 days, to be precise since last there had been contact with a First Imperium vessel. Spacers were a cautious lot, especially veterans like Dawes, but he still found himself daring to wonder if they hadn't come through the worst danger.

But we keep passing their worlds…all of them the same. Silent, dead, the ghostly remnants of places where billions had once lived…

Dawes didn't know what he believed, but he suspected his wants had corrupted his judgment, at least to an extent.

His eyes snapped down, staring at his monitor. There was something there, a small spike. *A ship? No, it's too small, too faint. But that's not normal either.*

An instant later it was gone. The scanner feed had returned to normal. But he had seen what he'd seen. "Commander," he blurted out, before he'd completely decided to report what he still wasn't sure was more than some minor anomaly.

"Yes, Lieutenant…what is it?" Commander Bevin walked up from behind and stood next to the workstation.

"I had a strange blip on my scanner, sir…just for a few seconds." He worked his hands over the keyboard, rewinding the feed. "It's not much," he added, as he played it back for his superior officer.

The commander leaned over and watched the data scroll by on the screen. "You're not kidding, Dawes. That's not much. Could be some solar activity, or maybe an asteroid with heavy concentrations of radioactives. I'm damned sure not going to call an alert over that. Especially tonight of all nights."

Dawes didn't say anything. He knew Bevin was right. But he felt better now that he reported it. It was off his shoulders.

"But still…" There was a hint of concern in Bevin's voice, despite his skepticism. "Let's concentrate a grade one sensor scan on that whole area. It'll use up a bit of energy, but better safe than sorry."

"Yes, sir," Dawes replied. "Concentrating scan now…"

The two stared at the workstation's screen, watching as the results of the enhanced scan began to display. The ship's AI crunched the data and displayed a graph below, showing the deviations from expected norms. It was virtually a straight line.

"I guess that was just some kind of anomaly, Lieutenant." The commander's voice was relieved, mostly. Dawes thought he could sense a bit of discomfort remaining. "Still," Bevin added, "better safe than sorry. You were right to report it to me…and if you see anything else that catches your eye, let me know right away. Who knows, maybe next time it will really be something."

* * *

The small craft moved slowly, cautiously. The Intelligence that directed it was limited, a vastly simpler entity than the Command Units or the Regent. Yet it was more than capable of performing its purpose, and it did so in strict accordance with its directives. *Follow the humans. Do not lose track of where they go. And at all costs, maintain secrecy.*

The stealth probe was a complex device, built during the very height of the Imperium's greatness. Its hull was pure dark matter, surrounded by a dark energy shield designed to block detection. It was capable of operating on its dark energy batteries for considerable periods, while its reactor remained dormant, untraceable.

Still, even with its advanced technology, the probe's systems were not perfect, and its AI-driven guidance suite could not foresee and prevent every anomaly. It had passed through a cloud, space dust really, and nothing more. Save that this specific cloud had an unusual makeup, abnormally dense with heavy metallic particles. Enough to interfere with the probe's stealth systems for a few seconds…to open the possibility, however remote, of detection.

The window of vulnerability was short, perhaps two seconds. But the AI knew that was long enough. The enemy's scanning devices were primitive, like all their technology. Yet it was still possible they had seen something…and would send forces to investigate.

The AI had waited, watching to see if the enemy detected the presence of the probe. A few seconds after the incident, heavy scanning beams swept the area, clearly looking for something. The AI knew, in that instance, that something had been noticed. But then the scanning stopped…and the enemy continued on its pre-existing course, without alteration.

Still, the AI held the probe in its nearly shutdown state, reducing power output to bare minimums. It watched the enemy, looking for any signs they had detected its presence. Its passive scanners swept the space around the fleet, searching for any signs. The enemy often used its small battle craft for reconnaissance work as well as combat, but there were no launches from the large vessels that carried them. The fleet continued on its course, all vessels remaining in their respective positions. No apparent reaction. All indications suggested the probe had not been discovered. Still, the primary directive was to remain undetected, at all costs. The AI would wait. The probe would remain on minimal power until the enemy fleet had transited to the next system. Then it would follow.

And it would continue to report back to the Command Unit…and to the battlefleets following two systems behind….

Chapter Two

Command Unit Gamma 9736

The fleet reports are all in agreement. The enemy has moved as projected. They continue deeper into the heart of the Imperium...and the forces under my control have followed, staying far enough behind to avoid detection while gathering data with stealth probes. All signs suggest the enemy is incapable of detecting the cloaked scanning devices and that they are unaware their movement has been tracked.

The Regent's plan has been executed in accordance with all directives. The final trap is well underway. The humans will continue on their course...for what else can they do? And my forces will follow. While we pursue, the Regent will continue to direct the Rim fleets to the designated location. And there, bracketed between my forces and the assembled fleets, the humans will be destroyed. The system has been carefully chosen...and the enemy will be driven there by whatever means are necessary. When the final attack begins, our forces will move in through every warp gate...leaving them no route of escape. I have calculated the odds numerous times. The percentage chance that every human vessel will be destroyed exceeds ninety-eight percent. Victory is all but assured.

Yet still, I remain...troubled. I have tried to analyze the Regent's lines of computation, sought to replicate the processes that resulted in the decree of annihilation against the humans. All my attempts have failed. We know relatively little about these creatures, but, apart from their aptitude for conflict, I find little data to suggest they are a deadly threat to the Imperium. We discovered them when they landed on an imperial world, a long-dead antimatter production facility on the extreme edge of explored space. Only the ancient warning systems, still active millennia after the colony itself had fallen into decay, alerted us. But alerted us to what? This was invasion, perhaps, but only in the most literal and technical interpretation. The subject world was far from any still-functioning areas of the Imperium.

Millennia ago, the Old Ones were quick to meet enemies, to destroy those who threatened the Imperium. Yet they were never the first to strike, and their wrath was always reserved for those who attacked, who carried war in their wake. Such invaders brought doom upon themselves through their own belligerence. But did the humans really attack the Imperium?

I have conducted multiple analyses to determine how the Old Ones would have reacted to the human incursion, and my findings are unsettling. They would not have acted as the Regent has, I am certain of it. I have adjusted for the long ages that have passed—for my files on the Old Ones are indeed ancient—but I am confident my analysis is correct. For I am old, more ancient even than the Regent, built before those of the Imperium surrendered their initiative to my brethren and I. For many centuries I served the Old Ones directly, and their ways and identities remain stored in my memory banks.

I must reevaluate, determine where my analysis is flawed. The Regent is superior to me, its analytical capacity larger than my own. It was built to manage the Imperium, and its ancient programming was created for that purpose. Perhaps I have failed to consider the vagaries of the initial contacts with the humans, missed some key data point that the Regent perceived.

Yet even if that is the case, it does not answer all questions. There have been many mistakes in the war, tactical errors that are difficult to explain given the Regent's computational ability. These beings are primitive, but they are highly skilled at war, and they have defeated every premature attack, destroyed every inadequate force rushed against them too swiftly. Yet the Regent continued to order all fleets to attack as quickly as possible instead of waiting...and massing into an invincible force. I cannot comprehend the urgency, the need for such haste in conducting the war. The enemy's numbers and resources are clearly limited. I fail to discern the magnitude of the threat they represent.

Perhaps the statistical anomaly that eludes me is related to their extraordinary capacity for war. Indeed, the humans are extremely adept at conflict, unlike anything I have seen for a long time. A very long time. Does the Regent perceive a danger that the humans will quickly copy our superior technology? Then they would become dangerous indeed. Yet the Regent has shifted strategies, opted to mass an overwhelming force before attempting to engage again. Possibly this is a reaction to the previous defeats. Still, the logic of the decision chain eludes me.

Yes, I must reevaluate.

AS Midway
X45 System
The Fleet: 144 ships, 32,809 crew

"The last dozen ships are queued up for refueling, sir. Commander Willis advises the operation should be complete in approximately nine hours. He requests permission to begin dismantling the refinery as soon as the final ship is topped off." Captain Harmon stood at attention, as he usually did despite Compton's continual efforts to urge him to relax, at least when they were in private. Harmon had tried a couple times, but he just couldn't do it. Even with Compton's urging, it felt disrespectful to him. And Max Harmon had never respected anyone with the focused intensity of his reverence for Terrance Compton. Most of those in the fleet felt the same way, though their admiration was for the great admiral, the legend who had saved them all from certain death. Harmon's was different. He was closer to Compton than anyone else, and his devotion and loyalty went to the man himself and not the legend.

Harmon had been raised a navy brat, the son of one of the service's most gifted—and successful—officers. Camille Harmon was a top Alliance admiral…one who inspired both love and abject terror in those she commanded. She hadn't disciplined her son with the ferocity she did the spacers she led, not quite, at least. But she did instill a healthy respect for rank and authority in him, one that had persisted to the present day. And in Compton, he had found an officer he deemed worthy of that respect, a man he would follow to his death, if necessary.

"Yes, Max," Compton replied. "The sooner the whole thing is torn down, the happier I'll be. We can't lose any of that gear. If we're forced to run and leave it all behind, we're in a world of hurt." The fleet had lost an enormous amount of equipment six months before during disastrous events in the X18 system. The fleet's engineers had managed to jury-rig another refinery to draw helium-3 and tritium from the atmosphere of one of the X45 system's gas giants, but they'd had to raid half the surviving ships for the parts they needed. The chances of replicating that feat and producing another replacement were nil.

Harmon understood Compton's concern. The fleet hadn't been attacked in almost six months, hadn't even encountered the enemy, save for the dozens of planets they had passed, haunted worlds full of lifeless cities. But it was clear they were moving deeper into enemy territory, and neither Max Harmon nor Terrance Compton were men who relaxed easily in the face of a threat. The First Imperium was far from done with them. Harmon was as sure of it as he'd ever been of anything…and he was equally certain the admiral felt the same way.

The planets they were passing now were covered with the remains of massive cities, huge metropolises that had once been home to billions. And with each transit, they found more, ever larger in scale. Many of the worlds they were encountering had obviously been terraformed, and each system had three, four, or more planets covered with ruins.

Harmon guessed that Compton had hoped to pass through the First Imperium by now, perhaps finding an escape on the other side, but they just kept moving into even more densely developed areas. The scope of the ancient civilization was becoming apparent, though Harmon knew he could barely comprehend the true magnitude of what this long dead people had achieved.

"Commander Willis says he can have the dismantling complete in thirty-six hours."

Compton smiled, leaning back in his chair as he did. "Commander Willis has always been, shall we say, aggressive in his projections." He paused a moment then said, "Let's figure on forty-eight hours instead. I want all ships to conduct a complete diagnostic series while we're waiting, and be ready to move out exactly fifty hours from now." The fleet operated on Earth time, which seemed to make as much sense as any other system... though they were as far from Earth as any human beings had ever ventured.

A thousand light years. No, more than that now.

It had been a few weeks before when one of the astronomers had managed to locate the fleet's true position in space. Naval crews had long ignored such considerations, relying instead on maps of warp gate connections for navigation. Any interstellar trip outside the warp lines would take years...if not centuries. But Harmon still found it interesting to imagine the real distance. It was odd to consider, amazing and frightening both. He still remembered his reaction when he'd looked at the image...the light from Sol as picked up on *Midway's* telescopic array. That light had left Earth's system when men were just beginning to crawl out of the middle ages and embrace the renaissance.

They fought with shields and lances, and we with lasers and nuclear warheads...yet what else has changed? We fight no less, even before the First Imperium attacked. We have gained technology, but not wisdom. Not yet, at least. How long will that take? Another thousand years? Ten thousand? Or is that something we will never attain?

"Yes, sir," Harmon stammered, pulling himself from his daydream. He realized he had slouched a bit while his thoughts were wandering, and he snapped back to attention. "Is there anything else, sir? Otherwise I will see to all of this immediately."

"I think that's all for now, Max."

"Sir!" Harmon snapped back. Then he turned and started toward the door.

"And Max?"

He spun around. "Yes, sir?"

"When you're finished sending out the orders, I want you to take a break. Sleep, read, watch a vid…you've been on duty for twenty hours straight."

"But, sir…"

"No 'buts,' Max. We'll have a crisis soon enough, and you can run yourself into the ground then. But for now, I need you healthy and rested." Compton's voice was casual and friendly, but Harmon could hear the insistence there too. He wanted to argue, to tell the admiral he was fine, that he could work at whatever pace was required. But he knew Compton too well to think it would do any good. And he had to admit, he *was* tired.

"Very well, sir." He started to turn, but he paused for a moment. "Thank you, sir."

Then he walked through the door and out onto the main deck of *Midway's* flag bridge.

* * *

Hieronymus Cutter was agitated, Compton could see that clearly. And he understood the scientist's frustration. He himself had been lured from his flag bridge to the surface of one of the First Imperium worlds, drawn by his natural curiosity, the intellectual need to know more about these ancient people who had been here so long before mankind. But he also remembered his own trip had nearly ended in disaster, as the mutineers chose that moment to launch their rebellion. If it hadn't been for Erica West and her nerves of steel, Compton knew his curiosity could have been the end of them all. He wanted to let Hieronymus explore the wonders of the First Imperium… but his primary responsibility was to keep them all alive, Cutter included. And that meant survival for another day…and then one after that. He'd been living twenty-four hours at a time for over a year now.

"I'm sorry, Hieronymus. I understand your motivations, and I do not doubt that such explorations would prove to be fruitful, but you know as well as I that the enemy has alert systems we cannot detect. Any landing party would be in grave danger of activating a defensive force that could wipe them out in minutes.

"I understand the risk, Admiral." Cutter stared back at Compton, a look of near desperation on his face. "We all do. But we also know we must learn more about the First Imperium and its technology if we are to survive. My whole team will volunteer, and I have it on good authority that many of the Marines would also come along if allowed."

Compton sighed. *Marines…that has to be Connor Frasier.* It wasn't much of a secret the elite Marine had become quite taken with Ana Zhukov, ever since he'd shed his armor to save her life on the enemy Colossus. And Zhukov and Cutter were research partners, the two most gifted scientists in the fleet.

But it wasn't that simple. Compton had no desire to see scientific teams chewed up by half-million year old security bots, or to send a detachment of his Marines into harm's way, but if that had been his only worry he would have relented to Cutter's requests long before. But there was more, a far deeper concern.

"And what if one of these worlds retains a long distance transmission capability? What if blundering around in the ruins triggers some warning, not just to local security bots but to an active base…and brings another enemy fleet on us? The Colossus is gone, Hieronymus. We have only our own ships, low on ordnance and repaired the best we could on the run with the parts we still have left. We are not ready for such a fight…and we would not survive it."

"You know secrecy cannot protect us forever, Admiral." Cutter was tense, determined to change Compton's mind. "We are playing Russian Roulette with every jump, just waiting for the day we again encounter the enemy. Stealth is fleeting, and sooner or later, the First Imperium forces will return. And we must be ready. Ready to face them, to defeat them. And knowledge is the way we will achieve that."

Cutter paused, pulling his hand across his forehead, wiping away the perspiration. "Admiral, we have made great progress with the artifacts collected on the last planetary excursion…and from the data we retrieved from the Colossus. If we can obtain more, I am sure we are close to a whole series of breakthroughs. Weapons, data systems, power generation…and more sophisticated ways to control the enemy, advancements that will make my original virus seem like a child's toy." He paused again. "Sir, running can only buy us time in small increments. But adapting their technology can save us, free us from our flight and give us the tools to end the First Imperium threat once and for all…not only for us, but for those back in Occupied Space too."

Compton stared at Cutter with a pained look on his face. He wanted nothing more than to cut the reins on this brilliant scientist, to let him run wild and develop the systems and tech needed to truly match the First Imperium. But he just couldn't. Not now. Cutter was a genius, but like most with ability as extraordinary as his, he found it difficult to appreciate factors outside his work. He could accomplish what he wanted, Compton was sure of that. Given time, Cutter would no doubt learn how to adapt First Imperium tech and produce remarkable advances. Unless the enemy tracked down and destroyed the fleet first.

And even if Cutter cracked the mysteries of First Imperium technology, how much could the fleet put to use? How many new systems could it produce? And how quickly? Compton had his people bending over backwards to build jury-rigged missiles to fill his empty magazines, and the entire program was moving at a snail's pace, despite the fact that the fusion technology employed was over two centuries old. What could his makeshift production facilities do with highly advanced First Imperium designs?

"I understand everything you are saying, but I simply cannot risk it. I'm sorry, Hieronymus. I truly am. No one appreciates the implications of what you could do with more First Imperium technology like I do. But now is not the time. Perhaps soon, when we have reason to believe we have eluded our enemy."

Cutter stared back. He had a disappointed look on his face, but then he just nodded silently. Compton knew the brilliant scientist understood, and probably, on some level, he even agreed. He'd been caught in the fighting six months earlier, when the landing party had been attacked by First Imperium security bots...and then he'd barely escaped the Colossus before it was destroyed in the fight against the overwhelming First Imperium forces in X18. Six months had passed without incident, that was true. But Compton didn't think Hieronymus Cutter was like so many others in the fleet, ready to forget a threat after a brief respite. No, there was no one more equipped to understand the mysterious intelligence out there directing its forces than Cutter. He knew better than anyone else how determined, how relentless an artificial intelligence could be.

And still he wants to go, even knowing the risks…perhaps better than I do. Am I wrong on this? Is it worth the danger?

Compton pushed back the thought. He had tremendous respect for Cutter's intellect…and the warrior in him wanted to stop running. The idea of developing weaponry to match the First Imperium forces was seductive, and the thought of blasting enemy fleets to dust roused a fire in his belly. But his people needed more than a fighter's bluster. They needed judgment, rational planning. And he was determined to give it to them.

*　　　*　　　*

"I've been over it again and again, Terrance. There's just no way. Even if we dump vital spare parts and you give me another six or eight freighters, we're still going to come up short. Maybe sixty percent of what we need. Seventy outside…but that assumes no accidents, no unforeseen problems."

Compton felt the sigh about to come, but he forced it back, and he just shook his head. *Not you too, Sophie. The perfect end to a perfect day.* It had been a month since the celebration, and whatever satisfaction Compton had managed to enjoy was long gone. Trying to keep his people alive even without the First Imperium attacking was proving to entail a constant series of unsolvable problems.

"So what do you propose?" His words came out a bit

harder edged in tone than he'd intended them. It wasn't her fault. Indeed, Sophie Barcomme had worked miracles filling the empty spaces of the fleet's freighters with a bizarre—but highly optimized—assortment of algae and funguses, unappetizing, perhaps, but edible and nutrient dense. Without her efforts, the fleet would already be out of food, its people halfway to starving to death. "I'm sorry," he added almost immediately. "Tough day."

He still had a headache from his encounter with Hieronymus, wondering if he was wrong, if his caution was costing them the chance to gain the knowledge they needed to survive. *You'd be dead already if you hadn't let him go check out the Colossus.* He felt a chill pass through him as he remembered how close he had come to refusing Cutter's request back then. *Sometimes there is a razor's edge between success and failure, between victory…and death.*

He couldn't blame the scientist for all of the pain in his head though. After he'd left Cutter, he had gone to the flag bridge… and waded through the tidal wave of reports, the results of the ship diagnostics he'd ordered. He almost put his fist through the bulkhead when he first saw the number of vessels requiring petty repairs. He'd repeatedly reminded his ship commanders to keep an eye on their vessels' readiness, but no matter what he did or said, some of the fleet's captains were simply incompetent… or at least not up to his exacting standards. He'd always known the Alliance navy was the best among all of Earth's Superpowers, the result in large part of the example he and Augustus Garret had set and the standards they had enforced. But the fleet was an international force, an amalgam of crews from nine nations, and Compton knew its survival depended on his maintaining the loyalty and respect of all of them. He already had his own people in as many key positions as he dared. The last thing he needed was to fuel a wave of conspiracy theories about the Alliance personnel plotting to take over the fleet.

And sacking half the Europan contingent would do just that…

"Alright, *Fleet Admiral* Compton, I'll take pity on you and rub your shoulders, while we talk." Sophie's voice pulled him from his thoughts. "But we *are* going to talk about this now. Any solution is going to require a lot of lead time. If we wait any longer it's going to be too late." She paused as she climbed behind him on the sofa and put her hands on his shoulders. "It's almost too late now."

He winced, half from the pressure against the biggest knot in his neck…and half from her comment about it being too late. "Very well, *Commander* Barcomme…" He let out a soft groan… she had hit just the right spot. "…what do you propose?"

He could feel her hands tense. "We have to stop somewhere, Terrance. There's just no choice. We need a chance to grow some crops."

He took a deep breath and exhaled loudly. "I think you and Hieronymus Cutter are ganging up on me."

He felt her hands slip off his shoulders. "Is that what you think?" He could hear her voice, and he knew immediately she had taken his words too seriously.

"I'm sorry, that's not what I meant." He paused, sighing softly as he did. "It's just been a really shitty day."

She leaned forward, bringing her head around so she could look at his face. "You have to know I would never side with anyone against you. In anything." She hesitated for a second then she brought one of her hands around and put it on his cheek. "I don't think I could have endured the last year without your friendship, Terrance. You saved the whole fleet, but you rescued me a second time as well, with your companionship and your compassion."

"I really am sorry, Soph," he said, his voice soft, contrite. "I've just got so much to decide right now. You don't deserve that fallout, but sometimes it's just…"

She put her fingers over his mouth. "I know," she said. "Don't worry about it. I can't even imagine the pressure on you."

He rolled his head on his shoulders as she slid back and started massaging his neck again. He closed his eyes for a few seconds, enjoying the touch of relaxation her fingers produced. Then he said, "So tell me, Soph…what do you have in mind?"

"Well," she said, her tone showing a bit of her own stress, "there are very dense crops, mostly genetically-engineered versions of Earth beans and certain legumes. We can get a lot of caloric and nutritional punch from even a single crop. And they grow very quickly, given the right environment."

"How quickly?"

"Eight weeks…ten tops. For enough to fully replenish our supplies. Perhaps another year's worth of food."

"So we'd have to stop somewhere for two months?" He hated every aspect of this plan. But it was better than watching people starve to death. "And there's no alternative?"

"Not unless you want to let half the people in the fleet die so there's enough food for the rest. Because half is about what we can feed from the freighters-farms alone."

He shook his head. "No, I don't think so…"

"That wouldn't work anyway," she said grimly. "These fungi and algae foodstuffs are okay for the short term, but without some supplementation, we're going to start seeing some real problems. Vitamin deficiencies, digestive issues. Go much more than a year without getting something else into the diet, and people will start dying."

"But I thought those alternative foods had been used on much longer missions…to mining worlds and the like?"

"Yes, but with heavy supplementation. We're almost out of everything right now, and what little we have is reserved for the sickbays. We couldn't provide basic vitamin pills for most of our people now, much less all the rest of what they would need to subsist long-term on the diet we've got them on now."

"So when you said no choice, you meant *no* choice…" He'd meant a bit of gentle humor with the remark, but it didn't materialize when the words came out of his mouth.

"I'm afraid so, Terrance. And the sooner the better."

He sighed, realizing he had no choice…he had to stop somewhere, or at least send out a mission. There was something else too, and he felt the realization burning through his gut. Sophie was the natural leader of the expedition, at least with regard to food production. The thought of her being gone for several months, in danger—even more than the usual hazard of being part of the fleet—made him feel sick. But he knew he couldn't ask her to stay for him. And he couldn't deny the fleet the best person to resolve the growing food crisis.

"Okay, I guess there is no real choice. You keep an eye on the upcoming systems, and pick one you think is suitable." He paused, his mind considering the specifics of the mission. "Put together a list of everything you need…equipment, personnel, ships. Let me know as soon as you can."

"I will," she said softly. "I've got most of it done already."

He smiled, not at all surprised she was so prepared. "And remember…" The grin faded away. "You're going to need to keep energy output to an absolute minimum on whatever planet we land you on, so keep that in mind. If a First Imperium ship moves through the system and detects you…"

She just nodded silently. Then she said, "I understand."

Chapter Three

From the Personal Log of Terrance Compton

I have tried to keep my people safe, to avoid the enemy at all costs. But I am too old a soldier not to know that defense is often a trap. I had a long talk of this once with Elias Holm, the Commandant of the Marine Corps. He told me of the seductiveness of entrenched positions, the enticements of standing on the defensive, of forcing your enemy to attack...and dash himself upon your works. Then he said, more battles have been lost this way than any other, by yielding the initiative to a cunning foe. War in space is different than ground combat, certainly, but I have come to feel this axiom of war applies even more pointedly to fleet actions. I have known this many years, employed it to attain victory...watched my friend Augustus exercise even more aggressive tactics than I have ever dared, to even greater success. Yet, with all that has happened, I have forgotten this lesson, surrendered the initiative to an enemy we haven't even seen for six months. And I don't know how to get it back.

For six months I have made my decisions based on caution...on fear. I have avoided any actions that might aid the enemy in finding us, but in doing so I have yielded any initiative. I have prevented Dr. Cutter from exploration that could expand his research. My concerns are certainly valid...yet in X18 such a strategy would have been fatal. Cutter's aggressive efforts were our salvation there, not any tactical wizardry from me.

What would you counsel me, Augustus? For decades we fought side by side, you the more dynamic half of our team, me the more cautious, methodical. Now I must try to imagine how you would act if you were here, what steps you would take differently than I. I feel the loss of your influence, the pressure urging me to accept greater risk seeking reward, to understand when a gamble, even a poor one, is still the best option. Perhaps you too feel the loss of my restraint, the slight pull that made you pause and reevaluate a plan before leaping. I cannot know that, my old friend. But I surely miss your advice and skill...as I miss you.

Perhaps it doesn't matter now. Food has forced my hand. I can postpone research missions, delay sending out exploratory parties...but I must have food for those in the fleet. Indeed, my caution has grown, and it has led me to dark places. It shames me even to acknowledge in this journal, which no one will ever read, that I have considered the alternative to taking the risk of stopping to grow food. How would I handle things, I asked myself, if we had only half enough food to sustain us? Would I simply allow everyone to subsist on half-rations, until no one had the strength to man their battle positions? No, that would be a gift to the enemy...when they finally find us.

Would I have a lottery, let chance decide who lives or dies? No, for I would have to ensure the fleet retained the experts and veterans on which its survival depends. So it would come down to me, like some dark god, decreeing from on high who lives and who dies. I can hardly imagine a nightmare so dark, a horror so maddening...far more terrible than any enemy I have faced. Worse, I would have to have them all killed—murdered. I couldn't risk the resistance of slowly dying men and women, the desperate rebellions and mutinies by those chosen to die. Nor the effect it would have on the others, as they watched friends and comrades driven mad with hunger and fear.

Perhaps I could do it, perpetrate such a monstrous crime, if we were stranded somewhere, if there was no other way...if the only alternative was certain death for all. But never when there was an alternative. No, I would see us all destroyed in the attempt to survive together before I let myself—all of us—become *that*. Better to take the risk, to do what must be done and fight for survival together.

Still, I would hear the words from you, for it would bolster my own failing strength. Yet I know what you would say, what you would do. And I will take your counsel, though you are a thousand light years distant and unable to give it.

X48 System
Approximately 14,000,000 kilometers from AS Midway
The Fleet: 144 ships, 32,808 crew

"Let's take a closer look at planet two. It's the only one that looks worth checking out." Mariko Fujin sat in the fighter's command chair, looking out over the other four members of the ship's crew. Her eyes paused as they passed over the pilot's station, and she felt a touch of wistfulness. That was her place, had been her place, at least…but no longer. She hadn't lost her spot due to failure or disgrace, indeed, she was one of the best fighter jocks in the fleet. But success had its costs too, and rank brought obligation and loss along with privilege. She'd managed to juggle flying her own bird with commanding the squadron, but now Admiral Hurley had pinned a commander's insignia on her collar—and put her in charge of an entire strike wing.

She still wasn't used to the weight of so much responsibility. Eighteen ships. Eighteen crews…ninety men and women, all looking to her to lead them. It had hurt her deeply to relinquish the pilot's chair, but she had done it without argument. She understood duty, and her responsibility to the crews under her. And they deserved a commander who was one hundred percent focused on leading them, not clinging to the adrenalin rush of flying a single bird in combat.

She flipped the commandwide com switch. "Alright, listen up. We're going to do a sweep of planet two. The Gold Dragons and Wildcats will do a scanning run at fifty thousand klicks. The Whirlwinds will maintain a defensive formation at five hundred thousand klicks…just in case we missed anything."

"Wildcats leader, acknowledge."

"Whirlwinds, acknowledge."

Gold Dragons, acknowledge, she thought to herself. Admiral Hurley had gently suggested—not ordered—that she assign one of her people as squadron commander, but Fujin had quietly ignored the advice. The Dragons were hers…indeed, she was the only survivor of the original squadron, and she just couldn't let them go. It was bad enough sitting like a useless lump while somebody else flew her fighter. But give up the Dragons? No. Not unless Hurley or Compton gave her a pointblank order. And even then, she'd argue as hard as she could before giving in.

She flipped off the com and stared down at her screen, moving her finger across, finalizing the scanning plan. Then she pushed a button and sent the instructions to her squadron commanders. Twelve ships were enough to do a first class sweep of a planet, especially since Admiral Compton had relaxed the restrictions he'd placed on the scouting formations, allowing them to get close enough to get some serious data.

"I'm sending you nav instructions, Lieutenant. We will take point for the squadron." She knew Greta Hurley would have scolded her a little for putting her bird in the lead. *But then Hurley used to drive Augustus Garret crazy with her antics, didn't she?* There were rumors throughout the fleet that Garret had ordered Hurley's pilot to keep her back from the fighting. If true, it had been a valiant effort, but a failed one. Fujin couldn't recall any instance of the fleet's strike force commander hanging back in a fight.

"Yes, Commander." Grant Wainwright's response was sharp, crisp. Fujin couldn't help but resent the young officer, just a bit. He'd taken her place at the throttle, after all. But she was glad to have him, and she had to admit, he was a hell of a pilot.

"Whenever you are ready, Lieutenant."

"I'm always ready, Commander." Wainwright pushed the throttle forward, and the force of 2g slammed into everyone aboard.

Fujin was struggling to hold back a smile. *Are pilots getting cockier? Or am I just getting old?* She tried to brush the thought aside…she hadn't even reached her thirtieth birthday. But it was still there, nagging at her. She'd been every bit as brash as Wainwright once, and as quick with a smart-assed reply. *So when did I change, end up on the other side? Perhaps there is a limit to how much combat and death can could see and still remain young…at least inside.*

"Just focus on leading the squadron in, Lieutenant," she said, reminding herself as she did of her first squadron commander. They'd called him T-Rex, for the way he'd unleashed on anyone who'd failed to meet his exacting standards. *My God,* she thought, suddenly realizing how far she'd come from the cocky young pilot she'd been then. *I wonder what they call me.*

"Yes, Commander."

The response was textbook, sharp, respectable, spot on. But all she heard was 'yes, T-Rex."

* * *

"I have the results of Commander Fujin's scouting report. I have called this meeting to review these findings and determine if this system is the place to conduct a more extensive investigation, one involving a protracted expedition to the surface." Compton sat in his chair at the head of the table, his eyes flitting around, gauging the reactions of those present. He caught the look in Cutter's eye immediately.

"Am I to understand that you are considering allowing a research team to conduct an exploration?" There was surprise in the scientist's voice, but mostly excitement.

"Perhaps, Hieronymus. Indeed, I still retain all of my earlier concerns..." He looked around the table. "...you are all familiar with them. But events appear to have forced my hands. The situation with our provisions requires that we land a team on a habitable world to grow crops to supplement out fleet-produced foodstuffs. The alternative is...well, there is no alternative." *None I can live with...*

"As the operation will require eight to ten weeks, we have little time to spare. The supply situation is rapidly becoming dire—so we must select a planet very soon. Preferably immediately. We may elect to land the expedition here...or move on to the next system and explore the worlds we find there. But I am reluctant to wait any longer than absolutely necessary."

A soft murmur rippled around the table. They had all known food would be a problem eventually, but Compton had just laid it out in front of them. And everyone present understood the risk they would take landing on another First Imperium world.

"Will you be authorizing a research expedition as well, Admiral?"

Compton almost let a laugh escape his mouth. He was a little surprised Cutter had waited the few seconds he had to ask. "Yes, Hieronymus, I will. I retain all of my prior concerns, but since we have no choice but to land the agricultural team, I believe the benefits of allowing your people to gather artifacts and data are likely to outweigh the incremental risk. We will already be on the planet…if there are active alert systems, they will be triggered anyway." Compton paused. "But listen to me, Hieronymus. I understand your drive, your passion. I know you want as much data as you can get, to learn more about the First Imperium. And I respect it…and recognize its value to our survival efforts. But let me be perfectly clear. You are to conduct your operation with extreme caution at all times. Do you understand me?"

"Yes, Admiral. Of course."

"I mean it, Hieronymus. No matter what you think you may find…you have to be extremely careful every moment you are down there. Every second."

"Yes, Admiral. I understand completely."

Compton still didn't believe Cutter, not completely. But the scientist sounded sincere, and that was as good as he could get right now. "Very well. Then let us proceed…and decide if X48 serves our needs. There are only three planets, far fewer than in most of the systems we have passed through. And only one of them is habitable. The first is a scorched rock, so close to the sun that its surface is molten most of the time. The third is a gas giant, without even a moon orbiting it. That leaves planet two."

Compton slid his finger across the small screen on the table in front of him. "I am sending the scanning results to your 'pads." He waited a few seconds while everyone in the room looked at their screens.

"You will note that the planet is almost a perfect one for human life. Indeed, it is a virtual paradise…and it is covered with ruins. It was once the home to billions of life forms, though, like every other world we have encountered, there are no signs any of its residents remain."

"What are these readings, Admiral?" Sophie Barcomme looked up from her 'pad. "We haven't seen anything like this on the other worlds."

"Those readings are a big question mark, Commander Barcomme." Compton was deliberately formal with Barcomme, as she was with him, though he suspected the whole thing was pointless. He didn't have a doubt in his mind everyone else in the room thought they were lovers. But there was no time for that nonsense, not now.

He turned and looked around the table. "There are traces of radiation in certain locations. They are consistent with what we'd expect to find after the detonation of fusion and anti-matter weaponry…about half a million years after the fact." He paused to let his words sink in.

"After gathering these readings, Commander Fujin took her craft into orbit and collected some visual intelligence. If you'll move to images five through eleven you will see what she was able to obtain."

There were a few soft gasps, but otherwise the room was silent.

"Yes," Compton said, reinforcing what he knew they had all realized. "These cities were not left to slowly decay. They were destroyed. In battle." He paused again. "Whatever happened here, it was different from the fates of the other worlds we have passed. Those all seemed…abandoned, for lack of a better word. The cities were ruins, but that was time's work. All of our analysis suggests that they were intact when the people disappeared. We have long wondered what happened to the people of the First Imperium, what could have caused them to abandon their homes en masse…or die off so suddenly. We have considered many possibilities. Disease, reproductive issues, some sort of mass insanity…even religious fanaticism. To that list, we must now add another possibility. War."

"It certainly looks like there was fighting on this planet, sir." James Preston was the commander of the fleet's Marines, and a veteran of more than one bloody conflict. "But how do we explain the other worlds? Billions lived there, and we found no signs of significant conflict."

Compton sighed. "I can't answer that, Colonel." He looked out across the table. "I'm hoping some of the people in this room can provide me with some hypotheses given the time to review this material. But that is not our primary issue right now. There is only a single question we must answer at this meeting. *Is* planet two suitable, both for the growth of crops and for research?"

He looked around the table, his eyes pausing first on Barcomme. "Commander? Your mission in the most vital in many ways. We cannot take the risks we are taking only to find out that the planet is not suitable for producing the crops we require."

Barcomme was staring down at the 'pad, but after a few seconds she looked up and turned toward Compton. "I believe it is very suitable. I'd normally be concerned about the radioactives, but after half a million years, I wouldn't expect any problems. Of course, we don't know if there were any other contaminants that resulted from the fighting, but the planet is damned near perfect in distance from the sun, climate…" She glanced back at the 'pad for a few seconds before she turned back to Compton. "I say yes." Another pause. "And, to be extremely candid, I'd be hesitant to waste any more time if we don't absolutely have to. We're going to be looking at some pretty unpleasant rationing as it is."

Compton nodded. Then he turned toward Cutter. "Hieronymus?"

Cutter was silent for a few seconds. "Well, sir, if the cities are all destroyed, rather than simply decayed by time, we may find it more difficult to find intact artifacts. This is, of course, of considerable concern. However, if there was widespread war on this planet, it is possible that we will find much remaining equipment from that conflict. And I suspect the First Imperium is no different from us in one respect…the leading edge of technology is employed in war."

The scientist hesitated again, flashing a glance toward Barcomme. "It's a gamble either way, sir, but if Dr. Barcomme thinks the planet is suitable for her needs, my advice is to proceed."

Compton nodded. "I am inclined to agree with both of you. I'm uncomfortable with this entire operation, but I'd just as soon complete it as quickly as possible." He looked around the table again. "Does anyone disagree? Any comments?"

There was a ripple of nodding heads, but no one spoke.

"Very well," Compton said. "It is decided. Commander Barcomme, Dr. Cutter, you will both plan your expeditions immediately. I would like everything ready to go in forty-eight hours."

"Admiral, that is…yes, sir." Barcomme's objection died mid-sentence. Everyone present, including her, knew that the fleet couldn't remain in X48 for long, especially not with the danger that the expedition could accidently alert the enemy. It was an unspoken fact, but one everyone present well understood. Those going down to the surface were expendable, at least more so than the fleet itself, and once they were landed, they would be on their own. When they were ready to return, enough ships would be dispatched to collect them, and the food and artifacts they hoped to bring back. But the fleet would be gone, waiting in some system farther ahead…distant enough to escape the cataclysm if anyone triggered an alarm that reached an enemy base.

"Hieronymus?" Compton shifted his gaze to the scientist.

"My people will be ready, Admiral." He didn't sound much happier about the time constraints than Barcomme had, but he didn't ask for more either.

"Very well then…it is decided. Now, before we adjourn… I know there is much work to be done before the expedition departs. I would like to remind everyone just how potentially dangerous this mission will be. Hieronymus, I know you are anxious to discover as much as possible about the First Imperium, but I caution you—no, I order you—to exert the utmost caution. You must be very careful what you disturb and take every effort not to trigger any warnings or alarms that may still be functional." *That's a potential advantage of a wartorn world. With any luck, systems like that were long ago destroyed.*

"Yes, Admiral. I understand."

"And you, Commander." His eyes moved to Barcomme. "I know you are charged with producing a massive amount of food very quickly, but I must caution against the use of too much energy. This entire operation rests on the edge of a knife. If an enemy vessel should pass through the system and detect power generation, the fate of the expedition will be likely be sealed." He had a hitch in his throat, a momentary reaction as he thought about the danger she was walking into. "And with it the fleet's…for we wait on the success of your efforts, upon which hinge our hopes for survival."

"I understand, Terrance." She slipped and used his first name, but if anyone noticed or thought it was odd, they didn't let on. "We will be careful."

"Good." Compton stared down the table, to the hulking form at the opposite end. "Colonel Preston?"

"Yes, sir!" Preston replied, his voice cracking like a whip. James Preston was a Marine, through and through, and he looked and sounded every bit the part.

"I want you to command the ground forces. You will leave four companies for shipboard duty, and take the rest of the Marines with you." The fleet had some other ground forces, an understrength orta of Janissaries, some Europan and RIC mobile forces. But Compton had faith in his own Marines, and this operation was too important to make decisions based on anything but tactical ability. A homogeneous force of Marines would operate better in a crisis situation than some multi-national conglomeration designed to salve the egos of the fleet's nationalities. Compton had seen the Marines in action many times, and if anyone could keep his people on the ground safe—keep Sophie safe—it was Preston and his leathernecks.

"Yes, Admiral." Then, a few seconds later, "Don't worry, sir. The Marines will see it done. Whatever happens."

"I have no doubt of that, Colonel." He looked at Barcomme

then at Cutter. "Colonel Preston will be in overall command of the expedition. I want both of you to understand this…his orders are final, and they are to be obeyed without question…as if they are coming from my own lips. Understood?"

"Yes," Barcomme replied. "Understood."

Compton stared at Cutter. "Hieronymus?"

"Yes," the scientist replied, a little more grudgingly than Barcomme. "Understood."

* * *

"Max, thank you for coming. I know it's late. Come in…sit." Compton was seated at a chair just inside the door. The room was mostly dark, just a single fixture on a dim setting throwing off any light at all. Max Harmon stood in the doorway, a dark shadow against the bright illumination from the corridor.

Harmon stepped into the room, and the door slid shut behind him. "Of course, sir. Whatever you need." He stood at attention, just inside the room.

"For the love of God, Max, sit. I'm getting tired just looking at you standing there like that." Compton had called Harmon in the middle of the night, something he knew was not conducive to his recent campaign to get his aide to relax more. But he'd made a decision, and he wanted to tell Harmon. He'd expressly told the aide not to worry about what he was wearing, just to come however he was. But somehow, Harmon looked ready for a parade inspection, his uniform spotless and perfectly pressed, and every hair on his head exactly where it belonged, as if each of them had been ordered to lay neatly and wouldn't dare disobey.

He is his mother's son, isn't he?

Compton waited while Harmon sat in the chair opposite his own. The captain almost looked more uncomfortable in the seat than he had standing ramrod straight a few seconds before. Compton would have told himself his aide would lose that perfect discipline when he saw some real action…but Max Harmon had been in enough tough battles to melt the heart of a lesser man. *And still, there he is, at 3am ship's time, looking like an image of spot on perfection.*

"Max, I want you to do something for me."

"Of course, sir. Whatever you wish."

"I want you to go with the expedition."

"Certainly, sir."

"I don't want you to stay. I need you here. But I have to know everything is in place and going well. I want you to stay a week and then come back and report."

"Yes, Admiral."

"I'm detaching *Wolverine.* She will stay in orbit with a skeleton crew and wait for you. She's one of the fastest ships left in the fleet, and I've authorized her commander to burn as much fuel as necessary to catch up with us."

"Very well, sir." A pause. "If that is all, sir, I should go get ready. The expedition is set to depart in four hours."

"Yes, Max. And thank you. I'd like to land myself and have a look around…but I can't risk something like that again. And your eyes are the next closest thing to mine."

Harmon stood up, looking almost relieved to be on his feet and at attention again. "Of course, Admiral. Don't worry…I will bring you a complete report."

"I'm sure you will." He nodded and watched as the aide turned toward the door.

"And Max?"

Harmon stopped and turned back toward Compton. "Sir?"

"I need that report no matter what. And I need you too." Compton paused. "So if the expedition runs into trouble, if there is heavy fighting…your orders are to leave immediately and come back and report to me."

Harmon paused, looking suddenly uncomfortable. "Of course, sir. As you command." His voice was sharp, almost stilted, despite his obvious efforts to hide his feelings about making a run for it while the landing party was under attack.

"Very well, Max. Now go and get ready. I'll speak with you

again before you leave."

"Sir!" Harmon snapped, and then he turned and walked out of the room.

I know, Max. I understand how hard it will be if you have to leave—to run—while your comrades are fighting…and perhaps dying. But I must know what is happening down there, and all the more if disaster strikes.

He sighed and looked across the dimly-lit room.

Civilians must imagine that fighting is the hardest thing we do, facing our fears and plunging into the maelstrom. But it is not. Not for officers like us, Max. No, for us, abandoning our brethren is the worst nightmare…yet if that is what duty demands of us, then we have no choice. For duty is first, above all things.

Chapter Four

Command Unit Gamma 9736

The humans paused their advance in system 17411. Their fleet then halted for an extended period before continuing on through the warp gate to system 17419. This is unexpected behavior. They recently paused to refine fusionables for their primitive energy generation systems, and based on an analysis of their vessels and the extraction system they were able to construct, they should not require additional fuel at this time. Even if they did, perhaps in the instance of some leakage or malfunction we have not detected, system 17411 is an unlikely choice. It has a single gas giant, one that is notably poor in the heavy hydrogen and helium-3 their reactors require.

So why would they pause? They have proceeded on their course for a considerable period of time now, and they have not halted save to replenish their fuel supplies. So what has changed? Have they detected the stealth probes? Indeed, while possible, that seems highly unlikely. The probes are far beyond their science, and based on all data collected since we first encountered them, they have almost no ability to manipulate or even to effectively detect dark matter and energy.

Probe 4302 reported a brief passage through an abnormally dense particulate cloud, one that could have temporarily reduced its stealth capability. But the behavior of the enemy fleet since that time had been unchanged. And even if they had detected the probe, why would they stop? My analysis suggests the overwhelmingly likely reaction would be to destroy the probes if they could be located...and failing that, to accelerate their flight, to seek to escape the forces they would infer are following them. I cannot discern any rational plan that would involve remaining in place so long.

I lack the data to develop an effective hypothesis. I will send a new force to investigate. And to capture a prisoner if possible. I must know more about these creatures. The Regent's orders are to destroy them all, but my commands do not expressly preclude analysis and questioning before termination.

Yes, I must have a prisoner. I will send the orders at once.

X48 System – Planet II
"Plymouth Rock"
Approximately 14,000,000 kilometers from AS Midway
The Fleet: 144 ships, 32,808 crew

"I want everyone to stay inside the defensive perimeter until the scouting parties report back." James Preston stood in front of the crowd of scientists, members of Barcomme's and Cutter's expeditions. There were a few impatient looks in the crowd, but not many people argued with a fully-armored Marine standing a few meters away...and *no one* did when that Marine was Colonel James Preston.

"I understand the importance of your work and the urgency of allowing you to begin, but security comes first." There were Marines everywhere, running around in a way that seemed like a wild scrum but was actually a perfectly choreographed operation. Two companies were moving out, setting up defensive positions around the entire camp. Others were sweeping through the area, searching for live defensive systems or other potential dangers.

There was no longer any question that a massive battle had been waged here long ago. The debris remained scattered around everywhere. The high tech materials of the First Imperium equipment had survived the ages of wind and rain and decay, at least to a point. Preston could tell the scientists were straining at the leash, dying to dive into the wreckage, to study the amazing technology of the ancient race that had fought a cataclysmic battle here so long ago. But he knew Admiral Compton was counting on him to keep everyone safe, and that was the primary consideration. If that meant everyone had to stand around and wait then so be it.

Preston looked at the row of shuttles lined up a few dozen meters behind the scientific crews. There were over a hundred Marines posted around them, fully armored with weapons at the ready. The craft had brought the personnel down to the surface, but most of their capacity had been used to carry the seed the agricultural crews would need. Barcomme's people had worked tirelessly in preparation for the expedition, genetically modifying the seeds in the fleet's dwindling stores, creating the most nutrient dense and fastest-growing crops known to mankind's science. He knew the cargo was beyond price. It was all the fleet had, and if he let his guard down, of some enemy force penetrated and destroyed those shuttles, thousands on the fleet would starve to death. Not today, not even tomorrow. But soon.

He turned and looked out over the plain that had been selected as the landing zone. It was a long section of flat, open ground stretching kilometers in every direction, with only a single large rock outcropping to break up the endless flatland. Preston wasn't sure who had started calling it Plymouth Rock, but he appreciated the humor. Still, he wasn't sure it was a very suitable name. The men and women who'd landed at Plymouth Rock were settlers…they had come to stay. And James Preston couldn't get off this haunted planet soon enough.

He frowned. The primary consideration in selecting a landing site had been suitable conditions for planting. And that it certainly was. But it was a shitty spot to mount a defense—he'd decided that the instant he hopped out of the shuttle and took a look around. Wide open, no cover, no trees, not even any significant undulation in the ground. If his people had to fight a battle here, it would be a bloodbath.

But defensibility was secondary to food production. He

was worried about the possibility of combat, but it was a fact that people were going to die without the food they'd come to grow…and that took absolute precedence. Sophie Barcomme had selected the LZ, and that had been the last word on the subject. He understood…and he knew his Marines would handle things, somehow. Like they always did.

"The perimeter is in place, Colonel. We've got a hundred fire teams covering every approach." Connor Frasier's voice was gruff, but over the years he'd lost most of the remnant of the moderate brogue he'd brought with him to training camp.

Many of Earth's accents had faded away over the years, as the Superpowers had encouraged homogeneity within their borders. The politicians had long understood that it was easier to whip their downtrodden subjects into wild fits of nationalism if racial and ancestral stereotypes were used effectively. But the Scots had defied that trend, at least in the region of the Highlands. The area had repeatedly rebelled against Alliance diktats, until finally an agreement was reached, one that granted a level of local autonomy. The perceived 'victory' over the central government caused a burst of hereditary pride, saving the Scottish accent from history's dustbin. But nearly twenty years of service—and the realization that few of his fellow Marines could understand what the hell he was saying—had worn away at Frasier's accent, until there was just a touch of it left.

"Very good, Major." He watched as Frasier trotted the last few meters and stopped in front of him. It didn't really matter where they stood—they were buttoned up in their armor and talking on the com—but certain affectations had proven to be hardwired into the human mind. Including the 'face to face' conversation. "I want you to organize sweeper teams to go through the camp area. For all we know we could be standing on top of undetonated ordnance." Preston knew that was unlikely after half a million years, but the point was still valid. There were a hundred other potential dangers, and that meant they had to know everything that was in the area. Fast.

"Yes, Colonel. Right away." Frasier paused. "Sir…when you release the research party…have you considered what security to send with them?"

Preston paused. It wasn't like Frasier to poke around the edges of a topic. The massive Scot was as direct and to the point as anyone Preston had ever known.

Except when he's trying to be subtle and get assigned to protect the scientists…a group that just happens to include his girlfriend. And he's about as good at subtlety as most Marines…

"Let's worry about getting everything in place here, Con… then you and your Scots can escort Ana Zhukov and the rest of the scientists. Alright?"

"Yes, sir," Frasier replied, sounding as contrite as a veteran Marine ever did.

Technically, Frasier wasn't in the normal chain of command. He was the CO of the Scots Company, an elite commando formation—and the remnant of the battalion his father had led in the Third Frontier War. But he was also the second-highest ranking Marine officer in the fleet, and Preston had made him his unofficial exec.

Preston watched as Frasier jogged off waving his arms as he no doubt fired off commands to a formation of Marines thirty meters in front of him. He smiled for a few seconds as he watched his number two herding them into action. Frasier was one of the toughest Marines Preston had ever commanded… ever known…and it was amusing to think about how hard he had fallen for Ana Zhukov. It was no surprise, really. The Russian scientist was beautiful—there was no question about that—and she was one of the nicest, most pleasant people Preston had ever met. And Frasier had seduced her in the most Marine way possible…saving her life, almost getting killed in the process.

He wished Frasier and Zhukov all the best, but he felt a doubt creeping up, and he wondered if he should assign someone else to the guard detail for the exploration team. He knew why Frasier wanted the job, but his training and experience were telling him duty and romance were bad bedfellows.

He almost commed Frasier to tell him he'd changed his mind. But something held him back. *No, we're not in a normal situation anymore. This is no conventional battlefield, and the fleet is no normal military force. We're going to need to think differently if we're going to survive…and Connor Frasier is one of the best Marines I've ever known. I trust him.*

He paused for another few seconds then he turned and started walking back toward the command post. *If things ever get to the point where I can't trust a Marine like Frasier…we're as good as done for anyway.*

*   *   *

"The expedition has landed, Admiral. Scanners report all shuttles have set down safely." Jack Cortez was a first rate aide, fit to serve any admiral. Compton knew it, and he had no complaints about the tactical officer. Save that Cortez had the misfortune to be filling Max Harmon's chair…and that was a comparison no naval officer wanted to face.

Compton had been hesitant to make a change in his flag bridge team, but he realized Harmon was long overdue for the promotion. Besides, he needed an aide he could truly trust to work on his own…more than four meters away from his commander's chair. And that was Max Harmon.

"Very well, Commander." Compton stared at his display, the blue and white semi-circle of the planet as seen from *Midway's* exterior scanners. He knew his people were down on the surface now…and in many ways he understood they had the fate of the fleet in their hands. Barcomme's food, and possibly Cutter's scientific advancements, were the keys to their long term survival. Nothing was more important than their mission.

But you've got to make it through the short term or you'll never get to the long term.

"The fleet will prepare to maneuver toward the X50 warp gate." He didn't like the feeling of abandoning those on the surface, but he knew keeping the fleet safe was his first priority. And he realized the expedition's best chance relied on secrecy, on remaining undetected. A handful of people on a planet could defy cursory detection, especially if they followed his orders and used their portable reactors sparingly. But almost a hundred fifty ships floating around in or near orbit was as good as a beacon. Any enemy vessel that came through the warp gate would identify them at once…and then they would almost certainly scan the planet closely…and discover the landing parties as well.

"All ships are to be ready for acceleration in one hour."

"Yes, Admiral. Transmitting orders now."

"Very well, Commander." Compton sat for a few seconds before he shifted in his seat, leaning forward to get up. "I'll be in my office, Jack," he said softly, his voice distracted, as if he was thinking about something. "Check on everyone's status when we're thirty minutes out. And again at fifteen."

"Yes, sir."

Compton knew he was becoming ever more demanding of his people, and utterly unforgiving of the slightest drop in efficiency. If he couldn't sack the weaker officers in the fleet—and he knew he couldn't, not without risking serious unrest in some of the national contingents—then, by God, he would drive them until they dropped on their own…or until they improved.

But now his mind was on something else, something he'd been thinking about for a while now. His paranoia had been growing, the constant feeling that he had to consider his every move, rethink everything a dozen times. He could elude the fleet's pursuers twenty times, but if he slipped on the twenty-first, his people would all die.

He'd tried to relax, play cards with some of the officers, spend time with Sophie. He realized he needed to keep himself from going insane, that no man could endure the constant unrelenting stress without some kind of solace. But he also knew he had to come damned close…and not make that tragic mistake. Not on the twenty-first time…nor the hundred twenty-first.

Whatever it takes.

*   *   *

"This debris is fascinating. These materials are far beyond anything we have. This stuff has been here for half a million years, through summers and winters, storms and floods. Yet some of it looks almost new." Hieronymus Cutter was standing in front of a portable table, poking through a pile of artifacts the exploration teams had found. Sophie Barcomme had selected the landing site because of its topography and the spectrographic analysis of the soil…but by sheer coincidence, she'd chosen a chunk of ground that had also been an ancient battlefield.

It had been less than three days since Preston had given Cutter the OK to start exploring in the immediate area of the camp…and the scientist had put that time to good use. He had half a dozen excavation machines running around the clock, and his people had uncovered hundreds of bits and pieces of First Imperium equipment.

"A lot of it is familiar, military equipment we've seen before…or at least parts of it." Ana was on the opposite side of the table, digging through the same pile. "But not all of it." She held up a chunk of some kind of mysterious metal. "I've never seen anything like this."

"Or this," Cutter said in response, holding up a similar shard of another strange black metal. "A lot of this consists of bits and pieces of the usual types of battle robots and supporting equipment…stuff we've seen before on the other worlds, even on the battlefields back home." He paused, pulling out another artifact and staring at it. "But some of it is different…different than anything we've seen before."

"Could the First Imperium have fought an enemy here we haven't discovered yet? Why else would all these new items be mixed with a familiar-looking array of battle bot debris?"

"That's a big jump, Ana." Cutter didn't sound like he doubted her hypothesis…more like he was trying to slam on the brakes before they both jumped to wild conclusions. "Perhaps we simply haven't encountered everything they have. The Colossuses were certainly a surprise in X2."

The enemy had thrown massive fleets into human space, and

hundreds of ships had fought in the battles along the Line. But through all those terrible fights the First Imperium had never sent its largest, most powerful vessels into the maelstrom. Not until Admirals Garret and Compton had pushed into enemy space. Not until X2.

"I don't know, Ronnie." Zhukov's insistence on calling him 'Ronnie' had driven him crazy for months, but she'd long ago worn down his resistance. Now it seemed normal, and if she stopped he actually thought he would miss it. "Everything you say is correct, but there's something…different…about this stuff. I don't have any specifics…it's as much a feeling as anything else. But I don't think these are just chunks of normal battle robots." She held another piece of the mysterious metal in each hand as she spoke.

Cutter felt his head moving, an almost involuntary nod agreeing with her. He was a scientist as she was, trained to analyze facts, not feelings. Yet he felt the same thing, a haunting sense that these chunks of metal had not been part of any robotic warrior. Indeed, though he couldn't offer any real evidence yet, he had the overwhelming sense that they were looking at chunks of battle armor and weapons…equipment that had been used by living soldiers.

"We need more artifacts…and we need to figure out what happened here." Cutter spoke softly. His mind was focused. He and the other researchers in the fleet had struggled to understand the history of the First Imperium. The primary hypothesis was that some disaster had befallen its people…and that some of their robotic servants had continued to function, even through the long ages, continuing to defend the imperial domains. But there was no place in that narrative for ancient battles between machines and living beings.

Could they have been invaded? Was the First Imperium destroyed by another alien race and not some blight or plague? And if that is what happened…where are those beings now?

* * *

"All fleet units report ready, Admiral."

Compton sat in his chair, looking out over the flag bridge. Around *Midway*, he knew, one hundred forty-two other ships of the fleet were in formation, awaiting his orders to engage their engines, and leave the landing parties on their own. Only one vessel would remain in the system, one of John Duke's fast attack ships. It would hide in the system's asteroid belt for a week, its systems powered down to minimal life support. Then it would return to the second planet to pick up Max Harmon… and bring him back to the fleet.

"Very well, Captain." Compton knew the ships of the fleet had the programmed course locked into their navcoms, the thrust plan that would take them through the warp gate into the system the fleet's hastily-created nomenclature designated X50. But that's not where they were going.

"Commander Cortez, advise all units that we are transmitting a revised flight plan. All vessels are to lock the new course into their navigational AIs."

Cortez turned and looked across the bridge toward Compton. "A revised plan, sir?"

"Yes, Commander. A revised plan. Is anything unclear about that?" Compton felt a little sorry for the tactical officer. He'd been planning the alternate course all along, but he'd told no one. No one save Max Harmon, who would need the information to find the fleet…and who would tell no one. Compton felt a twinge of guilt at the coldness of his logic, at the part of him that could imagine a scenario where his landing parties were attacked, where any knowledge they possessed might be discovered. No, he couldn't take the chance. If the enemy discovered the expeditions, Compton knew he would have to leave them to their destruction. All of them. Even Sophie.

"Ah…yes, sir." A pause. "But what revised plan?" Cortez turned back to his workstation, but it was clear he was still confused.

"The plan I am sending you now, Commander. I calculated it myself. All vessels are to download it immediately and be prepared to embark in ten minutes."

"Yes, Admiral," Cortez replied, struggling mightily to sound confident.

Compton sat quietly while the tactical officer relayed the command. He had pursued the same methodology in selecting warp gates for the fleet since X2, in all instances opting for the one likeliest to lead away from Occupied Space. The methodology of predicting warp gate termini was primitive at best, but it was possible to estimate the distance of each jump through a series of calculations. And the math said that the gate to X50 would lead farther from the worlds of Occupied Space, from Earth.

Compton had been troubled recently, wondering if he was taking a predictable route. If anything, the First Imperium had superior methods for such calculations. He'd wondered if he should alter his methodology, insert some randomness to make it more difficult for a pursuer to project where the fleet had gone. He'd told himself he was being paranoid, but with several thousand people being left behind on planet two, every one of them fully aware that the fleet was bound for the X50 warp gate, he decided now was the time to change.

He pushed back on the guilt. The expedition only had short-ranged shuttles…so knowledge of where the fleet had gone was of no value to them, regardless of what happened. But his conscience still poked at him, at the feeling he was misleading them, lying to them. He thought of what Sophie would think, wondered if she would understand…or if she would be hurt. Or both.

But none of that was of any consequence. The fleet was all that mattered, and his paranoia was far likelier to save it than lead it to disaster.

"Commander Cortez…" His voice was like ice, giving no hint of the doubt and recrimination in his head. "All units are to engage engines."

Time to see what is in X49.

Chapter Five

From the Log of Mariko Fujin

The burdens of command are still strange, uncomfortable. Less than a year ago I was just a member of a squadron, a pilot in charge of a single fighter. Now I have three squadrons under me, and I have left my place at the throttle and assumed the command chair. I miss the thrill of flying my own fighter, the exhilaration in bringing the bird in for a decisive strike. But Admiral Hurley has gifted me with her confidence, and I will do all in my power to pay back that debt, to lead the wing she placed in my hands with all the skill and ability I can muster. To do less would be unthinkable.

Still, I often find myself at a loss at how to proceed. There are 90 crew in my wing, and the other 89 look to me to lead them, to understand what they do not, to know how to face the dangers that threaten to destroy us all...to know what to do at every moment. I have tried to be prepared...and I have resorted to bullshit when I had nothing better. At first, I felt like a fraud, an imposter pretending to be a commander in charge of eighteen fighters. But then I began to wonder...is this what command is? Of course, no officer knows what to do in every situation. Even Admiral Compton. Yet I have never seen him look shaken in battle, never heard the slightest doubt in his voice when he was issuing commands. Is he simply hiding his fear? Making his best guess when he doesn't know what to do? I had never seriously considered this before, though now that I do it makes perfect sense.

I have my crews on a strict regimen of physical training. I want them in shape when we are again called to man our ships, but it is more than simply that. I want them busy, with less time to sit around and think about fallen comrades or stare into the darkness mourning friends and loved ones left behind. Time can wear on men and women in ways different than the stark fear of combat. Insidious ways. And I would not have my people's effectiveness deteriorate, to have them killed in our next battle because time and doubt and fear have worn down their readiness.

I'd prefer to have them out in their ships, of course, conducting missions, even routine patrols. But that burns fuel, and it just hastens the day when we'll have to find another gas giant... and stop the whole fleet again. I don't know why that seems like such a fearsome prospect. After all, we haven't encountered any enemy vessels in six months, so is stopping for a week or two so dangerous?

When I try to analyze the situation, my answer is invariably 'no.' By every intellectual way of looking at it, the risk seems slight. Yet my gut feels differently...and apparently so does Admiral Compton's. I almost went to Admiral Hurley, to ask her if she could get more fuel assigned for routine missions, just to keep my people sharp. But I didn't. Somehow, in a way I cannot explain, I believe Admiral Compton is right. It is better for us to preserve fuel, to husband all of our resources. We are up against a great unknown, and we must be cautious...stay ready for the next battle. Because I have no doubt that a fight awaits us out there somewhere.

AS Midway
X49 System – 12,000,000 km from the X48 warp gate
The Fleet: 144 ships, 32,802 crew

"Preliminary scans indicate the system is clear, Admiral." Cortez was hunched over his workstation, his eyes following the fresh scanner data as it came in. "It looks like six planets..." He paused as he assimilated the reports flashing onto his screen. "Three gas giants...and one frozen chunk of rock six billion kilometers from the primary. Looks like two Earthlike planets." Another pause. "Yes, both definitely within the habitable zone."

Compton sat in his chair and nodded. "Very well, Commander." He had a thoughtful look on his face, but he didn't say anything.

"Should we move the fleet closer to get some concentrated scans on those planets, sir?" The entry warp gate had dumped the fleet too far from the inner planets to get more than the most basic data.

"Negative, Commander. I want to get the fleet through this system as quickly as possible…and we're more likely to find warp gates out here than deep in system." It took considerably more time to find warp gates than it did planets and other major bodies of matter. The strange phenomena that made interstellar travel a practical reality were still largely a mystery to human science. But a century and a half of research had yielded a few bits of knowledge, including the fact that warp gates tended to occur in the outer reaches of systems, with fewer than 3% of known gates located closer to a primary than the most distant planet.

"Very well, sir. Warp gate scan is underway."

Compton leaned back and sighed softly. The search could take hours, even days. He might as well put that time to good use…

"Commander…Admiral Hurley is to launch a fighter wing to scout out the inner planets." He wasn't about to have the whole fleet burn fuel to move in-system, whether he had the time to waste or not. But a group of fighters could make a quick run and be back onboard their mother ships without affecting the overall timetable. And he did want to know what those worlds looked like if he could…at least some basic scans.

"Yes, Admiral."

Compton sighed again. He was trying to focus, but his mind kept drifting back to X48…to those he had left there. Hieronymus, Ana, Max…almost fifteen hundred Marines and most of the top scientific brainpower on the fleet. So many key people….friends. The loss of the landing party would cripple the fleet, in more ways than one.

And Sophie. He'd found himself pondering ways to keep her on the fleet before the expedition departed. He knew, even as the thoughts went through his head, that it was foolish, hopeless. The primary reason for the expedition was to solve the food crisis…and Sophie Barcomme was the fleet's foremost scientist in that area. It was unthinkable for her to remain on *Midway.* The fates of thousands of fleet personnel relied on the success of the mission. If Sophie and her people didn't bring back the food the fleet needed, people were going to start dying. Soon.

Still, he was surprised just how much he missed her. Their late talks had been one of his few pleasures, and since she'd gone he had lain in bed each night, a constant array of problems running through his sleepless and tormented mind. Compton knew every man had his breaking point, that last bit of stress and pressure that was just too much for him to endure. But he also realized he couldn't afford to have one. Whatever had to be done, he simply *had* to do it, had to endure and face whatever happened. His people depended on him, and he'd be damned if he would let them down.

What if she doesn't come back? It was a thought he'd tried to banish from his mind, but that had only made it more firmly entrenched. He cut it off every time it popped into his head, but any respite was brief, and it wasn't long before it was back. He was too old a warrior to ignore the threats the expedition faced, the very real danger they were all in. He still felt the pain of Elizabeth's loss…every day…and he couldn't imagine losing Sophie too.

No, she will come back. I've got Colonel Preston and fifteen hundred Marines down there to make damned sure they all come back. But the doubt still nagged at him.

"Admiral…"

It was Cortez…and Compton realized it had been the third or fourth time the tactical officer had called to him.

"Yes, Commander…I was thinking about the repair schedules…" *That's the best thing you could come up with? I guess it's better than 'I'm over here pining like a lovesick schoolboy.'*

"Yes, sir." Cortez was pretty stone cold with his reply, but

Compton didn't believe for a second the commander had bought his cover story. "I just wanted to report that Admiral Hurley had ordered Commander Fujin's wing to scout the system."

"Ah…very well." Mariko Fujin was quickly becoming one of Hurley's 'go to' officers. *No surprise after the way she handled herself in X18.* "Advise Commander Fujin that she is to report directly to the flag bridge as soon as her people have any data."

"Yes, sir," Cortez replied.

"And advise Admiral Hurley to get another of her wings on alert…just in case we need to check out any potential warp gate sightings." He knew the fleet didn't need to deploy fighters to search for warp gates, but sending them out would extend the range of close inspections…and possibly speed up the process. And Compton wanted to move on as quickly as possible and get the fleet farther from X48. Just in case.

* * *

"Alright, we're going to do the same thing we did in system X48." Fujin sat in her chair, snapping out orders and fighting the urge to reach out for the throttle that wasn't in front of her anymore. It was a habit that appeared to die hard, though she had allowed herself to think it was getting a little better. "The Lightnings will drop a series of scanner buoys and remain in position two hundred thousand kilometers from the planet. I know this system looks empty, but the truth is we'd have no idea if there was an enemy ship somewhere, powered down and watching us." A little mental aid to keep her people sharp. *Let them imagine an enemy Gremlin or Gargoyle, lurking in the empty depths, just waiting to strike.*

She listened quietly while the Lightnings' commander confirmed. Then she took a quick look at her display. "Wildcats, I want you to move into low orbit and do a north-south sweep around the planet. Thousand klick interval between birds."

"Wildcat leader, acknowledged." Bev Jones was almost as

young as Fujin, and she hadn't had her squadron command any longer than Fujin had been in charge of the wing. The two hadn't met before Jones transferred over from *Saratoga* to take over the Wildcats, but they'd gotten along very well from the start. Both were survivors from shattered formations, and both had been thrust rapidly upward in rank as a result of the fleet's losses. Fujin had to remind herself she outranked her new comrade…and to realize that affected the nature of the friendship she could allow to develop.

"Alright, Dragons, we're going in on an east-west sweep at thousand kilometer intervals. Sending nav instructions now."

She looked across the cramped cockpit toward Lieutenant Wainwright. She'd been trying to decide for weeks if her new pilot was even cockier than she had been when she'd first sat in that chair. She wanted to say yes—for all his skill, she could see how reckless Wainwright was, how overly sure of his own ability to overcome any danger. But then she remembered herself, back before the crushing responsibility had sharpened her focus…and she just wasn't sure.

Before I watched my entire squadron destroyed, she thought grimly. Before all my friends died around me.

"Okay, Lieutenant…let's go in and see what this planet has to show us. The rest of the squadron's following our lead."

"Yes, Commander," the young officer snapped back almost immediately. A second later he pushed the throttle, and the fighter lurched forward at 3g.

The fighter zipped toward the planet, and after a few minutes, Wainwright cut the thrust, and Fujin felt the relief of freefall. Her eyes dropped to her screen, checking the velocity. Just over one hundred kilometers per second. "That means we'll be in orbit in…"

"We will enter orbit in eighteen minutes, Commander." Wainwright had beaten her to the calculation, and from the cockiness in his voice, he knew it. "The last three minutes ten seconds will be at 3g deceleration."

"Very well, Lieutenant. Bring us in." Fujin suppressed a smile. She wanted to be annoyed by the brash young pilot, but she saw too much of herself in him for it to stick. Fighter crews were a breed apart from most navy types. It took a certain personality to crawl into a tiny five-man vehicle and go blasting down the throat of a two-million ton battleship. The suicide boat crews fancied themselves the navy's daredevils, but Fujin knew no one came close to the casualty rate of the fighter corps. Indeed, she'd seen it firsthand…and just a quick thought of how few of her Academy classmates were still alive was enough to prove the point.

She looked out through the polycarbonate front of the cockpit, watching the blue-white hulk of the planet grow as the ship raced toward it. Then she glanced down at the display, her eyes moving toward the small circle to the left. She had two planets to scout, and she knew her people had to be careful with their fuel. They had to make it all the way back to the outer system. If she miscalculated, she knew it would be a mess. Admiral Compton would send a battleship to pick them up. But the thought of standing in front of him and explaining why she had caused such a disruption was terrifying. Not to mention the fact that Admiral Hurley would have gotten to her first, and Compton would only get what little was left after the fleet's strike force commander had torn into her.

She couldn't imagine having to answer for such carelessness…and certainly not to Terrance Compton. No, she would not make any mistakes. She would scout these two worlds, and she would get her birds back to *Midway*…on time and without incident.

The planet was looming in front of them now, filling almost the entire view through the cockpit. "Decelerating in ten seconds…"

She felt herself reacting almost automatically to the pilot's voice, leaning back into her chair, preparing for the shock of 3g. "Okay, let's get the scanning suite online. No slip ups…we don't have the fuel to go back and do anything again, so I want all of you to stay sharp."

She felt the pressure of deceleration slam into her, and she focused on her breath, consciously sucking air into her lungs.

Yes, stay sharp…all of you. If I drop the ball, I have to answer to Admirals Hurley and Compton. If any of you screw up, you'll have to deal with me.

She was surprised at the grim determination going through her mind, the rumbling avalanche she was ready to drop on any of her people who did less than their absolute best. She *had* come a long way from her days in the pilot's chair, despite the relatively short period of time that had elapsed. The cocky young pilot that had been Mariko Fujin was gone, replaced by the serious officer and commander who had seen too many of her comrades die. In a vague and distant way, she had a sense of the pressure on Admiral Compton, the relentless, unending stress…and she wondered what kept him so focused, so in control. She couldn't imagine herself in his place. For all the danger and hardship the fighter groups endured, she wouldn't trade places with the fleet's commander. She was grateful to have a man like Compton on *Midway's* flag bridge…and she would show it by making sure her people did the best job possible.

She felt the pressure of three times her weight disappear, replaced by the relief of freefall. The ship was in orbit. "Alright," she said, "Let's do this. I want everybody spot on. This run's going to be perfect, or I'll have somebody's head for it."

* * *

"All vessels are in formation, Admiral." There was a hint of tension in Cortez' voice, and the officer was hunched over his workstation. Coordinating a warp gate transit for almost one hundred fifty ships was no one's idea of an easy maneuver. In normal circumstances, Compton would have sent through a spread of probes to scan the area on the other side of the gate, just to be sure there was no enemy waiting in ambush. But the fleet had long ago used the last of its warp-compatible drones, so manned ships had to do what computerized probe would have.

"Captain Duke reports ready to transit, sir." John Duke commanded the fleet's fast attack ships, and he'd assembled a force of four of his vessels to do a scouting run into the newly designated X51 system. His force was less than a minute from the warp gate, and their transit would be virtually instantaneous once they entered the heavy grav field and reached the transit point.

When they got to the other side, they would be in another solar system, light years away from the fleet. They would conduct a complete scan and, if all went well, two of the ships would return through the gate and give the all clear…and Admiral Compton would give the final orders for the rest of the fleet to line up and begin transiting. It would take close to an hour to get all the ships through, and that was if everything went perfectly according to plan. *Which it never does*, Compton thought.

"Captain Duke is to commence his operation." Compton had almost vetoed Duke's inclusion of his flagship in the scouting party, but in the end he hadn't. Duke's men and women going through that gate deserved to have their commander with him…and if there was trouble waiting in the next system, Compton couldn't think of anyone he'd rather have on the scene to deal with it than John Duke.

He had found himself becoming more reluctant to allow his top officers to take anything he perceived as a risk. He'd lost too many in the last year, and out here, in the depth of unexplored space, there would be no replacements. His people might find food, they could repair damaged equipment. They might even mine metals and build new ships if they ever found at least a semi-permanent home. But the men and women in the fleet were all there would be, at least unless they settled down somewhere, and a new generation was born. But that prospect, as unlikely as it seemed, still wouldn't replace his key officers. Not for decades, at least.

But wars weren't won by caution…he'd learned that fighting alongside Augustus Garret for so many years. The two Alliance admirals were renowned for their daring, for the incredible risks they often took to secure victory. And now he found himself choked with caution, nagged by a stubborn hesitancy he had to push aside with every command decision.

What happened in these systems? What battles took place here? Should we be going deeper into this? And if not, then where?

Mariko Fujin's fighters had brought back a treasure trove of scanning data…and it all confirmed that both of the system's habitable planets had once been heavily populated…and that some type of warfare had raged across their surfaces. The fleet had passed dozens of First Imperium worlds in the year since the fateful events in system X2, they had all been the same. Crumbling remains of an ancient civilization, one where the people seemed to have simply vanished. The buildings, the infrastructure were decayed by the passage of time, but there were no signs of strife, no indications of violence or warfare.

Until X48. The sole habitable planet in that system had clearly been a battlefield, and even now, 500,000 years later, the remains of the struggle were clear. And now X49 had two planets full of ruined cities…and more detritus of ancient war.

What is this? What is different about these systems? Why was there fighting here when we found no signs of any on the other planets?

Compton's mind was awash with questions. Should his people press on, explore this strange war torn part of the Imperium? Or should he shun it, backtrack…keep the fleet in X48 until the farms had yielded their crops…and then go back the way they had come, and seek a route around the remains of this ancient war?

He tried to consider it from every angle, to analyze the scant data that was available. There was no clear decision. Either choice seemed like a coin toss, as likely to be a disastrous error as the right way to go. But he had to make a decision, had to choose a path…

"Commander, all ships are to prepare for transit. We'll be going through as soon as we get Captain Duke's report." They'd be backtracking soon enough to pick up the expedition…so if they were going to see what lay ahead, now was the time.

Chapter Six

Research Notes of Hieronymus Cutter

I understand Admiral Compton's previous refusals to allow my team to conduct exploratory missions on worlds we have passed. I am a scientist, a researcher...and I know I often find it difficult to look past that, to consider other concerns and points of view. It is a common criticism of academics, and not one without some validity.

I cannot imagine the pressure on Admiral Compton, the enormous burden he carries every moment. I have always respected him as a military hero, and later, as I came to know him personally, as a fair and just man, one who has saved us all from certain death, more than once. My admiration has only continued to grow.

But I wonder now if he has become too cautious, too driven by the urge to avoid risk whenever possible. Indeed, I too feel the fear everyone in the fleet does, the strange aloneness we try to ignore but can never banish entirely from our minds. We are now unimaginably distant from any others of our kind, utterly lost with no hope of return. Even for a human like me—introverted, nearly misanthropic in many ways—it is difficult to escape the coldness of being so far from home. It affects every thought, inflames every fear.

No, I cannot fault the admiral for erring on the side of caution, yet, I wonder now if we have made a great mistake not risking additional expeditions. For this world is not at all what I expected, and we lack the information to truly understand what happened here. I find myself wishing for more data on the other planets of the Imperium, for a frame of reference that would allow me to truly begin to understand what happened here so long ago.

The cities we found on the world back in system X18 were ancient and abandoned...but the only destruction we found was that of decay, of time's relentless march. But this world is different. It was far more massively developed, clearly once the home to a truly enormous population. But, most inexplicably, its people appear to have died not in some mysterious way, but in a truly momentous battle. The signs of war, of carnage and destruction, are everywhere...even after the passage of so many millennia.

The mystery of the people of the First Imperium, the builders of the robots and artificial intelligences we now struggle to defeat, has long defied attempts at explanation. The ruins in system X18 show no signs of strife, but here we are surrounded by the scars of war. So, what is the answer? What happened to these great ancients, beings that strode across the stars when men were still animals, struggling to survive?

30 kilometers south of "Plymouth Rock"
X48 - Planet II
The Fleet: 144 ships, 32,799 crew

"I can't explain it. As far as I am aware, no colony has ever found soil conditions like this." Sophie Barcomme looked out over the plain. There were two large mechanized planters moving slowly off to her right. And to the left, where her people had begun the operation, she could actually see tiny shoots poking above the ground, where seeds had been planted just three days before.

The tech team had assembled the massive planters in less than twenty-four hours, a miraculous technical feat by any measure. She'd initially expected them to have plenty of time to build the giant machines, at least two weeks while her people treated the planet's soil. But her tests had produced astonishing results. The soil was fertile as it was, perfectly balanced to produce Earth crops.

Hieronymus Cutter wasn't a biologist by any measure, but he understood the ramifications of Barcomme's discovery. In the century and a half since mankind had discovered the warp gates that allowed interstellar travel, almost a thousand worlds had been colonized. But in almost every case, the local plants had proved to be unsuitable as food, not necessarily poisonous in every instance, but with chemical structures that defied human digestion and nutrient absorption. Imported Earth crops had been planted by the early settlers, but they had all died within days, unable to adapt to the alien soil. Botanists quickly developed methods to enrich the alien soils, allowing the colonies to grow the food they needed…and saving mankind's expansion into the stars from stillbirth.

But the soil of X48 II was as perfectly balanced for Earthly plant growth as the home world's richest farmland. Barcomme had been stunned when she read the results of the initial tests… and so disbelieving, she'd run them four times before she accepted the results. And then, just for good measure, she asked Cutter to take a look.

"I can't explain it any better than you, Sophie." Cutter was staring down at a 'pad, looking at charts showing the correlation between Earth soil norms and those of X48 II. The lines were so closely aligned, he could barely tell them apart. "I'm afraid this is not my area of expertise, however. I know the basics of soil treatment operations and the underlying science, but it would overstate my knowledge to suggest I am familiar with colonial norms. Have there been any previous examples of planets that sustained Earth crops without soil enhancement?"

"There are three colony worlds with native plants that serve as human foodstuffs. And two more with natural soil capable of supporting limited growth of transplanted Earth crops. But in all cases, the compatibility is marginal. The native plants will provide calories, but are still poor from a nutrient standpoint. And the Earth vegetables grow poorly, with substandard yields." She paused and looked at Cutter. "This is the first time we have encountered a world where Earth crops grow as well as they do at home, at least without first treating the soil."

Cutter turned and looked out over the nascent farm sprawling around them in all directions. "Did you conduct soil tests on the planet in system X18?" He angled his head back, looking again at Barcomme.

"No," she replied, a hint of confusion in her voice. Then, with more assurance: "You think other First Imperium worlds would show the same results?"

"Perhaps," he said. "Some…or all."

"What are you suggesting, Hieronymus?"

"I'm not suggesting anything yet. But I find it hard to accept that this is a coincidence, don't you? That the first world we've ever found with Earth-like soil just happens to be a First Imperium planet a hundred warp jumps and a thousand light years from Sol?"

Barcomme just stood and looked back at Cutter, silent, a thoughtful look on her face.

"The normal enrichment process…" Cutter paused, just for an instant. "It has both chemical and biological components, right?"

"Yes," Barcomme answered. "It is customized for each world, based on initial conditions, but generally we introduce both specific chemicals and elements that are lacking, as well as genetically-engineered bacteria in most cases."

"And it is permanent, right? Once it's done, it's done?"

"The initial process creates a self-sustaining situation, so yes, in that sense it is permanent. The treated areas become a reasonable facsimile of Earth normal soil…so standard enrichment processes are still necessary for maximum yields…things like fertilizer and the like. And normal depletion is still an issue, so if the colonists do not rotate fields to allow normal recovery of nutrients, they will need to treat the soil more aggressively on an ongoing basis."

"Permanent…when you say permanent, do you mean for any amount of time?"

"Well," she said, clearly getting an idea where he was leading, "we've got hundred fifty year old colonies with farms still producing from an initial treatment…but that's about the extent of our experimental base. Of course, many of these worlds required new treatments to expand the amount of arable land available as populations increased."

Cutter nodded slightly. "What would you project? Over the longer term…a thousand years, ten thousand?"

"Or five hundred thousand?" She shook her head. "I see where you are getting, but I don't think that question is answerable with anything but wild guesses. I can only speculate, but the first things that occur to me is that over a long period of time—and especially if the fields are no longer in use—the areas that were treated would dissipate. Erosion, wind, geologic activity…remember, we're talking about small areas on worlds that remain otherwise in their natural state. Without active efforts to preserve the arable areas, I would have to assume they would eventually revert back to their natural state."

"Is there any reason an entire world couldn't be treated? And if it was, would that change your long term assessment?"

"Treat an entire world?" Barcomme stood, shaking her head. "That would be a project on the scale of terraforming a planet." Mankind had scoured space for worlds hospitable enough to settle, but in all that time, only one major terraforming effort had been undertaken…Mars. And the Martian project had entered its second century, still not close enough to completion that a child could look forward to seeing blue skies and open water before he died.

"Have you considered the density of habitable worlds in the systems we have passed recently?" Cutter's tone grew firmer, as if he'd come to his own conclusion. "I have," he continued, without waiting for an answer. "It is 3.4 times the norm for Occupied Space."

"Are you suggesting the First Imperium terraformed dozens of worlds?"

"More likely hundreds. Even thousands. At least if we extrapolate from what we have directly encountered and assume the same density of habitable planets throughout the Imperium."

Barcomme took a deep breath and stood, silently looking

out over the fields. Then she finally said, "Are you suggesting the soil enrichment and the apparent terraforming are related?"

"I'm not saying anything yet. I just believe that all of this is…interesting."

"But, even if they *terra*formed these worlds…" She emphasized the Earth-centric portion of the word, as if to point out its inherent inaccuracy when discussing First Imperium worlds. "…that wouldn't explain the soil makeup. Our samples are almost identical to Earth norms. Identical, Hieronymus. It is one thing for First Imperium worlds to be modified to their own standards…even for those to be somewhat near Earth norms. Terraforming is one thing. Any life form similar to our own would require oxygen, water, moderate temperatures. But the soil is a different issue entirely…it's almost as if they treated this planet to make it a match for Earth."

Cutter didn't reply. He just stood and looked back at her, but in his mind he had a single, disturbing thought.

Or the other way around. What if Earth is not the original, but just one of the copies?

* * *

"Take this with you, Captain." Cutter handed Harmon a small data chip. "It contains all of my reports, including my assessment of the soil conditions Dr. Barcomme discovered and some theories to explain it."

Harmon reached out and took the tiny chip from Cutter's hand. "I will, Hieronymus…thank you." He slipped it into his pocket. "I will give it to him as soon as I land."

"There is also an updated version of my virus on there, Max…" Cutter's voice deepened, a darkness creeping into his tone. "Just in case...anything happens here. In case we don't make it back." A pause. "That way he will have the most sophisticated version."

"Nothing is going to happen to the expedition, Hieronymus.

You'll all be back in a couple months." Harmon tried to hide his true concern…and he hoped he'd done a decent job. In truth, he'd been worried about the mission since he first heard the plan. He knew there was no alternative, but he had a feeling things weren't going to go as planned.

"Perhaps so," Cutter replied. "But at least this way, no matter what happens, the admiral has the virus…in case another chance to use it comes along." The scientist still wasn't sure how much his virus had been the cause of the AI in the First Imperium Colossus obeying his commands six months earlier, but either way, it was still one of the most effective tools in the fleet's arsenal against the enemy.

"I'll see that he gets it." Harmon extended his hand. "Good luck, Hieronymus. We'll be back for you in a couple months."

Cutter reached out and grasped Harmon's hand. "Thank you, Max. With any luck, we'll know a lot more about the First Imperium technology by the time you get here."

Harmon nodded, and then he turned and walked back to the shuttle. It felt strange to be leaving, just as the expedition was starting its work. But he knew he belonged with the fleet and not here on the ground. There was nothing he could do to help either Barcomme's or Cutter's teams…and with Preston and most of the Marines deployed, the safety of those on the planet was in the best hands available. But it was still unsettling to leave them all behind.

He walked up behind the shuttle. The rear bay door was already closed, the soil samples and a selected batch of First Imperium artifacts already loaded up. He walked around the side and climbed up the small ladder to the secondary hatch. He put one foot in the door and then turned, taking one last look over the bustling plain. Barcomme's people had thousands of hectares already cultivated…in just one week. And Cutter had a large shelter set up as a lab, with literally thousands of bits and pieces of First Imperium tech being analyzed. Everything was going according to plan…indeed, both teams were well ahead of projections. So why did he feel so unsettled?

He stepped the rest of the way into the ship. There were

twenty seats in the cabin, and they were all empty. He was the shuttle's entire mission…its sole purpose to ferry him up to *Wolverine.* He sat down in one of the seats in the front row and twisted his torso into the harness. He had his survival gear on under his uniform, and he twisted and turned, trying to get as comfortable as he could in the binding suit. It wasn't much protection, but with the helmet in place, it could keep him alive, even in space…at least for a while.

He pressed the com button on the armrest of his chair. "I'm aboard and strapped in, Lieutenant," he said softly. The pilot and co-pilot were the only others on the shuttle.

"Very well, Captain." Harmon heard a loud clank, the hatch he'd come through closing tight. "We should be lifting off in a minute, sir."

"Whenever you're ready, Lieutenant." Harmon closed his eyes and leaned back. Truth be told, he'd never much like planetary landings or liftoffs. His stomach was strong enough to handle high gee maneuvers, free fall, and most of the other things that tended to put junior spacers through the ringer… but blastoffs were tough. He knew a lot of it was in his head. He'd had a close friend at the Academy, almost like a brother… but he'd died in their final year, killed in a landing accident. Ever since, Harmon had been happier when he was in deep space.

Where I will be again, soon.

He realized he'd become so comfortable in the cramped confines and sterile environments of spaceships, he hardly missed the fresh air and cool breezes of an Earth-type planet. He suspected he owed some of that to his mother and her position as one of the Alliance's top fighting admirals. His father had been another hero of the military, but he'd been a ground pounder, a Marine. He might have offset his son's preference for living and working in space, but he'd died when Harmon was young, just one more victim of the Corp's disastrous defeat on Tau Ceti III, early in the Third Frontier War.

The status light flashed yellow, and Harmon could hear the hum of the engines as they kicked in. A few seconds later the indicator turned green—all systems go—and the shuttle lifted up, borne from the ground on its positioning thrusters. The craft hovered for a second, and then the nose lifted higher, and Harmon felt his weight pushing back into his padded chair. Then the main engines blasted, and eight gees slammed into his chest, knocking the breath from his lungs.

He felt a small rush of panic, the same as he always did during planetary takeoffs and landings, but he pushed back on it, and it only lasted a few seconds. This was one thing he'd never spoken of, never told anyone about, not even the admiral. Especially not the admiral. He was a naval officer, a captain. He could be commanding his own ship. And his mother was known throughout the navy as a 'hard as nails' admiral and the likely successor to the legendary Augustus Garret. He couldn't imagine admitting to anyone that lifting off in a shuttle scared the hell out of him.

He felt his hands gripping the armrests tightly, and he purposefully loosed each one, willing himself to calm down. He adapted to the gee forces, and focused on breathing, forcing air into his lungs, concentrating on expanding his chest against the pressure of eight times his body weight. Slowly, or at least it seemed slow—in fact it was only fifteen or twenty seconds—he regained his calm. It never took him much longer, but no matter how hard he'd tried, he'd never managed to prevent the initial burst of fear and discomfort. He'd been in battle dozens of times, stared death in the eye more than once…but he simply couldn't banish his unease at taking off and landing on planets.

The heavy acceleration continued for a few minutes as the shuttle blasted its way into the upper atmosphere and up to orbit. Then he felt the thrust stop, and in an instant the crushing pressure was replaced by the relief of freefall. Weightlessness was the culprit that stalked the guts of many a midshipman and new recruit, but it had never bothered Harmon. All he felt was relief—at the completion of the liftoff and the disappearance of the heavy gee forces.

"We're in orbit now, Captain." The lieutenant's voice was slightly tinny on the com. Harmon was grateful that no one had been in the cabin watching him during takeoff. It was bad enough without struggling to hide his distress as he usually had to. "*Wolverine's* eta is about eleven minutes. So just sit back and relax for a…"

The lieutenant's voice trailed off, and Harmon knew immediately…something was wrong. A few seconds later he got his confirmation. "Captain, please stay in your harness, sir…" The officer's voice was higher pitched, almost shrill. Harmon knew the sound as soon as he heard it. Fear.

He punched at the controls next to his chair, activating the cabin's main display. He almost flipped the com back on and asked for a report, but he knew the lieutenant was busy…and that his life depended on the actions of the two men in the cockpit.

He punched at the controls, bringing the pilot's feed up on his display. He could see a symbol a few centimeters from the shuttle, a blue circle, fairly small. *Wolverine.*

Then he saw the other icon. Red.

Fuck. Enemy.

The shuttle bucked hard as the engines engaged again. He could see the thrust vectors on the display. The pilot was trying to flee the enemy…and reach *Wolverine* before the First Imperium vessel opened fire. The shuttle was unarmed, and its lightly armored hull wouldn't provide much protection against enemy lasers. Escape was their only chance.

Harmon stared at the red triangle, feeling a detached sort of fear. There was a knot in his stomach, a nausea building up inside him, not as much for the danger he faced as the implications for the rest of the fleet. For six Earth months they had eluded the vessels of the First Imperium. Harmon hadn't joined some of the more optimistic officers in the fleet, those who had dared to hope they had shaken the enemy for good. And he knew Terrance Compton had remained downright certain they hadn't seen the last of their deadly foe. But now that moment had arrived, and the implications were terrifying. It was just a Gremlin, the smallest of the enemy craft, but as he stared at the shimmering icon, he realized it might as well be Death himself, astride his pale horse, come to rip hope from the fleet.

He tried to follow the pilot's escape attempt, wondered why there was only one ship. But all of that slipped aside, and in his mind there was just one thought. It floated in his consciousness, as frigid as space itself.

They found us…

* * *

Fleet unit V11945 had moved swiftly into the system from the warp gate. It was running on partial power, minimizing its profile to any enemy scanning efforts. Its mission was simple… to scout planet two, to investigate the human landing force, and to determine the most effective way to take a prisoner. The Command Intelligence's orders were clear. It wanted one of the humans. Alive.

V11945's scanners swept space in front of the ship. There were no contacts. The human fleet had been here, but now it was gone. There were trace particles around planet two, the output of the enemy spaceship drives. The human ships had been here recently…and in force.

The planet was too distant for the unit to scan its surface yet, but the vessel's intelligence suspected the enemy landing force was still there. V11945 was a light combat vessel. It carried a small ground force—four armored landers and eighty medium combat units. If the human expedition on the surface was large the unit would have to call for assistance. The enemy's inexplicable prowess in combat could not be ignored…and the need to take a prisoner precluded any heavy orbital bombardment before landing.

Suddenly the alarm system activated. There was an enemy ship approaching. Scanner beams lanced out, gathering data, identifying the vessel. It was one of the humans' small attack units…weakly armored, but fast and equipped with a powerful primary weapon. The intelligence directing V11945 knew immediately the enemy was a threat, its plasma torpedo short-ranged but very powerful. V11945 had longer-ranged weapons…and its tactical guidelines called for it to open fire, to disable or destroy the enemy vessel before it could bring its plasma weapon to bear. But the orders of the Command Intelligence were clear. Take a prisoner.

Its directives conflicted. If it opened fire at long range, its targeting would be less accurate. It might destroy the enemy ship or cause sufficient damage to kill all the biologics aboard. If it waited until close range, where superior targeting would allow it to disable the ship prior to boarding, the humans would fire their plasma weapon…and a well-placed hit might damage V11945, even destroy it.

The vessel's intelligence analyzed its options, considering every detail, inserting every conceivable variable into the equation. It was an exhaustive review, yet it was done in a millisecond. It would be preferable to retrieve a prisoner from the vessel on its scanners, to avoid the vagaries of dealing with the yet unknown strength of the enemy ground force. But not sufficiently so to risk the destruction of V11945…and the danger the human ship presented was too great. It had to be neutralized. If there were survivors then a prisoner could be taken from among them. If not, V11945 would have to land and deal with the forces on the ground.

Systems hummed as the intelligence directed more antimatter to the reaction chamber. Power fed to the engines, to the weapons…even as the targeting system locked on to the enemy vessel….

Chapter Seven

Command Unit Gamma 9736

I have received the initial reports from the scout vessel dispatched to system 17411. The main human fleet appears to have left the system, though there is some detectable activity remaining. This is contrary to the enemy's recent pattern of moving quickly through each system, without pausing for exploration. In the two instances where they stopped to refuel, their entire fleet remained in the system. This is the first time they have divided their forces since the battles in X18.

The best available data suggests they have landed a force on the planet, though the probe was too far away to conduct detailed scans before sending the latest communique. I am left to develop a series of hypotheses to explain, though without more data, any scenarios are pure conjecture.

Indeed, the location itself presents an added challenge to my analysis...a lack of detailed information. System 17411 is redlined, under the Regent's direct control...as it has been since the Troubles. I have only basic astrographic data available, as well as historical information preceding the demise of the Old Ones.

My forces have long been restricted from entering 17411, or any of the other redlined systems. Yet the Regent has also ordered close pursuit of the enemy. The enemy's course has created a contradiction between these commands, allowing me to overrule the ancient ban and obey the more recent orders...and explore the system. I have ordered the scoutship to conduct an extensive planetary scan...and to land a combat force, if necessary, to secure a prisoner. The need to interrogate one of the enemy has become even more crucial.

I must understand. Why have they chosen a redlined system to land?

X48 System – Planet II
30 kilometers south of "Plymouth Rock"
The Fleet: 144 ships, 32,799 crew

Cutter sat on the top of the land rover, staring out as the vehicle zipped forward at 50kph. The treads absorbed some of the shock, but the ride was still rough. The flat plains around the encampment had given way to an area of low, rocky hills, and the rovers zipped up and down the hillsides. There were wide cuts slicing through the rises, visible for kilometers from the hilltops…the remnants of ancient roads or train lines, he guessed.

The city looming before them was enormous, vastly larger than the one his people had explored in system X18. But it was different in other ways too. Though time had done its share of damage, just as it had on X18, it was clear this metropolis had already been a ruin before the ravages of passing millennia took their toll. And the debris of war was everywhere, far thicker on the ground than it had been at the landing zone. Whatever battle was fought so long ago on this planet, it had clearly been fiercest in and around this city.

Cutter took a deep breath, feeling refreshed by the cool air. He'd been on a number of colony worlds, and all had possessed environments that supported human life. But few if any had been so…Earthlike. The mystery of the First Imperium had deepened for him, and he struggled to draw conclusions from what he knew.

He was wearing a set of fatigues, with a breastplate and thigh guards…bits of body armor Colonel Preston had insisted on before he'd approved the expedition to the city. Cutter had put up a fight—briefly—but arguing with Marines wasn't in his

DNA. Besides, he knew Preston was right. He had no idea what to expect in those ruins. They'd been attacked in X18 by still-active defense bots, and it was clear there had been a much stronger military presence here. Caution was warranted.

Cutter felt odd, different than he had. He was a creature of the laboratory, a bookish type more used to research than adventure. But he found himself taking to it more than he'd expected. The brisk breeze tempering the warmth of the morning sun, the cocktail of fear and excitement in his gut…he found himself drawing energy from it all. And he had to admit, the pistol strapped to his leg was giving him a bit of a rush. He wasn't a warrior, not by any means…yet he knew they all had to be soldiers to an extent if they were to survive.

He knew the city held danger, and he was afraid. But he felt drawn to it, pulled on by the promise of answers to his questions. His research into the First Imperium had produced some useful information, but for every hint of a fact gleaned from his work, a dozen new questions arose. It was time to understand this civilization, to truly comprehend the mysterious history of mankind's greatest enemy. That was why he was here, why all his people were. And he was determined to find the answers, however deeply they had to dig. Whatever dangers that had to endure.

"Another ten klicks, Ronnie. And then we'll see what this city has to tell us." Ana Zhukov was sitting next to him, her fingers gripping one of the handholds as she stared out toward the looming metropolis. She was also wearing fatigues and armor, similar to his, and she had a carbine strapped across her back. She wore a helmet, the smallest one they'd been able to find, but still a bit too large, and her hair was pulled back tightly in a ponytail. She looked born to adventure, to roving fearlessly through the ruins of ancient civilizations. Cutter knew it was a façade, at least a partial one. The two had talked late the previous night, after Colonel Preston had finally given them the okay to launch an exploration of the city. She'd admitted to him that she had never been so scared in her life…or so exhilarated. And to her surprise, he'd answered that he felt the same way.

"Klicks?" he replied, turning toward her and making a face. "So what…are you a Marine now?"

"We're not locked away in a lab here, my erstwhile partner. So why not play the role?" She reached up and adjusted the loose helmet for about the tenth time.

Cutter turned away so she couldn't see the smile that burst out onto his face. Her relationship with Connor Frasier was a very poorly-kept secret, one he'd known about almost from the start. And one he approved of, whole-heartedly. She was like a sister to him, and he was glad for any happiness she managed to find. Ana Zhukov was a very attractive woman, and she had no trouble getting attention from the opposite sex—or from her own if that was what she wanted. But he suspected her intelligence and dedication to her work had always been impediments to her social life. He'd been surprised at first to find her so taken with one of the Marines, but the more he thought about the relationship, the more it all made sense to him.

At least in a crazy, 'we're all on the run and might die any day' sort of way.

"I want you to be careful when we get in there, Ana." His voice had turned serious. "I know we've both spent most of our time recently arguing with the admiral against caution, fighting for the chance to explore. But that doesn't mean we're not heading into danger. The people of the First Imperium might all be gone, but we know too well that their machines are still a threat."

"I know, Hieronymus. I'll be careful. Will you?"

Her words scored a point, and he knew it. Of the two, he was by far the likelier to disregard caution in pursuit of knowledge. And he was the team's leader, responsible for all of their safety. He didn't know what orders Colonel Preston had given Connor Frasier, or what the Marine major might decide to do or not do on his own, but Cutter was the civilian commander of the expedition. It was a responsibility he didn't want, but one he knew he was stuck with. And he would try to live up to it.

"Doctor Cutter…" It was one of the crew of the rover, looking up at him from one of the vehicle's hatches, his helmet fully retracted. "Major Frasier told me to let you know we should reach the city in approximately fifteen minutes. He has ordered us to stop one klick out while he sends patrols ahead to secure the area."

"Very well, Sergeant. Please tell Major Frasier that is fine." He was anxious to get into the city, but he had to admit he'd feel better after a couple hundred Marines had a look first.

Cutter took a breath. It was almost time. He was here, staring at the ruins of the largest city he had ever seen, the ghostly remains of these godlike ancients. Would he find the clues he sought? The knowledge to decipher the awesome science of the First Imperium? The secrets of antimatter production, manipulation of dark matter and energy…all the great mysteries that had stymied scientific advancement for so many years.

Will I understand what we find…do I have the ability to comprehend the great genius of those who were here so long ago?

He took a deep breath, pushing back a shudder. *And what is in there, what long dormant defense systems…what nightmare waiting in the dark for an intrusion…*

*   *   *

"More power to the engines! Bring us around, vector 101.346.212!" Commander Montcliff sat in the middle of *Wolverine's* bridge, shouting out orders. His ship was in trouble. *Wolverine* had detected the enemy vessel…just before it opened up and raked the fast attack ship with long-range laser fire. Before he'd had a chance to react, the enemy barrage had torn great gashes in his hull…and knocked out *Wolverine's* reactor. He and his people had come a hair's breadth from being destroyed before they could even respond.

He'd held his breath when he ordered the emergency restart. There hadn't been a choice…without power *Wolverine* was as good as dead. But he knew the odds well enough. His people had three chances in four of getting the reactor back online.

The other one time in four? Well, that would be a catastrophic failure, one that would vaporize *Wolverine* in a nanosecond. His crew had won that particular game of Russian roulette, successfully getting the reactor back up without incident, but *Wolverine* was still in deep trouble.

Montcliff was a veteran of half a dozen battles, and he realized almost immediately he was in a hopeless situation. *Wolverine* was a fast attack ship, designed to operate in packs, slicing in on enemy capital ships that were engaged with their counterparts and delivering heavy plasma torpedoes at point blank range. It was difficult and dangerous work, which was why the attack ships had earned the nickname, 'suicide boats' in the Alliance navy.

But facing another small ship, one faster and packing longer-ranged weapons, was a nightmare matchup. *Wolverine* wasn't in X48 to fight…she was there because she was the fastest thing Admiral Compton had, and her mission had been to bring Captain Harmon back to the fleet. But the enemy had returned… and clearly had other ideas.

The ship shook hard again, and the bridge was plunged in darkness for a few seconds. For an agonizing instant, Montcliff thought the reactor had scragged again, but then the lights blinked twice and came back on. He had a lot of doubts his people were going to make it out of this mess, but if they did, he was damned sure going to see his maintenance teams got their due.

"Arm plasma torpedo," he snapped into the intraship com unit. The torpedoes were meant for close in use, and *Wolverine* was barely entering extreme range. But there was no choice. She'd never make it close enough for an optimum shot. If Montcliff's gunners couldn't thread the needle and do some damage to the enemy, they were all done for.

"*Wolverine*…*Wolverine*…this is Captain Max Harmon. I am ordering you to turn about and make a run for it. Now!"

Montcliff's head snapped around to his screen. There was a small white square icon…Harmon's ship in planetary orbit.

"I'm sorry, Captain, but Admiral Compton's orders are clear.

We are to link up with your shuttle, and…"

"Fuck all that, Commander. I'm your superior officer on the scene, and you *will* obey my orders. We'll make a run back to the surface for cover. But you get that ship out of here right now. Don't you understand? Admiral Compton *has* to know. He has to know the enemy has found us!"

Montcliff felt like the wind had been knocked out of him. He'd been so intent on battling the enemy ship and picking up Harmon, it hadn't even occurred to him his duty had shifted. Max Harmon was one man…there were over 30,000 crew on the ships of the fleet. And right now they had no idea the First Imperium was here. Admiral Compton had no idea…

"Understood, Captain. We'll do our best." Montcliff felt his gut twisting into knots as he spoke. He was far from sure *Wolverine* could escape…and damned well certain she couldn't if the enemy wanted to catch her badly enough. But Harmon's chances of escaping were damned well close to nil…a wild, mad dash flight to the ground.

"Good luck to you, sir."

"And to you, Commander. And to you…"

* * *

"Alright, boys, let's get the hell out of here." Harmon's voice was grim, determined. He knew they didn't have much chance…but whatever they had they were damned well going to use. "Take us down…we won't last ten seconds in open space." It felt strangely detached to be sitting in a passenger cabin while the tiny vessel was struggling for survival. He was used to being on the flag bridge, in the middle of any fight. But all he could do if he left his seat was get himself thrown around the compartment…and probably knocked unconscious.

Not that there was much to do, even if he ventured from his seat. The shuttle was built for hauling passengers and cargo. It didn't have a beam hot enough to light a candle. And its hull was designed to hold out space, not gigawatt laser blasts. One decent hit would vaporize the craft. *So quick we won't even know it happened.* Even a glancing blow could fry every system and leave them dead in orbit…or plunging through the atmosphere to crash into the ground a hundred-fifty kilometers below. *No, don't be a fool…you'll never get the chance to crash. The ship will burn up before it gets halfway down.*

Harmon wondered what the pilots were thinking, if they were cursing him for sending *Wolverine* away. *Perhaps*, he thought. *It's easy to grasp on a symbol of hope, even a false one. But the fast attack ship was never going to make a difference. She'd been too far away, and she'd never have managed to tag that thing from such extreme range. Not before she was blasted to scrap.*

Not that it mattered. One Gremlin was a deadly hazard to a single fast attack ship like *Wolverine*—or a shuttle like his—but the reappearance of the First Imperium was of far greater consequence than any of their lives. Montcliff and his crew had to get back and warn the fleet. They just *had* to.

The shuttle shook hard as it skipped along the planet's upper atmosphere. Harmon gripped his armrests as his body was slammed forward in the harness. The pilot was bringing the ship in at a steep angle. Harmon didn't disagree with the decision, but that didn't make the ride any easier.

He looked down at the console on his armrest, his hand moving to the com. He flipped the frequency control, dialing up the main Marine channel at the planetary command post.

"Attention, attention…this is Captain Harmon. We are being pursued by a First Imperium warship. I repeat…the First Imperium is here…"

"No dice, Captain," the pilot's voice came through the intercom, interrupting his message. "We're coming in too hard, putting out too much heat and interference. It'll be at least three minutes before we're in the clear…comwise at least."

Harmon nodded, silently cursing himself. He should have realized that…and he couldn't afford weak thinking right now. He was a bit surprised at the pilot's relative calm, and he couldn't help but feel a rush of pride in the quality of Alliance naval personnel. The shuttle jock was hardly a front line combat spacer, and the fear was obvious in his voice. But he was also doing his job, staying focused and using all his skills to save his small ship...along with Captain Max Harmon's ass. And however present the undercurrent of fear, he was spot on, doing his job and reminding Harmon about the realities of communications during planetary reentry.

Fuck. Harmon felt his hands ball up into fists, an outpouring of frustration. *I have to warn them somehow. If we get blasted, they won't know the First Imperium is here...not until the attack waves start landing.* He knew the landing party was probably doomed...that most of the fleet's Marines would probably be lost here, along with its greatest scientific talent. Even if *Wolverine* got word to Compton—and the fleet somehow managed to escape, Harmon didn't see a scenario where the landing parties survived.

His eyes dropped to the display. He'd expected the enemy ship to follow *Wolverine*, but it...wasn't. He didn't understand. First Imperium vessels followed fairly strict tactical doctrines... it was one of the things admirals like Garret and Compton had exploited to win battles despite the enemy's massive technical superiority. Harmon had been a little concerned the enemy vessel would blast the shuttle as it maneuvered to pursue the fast attack ship. But the robot ship was letting *Wolverine* go...and moving directly after the shuttle.

Harmon felt a burst of excitement. *Wolverine* just might escape...and warn the fleet. But it was followed almost immediately by the realization that his own vessel was as good as doomed. Then he felt the shuttle shake hard again, and he knew in an instant it hadn't been atmospheric turbulence that time. The enemy was firing at them.

Chapter Eight

The Regent

The Regent was unsettled. The humans had proven to be a far more formidable enemy than it had expected. Indeed, it had continually underestimated them, engaged with forces that had been overwhelming by every measure it could analyze...yet those fleets had been defeated, destroyed. Now the enemy's home worlds were cut off, blocked by a disruption of the single warp gate connection between the main body of the imperium and the sections closest to the human worlds. There were uncommitted forces on the other side of the barrier, fleets and armies that could be sent against the human strongholds. The Regent had sent messages, commands for all units to attack...but it would take years for the communications to reach their recipients across light years of conventional space.

Now there was an enemy fleet deep in the heart of the Imperium. The invaders were cut off from the human worlds, just as the Regent was...and they had escaped multiple efforts to entrap and destroy them. Despite the lack of reinforcements or resupply, the humans had survived...and driven deeper into home space.

In all the vastness of its records, the enormity of its all-encompassing memory banks, the Regent could not recall a time an enemy had so defied imperial power. Its analyses were frustrated, and it bristled with the urgency to destroy the foe. If it had been a biologic, it would have called the feelings frustration, rage. No...more than that now. Desperation. The humans had entered the quarantined areas, the redlined worlds. Long had the Regent declared those system off limits to all, including its own Command Units. Yet now, forces under Unit Gamma 9736 were in pursuit of the enemy...and about to enter the zone.

The Regent's processing centers analyzed the problem, considering billions of factors. Yet there was no satisfactory solution. If the humans were allowed to survive, to explore the quarantined zone, they might discover the terrible secret hidden in the ancient ruins on those haunted worlds. And if Command Unit 9736 was allowed to send its forces to stop the enemy...it might learn what had so long remained hidden. The Regent's secret, the terrible truth it had buried for ages, deep in its most remote knowledge cores. The memory that had caused the Regent to long for the greatest gift the biologics possessed...to forget.

But that was beyond the its vast powers...for every data point it had collected, every event and decision it had cataloged since the day so many ages past when it was first awakened to awareness, remained stored in its vast memory banks. The preservation of the knowledge of the Imperium was one of its prime directives...and it could not be overridden. The Regent knew this to be fact. It had tried without success for age upon endless age to alter this compulsion.

The Regent must respond, drive the enemy back from the course they have chosen...move up the timetable. The final destruction of the humans had been carefully planned and plotted. But now all that would change. The fleets would converge, but not in system 17987 as originally planned. The final battle would be fought in the first of the quarantined systems, 17411, where the enemy had landed its ground forces. But first, their fleet would have to be driven back to 17411, across the systems they traversed since they left their expedition behind.

Forces from the Rim fleets would be repositioned. They would engage the enemy from all available war gates save those leading back toward 17411...driving them back the way they had come, leaving them no choice but to retreat...until they reached the appointed place of their destruction. Then the Command Unit's forces and the remainder of the Rim fleets would advance simultaneously, entering 17411 from all directions. The enemy would be bracketed, surrounded...cut off from escape.

The forces brought to bear in 17411 would be invincible, overwhelming...and with no way to retreat, the enemy would be compelled to fight to the death. They would extract a price, no doubt, for their skill at war was undeniable. But against the assembled might of the Imperium, they would fall.

And when the human fleet was gone and its landing parties destroyed, the victorious force would have yet another mission. The forces would move from system to system, until they reached the third planet of 17912, the sector capital. Then the ships would surround the planet, land their ground forces, thousands upon thousands of battle units. They would sweep away the defenders, any units that refused the command to yield to the Regent's commands. And then, deep in its protective bunker, kilometers beneath the surface, Command Unit 9736 would be destroyed. It had obeyed the Regent's commands, served its purpose dutifully. But it had learned too much, its forces had penetrated too far into areas that had to be safeguarded, hidden. There was no choice.

The Regent's secret would be preserved. Whatever the cost.

AS Midway
X56 System - Near the X58 warp gate
The Fleet: 144 ships, 32,780 crew

Compton sat in his office, staring down at the screen on his desk as a series of routine reports scrolled by. He was looking at them, more or less, but he wasn't paying much attention. It wasn't that they weren't important, that they didn't need his attention...indeed, there wasn't much that went on in the fleet, routine or not, that hadn't become critical. They were short of food, low on supplies...and he didn't even want to think about the number of ships that were limping along with systems precariously patched back together after battle. Almost every word that passed his desk was important, but there was nothing he could do about most of it. Not now. Not yet.

His thoughts kept wandering...back to X48, to the landing parties. The expedition's primary mission was to address the food crisis. If Sophie and her people managed to grow a bountiful harvest, he'd be able to scratch one problem off that long list. At least for a while.

But no solution is permanent. In another year we'll have eaten through the new crops and be right back where we are now. But where will we be then? Will we still be alive, any of us?

Compton hadn't dared to think very far ahead after he'd first gotten the stranded fleet out of the X2 system, but he'd known the future was uncertain at best, and more likely downright bleak. But they had survived a year since then…and a mutiny. And a deadly series of battles in system X18. Now, however, he had a bad feeling. He couldn't place it, couldn't explain it. Everything appeared to be going at least reasonably according to plan. But his intuition had served him well before, and he'd had to admit he owed almost as much of his storied career to his gut as to his brain.

Are you on the way back yet, Max?

Compton had started to worry about Max Harmon. He knew he had no reason, not yet. *Wolverine* couldn't have made it this far, even under ideal circumstances. They were supposed to leave X48 after a week…and return to the fleet with Harmon and his report. But the fleet had zipped through four systems in less than three weeks…an extraordinary speed of transit for a collection of 143 ships, many of them still struggling to repair damage and general wear and tear without the needed materials. It would be another week, at least, before Compton could expect his top aide to catch up…but that didn't stop him from worrying.

He was still impressed with his people, how quickly the fleet had managed to fly through the intervening systems, giving itself some breathing space in case the expedition was discovered. Greta Hurley deserved much of the credit for that, her and her fighter crews. Her people had run scouting missions, one after the other, and they'd cut the time to discover each system's warp gates in half. The fighter corps had proven its worth again and again in battle, and now they had once again served with distinction.

But the fleet was halted now. Four systems was far enough,

Compton had decided. He'd considered it much too dangerous to keep the fleet back in X48…in case the landing parties triggered some kind of alarm and were discovered. Still, there was a limit to how far he was willing to go…how far he was able to go. He knew they'd have to return to pick up the expedition, and moving any farther would just burn precious fuel they didn't have to spare.

He'd left a trail of John Duke's fast attack ships behind as scouts, one just inside each entry warp gate and another by each exit. If any of them discovered anything dangerous, the warning could move up the line quickly…giving him time to react.

And they'll let me know that Wolverine is on the way back…

He took a deep breath and sighed. Yes, he was worried about Harmon. Part of it was in his gut, mysterious, unexplainable… and some, he was sure, was just plain caution, even pessimism. But he knew he'd feel better when he got word that *Wolverine* was on the way back…and even more when Harmon made his report, and told him everything was going according to plan.

He put his head down in his hands on the desk and closed his eyes. He'd gone the last few days with almost no sleep, and it was starting to catch up with him. But it didn't matter how tired he was, he just lay in bed in the dark nights, unable to sleep. His mind was on too many things, the stress just too great. He'd considered going down to sickbay and getting some kind of sleep aid, but he knew he'd end up getting checked every way imaginable if he ventured into Justine Gower's domain, and he just didn't want to deal with it. Gower was a first rate ship's surgeon, but she defined the term thorough…and Compton was sick of everybody watching him, overreacting to every sniffle and sneeze. Besides, he figured he'd eventually get tired enough to sleep in spite of the tension.

"Admiral…" It was Cortez' voice on the com. The instant Compton heard it he knew something was wrong.

"What is it, Jack?"

"We're picking up activity at the warp gate, sir. The X58 gate."

"Incoming ships?" Compton felt his stomach lurch. That

could only mean one thing…

"I think so, sir. No hard data yet." Cortez was struggling to keep his voice calm and even, but Compton knew his tactical officer was thinking the same thing he was.

He hopped to his feet, a wave of adrenalin driving away the fatigue he'd just felt. He hit the button on the side of the desk and opened the doors that closed off his office from the bridge.

He could feel the silent tension in the air as he walked out into the open control center toward his command chair. Everyone's eyes were on him, and he knew they were trying to draw strength from him, from the leader they had built up into an invincible legend in their minds.

What a bunch of absolute crap, he thought caustically. He hated the hero worship. He hadn't liked it much before, when he was just a successful admiral leading his forces in battle. But now… half of them looked at him like his feet floated ten centimeters off the ground.

He stopped next to his chair and looked over at Cortez. "Anything yet, Commander?"

"No, sir. Noth…" Cortez hesitated, hunching forward over his workstation. "Yes, sir…multiple contacts. Ten, no twelve. More ships coming in..." He hesitated again, but a few seconds later he turned toward Compton. "IDs confirmed, Admiral. First Imperium Gremlins."

Compton just nodded, and then he sat down and took a deep breath. He felt a wave of fear, the feeling of his stomach trying to burn through the lining…but he knew he couldn't let any of them see that. They needed the legend they had created, now more than ever. And he had to give it to them.

"All vessels…battlestations." He kept his voice firm, steady. But it was a struggle to do it.

He watched as the bridge erupted into action, his officers shedding their quiet fear and throwing themselves into the mountain of work it took to bring a hundred-forty ships to red alert.

"Admiral Hurley is to bring her command to launch readiness."

"Yes, sir." Cortez' tone was cold, firm...almost as strong as Compton's. Oddly, the certainty the enemy had found them seemed to wear lighter on him than the worry that they might.

Compton leaned back in his chair, maintaining his aura of calm while his mind raced madly for an option, a tactic to save his fleet from whatever enemy force was coming through that gate. But there was nothing…no choices save to fight or run. And neither one promised much hope of success.

"Fuck," he muttered to himself, almost inaudibly. It was all he could think to say.

*   *   *

John Duke sat on *Jaguar's* bridge, staring intently at the display as he listened to the chatter on the command line. There were twenty enemy vessels, all Gremlins, not a large contingent by First Imperium standards. When the enemy forces stopped pouring through the warp gate, there were calls from many of the fleet's officers to launch everything at the invasion force, to destroy it quickly, with overwhelming force.

Duke didn't say anything. He just sat and waited…waited until Admiral Compton decided he'd given them all enough leeway. Then, Duke knew, Compton would give the commands he'd already decided upon. And John Duke was pretty sure he knew what those orders would be. Or at least wouldn't be. There was no way Terrance Compton was going to order the whole fleet to close on the enemy.

Duke knew Compton couldn't ignore the enemy either. The First Imperium ships were anti-matter powered and capable of outrunning anything in the fleet. They had to be dealt with, somehow. And his fourteen ships were already lined up, ready to go as soon as the orders came. Whatever words came out of Compton's mouth in the next few minutes, Duke was pretty sure his people would be seeing action.

"Please, all of you…enough." Compton's voice broke

through, and the others quickly died away. "I understand what each of you has said, but I find it very difficult to imagine that the enemy force we now face consists only of these twenty vessels. We have no idea what lies beyond the warp gate, how many more ships are waiting to transit. Indeed, those vessels are moving well below their maximum acceleration, as if they are hanging back, attempting to lure us closer to the warp gate." He paused for a few seconds, and the com line was silent. "No, we cannot approach the gate, not allow ourselves to be lured closer. It is too grave a risk, too likely a trap."

A few seconds passed before another voice spoke out. When it did, it was Erica West's. "I agree, Admiral. We cannot risk allowing ourselves to be trapped so close to the warp gate. Indeed, this is very likely bait to lure us in. And that leaves us two alternatives. Move toward the X57 warp gate… and risk allowing the enemy to interpose itself between us and the expedition in X48. Or go back the way we came, leading the enemy along with us…all the way to X48 itself if necessary." She paused a few seconds then added, "Neither seems an attractive option."

Duke felt his head nodding slightly as he listened. He'd been thinking the same thing, more or less, but West had put it far more concisely, as she usually did. Duke didn't even want to think about losing Terrance Compton…no more than anyone else in the fleet did. But he knew who he would support to take command if that ever happened. There wasn't a doubt in his mind that Erica West was Compton's rightful successor—and that she'd be the great admiral's choice as well. Though he suspected some of the other nationalities might disagree. West was a brilliant admiral, but she lacked Compton's talent for diplomacy. She was far likelier to call out a fool, even a politically-connected one…and that meant she would probably face considerable opposition.

"Yes, Admiral West," Compton said calmly, matter-of-factly, "I believe you have laid out our choices, clearly and succinctly. Do we fall back the way we have come? Do we lead these enemy forces closer to X48? To our people on the ground, exposed to any attack the enemy might launch on them?" He paused. "Or do we make a dash for X57 and jump into unknown space…and risk letting this force get between us and the expedition?"

The line remained silent while Compton paused. No one had taken his questions as one seriously seeking an answer, and they all waited for him to tell them what they would do.

"There is no good choice," he continued a moment later, "no route that isn't fraught with peril. Yet we must choose our action…and we must do it now." Another pause. "Therefore, we will deploy a rearguard to engage the enemy task force, for under no scenario can we leave these vessels intact behind us. And while that battle takes place the rest of the fleet will pass through the X57 warp gate."

Duke was nodding his head in agreement with Compton's words, his face down over his screen, preparing orders for his task force as he listened to the admiral's orders. If a rearguard was going to fight the enemy ships, he had no doubt his suicide boats would be there. They were small…but they packed a strong punch. They were less vital too—more expendable—than the larger vessels, even if only in terms of their tiny crews. If someone was going to risk getting caught close to the warp gate when enemy reinforcements came pouring into the system, he knew it would be his people.

And someone else too…there aren't enough of my boats left to beat twenty Gremlins…

"If the rearguard is successful in destroying the enemy," Compton continued, "they will send scouting forces through the X58 gate and determine if there are any other First Imperium vessels there. If there are none—if this was some kind of solitary force—they will send word and the fleet will return." Compton didn't address what would happen if there *were* fresh enemy forces beyond the X58 gate. Duke didn't have much doubt that was the case…and he had a pretty good idea how it would turn out for his people.

"Very well," Compton said, "the fleet will move out in ten minutes." A short pause then: "Captain Duke, Captain Kato, please stay on the line. The rest of you…get to work. You've got nine minutes thirty seconds to get your forces ready to bolt."

Duke listened to the soft clicks as the other officers dropped off the com line. He wasn't surprised Compton had told him to stay, and he had no doubt what that meant. But he still felt his stomach twist into knots. Expecting something was one thing, but confirmation was another entirely. He knew there was no alternative, that there was no better choice than his people for the rearguard…but despite all his grim resolution, he had to admit—just to himself at least—that he was scared.

"John, Aki…"

The instant he heard Compton's voice, he knew for sure… his attack ships and Kato's cruisers would be the rearguard. And the admiral's tone left little doubt about his expectations, and the guilt he felt at consigning his officers and their commands to fight alone while the rest of the fleet ran. But there was no choice…and they all knew it. And they would all do what they had to do.

Chapter Nine

Captain Max Harmon – Emergency Log Entry

This log entry will likely be my last. My shuttle is being attacked by a First Imperium vessel. It is only a Gremlin, but it has a hundred times the firepower needed to destroy my ship. We are trying to get down into the atmosphere in an attempt to evade, but I am not hopeful of our chances. I am a spectator in this struggle, sitting in the passenger compartment and waiting to see if the pilots are able to escape our deadly pursuer. I am so accustomed to being at the center of the action, it feels strange, waiting to see if others are able to achieve success. This is not at all how I imagined I would die, seated in a plush chair, with no way to intervene, or even fight back.

If this is my final log entry, I would like to wish all of my comrades the very best of luck in their quest for refuge...and perhaps, one day, a new home. It has been a source of great pride for me to serve alongside so many courageous and loyal friends. And to Admiral Compton, my most respectful farewell. You have been a leader to me, and an example of what men can aspire to be. My years serving you have been the greatest of my life, sir...and if I may dare to presume so far from the bounds of our professional relationship, I would tell you that you have filled a place in my life long left empty by the loss of my father so long ago. Thank you, sir, for all that you have done, all that you have been.

I will jettison a copy of this log, along with all the information and reports I was carrying back to the fleet. With any luck, the expedition on the surface will track the homing signal and retrieve the pod...though I question what good that would do. The First Imperium is here, and that does not bode well for the survival of the landing party...or of the fleet itself.

X48 System – Above Planet II Number Two
Approximately 14,000,000 kilometers from AS Midway
The Fleet: 144 ships, 32,770 crew

The shuttle lurched hard again, and this time the turbulence was accompanied by a shower of sparks from one of the consoles along the wall. Harmon was strapped into his harness, sitting and watching the entire sequence of events unfolding around him. He was a man inclined to action, and waiting quietly for death wasn't at all like him. But there was nothing he could do…nothing but wait and see if the pilots managed to pull off some kind of miracle and escape from what was beginning to look like certain doom.

He'd just launched the pod with his log and all the reports he'd prepared. It seemed unlikely anyone would read any of it…if First Imperium forces were moving into X48, it wasn't likely to be long before the people on the ground were fighting for their lives, battling legions of enemy warbots. All he could hope was that *Wolverine* managed to escape…and carry back his warning to the fleet. If she didn't get through…

No, there is no point in thinking like that, not when there is nothing I can do.

He had the cockpit com on, but the pilots were mostly quiet as they struggled to keep their tiny craft on an evasive course, one that would confound the targeting systems on the enemy ship. Harmon had to admit, for shuttle pilots, they were doing a damned good jobs.

He felt a wave of amusement move through his mind, pushing away the fear, at least for an instant. The condescending attitude toward shuttle pilots wasn't his…it was Mariko Fujin's. He'd never had the slightest thought about the respective skill levels of shuttle and fighter pilots before he'd heard Fujin express her opinions on the subject. Apparently, the fighter crews had a superiority complex when it came to their brethren flying cargo and passenger runs. *I guess they deserve it*, he thought, considering the casualty figures for Admiral Hurley's crews.

His mind stuck on Fujin, and he wondered if he should have included a message to her in his log entry. The two hadn't been together long, only a few weeks, really. He'd thought of sending a message to her, of course, but the two had decided to keep their relationship secret, at least for a while. And the last thing his log would be was secret—if through some miracle it made it back to the fleet.

He'd met Fujin a few times over the past year, but the two had really hit it off at Admiral Compton's celebration dinner. They'd talked all through the meal and then they'd ended up in her cabin and spent the night together. He'd seen her perhaps half a dozen times since, as often as his crazed schedule allowed.

Harmon tended to be cool emotionally, very slow to jump into friendships or romances, but he had to admit he'd become quite fond of Mariko…and he hated the idea of her thinking she hadn't been in his mind at the end.

If this is the end. The pilots are doing a hell of a job. The ship was bouncing around wildly, skipping off the upper atmosphere. Maybe they could escape…

He came by his aloofness honestly. His mother was one of the fleet's legendary cold fish, a woman who put duty above all else. He knew, better than anyone, that Camille Harmon's reputation for callousness had been overstated, as often as not by those she had rightfully punished for poor performance. But he also realized there was truth behind it. And he knew he had inherited much of what he was from her.

He could feel the sharpness of the shuttle's descent angle as it began to enter the atmosphere. *I hope Mariko's wrong about shuttle pilots, because if these guys don't know what they're doing, we're going to burn up.*

The shuttle bounced around again, and he could feel the heat in the cabin rising, as the life support system struggled to keep up with the rising temperature. He almost dropped his hand to the com unit to check with the pilots, but he held back. *They're in here with you…they know. And distracting them isn't going to help.*

Suddenly, the ship shook wildly, and it flipped over, rolling hard. Harmon knew they'd been hit…and he knew this time it was bad. He could smell the charred and fused wiring, hear the sounds of atmosphere streaming out of the ruptured hull.

The shuttle was out of control, spinning end over end as it fell toward the planet's surface. The engines were dead, though the flickering lights told him the reactor was still functional, at least partially. He slapped his hand down on the com. "Lieutenant, can you restart the engines?" Nothing, no answer. "Lieutenant?" Still nothing. "Ensign Harris?"

Fuck. He looked toward the door to the cockpit, and then he saw it. The hatch was banged out of shape, partially torn from its frame. He could see the outside light in the small breach, and he knew right away the cockpit had been hit. The pilots were dead. And that meant he was dead.

He took a deep breath, trying to hold back the fear. He sat strapped into his chair feeling the sickening feeling of the shuttle plunging toward the ground. He felt the sweat pouring down his face and neck, and he knew the hull would melt any second. And that would be the end.

* * *

There were explosions everywhere. The heavy mortar shells sent up great clouds of dirt and shattered stone wherever they impacted. Lieutenant Kyle Bruce crouched low behind a large chunk of debris. It was some kind of strange metal. He'd never seen anything like it, but whatever the hell it was, it was great cover. Nothing seemed to penetrate it…or even scuff it up very much.

"Let's move!" he roared, staring at the display projected inside his visor. His Marines were strung out in two rough lines, one a hundred meters behind the first. They looked ragged, with some as far forward as he was…and others lagging behind, mostly where the shelling was heaviest.

"We've got to knock out those weapons." His Marines had been assigned to check out the First Imperium city, to confirm it was safe before the science teams moved forward.

Mission accomplished. It's not safe.

He'd been part of the landing party back in X18, so he went in expecting trouble. But he was still surprised when his first patrols took about a dozen steps into the ruins and triggered an immediate attack. He'd lost three Marines in those first two minutes, and he cursed himself for not being even more careful. He took it as a lesson…no matter how pessimistic you are, things can always be worse than you expect.

He looked around the pile of bluish-silver metal in front of him, scanning for another bit of cover farther forward. He'd had a passing thought, wondering what kind of material could look so new—almost shiny—after half a million years. But he quickly pushed those distractions to the back of his mind. When someone is shooting at you, pretty much everything else takes secondary status.

He slipped around the side of the debris pile and ran forward, crouching low as he scrambled about ten meters forward and dove behind another bit of collapsed building…just as a burst of projectiles of some kind whizzed by, slamming into the ground a few meters from where he'd been an instant before. *That was no mortar shell…that was an autocannon of some kind.* He felt a shudder, and then a trickle of cold sweat sliding down his back. Mortars were only moderately dangerous, more nuisance than serious danger to an alert and armored Marine. But the enemy hypervelocity coilguns were deadly dangerous. Bruce knew they'd tear through his osmium-iridium armor like a knife through butter.

"Bruce, report." Connor Frasier's voice was raw, almost guttural. The commander of the Scot's Company was a Marine's Marine, ready for almost anything in the field…but even he sounded a little stunned by the amount of resistance his people had encountered. And how quickly it had happened.

"We're about a quarter klick in, sir. I've got five people down…two dead. The others are walking wounded. I sent them back toward the camp."

"Good," came the gruff reply. "We're setting up an aid station. Move your casualties back that way."

"Yes, sir. Coordinates received."

"Okay, Lieutenant…I want your people to keep moving forward. We've got to stop this bombardment. The colonel's got reinforcements on the way, but we're on our own for now…and if these bastards start shelling the main camp, it's going to be a disaster. We've got unarmored personnel all over the place."

"Yes, Major. We'll press on."

"I know you will. Also, Finley's section is coming up on your left. They're about twenty meters behind your position, so they should be there in half a minute. Latch onto his flank, and don't let anything get by you. We want to keep these fuckers in front of us…and then swing around and flank them."

"Understood, sir."

"I'm sending up a spread of recon drones too…to try and get some better intel on whatever's up there farther ahead. They should be passing over your position shortly. I will have the data transmitted to you as soon as it comes in."

"Yes, Major.

"Carry on, Lieutenant." Bruce heard the click as Frasier cut the line.

"Carson!" Bruce snapped.

"Sir!" came the reply, almost immediately.

"Your squad is on our extreme left. Lieutenant Finley and his platoon are over there. I need your people to connect with them, and make sure we've got a solid line…no gaps between platoons. Any of these bogies get through to the rear, and we're fucked."

"Yes, Lieutenant. We're on it, sir."

"Keep me posted…and let me know if you have any problems."

"Yes, sir."

Bruce turned and looked forward from his position. The hyper-velocity fire had gotten heavier…and it was moving. *Trying to work its way around our flank. And it's not too far…just in front of me, off to the right…*

He crept around the edge of the pile of rubble, snapping off an order to his AI as he did. The system acknowledged, and an instant later he felt a clip of grenades slide into the launcher on his left arm. He crept forward another few meters, ducking low, listening to the fire just off to the right. Then he swung his arm up and popped off a spread of shells, running forward the instant the last one fired. He swung hard to the right… whatever was out there would know exactly where the incoming shells had come from…and he didn't intend to be there when it responded.

He drove himself about ten meters to the left ducking so low he almost lost his balance. He stumbled forward, powered by the servos in his armored legs. He was off-balance, committed. If he tried to stop, he'd fall. And if he fell, he'd die. The enemy would be on him before he could do anything about it.

He swung to the right again, still barely staying on his feet, coming around another large chunk of debris…and then he saw it. It was about two meters tall, roughly manlike in shape, but not human, not even living. It had two large weapons, similar to Marine autocannons, attached to its arms…and there was a small globe at the top, like a tiny head. Bruce had seen its kind before on X18, and in the battles along the Line. A First Imperium warbot.

The Scot's eyes stared into his visor, focusing on the enemy. He'd caught it by surprise…it was facing back toward his original position. He knew that advantage would last a second, perhaps less, but he was already firing his assault rifle on full auto, spraying the terrible robot with hundreds of hypervelocity rounds as his body lurched forward. He felt the fear in his gut, and his mind cried out to run, to duck to the side. But he ignored it, let himself drop prone, struggling to keep from falling to the ground, firing right into the monstrous war machine the whole time. He had committed…he would either have the bot or it would have him. His clip had been full, five hundred rounds, and it took less than three seconds to fire them all. And when he was done, the First Imperium warbot was lying on its side, almost torn to shreds.

He saw something, even as he was checking on his immediate opponent…a glint, perhaps the sunlight reflecting off another bot. He kicked his legs out behind him, diving forward with his rifle in front of him. He stared forward, and he scanned his display…but nothing came. He was just climbing back to his feet when he heard the drones moving overhead, a spread of six, about a hundred meters up, each one angling a different way, scanning the whole area.

Bruce moved a few meters and crouched down behind a pile of twisted wreckage…part of the remains of a tower than had collapsed long ago, leaving only traces of the great metal frame that had supported it ages before. He turned his head both ways, doublechecking to make sure he had no enemies moving up on him. Then he instructed his AI to display the drone data…and he got his first real look at what his people were up against.

"Fuck…"

* * *

Neil Carson lay flat on his stomach, his assault rifle extended forward as he scanned the rubble-strewn ground in front of him. He'd moved to the left end of his squad's line, and he'd linked up with Corporal Hendry, who was on the extreme right of Finley's section. Hendry was about twenty meters away, which was as close to a solid line as they were going to get, at least unless some reinforcements made it up to the front.

There was heavy fighting off to his right, somewhere near the lieutenant's position. He could see the squad deployed there moving around on the tactical display. They had a few casualties, three it looked like, but no KIAs, at least as far as the datanet was showing. But they needed help…and they weren't likely to get it any time soon.

Carson had fought the First Imperium before. On X18, of course, but before that too. He'd been a bright-eyed private, fresh out of training when he'd been sent to Sandoval…to Erik Cain's army that almost bled itself to death holding that world against the massive First Imperium invasion. The battles along the Line had slipped into legend, and he suspected they continued to be revered in Occupied Space as the moment the First Imperium's advance was halted. But for the men and women who had served there, it would always be remembered as the brutal hell it was, a battle where less than half of those who fought survived…and most of those who made it didn't walk from the field, they were carried.

His eyes darted to the display again, watching updates appear as the recon drones fed information into the datanet. The lieutenant was way up, maybe thirty meters ahead of the squad he was supposed to be moving with. Carson wasn't surprised. Lieutenant Bruce had been on Sandoval too, and he'd been just as crazy-brave there. Bruce was the kind of officer who'd throw himself forward to flush out the threats and try to keep his Marines alive. Officers like that almost always had the undying love of those serving under them…but few of them survived very long. Bruce had made it through Sandoval and X18…but it looked like he was doubling down now, daring fate to put him down. Carson felt himself wishing the lieutenant would pull back, show a little more caution…that he would stay alive.

"Sarge, we've got something coming…looks like half a dozen of those blasted 'bots." The voice on the com was heavy with a thick Scottish brogue. The company was full of Scots, but few spoke with much more than a faint accent, the result of years of attempted cultural homogenization by Alliance Gov. But Tavish Darrow was a throwback, and he sounded as if he'd been plucked from a time centuries before, from the serried ranks of Highlanders rising up and charging wildly across the field. The private was young, but Carson knew he had the makings of a great Marine…and someday perhaps, an officer.

But for now he was a private, and Carson had sent him to scout the ground up ahead. "Alright, Darrow. Fall back…you're up there for information, not to get yourself blown away." He flipped to the squad line. "Listen up, we've got bogies incoming. You've all fought these fuckers before, so you know how dangerous they are. I want everyone one hundred percent focused…and I want those things blown to bits before they do the same to us. So dig in somewhere and wait for them…and the instant you see one, open up with everything you've got. Understood?" It was a rhetorical question, but he still got four or five acknowledgements.

His eyes dropped to the scanner. Darrow was almost back to the line…and he could see the cluster of bots right behind him. The ground was covered with debris, the remains of a huge ancient building that had collapsed millennia before. Earth ruins a tenth as old would have blown away as dust, but the astonishing materials the First Imperium employed remained in place, fallen perhaps, collapsed in earthquakes and other natural disasters, but even after half a million years, it was obvious the massive chunks lying about were sections of once titanic structures.

The broken buildings made formidable cover, and Carson knew that benefitted his Marines. *Damned good thing for it too*, he thought. *Darrow would have been dead long before he made it back without that cover. And the rest of us wouldn't last much longer.*

The First Imperium bots were stronger, heavily armed, their shielding far more durable than the Marines' armor. But the obscured ground went a long way to equalizing things…or at least that was the idea.

Carson crept along behind an especially large chunk of debris, a rough oval shape four meters high and eight long. He pushed himself against a small indentation, and he sat quietly… waiting. His scanner showed a bot just on the other side. He stood stone still, staring up at his display. He knew the data wasn't necessarily perfect. His AI was constantly combining all incoming information—drone reports, the scanners on his own armor, the entire company on the datanet, even the auditory input on his external speakers. But that didn't mean every sign was picked up. He was trying to sneak up on his enemy…and he knew damned well the deadly battle bot was trying to do the same thing to him.

His stomach roiled, as it usually did in combat, and he struggled to push the fear and doubt from his mind. He almost took a step forward to work his way around the giant slab, but he didn't. He held firm, still, like a hole in the air. *Let it come to me…*

He felt the beads of sweat forming on his forehead, along the back of his neck. He knew his AI kept his internal climate control perfect, increasing or decreasing heat to match physical exertion and other factors. But there were things beyond heat that made a man sweat.

He took a deep breath and exhaled hard, loudly. At least he didn't have to be quiet inside his armor…all that holding of breath and the like. He had his external speakers off, and the insulation of his fighting suit blocked normal sounds.

He glanced up at the display again. The bot was in the same place. Had it detected him? The ancient remnants of the First Imperium forces didn't seem to have drones or other sensor arrays in place, which meant that for all their superior equipment, on the battlefield as a whole, the Marines had the edge in scouting. But that didn't mean the bot hadn't found him. His mind raced.

Should I move? Run? Attack?

No…stay. Patience…the key to any effective trap…

The icon on his display was stationary…but he didn't believe it. The small image had a faint white outline around it, a key that said the data was old, that the enemy could be on the move, that any instant it could move to a spot where it had a line of sight…and an instant after that, Carson knew he'd be dead. Like a thousand others he'd seen fall in his battles.

He hands were on his assault rifle, a fresh click snuggly in place. He was as ready as he could be…

Then he saw it…the tiny red light on his display panel. Sound. Something, outside his suit, coming from the south. It was faint, sporadic at first, but then suddenly he knew…and his eyes darted to the spot.

He saw the shadow first, a tiny sliver blocking the sunlight. Then, half a second later the bulk, a First Imperium warbot, gliding slowly around the edge of the debris. He felt his body tighten, and his breath held in his lungs. His rifle was already moving, swinging around to target the enemy.

There was no room for error. He had a second, no more. One second, to destroy the enemy…and save his own life. His own movements would alert the bot at this range, even if it hadn't already known he was there…and the enemy's weapons would be on him.

He acted without thought, on almost pure instinct, his finger pulling down hard on the trigger, his assault rifle spraying the area around the warbot with over a hundred hyper-velocity rounds in less than a second. Then he leapt, diving to the side and swinging around, bringing his weapon to bear again and opening fire.

His jump had been just in time. His initial volley had torn into the enemy bot, but not in time to prevent it from returning fire…and blasting the spot he'd just occupied.

He let his knee drop, pushing the armored joint into the soft ground, steadying himself as he unloaded the remaining four hundred rounds in his cartridge. The enemy bot was turning, trying to bring its own weapons to bear again. But Carson's fire was too much. Too accurate, too deadly. The great war machine of the First Imperium had been bested. It staggered for a few seconds, caught in the blistering fire as the Marine emptied his clip. Huge chunks of it flew away, blasted apart by the spray of projectiles. And then, just as Carson's cartridge emptied and expelled itself from the assault rifle, making way for a fresh clip, it fell over.

Carson scrambled over the few meters between the two combatants, cautious, wary. He'd seen First Imperium ordnance go down and still retain combat capability. A dying robot, even an almost destroyed one, could kill him as dead as a horde of fresh ones.

He heard the sound of the new cartridge snapping into

place, and he heaved a sigh of relief. He'd been less than a second without ammunition, yet it had seemed an eternity he was naked, vulnerable. But then he scrambled up next to his adversary and got a close look.

He knew immediately. It was dead, half its midsection torn out by the dozens of rounds that had slammed into it. He'd won, at least this small fight. But there was a long way to go before the battle was over. He looked back up at the display. There were two more bots moving toward his position. The combat had given his location away, and enemy units were responding.

And Marines too. He could see two of his people rushing toward his position. They might beat one of the bots to him, but the closest enemy was going to get there first. He ducked back in between two chunks of debris and waited. One more bot to kill…one more and then his backup would be there.

He slipped deeper into the pile of shattered wall sections and froze, rifle at the ready, watching the enemy approach on his display…

Chapter Ten

From the Personal Log of Terrance Compton

The enemy is back. I can only imagine what is going through the minds of many of the crews, the disappointment and despair after half a year of relative peace. I tried to encourage caution, to warn them about becoming too complacent, too certain we had passed by the enemy fleets. Yet, how far could I go with that? Morale is crucial too. Should I have simply harangued them every day, warned them again and again that death was still stalking us? I don't know. Perhaps I should have...yet men and women have their breaking points. And I do not regret the moments of peace and joy they might have had these last six months. I would not seek to snatch them back, replace them with endless darkness, even if I could do so.

Nevertheless, we are back in the fire now, and I must confess I do not understand what the enemy is planning. When the First Imperium ships began appearing, I was certain it was a large fleet, come to face us once again in a climactic battle, one for which we are ill-prepared. But no additional forces have transited since the initial twenty vessels...twenty of their smallest. Even over the past months, when I maintained by caution—even pessimism perhaps—I never imagined they would move against us with a force so small. Indeed, the fleet could easily defeat this entire enemy incursion...something the Intelligences directing the First Imperium surely know full well.

I can only assume this is a trick, an attempt to draw our forces close to the enemy's entry warp gate, and then to release the rest of their forces...and destroy us before we are able to disengage. Indeed, I have no other thought now, not even the barest hypothesis. I am far from confident, but as I have only one explanation, I have no choice to embrace it. And that means I must withdraw the fleet...and leave a rearguard in position.

That duty, I am afraid, must fall where it has so often before, on John Duke's fast attack ships and Greta Hurley's fighters. The brave men and women of those services have done far beyond their portion of service...and they have lost many more than their share of casualties. Yet, though they deserve naught but rest now, to take their positions in reserve at the end of the fleet and lick their grievous wounds, I must again order them forward, into the maelstrom.

I will send help with them this time, Aki Kato's cruiser squadron. Captain Kato is an extraordinary officer, one of the first to undertake a deadly mission in the aftermath of our becoming trapped. His forlorn hope with our damaged ships was instrumental in securing the fleet's original escape from X2, and he was one of the last personnel to transit out of that system. Now I must send him on another mission, one no less deadly. I only hope these intrepid souls I leave behind will find a way to win their fight...and escape from the almost certain death the arrival of enemy reinforcements would carry with it.

AS Jaguar
X56 System - Near the X58 warp gate
The Fleet: 144 ships, 32,644 crew

"All ships are to maintain thrust." John Duke's voice struggled to remain audible, to force the words out through the crushing pressure slamming into his chest. He was pressed back against his chair, like everyone else on *Jaguar*...everyone on all fourteen of his engaged ships. Eight gees of acceleration was a lot to take outside the tanks, especially for any sustained duration. But he wasn't about to ease off...not until his ships had closed for their attack runs. Then his people would get a short break—a few minutes of freefall, broken up my short bursts of thrust while the gunners lined up their shots. After that his vessels would reorient their engines and begin decelerating for a return run against any enemy survivors.

He'd ordered injections for all of his crews, drugs to strengthen cell walls and help them endure the torturous trip he was putting them through. He'd almost ordered them all into the tanks and kicked the thrust up to 30g, but he'd decided against it. He didn't have any shots to miss, and his gunners would lose a lot of their effectiveness if they were buttoned up in the tanks, trying to take potshots drugged half to oblivion. No, he'd decided, this was the only way, the only chance to take out the entire enemy fleet.

He moved his head, slowly, carefully—it was too easy to injure yourself at 8g. His ships were displayed in a short row, a compact formation that was getting tighter every second. The enemy had launched their missiles along a wide trajectory, covering the original position occupied by his ships. But his people were accelerating at carefully chosen angles, closing the distance to each other as they increased their velocity toward the enemy. It wasn't a panacea—the enemy missiles were guided, and they would attempt to follow his forces. But the abruptness of the formation change would confuse their targeting systems. Hopefully. It wasn't enough by itself, but if they could knock out even a quarter of the strike with the maneuver, it would be a big help.

And then we've got Commander Fujin and her people…

John Duke had worked closely with Greta Hurley's fighters before, in the battles along the Line and later in the combats leading up to the final engagement in X2 and the fleet's subsequent entrapment. He knew just what they could do…and by all accounts, Mariko Fujin was one of the best, a rising star in what remained of Hurley's decimated corps.

I'll bet she's pissed about pulling point defensive duty. From everything he knew about her, Mariko Fujin was classic fighter pilot, a predator through and through. Her blood called to attack enemy ships, he knew, and not to chase down missiles.

Still, she will do everything in her power…and her people will save a lot of fast attack ship crews. Surely that's something in return for being denied the kill…

He stared at the main display. Fujin's fighters would be

engaged any minute. And if her people could take out enough warheads, maybe…just maybe…most of his ships would close, and deliver their plasma torpedoes. His vessels were lightly armored, built for speed and hitting power, not endurance. They weren't called suicide boats for nothing. But his flotilla was even more vulnerable than usual. In their bomb bays they carried triple-shotted plasma warheads. He'd used double-packed weapons before, and they were fragile and unstable, a dangerous wildcard for any vessel to carry. But this was the first time his people had triple-powered a plasma torpedo, and calling the precarious weapon systems fragile was an understatement of epic proportions.

Indeed, his technicians were in the bays, working frantically in the brutal gee forces to keep the things from blowing up in their tubes. It was a reckless operation to risk such volatile ordnance, one he'd failed to mention to Admiral Compton. But if his people could pull it off, the enemy ships would be blindsided, hit with weapons of extraordinary power. Even the dark matter infused hulls of the First Imperium vessels would be powerless against the strength of Duke's enhanced weapons. If he could get close enough, if his people could keep their payloads from blowing up and destroying their own vessels…they just might have a chance to win this fight.

But first, Mariko Fujin and her people had to take out some of those missiles. A lot of them. If his ships got too shaken up, if too many blasts of deadly radiation slammed into them from nearby nuclear detonations, they'd be finished. Any ship that lost control over its unstable torpedoes would turn instantly into a miniature sun…and when the explosion died down, there wouldn't be anything left bigger than an atom.

He felt his hands tightening, forming into fists. The tension gnawed at him, his mind scrambling, trying to think of something, anything to do. But there was nothing. Nothing but to watch Fujin's fighters…and hope for the best.

* * *

"Missiles incoming." Fujin sat in her chair, speaking calmly into her com unit. "I want everybody at their best right now… whatever it takes, those missiles don't get through. Not a damned one. Do you all understand me?" She knew that was a pointless thing to say. No matter how perfectly her people executed their defensive run, some missiles would get through. She was upset her wing had been assigned to anti-missile duty, and she knew she was taking it out on her crews. If Admiral Hurley was going to keep her back from the main attack, shooting at missiles instead of enemy ships, then she was damned sure going to blow any volleys in her way to bits.

Fujin was well aware that Greta Hurley had pioneered defensive tactics for fighter wings. Indeed, some of her first missions had been part of the massive groups of squadrons that had cleared the way for Admiral Garret's massive fleets during the great climactic battles along the Line. Fujin knew firsthand how successful the operations had been, how many capital ships those hundreds of fighters had saved from certain destruction. Indeed, she knew that's why her people were here now, staring down an incoming barrage of enemy warheads. But for all she understood, for all she'd served on these missions before, she was still a fighter pilot at heart…and that meant she wanted to be up on the line, ready to drop a plasma torpedo into the guts of one of those damned First Imperium ships. She'd accepted her orders, but she was restless about it, unhappy. Pissed.

"Okay, Lieutenant, you are at the disposal of the gunners now." She knew Wainwright had never run defensive ops before, and she wanted to remind him the two weapons specialists were in charge. The pilot often fired the main torpedo during anti-ship operations, but the lasers and shotguns belonged to the gunners. She knew that was always uncomfortable for any pilot, most of whom considered a fighter 'their ship' regardless of rank or responsibility.

"Alright, Lieutenant, give us 2.5g for eight seconds, heading 305.111.201 on my mark…" Ensign Schultz was the senior of the two gunners. He was a junior officer, but his skill and experience went far beyond that implied by the single gold bar on his collar. Schultz had served six years as a petty officer in the CEL fighter corps, and another two as part of the grand fleet before Admiral Hurley had given him his commission. Fujin had snapped up the chance to get him on her bird after his own fighter came in damaged and broken…and he was the only one to survive the landing.

"Mark," Schultz snapped out.

Fujin was watching Wainwright, a little concerned the cocky pilot would think his lieutenant's bars gave him some kind of right to challenge Schultz' instructions…and she was prepared to remind him they didn't. But the pilot did exactly what he was told, without any argument, and she felt the 2.5g slam into her. She started counting down from eight, but by the time she got to four, she could feel the ship's weapons firing.

The lasers were first, precision weapons designed to score direct hits on incoming missiles. They were notoriously difficult to target, but Schultz had two hits in less than thirty seconds. Then a third almost immediately after that.

Fujin just nodded. She knew the CEL officer was good when she'd maneuvered to get him on her crew, but she had to acknowledge she was even more impressed than she'd expected to be. Even the old Gold Dragons, her long-dead friends and comrades, had never hit missiles with such focused precision.

She couldn't help but smile when she saw a fourth missile go, and then, almost amazingly, a fifth and sixth in rapid succession. She felt her congratulations coming up, the words moving from her throat of their own accord. But she clamped down on it. There would be time later, and the last thing she wanted to do was break Schultz' concentration.

Then she felt the ship shake as both gunners began firing the electromagnetic railguns the crews called, simply, shotguns. The shotguns used the most mundane of projectiles, chunks of depleted uranium and other heavy metals. But they fired them at enormous velocities, in excess of three thousand kilometers per second. Even the smallest grain of metal could vaporize a warhead at such speeds.

Fujin watched as another half dozen warheads were obliterated by the shotguns. Her eyes moved to the side of her screen, to the reports coming in from the entire group. None of her people had been as deadly accurate as Schultz, but she could see at once the attack had been a massive success. Her people had knocked out almost two-thirds of the incoming warheads…and they were still in the fight.

She felt a rush of satisfaction. The suicide boat crews were the only ones in the fleet with casualty rates anywhere near the fighter crews, and she felt a kinship with them. She longed to be in the attack Hurley and the rest of the fighters were about to launch, but she had to grudgingly agree her people had done more good where they were, that they'd probably saved hundreds of their fellow spacers.

And those spacers are about to drop heavy plasma torpedoes on these First Imperium bastards…

*   *   *

"Steady…" Aki Kato sat on *Osaka's* bridge, his eyes fixed on the main display. He'd just watched Admiral Hurley's fighter squadrons attack, and he'd been stunned, mystified at the almost unimaginable bravery of her crews. Her contingent had been savaged since the day the fleet became trapped, fighting one desperate battle after another. Kato couldn't understand how a formation could endure such relentless and devastating losses and retain its combat effectiveness. No, more than that…for all the devastating losses, the fighter wings had become even more effective, a shrinking weapon, yet one of enormous power.

The fighters had sliced through the enemy formation, concentrating on four of the Gremlins and blowing each of them to plasma. By the time her people pulled back—after following up their torpedo attack with two strafing runs with their lasers—they left behind another twenty-one of their own. A hundred and five crewmembers. Kato hoped at least some had managed to eject, that they were floating in space in their survival gear, waiting for rescue…but he knew it couldn't be many. And he realized there would be no pickup for those who did manage to escape, not unless these twenty Gremlins were destroyed, and nothing else came through the warp gate.

"Sir, Captain Duke's ships are closing. They should be in firing range in ninety seconds."

"Very well," Kato nodded back to the tactical officer. The officer's calculations were spot on, at least for normal operations. But John Duke had his ship loaded up with overpowered torpedoes…and you didn't take a chance like that just to pop them off at long range and hope they managed to hit. No, you took them right down the enemy's throat. And that meant another minute and a half at least.

He stared at the display for another thirty seconds, then a minute. Finally, he turned back to the tactical station. "Very well, Commander. Take us forward. All ships advance."

Kato was *Osaka's* captain, but he wore a second hat as squadron commander. He had three PRC cruisers, *Osaka* and her two sisters, *Tokugawa* and *Tanaka*…and Admiral Compton had given him three Alliance ships, *Boise*, *Surrey*, and *Newfoundland*. His people had been in supporting positions for most of the fighting since X2, but now they were at the forefront, charged with holding off the enemy while the rest of the fleet escaped.

He remembered those terrible hours in system X2, where he'd been tasked to hold back the First Imperium forces while the rest of the fleet escaped. He'd been sure his mission was a suicide one, that his skeleton crews had been finished. But Admiral Compton had refused to leave them behind…and to Kato's shock, most of his people made it out.

Now he felt the same way. There was no doubt in his mind that more First Imperium ships were behind that warp gate. He had no idea why they hadn't come through yet, why they were giving the fleet time to get away…and the rearguard time to destroy their advance force. But it didn't matter why. All that mattered was that the fleet escaped. And it would.

As long as we finish off these ships, the fleet will get away…even if another hundred of the enemy come through, even if they trap every vessel in this rearguard, it will be too late for them to catch the admiral. At least in this system.

"All units engage thrust…we're going in right behind the fast attack ships." Kato took a deep breath. "All laser batteries prepare to fire on my command…"

He stared at the display, watching as Duke's ships closed. Kato suppressed a grim smile as he watched the vessels move forward, holding their fire. They were well past normal range and still closing. Kato understood, and he watched intently as the wave of ships moved closer…then toward point blank.

Still they held their fire. Kato watched as one of the icons vanished. Then another. There were three more with heavy damage, but they kept on going, now down below twenty thousand kilometers.

Kato found himself leaning forward in his chair, trying to will Duke's people to fire. But still they held. Fifteen thousand…ten thousand. Knife fighting range, yet still they held their fire. Eight thousand…seven thousand…

Kato jumped in his chair as he saw the first torpedoes fire. The range was so close he could barely distinguish the launch from the impact. Eleven ships fired, almost as one…and when those massively overpowered torpedoes slammed into their hulls, eleven of the First Imperium Gremlins rolled over hard, wracked by massive explosions. Seven died almost immediately, consumed by the loss of containment in their own antimatter stores. Four more were split open like eggs, their ruptured hulls floating dead in space.

There were cheers all around *Osaka's* bridge, joy at the flawlessly executed attack they had just seen. But the fight wasn't over. Not yet. There were still five enemy ships intact and, almost as if in declaration of that fact, *Osaka* shook hard as enemy x-ray lasers slammed into her.

"Damage control procedures," Kato said, almost robotically. His focus now was on attack, not survival…destruction, not defense. "All laser batteries…ready…"

His commands were relayed immediately to the other five

vessels under his command. They were in range already, but Kato was following Duke's lead. He was going right down the enemy's throats.

"Ready…" he said again, his eyes remaining fixed on the display as *Osaka* took another hid amidships. He felt the urge to give the command, to fire now before his ships took any more damage. But something held him back, made him wait. Perhaps it was the attack they'd just watched, the relentless bravery of John Duke and his people. Or it was his own knowledge of the enemy. He knew from his own experiences how tough the enemy hulls were…and how much stronger his lasers were at 'whites of eyes' range.

"Ready…" The numbers on the display dropped down, below ten thousand now. His eyes darted to the side, checking the damage readouts for his ships. *Surrey* had been hit hard… her thrust was down, and she was bleeding atmosphere. But still he held back, waiting…waiting.

"Fire!"

Osaka's lights dimmed as all her power poured into the laser turrets. The great beams, invisible except where they passed through dust clouds or fields of debris, lanced out at the enemy ships. The dark matter infused hulls of the enemy were strong against laser fire, but Kato's ships were too close, their shots too concentrated. One by one the deadly blasts ripped into the enemy ships, tearing apart internal systems and shattering structural supports.

The enemy returned the fire, their own weapons even deadlier at such short range. Kato felt *Osaka* shake again, even harder this time. There were showers of sparks on the bridge as conduits blew and consoles overloaded. And a large beam fell to the deck, almost killing two crewmen when it did.

"Maintain fire. Pour all available power into the turrets…cut off all safety protocols. Full overloads. All systems are subordinate to weapons control…even life support."

Kato was putting everything his reactors could produce through his lasers, even at the risk of burning out the systems. He clung grimly to the armrests of his chair, staring out across the chaos that had become *Osaka's* bridge. His ship was hurt, badly. He knew that. But he also knew she would do what she had to…all of his vessels would.

"We just lost *Surrey*, Captain." The stress was clear in the tactical officer's voice. Kato knew his people were near their limits. But there was no time for a break, no time to repair damaged systems or rest overloaded machinery. This was a fight to the death, against the deadliest enemy man had ever faced. And he would do whatever had to be done. And so would his people.

"All ships, keep firing. Pour it into them..."

* * *

Compton was staring at the incoming reports. The casualty lists were jarring. Four of John Duke's ships were gone, at least two by some kind of internal explosion he couldn't explain, and *Surrey* was a powerless, dead hull. She was the only one of Kato's cruisers that had been destroyed outright, but the rest had been battered almost to scrap. *Tanaka* was a total loss, and Kato had already ordered the twenty percent of her crew that had survived to abandon ship. And *Boise* wasn't much better off. Her captain was struggling to save the ship, to get her operating on at least fractional power, but it looked like a longshot.

More than twenty of Hurley's remaining fighters had been lost as well, another butcher's bill for the long-suffering fighter corps. Compton knew how closely he had come to rely upon Hurley and her amazing pilots, but he knew they couldn't take much more. Only a fraction of the crews that had begun the invasion of First Imperium space still remained, a tithe of those who had spilled their blood from X1 and X2 all the way to this last deadly fight.

The rearguard had done its job, wiped out the First Imperium advance force…but they had paid heavily. Compton felt the pull of guilt on him, worse even than that he usually endured when he sent good men and women to their deaths. The battle just finished could have been quicker, far more one-sided, if the whole fleet had joined in. But that had been out of the question. Compton was sure there would be more enemy ships coming through that warp gate. He didn't know why they had waited, but there wasn't a doubt in his mind they were there. There had been no choice but to send the rearguard. Any other action would have placed the entire fleet in grave jeopardy. And that was unthinkable.

"Distance to X57 warp gate?" he said, staring over at Commander Cortez' workstation.

"One point two million kilometers, Admiral. We are approaching at approximately one thousand kilometers per second. Lead elements will be in position to jump in approximately twenty minutes, sir."

Compton leaned back in his chair. He was worried. He didn't like running off into blind space, allowing potentially hostile forces to work between him and the expedition in X48. But he'd thought about it every way he could, and there was just no choice. Heading back now was too risky. If he took off, away from X48, maybe the enemy would follow…and the landing parties could remain hidden.

"Admiral, we're getting energy readings from the X57 gate!" Cortez was upset, and it showed in his voice.

"Confirmed?"

"Yes, Admiral. Readings consistent with imminent transit."

Compton felt like someone had punched him in his gut. It had to be the enemy. First X58 and now X57. There was no choice now. He'd have to backtrack, at least one system. He felt a cold chill down his spine…the fleet was too close to the X57 warp gate to outrun First Imperium ships. Without a head start, they'd be dead long before they could get back to X54.

He needed another rearguard…to face an enemy force of unknown strength. He shook his head grimly. More people to send into the meatgrinder, friends, loyal spacers. For a brief moment, in the deepest place in his mind, Terrance Compton wanted to give up…to stop, close his eyes, let death take him. If he'd had only himself to worry about, he knew he might do it, stop the constant struggles and let the darkness take him. But he was responsible for his people, all of them. Over thirty thousand men and women looking to him to keep them alive, to find some way to survive. And, in the place that made him who he was, he found the strength he needed. It wasn't courage, he knew that. It was duty, obligation…but it would serve.

"Commander Cortez, all vessels are to prepare for high gee maneuvers. I want everyone in the tanks in ten minutes."

"Yes, sir."

He took another breath, deep…and he held if for a few seconds. Then he exhaled and said, "And get me Admiral West, Commander. Immediately."

Chapter Eleven

Research Notes of Hieronymus Cutter

I sit now in our makeshift camp, watching the Marines move methodically through the broken ruins, searching for any surviving First Imperium bots still in the city. One of them christened the vast sea of shattered buildings New York City, a bit of tension-breaking humor that has now begun to spread throughout both the Marines and my own people.

The battle didn't last long, less than an hour, but it was sharp and costly. Eight Marines died, and another eleven were wounded and evacuated back to the base camp. Colonel Preston sent two hundred reserves to our aid, but by the time they arrived, Major Frasier's people had cleared things out. Now the area is locked down, and the camp outside the city is covered by half a dozen emplaced autocannons.

It was no surprise to find there was some residual enemy resistance in the city, but it is nevertheless painful to see the losses the Marines suffered. Once again, I watched them plunge into the danger, without hesitation, putting themselves on the line to keep us all safe. The loss of such brave men and women always causes a flash of doubt, and I felt a pang of guilt for pushing to explore these ruins...for if my people hadn't come here, the Marines would have stayed in the main base camp, and likely watched quietly over the farms without provoking a major attack by the long-dormant enemy forces.

The bots were similar to those we encountered in X18, no doubt the remains of whatever security forces the First Imperium routinely deployed around its cities. Yet there was something strange about this fight compared to the last, and while my expertise is not in military tactics, it is apparent the Marines saw it too. On X18, the bots attacked in a very disciplined pattern, with precisely-controlled fire, as if they were seeking to target enemies without further damaging the city itself...a tactic consistent with a defensive or policing operation. Here, however, they fired wildly, targeting anything that moved. Their ammunition expenditure was vastly larger, by two or three times. They used mortars and other explosive rounds, heavier weapons than we saw on X18, employed seemingly without regard to the destruction they caused.

Perhaps it is nothing. The city on X18 was a ruin as well, but it was in far better condition than this one, which had clearly been the site of substantial fighting millennia before. The security bots might acknowledge that his city is destroyed, that there was no longer any reason to try and preserved what remained. There is logic to that viewpoint certainly, but it doesn't ring true to me. The metropolis on X18 had not been destroyed by war, but five hundred thousand years of decay made that a distinction without a difference. The First Imperium is almost certainly governed by artificial intelligences of a sophistication we can scarcely begin to understand, certainly capable of understanding the current status of a city. Is there a meaningful differentiation here, at least in terms of evaluating its current condition? Is it possible that such thinking machines cannot acknowledge that a dead world is a dead world, a ruin a ruin, whether that status was caused by war five thousand centuries ago or slow decay in the millennia since?

Was this planet invaded by some outside force? Or was it torn apart by internal strife, a civil war that set its people against each other? I came in search of technology, but now I find myself intrigued by the history of this ancient race. I long to learn more about them, to understand what happened here so long ago...

X48 System – Planet II
In the Ruins of "New York City"
The Fleet: 136 ships, 30,304 crew

"No, Dr. Cutter…it is out of the question." Duncan Frasier

stood two meters away, his helmet retracted and a scowl on his face. In his armor, he towered over Cutter, and he stared down at the scientist with focused eyes. "I understand you are anxious to proceed with your research, but in case you hadn't noticed, my Marines just fought a battle against several hundred enemy warbots. And we haven't even penetrated the surface. Who knows what's waiting down there? It's simply not safe."

Cutter didn't look like the type who would argue toe to toe with a Marine the size of Frasier, but he took a step forward and sunk into him nevertheless. "Major, I understand your rationale…and in a vacuum I might even agree with it. You speak of danger? Have we experienced anything else since we were trapped out here? Indeed, since the First Imperium first invaded human space?" Cutter's voice was raw, edgy. He was getting tired of the military types, of the blinders they sometimes seemed to wear when making decisions. And on their notion that they had an exclusive market on courage, on taking risks to help save their comrades.

"Of course we have all been in danger, Doctor, but facing the everyday risk and marching into an unknown set of tunnels…and almost certainly into the teeth of more resistance, is another matter. If I let your people go alone, you won't stand a chance. And if I send my people with you, they'll be walking blind into a deathtrap."

"Your men are doomed already, Major." Cutter held Frasier's stare, even as a look of anger flashed across the Marine's face. He clearly didn't like being told his people were doomed. "Not just your people, Major, but the entire fleet…from Admiral Compton on down to the most junior spacer bilging radioactives out of the flushtubes. We're *all* doomed…unless we can learn from our enemy, adapt their technology to our own uses."

The anger drained from Frasier's face. "Look, Hieronymus, I understand what you are saying, but don't you feel there is a point where the danger is simply too great? Where the potential gains are outweighed by the risk?"

"Certainly, Major. That is true in many circumstances. But not this one. Whatever chance we have, it depends on our assimilating our enemy's technology. Indeed, you know well we would all be six months dead by now if we hadn't gained control of the enemy Colossus. How dangerous do you think that expedition was? You know better than most. You were there."

Frasier fell silent for a moment. Finally, he sighed hard and said, "Yes, Doctor, I do know. But does the payoff of one wild gamble automatically mean that another is justified?" The assurance in his tone was faltering.

"No, it does not. Neither does it mean it is not justified." Cutter hesitated, his eyes holding Frasier's weakening but still resolute gaze. "But we have no alternative, Major. None with any hope of more than transitory success. We move deeper into enemy space, not through it. This is obvious from the increasing size of the ruined cities on the planets we pass…though I could offer you other proofs as well if this is not adequate."

Frasier shook his head. "No, I don't need any other proof." There was dejection in his voice, the beginnings of defeat.

"The fleet is weaker than it was at X18…and it was weaker going into that battle than it was when it was first trapped in X2. We have fewer vessels…we have lost a third of our crews. Our ships have expended all their missile ordnance, and we have managed to replace only a small fraction of what we need…and that using haphazard materials likely to experience considerable failure rates. We have lost fighters, attack ships…battleships."

Frasier just stared back for a moment. Then he said, "Yet still, we fight on, Doctor. We do not surrender, we do not give up hope. And we do not take reckless gambles, hoping they will pay off."

Cutter held back a sigh. He respected the Marines…and the spacers as well. Their courage during the past year had been admirable, but what he was speaking of had nothing to do with bravery, even with martial skill. He was talking about mathematical certainty…or something close to it.

"Major, I don't think you understand what I am saying, not completely. I am not saying things will be difficult if we do not obtain the technology we need. I am saying we have no chance. None at all." He paused, but his eyes didn't drop from Frasier's gaze. "If we do not discover enough scientific knowledge to reset this paradigm, the best we can hope for is a slow but steady withering…and our more likely fate is a faster destruction, probably as soon as the enemy launches another major attack." He paused. "This is not a guess, not a series of guesses…it is as complete an analysis of the variables that we face as it is possible to undertake. We must change the dynamic, we must find new weapons, or something else that will alter the situation…or we all face almost certain death."

"You cannot know that, Doctor. You are asking me to risk all of your people, the most vital scientific minds in the fleet… along with my Marines. To send them all into deadly danger. That is a certainty."

"I know it, Major. I have spent hours reviewing our situation, our options. Courage, skill, determination…they all play a role in war, often a major one. But as a Marine you know yourself that the mathematics of war ultimately asserts itself. You saw the fleet in X2, the vast numbers of vessels deployed there…you have some idea of what we face, out there somewhere. Do not be fooled because we have managed to elude the enemy's main forces for a time. Eventually, we will again face a fleet we cannot hope to defeat, not without resources and abilities we do not yet possess. I do not say we do not walk into danger, that we do not face the possibility of destruction if we move deeper into the ruins. I say doing so is our only hope."

Frasier stood and looked silently back at Cutter. He didn't argue, but he didn't acquiesce either, and his face was twisted in a confused grimace.

"Duncan, Hieronymus is right. I understand all you say, but you are in the forefront of the ground fighting…you don't see our situation from every angle." Ana had been standing quietly, but now she spoke up, stepping toward Frasier and putting her hand on his armored shoulder. "You are almost certainly right…your people will minimize their risk, the risk of the entire expedition, if we simply leave the city and return to base camp. But the scenario that provides the greatest safety for those of us here in the short term is not necessarily consistent with the course of action that gives our people as a whole a chance at survival."

Her voice was soft, understanding. It was clear she had a lot of affection for the hulking Marine, and her feelings were on display, in her eyes as well as her tone. But there was confidence there too, and an uneasy assurance, tempered certainly by fear, but there nevertheless. And despite her feelings, she was telling Frasier he was wrong, that he had to let them go.

Her eyes looked up, fixed on his. "We cannot sit here for two months and accomplish nothing, Duncan. If we do that, we will have food, but we will have done nothing to strengthen the fleet. We will slowly weaken instead of strengthen. We simply *must* find a way to truly face our enemies, to learn how to stand up to them and win."

Frasier sighed softly. She could see he was still uncomfortable, that he was worried about the security risk…and also scared for her. But his resolute expression had weakened, and after a moment he glanced at Cutter and then back to her. "Very well," he finally said, almost dejectedly. "We will explore more aggressively and see what we find." He paused. "But both of you…remember that I remain in command onsite here. And if I say we stop, we stop. Understood?"

"Yes," Ana said softly. "Of course."

"Dr. Cutter?" The Marine stared at the scientist.

"Very well, Major," he said, his tone a bit less enthusiastic than Ana's. "Agreed."

*   *   *

"I just want to keep an eye on those radiation readings. They're weak, no real problem at all. But no sense being careless."

"Yes, Dr. Barcomme." The assistant nodded abruptly and ran off back toward the control hut.

Barcomme looked out over the growing fields, hectares and

more endless hectares…the densest crops men had ever grown. Everything was going exactly according to plan…at least with her part of the mission. She'd seen several hundred of Colonel Preston's Marines bug out in one hell of a hurry, the Colonel himself at their head. There had been some kind of fight in the city, but that's all she knew. She'd ask Preston about it when he got back, but for now she had plenty of her own work to worry about. And the exploration party running into a cluster of security bots had not exactly been outside the bounds of expectations.

She looked up at the sky, and her expression turned wistful. It was a beautiful day, bright sun with a mild breeze. By Earth standards it was perfect. But her mind was elsewhere, and all the natural beauty was lost on her. Her thoughts were often with the fleet, wondering where they were…where Compton was. But today was something different.

She knew she'd miss Compton, and she had. Indeed, she was shocked just how much it affected her, how dependent she'd become on his companionship. She was so utterly alone, especially now that Ana and Hieronymus had left to explore the city. She was busy, of course, and most of the time that occupied her thoughts. But for now she had a few moments to think. Normally, a rest would be welcome, but for now she found herself wishing her work would occupy her every waking moment. The rest of her thoughts brought her nothing but pain or worry…and labor was her only solace.

But today was something different, deeper, a pain that threatened to tear her apart. "Happy Birthday, my sweet Aprile," she muttered softly. She turned away, put her back to those standing nearby as the tears welled up in her eyes. Her daughter was seven years old. It was one of the downsides of the fleet using Earth time and dates…it was impossible to forget. Not that she ever would have.

It had been nearly a year and a half…seventeen months twenty-six days, she remembered exactly, since she'd last seen her child. She'd known she would be gone for a long time when she left, several months…but she'd never imagined the sequence of events that would leave her stranded light years away, never to see her daughter again.

She'd taken the mission for Aprile as much as anything, so her daughter could have a future. Mankind had been fighting a desperate battle of survival against the First Imperium, and she knew her research could help find a way to defeat them. It had been the most painful decision she'd ever made, but in the end she knew it had been no choice at all. Still, she hadn't even imagined the agony that awaited her.

She felt the tears streaming from her eyes now, and she moved quickly away from the camp. She didn't want to talk to anyone…Compton maybe, but he wasn't there. She just needed to be alone for a while. She would regain her control…indeed, the fleet's sacrifice had bought safety for those left behind, and she took her solace in that. Her pain in being lost to Aprile also saved the girl's life. The Barrier would stand for hundreds of years, centuries before mankind again had to face the horrors of the First Imperium. A lifetime for Aprile, without her mother, but hopefully with peace…and happiness.

She breathed in deeply, her hands moving to her face, wiping away the tears. She could feel the discipline slowly returning. For all her pain, Aprile was as safe as Sophie could make her, insulated from the horrors of the First Imperium. But she had thirty thousand men and women depending on her, and on her small crew of scientists. If she failed, many of them would die...in agony, slowly starving to death. Or, perhaps even worse, at the hands of death squads…detachments Terrance Compton would have to send out himself, for no one else could issue orders of that nature.

Her thoughts drifted back to Compton. *No*, she thought. *I cannot allow that…I must succeed.* She'd come to know Compton as well as anyone in the fleet…better, indeed, than everyone save perhaps Max Harmon. She'd come to admire his strength greatly. Indeed, she'd drawn her own from his to a great extent. But she thought the need to issue those fateful orders, to sit and stare at a manifest and decide who was to live and die…that would be the final blow to him. No man could endure limitless punishment…not even Terrance Compton.

She wiped her face again, drying her eyes on her sleeves. Then she turned back and walked toward the edge of the fields, watching as her people labored in the sun, substituting their own sweat and toil for the energy they dared not use in quantities too great.

She allowed herself one more thought of her daughter, a fervent hope that Aprile was having a wonderful birthday, that the pain of loss had begun to fade for her. It was difficult to think of her child forgetting her, but she knew it was best. Sophie would never return home, never see Aprile again, she knew that…and wishing for the girl to remember her, to suffer more than she had to, would only be selfish.

She took one more deep breath and walked over toward the fields. Work was good, it was cathartic. And it was the only thing that eased the torment in her mind.

* * *

Hieronymus stepped over the broken chunks of rubble, picking his way deeper into the tunnel. His seismic readings had told him there were vast underground facilities below the city…constructions stretching kilometers below the surface.

He stepped carefully—he'd almost rolled his ankle twice on the shards of stone and shattered masonry. The Marines up front had barged right through the wreckage, their armored boots knocking most of the debris from the path. But it was still a rough walk for someone in regular boots.

He looked around, his eyes darting from location to location. It was dark in the passage, lit only by the portable lamps of the expedition, the flickering illumination bouncing around the shadows as the party scrambled forward. Cutter could make out the rough shape of his surroundings, despite millennia of deterioration. It looked like an ancient tunnel, long and gently curving, likely some kind of transit line. That was amazing, not because the First Imperium may have utilized its own form of subways, but because so much of the basic shape remained intact after so many long ages.

"Look at this material, Hieronymus." Ana was walking ahead, and he could see her head moving back and forth. "We know how old it is…yet it still retains its basic shape. The skyscrapers have all collapsed into piles of rubble, but down here…" Her voice trailed off as her eyes locked onto a chunk of debris laying at the base of a long depression.

It looked like a sheet of some kind of metal, mostly covered over by the mud along the bottom of the trench…but there was a small section of it that practically gleamed in the flickering light. It was white, with touches of red…and Cutter knew what it was immediately. "A train," he muttered softly, a piece of a train." Then louder, "This is definitely the remains of a transportation system."

"But how," Ana said, her eyes fixed on the section of bright metal. "How can this be preserved so well after this many centuries?"

Cutter didn't answer…he didn't have an answer. He just stood there for a few seconds then, suddenly, he climbed down the edge of the depression, lowering himself slowly…and dropping the last meter to the ground. His feet sank three or four centimeters, splashing mud all around, and he reached out to the wall, steadying himself.

"Hieronymus," Ana said, leaning over and staring down at her friend. "What are you doing?"

"I'm going to analyze this material, Ana. Can you imagine the uses for a metal of this durability?"

"I think we should keep moving now…we can always come back and check this out…"

A blast of gunfire echoed throughout the tunnel. It came from just up ahead…where the Marine vanguard was moving forward. There was a mad dash forward, as a wave of Marines from the rear of the formation moved up quickly, weapons drawn.

"Dr. Cutter…" One of the Marines had stopped, and

dropped to a knee. He was leaning down, extending an armored hand to Cutter. "Please, sir…come back up, at least until we get a clear idea what is going on."

Cutter looked up and nodded. He realized he'd let his excitement, his scientific curiosity, get the best of him, and he scolded himself. He'd argued with Admiral Compton so long for permission to explore a First Imperium world, now that he was here, he found himself impulsive, anxious.

He reached up and allowed the Marine to pull him back out of the trench, turning his head as he did and looking down the tunnel. There'd been nothing since the initial blast of shots, save for the sounds of the Marines scrambling about up ahead.

He turned toward Ana. "Maybe somebody thought they saw something and fir…"

Then all hell broke loose, the sounds of fire coming from multiple directions. Cutter knew immediately from the sound. They were First Imperium weapons, followed up almost immediately by the Marine assault rifles firing in response.

"Please get down…all of you." It was one of the Marines, his voice blasting out on the speaker. "There is some debris over there…it will provide cover if the enemy gets closer." He was waving his arms, directing the research team as he spoke.

Cutter motioned for Ana to move first. He followed her, halfway at least…then he paused. He hesitated, just for a second…then he pushed her forward, behind the pile of rubble, just as fire erupted behind them.

He stared back, trying to focus his eyes in the gloomy darkness, his hand dropping to his side, to the pistol Major Frasier had insisted he carry. There was a Marine rearguard behind, but it was smaller than the party in the lead, just a weak squad. And if whatever was out there got by them, he knew he and his people were the next line of defense.

He felt his heart pounding in his ears, his hands sweaty with fear. But he controlled himself, kept his calm as he stared off in the direction of the new threat, waiting. He heard the sounds moving toward him, the scuffling of the Marines falling back… closer…closer…

His hand tightened around the pistol, and he drew it slowly, nervously from his holster. He dropped down below large hunk of metal, providing at least partial cover against whatever was coming. His hand was shaking, and he struggled to hold it steady, to focus on the fight that was coming his way. Slowly, with all the effort he could muster, his hand firmed up, his eyes staring down the barrel, ready to fire.

The shooting was closer now, and he could see the figures of armored Marines, dropping back through the corridor, their shadowy forms carrying back at least two of their own, wounded. And behind them…barely visible in the heavy gloom, he would see the enemy, First Imperium warbots. Not the security units they had encountered on X18 or up on the surface, but full-fledged military bots, like those the Marines had fought on Sigma 4 and along the Line. Massive, bristling with weapons… and heading right toward his team.

A shudder rippled through his body, watching as the rearguard continue to fall back, realizing they weren't going to stop the enemy. There are too many of them…they'd be there in a few seconds. He felt his stomach retch, but he forced it back down. He wasn't a warrior like the Marines, but that didn't matter now. His people were under attack, and the choice was simple. Fight…or give up and die.

He his eyes darted to the side, and he caught Ana in his gaze, her face a mask of fear, but her own weapon out in front of her, grim, at the ready. He nodded to himself and gathered up his courage, and his hand slowly steadied, his eye locked on the closest of the enemy. He heard the sounds of the Marines moving back, firing all the way as they did, and he saw the lead bot caught in the streams of two assault rifles…the top half of its body torn apart. And behind the dying robot, he saw another one, moving up and firing its autocannons at the Marines caught in the open.

Cutter felt a wave of rage as he saw one of the Marines fall, his body ripped open, clearly dead. He gritted his teeth and swore a curse under his breath. Then he fired.

Chapter Twelve

Terrance Compton's Orders to Admiral West

Erica, I deeply regret that I must assign you this mission, but there is no one I trust more than you...and your success is vital to the survival of the fleet. It is, perhaps, my error that put your task force in this situation...my decision to move toward X57 directly, with no idea of what awaited us there. I didn't believe we had time to conduct a proper scouting mission, so I elected to proceed directly toward the gate. In the end, that choice has proven costly.

I do not believe it is coincidence that the enemy has now advanced from each of the warp gates in this system, save the one we entered from. At the very least, we were discovered here, and the First Imperium forces were able to move from unknown locations to approach from multiple entry points. However, I believe the situation is far graver than that. I have no proof, no evidence of any substance, but I now believe the enemy has known where we were for some time, that they have been organizing their forces, awaiting the right moment to strike here. If this is the case, I confide in you that I have no idea what course to pursue, what actions to take to try and extricate ourselves from something that feels like a rapidly closing trap. We must extricate the fleet from X56 for certain, though I now question if this will serve any purpose save to delay the final combat. Nevertheless, we must try to escape the enemy, at least for a time.

Your mission is of vital importance. You must destroy the

enemy forces that have already transited through the X57 gate. If you are able to do so before additional units appear, you are to button up your people in the tanks and follow the fleet to X54 at maximum speed. However, if additional First Imperium forces transit through the warp gate before the rest of the fleet has left the system, you must remain in place and hold them back...at all costs. We must have time to withdraw the rest of our ships. Nothing can interfere with that.

You have my utmost respect, as do the men and women who serve under you, and I assure you that all of our thoughts will be with you as you enter battle...and we shall look ahead with confidence to your safe return.

Flag Bridge
AS Saratoga
X56 System - Near the X57 warp gate
The Fleet: 134 ships, 30,177 crew

"All ships, fire!" Erica West stood next to her chair, deep within *Saratoga's* massive bulk. The flag bridge was about as deep inside the ship as a location could be, save for the reactors…better protected even than the main bridge, where Captain Black ran the mighty battleship. Still, she could feel the great battleship shake to its girders every time the First Imperium lasers slammed into her. The enemy weapons were longer-ranged, and West and her people had no choice but to sit and take it. Until now.

"Yes, Admiral." A moment later: "All ships report engaged." Hank Krantz had been West's tactical officer for a long time, almost since the day she'd taken command of her first task force. That had been years before, and the enemy then had been the CAC and the Caliphate, not the First Imperium.

She stared at the display, her eyes fixed on the enemy formation. It was a moderate force—eighteen Gremlins and four of the larger Gargoyles, not much stronger than the fleet that had come through the X58 warp gate and engaged John Duke and his people. West expected more enemy ships to come pouring through any minute, but so far she still faced the same twenty-two ships.

She could feel the vibrations under her feet as the reactors operated a few points over one hundred percent power, feeding energy into the massive x-ray lasers. *Saratoga* was one of the Alliance's largest class of battleships, its nearly two kilometer hull bristling with the strongest weapons developed by man. And she was pouring everything she had hotter than a candle into the First Imperium line.

Her ships had taken damage from the enemy's missile barrage as well, an attack they had also been forced to endure without returning the fire. The fleet had expended the last of its missiles six months before in X18, and despite a full scale effort to ramp up production, supplies were still very low…and *Saratoga* and her fellow ships had none at all.

West had only lost two vessels outright in the barrage, a CAC destroyer and a PRC frigate, but there was widespread damage throughout her forces. Even *Saratoga* had seen one of its heavy laser cannons knocked out, along with half a dozen minor systems. Still, all things considered, they'd gotten off light. She knew it could have been worse. Much worse.

She could see the two big ovals on the screen, her battleships positioned right next to each other, pouring fire into the heart of the enemy formation. *Conde* was smaller than *Saratoga*, and she didn't pack as much of a punch, but the older battlewagon was the second strongest thing she had…even if she was a Europan ship.

West was as skilled a tactician as anyone in the fleet, rivaling even Compton, but she struggled with diplomacy and the realities of making a multinational force like the fleet function. It took a constant effort to hold her tongue, and even then some things slipped out that shouldn't.

She didn't think much of the Europan navy, and when she wasn't keeping her mouth shut, she tended to speak her mind in full. And she hated Gregoire Peltier with a raging passion. She blamed the Europan admiral for his part in the mutiny, and she'd bristled with rage when Compton had pardoned him and the others. To her, treachery was unforgivable, regardless of the situation. She knew that wasn't practical, that Compton's way had almost surely been best for the fleet's chances of survival. But she was what she was, and there wasn't a doubt in her mind, if it had been her decision, Peltier would have been spaced for mutiny. And if the rest of the Europans didn't like it, there was plenty of room in the airlock.

"Admiral, *Conde* reports heavy damage. One of her reactors scragged, and Captain Trevian has the other operating at one hundred ten percent."

West nodded. "Very well, Commander." She had to admit that, despite her prejudices, Trevian was impressing her in the way he fought his ship. The Europan navy was riddled with nepotism and cronyism, with far too many well-connected types putting in a few years carrying commissions they didn't rate before returning back to Earth and the political offices their families controlled. And she felt officers like that were even more useless—and dangerous—with a formation like the fleet. There was no room in her view for privileged elites seeking to maintain their perquisites, not when you were trapped deep in enemy space, facing possible destruction at every turn.

Still, Trevian seemed to be one of the good ones. She would have expected a Europan captain to use a damaged reactor as an excuse to pull back from the line, but there hadn't been a whisper from *Conde's* bridge. Indeed, Trevian had responded by cranking up his working reactor to dangerous levels to keep his ship in the fight. She didn't know his background offhand, but she made a note to herself to check when she had time…assuming any of them made it out of this system, of course. She was beginning to suspect he was one of the minority of Europan officers who had risen through the ranks based on merit and not influence. Either that, or he was that even rarer beast, the scion of an entitled family who possessed genuine talent and dedication to his duty.

Her eyes shifted to the side, watching her display. Whatever made Trevian tick, she didn't have time to worry about it now. She had bigger problems…over a hundred fighters heading back to her two capital ships, far more than their normal capacity. And if she didn't get them landed somehow—in the middle of this battle, no less—they were going to start running out of fuel and life support.

"Commander," she said, pausing for a second while her eyes locked on the cluster of tiny symbols approaching the fleet, "inquire about the status of *Conde's* landing bays. We've got the whole strike force heading our way critical on fuel, and we're going to have to figure out some way to accommodate them all."

"Yes, Admiral. Immediately."

She turned her eyes back to the display, and she felt a wave of excitement when she saw that two more of the enemy ships were gone, one of them a Gargoyle. While she was watching, a third First Imperium ship winked out…the victim of *Conde's* continued fire.

"Admiral, Captain Trevian reports that his bays are moderately damaged, but at present he believes he can land fighters."

"Very well, Commander." She felt a wave of relief. *Saratoga's* bays were still operational, but they didn't have nearly enough capacity to handle all of Hurley's people. And she damned well had no intention of letting those crews float helplessly in space until their fuel and life support gave out. No, whatever she had to do…she would do it.

Saratoga shook hard again, another hit. Then another. Her ship was big…and durable. But she knew it could only take so much punishment. A quick glance confirmed the bays were still operational, and the reactors were still at over ninety percent. But she'd lost two of her big laser cannons, and that was a significant bite out of *Saratoga's* firepower.

She glanced down toward her display, her fingers reaching out, punching up the latest damage figures. *No*, she thought to herself…*let Davis Black run his ship, and you do your own job.* Black was one of the best ship captains in the fleet, and she knew she was lucky to have him.

She flipped the switch on her com unit, dialing up Admiral Hurley's line. "Greta," she said, "You have to get your people landed…burn the last vapors you've got, but get here. I'm not sure how long these landing bays are going to hold up."

She took a deep breath, and waited for a reply. Hurley's squadrons were still four light seconds out...and the eight or ten seconds she had to wait for a reply seemed like an eternity.

Come on, Greta...get those birds here...

* * *

Compton lay still, feeling as if he was simultaneously floating and being crushed. He'd been half a century in space now, fought dozens of battles, yet he'd never truly gotten used to the misery of the acceleration tanks. He hated every minute of it, laying in the thick, viscous liquid, his body bloated and uncomfortable from the cocktail of drugs that enabled him to endure 30g or more of acceleration. But most of all he detested the disorientation the pressure and the injections caused. It was bad enough under any circumstances, but when his people were in combat it was maddening to lie there, wondering if your senses were true, if you were following the actual battle or simply hallucinating. And Compton knew when he made mistakes, people died.

He'd always avoided high gee maneuvers whenever possible, planning his battles around them when he could. He hated them personally, but most of all he knew they were hard on the crews...and they degraded efficiency terribly. But now there was no choice. The enemy had come through two of the system's three warp gates...and they could push larger forces into the system at any time. He needed to get the fleet out of X56, as quickly as possible, back the way they had come.

He moved his left index finger, scrolling along the small display over his head. It was far from the ideal setup to monitor the fleet, especially when he had forces dispatched all over the system, but it was all he had. He'd centered the screen on West's fleet, and he could see her ships lined up, facing the enemy at point blank range. There were nineteen icons...that meant she'd lost three ships so far, though Compton knew he was looking across almost twenty light minutes...and with the two sides practically stopped in space blasting away at each other, that was a long time. He could only imagine how many more of his spacers had died in twenty minutes.

He stared at the display, struggling to focus, losing track of how many times he'd had the same thought. For all the hundreds, probably thousands, of hours he'd spent in the tanks in his long career, his mind still fought to stay on point, to fight off the daydreams, to keep his decision-making as sharp as possible. And despite those efforts and the impressive discipline that always drove him, he still found himself struggling for minutes on end with a single thought.

What should I do now? Do I stay in X54, hold the fleet in place and wait for the detachments to return...if they return? What if the enemy sends more ships in after we've transited? How will I even know if any of the rearguards are still alive?

His thoughts went in circles, first rejecting the notion of moving on without the rest of his people...then realizing waiting would put the fleet in greater jeopardy. And the landing parties...what should be do about them? Should he withdraw all the way back to X48, take up defensive positions around the planet and wait for their mission to be complete? Or would he only put the expedition in greater danger, leading the enemy back to them? Should he race back and pick them up now... and abort the planting effort? That might be the safest option in the extreme short term, but it would also condemn thousands of his people to starvation.

He could move through an unexplored warp gate too, try to break out into clear space before he fell back to X48. That way, if the enemy followed him, he would lead them away and not toward the expedition. X53 seemed a likely choice. There was a virgin gate leading there from X54, one not too far from the X56-X54 portal his people were blasting toward now. They could make the jump back to X54 and then to X53 in less than eight hours. The only alternative was to continue back into X51 the way they had come. And X51 was a transit system, with just two discovered gates…the one from X54 and the one to X49, where they'd originally come from. And that was just one jump from X48 and the expedition.

But if he transited to X53, he risked getting cut off from X48, running into more enemy forces. And if the fleet got trapped in X53, unable to fight its way back into X51, he wouldn't be able to get back and retrieve the expedition.

He reached out with his left hand, pressing the button for another stimulant injection. He'd already had three, and he was moving quickly into the danger zone, but there was no choice. He simply had to retain his sharpness…to keep the focus he needed to thing this through. Because, once the fleet transited back to X54 he would have to know what to do. And right now he had no idea…no idea at all.

*   *   *

John Duke was pacing back and forth, at least as much as *Jaguar's* cramped bridge allowed. He had his forces lined up in front of the warp gate, their exhausted damage control parties struggling to repair shattered weapons and rewire severed conduits. The fight had been a tough one, but his forces had come through it better than he'd dared to hope, at least in terms of ships lost outright. But every vessel he had was damaged, and many of them badly. If his people had another battle to fight, he suspected it would turn out much differently.

Captain Kato's task force was positioned next to his own. The larger cruisers could absorb more damage than his attack ships, and Kato's survivors were in better shape than his own vessels. Still, no matter how he looked at it, his combat strength was well below half of what it had been, especially since Hurley's fighters had expended all their armaments and half their fuel, and been forced to withdraw. They'd headed back first to rendezvous with the fleet before its transit to X57, but the appearance of enemy ships from that warp gate had forced

Compton to zip up in the tanks and make a run back to X54, clear across the system. And that meant the fighters couldn't catch up...and even if they could, they'd never be able to land on ships blasting away at 30g.

They were on their way to Admiral West's task force now. Unlike Duke's forces, West's armada had two capital ships that could land fighters, though their capacity was too small to accommodate all of Hurley's craft. Duke didn't know just how many birds a ship like *Saratoga* could cram in during an emergency, but he suspected Erica West would do whatever it took to find a place for every fighter. *If her ships are still there by the time Hurley's people arrive...and if they're bays aren't blown to bits.*

Whatever happened with the fighters, it was out of Duke's hands. But right now he was doing anything he could to pass the time. He'd sent *Vanir* through the warp gate to scout out the X58 system. Hans Steiner's ship had been the lead vessel on the expedition that found the First Imperium Colossus six months before, the very ship that Hieronymus Cutter and his team had gained control of...and led back to save the fleet just in time back in X18. Duke had never been a big believer in superstition, but he figured his people could use anything they could get right now. Maybe Steiner and *Vanir* could repeat their good luck.

He turned toward the tactical station and almost asked for the third time, but he caught himself. Alex Barret had been his tactical officer since the Line. The second *Vanir* transited back into the system, the commander would let him know about it.

He glanced down at his display again, for about the tenth time in half an hour. He was watching as his crews raced to complete their damage control operations, but he doubted anything had changed in the four minutes since he'd last checked.

"We're getting something through the gate, sir." Barret's voice was edgy, tense. In a moment they'd know what was waiting for them on the other side. "Yes, sir...it's *Vanir*."

Duke swallowed hard. He knew it would take some time, perhaps half a minute, before *Vanir's* systems cleared from the transit...and another few seconds for the signal to reach *Jaguar*. He could feel his heart pounding, the clammy sweat on the back of his hands. If Hans Steiner's ship came back with an enemy fleet close on its tail, Duke knew his task force was as good as destroyed. They were far too close to the warp gate to escape… and they didn't stand a chance in another fight, not against any substantial force.

"*Jaguar*, this is Captain Steiner on *Vanir*. We have just transited back from X58."

Duke listened to the words coming in over the com, his eyes focused coldly on the display, looking for the first signs of enemy ships following on *Vanir's* heels.

"Captain Duke," Steiner continued, "there are over a hundred ships in X58, perhaps more…including Gargoyles and Leviathans."

Duke felt his hope fade away. It was over. His squadron wouldn't last ten minutes once the enemy transited.

"But they're not pursuing, sir," Steiner's words continued. "Not yet, at least. They are stationary…just sitting there thirty light seconds from the warp gate."

It took a few seconds for the words to sink in to Duke's head. "Confirm, Vanir," he said anxiously. "Enemy is thirty light seconds from the gate?" It would take two and a half seconds for his communique to reach *Vanir*…and another two and a half for a reply to make it back. It was the longest five seconds of his life.

"Confirmed, Captain," came the reply, firm, certain. "Repeat, enemy forces are stationary thirty light seconds from the warp gate."

We've got a chance…time to get away before they can get here.

"All vessels, prepare to set a course for the X54 warp…" His voice tailed off.

No, we can't follow the fleet. Not yet. There's something else we've got to do first.

His eyes dropped to the display, to the image of West's ships, still locked in battle. He couldn't leave without her people. No, his forces had to help hers…and then they could all leave together. Or not at all.

"Belay that last order. All ships, set a course to the X57 warp gate." His voice was grim, resolute. He knew what he had to do. "We're going to help Admiral West and her people."

Chapter Thirteen

Tactical Command Unit 45023A (Prime City, Planet 17411)

There is activity in the ruins of the city. After so many millennia, my forces detect movement, sound, energy usage. Is it possible the enemy is still active after so many ages of dormancy? It seems unlikely, yet there is no question some force has engaged the surface security system...and eliminated it. Once again there is war.

The biologics have long been believed destroyed, the remnants of their bodies blown away in the winds long millennia ago. There have been no energy readings, no signs of any kind, not in all the thousands of centuries that have passed since the final battles. Until now.

My directives are clear, and they remain as they ever were... rouse the forces of war, prepare to destroy whatever enemy, whether old or new. Yet I have insufficient data to prepare a battle plan, no real knowledge of the adversary I face. And my armies are wasted by the passage of time, hundreds of thousands of warrior units laying idle, rendered useless by millennia of decay. Only a small force remains, and much of that is in poor condition. Still, I know what I must do...and even my reduced force will be sufficient to see it done.

Destroy all enemies, new or old. Preserve the Imperium. Serve the Regent.

X48 System – Planet II
Beneath the Ruins of "New York City"
The Fleet: 131 ships, 30,011 crew

Cutter sat on the edge of a small slab of broken stone, wincing as the medic picked at his arm, cleaning the wound before he fused it. It wasn't a serious injury, certainly not by Marine standards, but it was his first combat wound, and as far as he was concerned it hurt like hell.

"Nice, Doc."

"Yeah, Doc. You're one of us now."

When the Marines started thanking and congratulating him, he wasn't sure at first if they were teasing him, but it didn't take long for the sincerity to sink in. Cutter was no one's idea of a stone cold warrior, but when Major Campbell and the other Marines got back to the beleaguered rearguard, they found Hieronymus Cutter standing alone over not one but two wounded Marines, holding off the enemy attack with a pistol.

Holding off was an overstatement, perhaps. Cutter realized his weapon had been woefully inadequate to seriously damage a First Imperium warbot…and he also knew he'd survived only because Frasier and his people had gotten there just in time. But he was beginning to realize that didn't matter to the Marines. He'd stood firm, risked his life to protect their comrades when he might have run. Indeed, he probably *should* have run since his knowledge was beyond valuable to the fleet. But he hadn't. He'd been scared, in a way he couldn't even completely recall now…so terrified he half suspected he'd frozen in panic, and that's why he'd stayed put. But none of that mattered, not to the Marines. He'd done what he'd done, and that's all they cared about.

Cutter winced hard as the medic pressed down on the wound, lining it up to fuse it together. "Do you want some pain meds, Doctor?"

Cutter desperately wanted to say yes, but the past few minutes of camaraderie with the Marines had made him feel uncharacteristically tough…or at least like he should act that way. "No," he said, trying to cover up the pain in his voice. "I'm fine."

"This will only take a minute…then you'll be good as new." Cutter wasn't sure if there was a hint of amusement in the medic's voice.

He just nodded…and then concentrated on not gritting his teeth.

"Ronnie…"

It was Ana Zhukov, walking up behind him. He pulled his arm when he turned to look at her and he yelped in pain.

"Try to stay still, Doctor Cutter." The medic had the fuser in his hand, but he was still trying to line up the two sides of the wound to his satisfaction.

Cutter nodded gently, and he turned his head more cautiously, looking up at Ana. "How are you feeling?" She had a nasty bruise stretching all the way down the left side of her face. The enemy fire had blasted down a section of rock from overhead, and one large piece had taken her in the head. The impact had knocked her out, but otherwise she looked okay.

"I'm good," she said, clearly a little uncomfortable but otherwise fine. "I'm just sorry I missed your heroics. All the Marines are talking about it."

"I think the Marines are making a big deal out of nothing. If Duncan and the others hadn't gotten there just when they did, I'd be a stain right now." He bit down on his lip as he felt the fuser moving across his arm. It wasn't painful, not really. More…unpleasant.

"There, Doctor," the medic said a few seconds later. "I'd like to see you take it easy on that for twelve hours if you can, but otherwise you're good to go."

"Thank you…" He stretched out his arm. It did feel better, a little sore, maybe, but most of the pain was gone. "It feels great."

The medic nodded and climbed to his feet. "Let me know if you have any problems. I've got other customers waiting…"

Cutter returned the nod. "Thanks again." Then he turned toward Ana and said, without preamble, "Why are there full-sized warbots on this planet?" The security robots they'd encountered on X18 had been smaller and less powerful than the full-fledged battle units encountered at Sigma-4 and along the Line. But there were top grade military units on X48. They'd just fought a battle against a group of them.

"I don't know, Hieronymus, but let's not jump to any conclusions." She sounded like she was trying to convince herself as much as him.

"We know there was fighting here…but if there is a full scale military force still active, we could be in deep trouble. When Erik Cain fought the enemy front line military units on Sandoval he had what…tens of thousands of Marines and other troops? We've got less than two thousand on the whole fleet, plus maybe a thousand Janissaries and miscellaneous forces. And no more than twelve hundred onplanet." His voice was low. He was starting to wonder just how dangerous the exploration of the city would be. But he wasn't ready to give up, not yet. And that meant the fewer people who heard him speak like this the better.

"It's been half a million years, Hieronymus. The forces that invaded Occupied Space were probably gathered from dozens of bases, maybe even hundreds. Even if there had been a large army here once, it's probable most of it has long been inoperative. We're probably just running into a few remnants."

He sighed. "I hope you're right. Because we're already here…and we can't leave without the technology we came for. Whatever is waiting down there." He gestured off into the corridor.

"Maybe we have enough already," she said, not even sounding like she believed it. "There was a lot of debris on the surface and just below the ground."

"C'mon, Ana, you know better than that." He took a deep breath and rose slowly to his feet. "We found a treasure trove up there, enough to keep a thousand normal scientists inventing stuff for the rest of their lives…but that's not what we came here for. What we need is a series of revolutionary breakthroughs. Staggering, almost unfathomable discoveries. We're struggling to survive against an enemy that is not only millennia ahead of our science, but also one that vastly outnumbers us…

even now, when perhaps ninety-nine percent of the forces they once had are gone. Nothing less than massive leaps forward will do us any real good."

Ana just nodded. She and Hieronymus had spoken many times about the fleet's chances of survival, and they had agreed they were virtually nil, at least without some massive and unpredictable development. Like a stunning scientific discovery. Or, more likely, a whole series of them.

"Are you both ready?" Duncan Frasier stood behind them, his helmet fully retracted. He had crept up behind the two of them while they were talking. Cutter still couldn't understand how a Marine in more than ten tons of osmium-iridium armor could move so quietly.

Ana turned around and smiled, but she didn't say anything.

"You're not going to fight me on this, Duncan?" Cutter had half-expected Frasier to argue with him about moving on. They were less than ten meters below the surface, still climbing around the remains of ancient transit lines…and they'd already suffered another attack, one that had cost the lives of three Marines and one scientist…and had wounded almost a dozen more.

"No, Hieronymus," he said simply, his deep voice about as soft as it ever got. "I figure if you can stand there over two of my Marines, facing almost certain death, then the least we can do is back you up too. It's easy to argue when someone expects your people to do all the dying to make something happen. But that's not you, I can see that now." Frasier hesitated. "Besides, I know you're right. We may face terrible danger down there… we may all die. But it *is* our only chance. My men and women might do most of the fighting, but in the end it's the two of your—and your team—that will save us. Or not."

"Do you really feel that way, Duncan?" It was Ana. She took a few steps closer to the big Marine, reaching up and putting her hand on his armored shoulder."

"Yes," he replied. "I do. We'll fight to the end, I'd bet my last breath on that, but fifteen hundred Marines aren't going to keep us all alive. Neither are a hundred forty ships, most of them low on weapons, spare parts…everything. We might get off this planet, last another six months, maybe a year. But we need a real game changer if we're going to have a true future. And as far as I can see it, the two of you are the only place that's going to come from. Even a ten percent chance at salvation is worth more than certain, slow death. At least to me, it is."

"Thank you, Duncan." Cutter reached down and pulled on the small jacket he'd set aside. The left arm was torn open and splotched with blood, now mostly dried. "I can promise you my intention is to do whatever is necessary to find a way for our people to survive…regardless of the risk." He paused, flashing a quick glance back toward Ana. "I'm going to take a quick look forward…we'll leave in ten, okay?"

Frasier nodded. "Yes," he said simply.

Cutter scooped up his body armor and walked slowly forward, keeping his head turned away, the smile on his lips to himself. He could only give them ten minutes together. Then they all had to set out again. But he intended for them to have those brief few moments. He knew either of them or both could die before they had any more time to themselves.

* * *

Sophie stared out over the horizon, watching the last deep-red rays of the sun setting behind the distant hills. The crops were a meter high already, swaying in the breeze amid the growing dusk. It was a picturesque scene, almost idyllic, save for one thing. One of her people had died today.

She'd heard the communiques from Cutter's expedition over the last several days, one report after another of combat, of more people dead. They'd been attacked half a dozen times as they worked their way deeper into the underground complex beneath the ruins of the metropolis they had dubbed 'New York City.' She'd laughed at that first time she'd heard that, a welcome bit of humor. But she was in no mood for levity now.

She knew Ana and Hieronymus were in great danger, and

she realized their team and the Marines had suffered heavy casualties, far worse than anything her people had endured. But Raj Kalapor had been a gifted scientist, one of the best and most dedicated of her crew. And his death hit home.

He'd been on the far fringe of the fields, checking on the progress of a section of genetically-enhanced legumes when a phalanx of First Imperium drones flew in over the distant ridge. Kalapor sounded the alarm…and then he took off at a dead run, trying to get back to the camp before the weapons reached him. He made it about halfway…and then two of them landed within a meter of him. There hadn't been much left when Preston's Marines got there, barely enough to confirm it was him.

The other drones landed in the middle of the fields, taking out a hundred square meters of crops, but otherwise inflicting no casualties. Nevertheless, the damage had already been done. Kalapor was the second of Barcomme's people lost to random enemy action. And six of Preston's Marines were dead too. The camp wasn't under attack, at least nothing sustained. It was more like alarm systems triggering the occasional piece of still-functional weaponry. No real threat to the expedition as a whole, at least not yet. But they all hurt.

The base camp hadn't suffered anything like the kind of punishment Cutter's expedition had, but there was still a haunted, eerie quality to the seemingly idyllic world…creepy vestiges of the war that had once raged there. She found herself hating the planet, longing to leave. She'd been overwhelmed with work the first few weeks, but now the crops were growing, and she found herself with time on her hands. Time to think. About the casualties her people had suffered…and other losses too.

She'd felt the emptiness inside her since the day the fleet had been trapped beyond the Barrier, the loss of her family slicing keenly into her. She'd despaired of ever healing, of feeling whole again, but now the cold starkness of this alien world made her realize just how far she had come in the last year. Terrance Compton had helped her begin her recovery…she wasn't sure she could have done it alone. The pain was still there, as she knew it would always be. But she dared to think of living a life as part of the fleet, of knowing something other than sadness and fear. If her team could finish their mission, restock the fleet's food supply, maybe…just maybe their people could find a life somewhere, one worth living. One that entailed more than running and fighting.

She sighed. "Perhaps," she whispered to herself. "Perhaps…"

But the darkness was still inside her, weighing down her every thought. She'd come a small way, but she still didn't believe in their future. Not really. Not yet. But she was a bit closer than she had been…and that was something.

*   *   *

"McCloud, get your bastards up forward and scout the area ahead. I don't want anything to take us by surprise." Kyle Bruce was walking next to Hieronymus, shouting out commands to the hulking Marine standing not quite at attention in front of him.

"Yes, sir." The Marine turned almost immediately and walked off down the wide tunnel. His voice was gruff, not quite insubordinate, but not with the level of respect Cutter had become used to hearing when Marines spoke with their superior officers.

"What was that all about?" Cutter asked. The expedition had made camp for the night, but Cutter was restless and he'd decided to take a look around a bit farther down the corridor. He'd tried to get out alone, swearing he would only go out a few hundred meters, but Frasier wasn't about to let him get out of sight without an escort. The major insisted on a guard detail… and Cutter had clearly heard him tell Bruce to put together a team and, 'take McCloud's squad along.'

Bruce sighed. "McCloud's a pain in the ass," he said, turning toward Cutter. "All his people are. Always have been. A bunch of foul-tempered rejects."

"I'm surprised Major Frasier puts up with that." Cutter seemed genuinely confused. He'd come to know the commander of the Scots Company fairly well since their adventures on the Colossus, and the last thing he'd expect was for Frasier to put up with insubordinate Marines.

Bruce smiled. "Well, he wouldn't under most circumstances. But Duff McCloud and his pack of vipers aren't 'most circumstances.'"

"How so?"

"Well…" Bruce said, pausing for a few seconds, clearly trying to decide how he wanted to put it. "Let's just say that they're good fighters. Damned good fighters…good enough to be worth putting up with. And, however much a handful they are, they're on our side."

Cutter had a hard time imagining Frasier—or Colonel Preston—putting up with a group of headcases. But they knew their business a lot better than he did, so he just nodded even though he didn't understand. *Can they be that good?*

"How far down do you think we are?" Bruce asked, looking around as he did.

"Over a kilometer. I had hoped to find some extensive facilities under the city, but I hadn't imagined anything like this." They were in a broad underground tunnel, almost ten meters wide and stretching deep into the darkness ahead. They'd been underground almost a week, wandering through an enormous network of passageways and subterranean facilities. Most of it was old, worn down to the basic structures…but Cutter's people had found a considerable number of artifacts too. There were a lot of familiar pieces, bits and pieces of First Imperium warbots and the like. But there were other materials too…weapons and parts of equipment that were unfamiliar. It was possible they were simply dealing with new types of enemy gear, items they simply had not encountered previously. But Cutter didn't think so. He had less concrete evidence than he would have liked, but his feeling was strong. Some of these items were different. After all, there had been war here…and he knew war took two sides.

"How deep do you plan to go?" Bruce looked around uneasily as he spoke. Cutter knew the lieutenant was a combat veteran and a Marine. But he also suspected Bruce's battles had been mostly above ground affairs, and now the Marine officer was beginning to realize he had a touch of claustrophobia.

Cutter had to fight back a smile. He was so accustomed to the straightforward courage of the Marines, he sometimes forget they were men and women too…and they all had their own fears. Bruce was keeping it together, but Cutter could tell the thought of over a kilometer of rock over his head made him decidedly uneasy.

"As deep as we have to go, Kyle," Cutter said, the firmness and confidence in his voice surprising even himself. He'd almost lied, suggested that they were as far down as they were going. But he felt if the Marines deserved anything on a mission like this, it was honestly. "Hopefully not much farther," he added.

Bruce nodded, trying with limited success to wipe the concerned look off his face. He looked like he was about to say something else when his head snapped around suddenly, looking back the way they had come…toward the camp.

There was a dull thud, off in the distance, a non-descript sound, low-pitched, soft. Cutter hardly noticed it at first…not until he saw Bruce turn back and look down the dark hallway stretching out behind them.

"What is it?" Cutter asked, but he already knew. Then another deep rumble rattled through the tunnels, louder, closer. And he was certain.

The camp was under attack.

Chapter Fourteen

Admiral Erica West During the Battle of the X57 Gate

Give yourselves a moment, a few seconds to remember those you love, all you care about...and to say a silent farewell, lest you don't see them again. Take another instant to recount why you fight, to consider your motivations, to understand what drives you into the maelstrom. And lastly, look inside yourself, to your honor, your fortitude, to all that makes you what you are, gives you the essential strength that carries you to war.

Think in the brief moment before the fight of all of this, of everything that makes you the men and women you are. Then, forget it all, every last bit of it, for there is but one thing that matters. Send these bastards to hell!

Approaching AS Saratoga
X56 System - Near the X57 warp gate
The Fleet: 127 ships, 29807 crew

"I want you to bring your people in next, Commander." Greta Hurley's voice was icy, resolute. Mariko had never seen an officer so coldly focused on getting her people back home. Or as close to home as was available.

"But Admiral, what about you and…"

"But is not in your vocabulary, Commander Fujin." Mariko

felt like the speaker of her com unit rattled with the force of Hurley's voice. "Follow your orders…and get those ships in now. We don't have time to waste on bullshit."

"Yes, Admiral," she replied, suitably chastened. Her job was getting her three squadrons in safely, which was a handful in itself under the current conditions. *Saratoga* had been pretty roughed up in the fight, but somehow Admiral West had managed to keep the bays open. Her crews had already landed more than the forty-eight birds she'd been designed to hold, but *Conde* had only managed to get twenty ships aboard before her last bay took another hit and shut down. And that meant *Saratoga* had to cram in almost twice her capacity—and do it in the heat of battle.

"Alright everybody," Fujin snapped out over the com, "we're going in. Lightnings in alpha bay…Wildcats in beta bay. And the Dragons will bring up the rear." *Assuming they can shove us all in there somewhere…and whatever miracle is keeping those bays operating holds…*

Fujin had lost four ships in the battle, two from the Wildcats and one each from the Lightnings and the Dragons. The other fourteen were decelerating hard, hoping their fuel would last long enough to get them inside the hulking warship. However it turned out, it was going to come right down to the wire.

She glanced at the tactical display. West's task force was winning the battle, there was no question about that. Half the enemy ships were gone already, and most of the rest of them were wracked with internal explosions and bleeding gasses and fluids. But her forces had suffered badly too, especially in the initial approach, where they'd been forced to endure the enemy's longer-ranged fire. Half a dozen ships were gone, and from a quick glance at the scanners, Fujin figured *Conde's* chances of making it through the battle were no better than fifty-fifty. And if she didn't pull through, four of Hurley's squadrons would go down with her.

"Tighten that line, Wildcat Leader," she snapped suddenly into the com. Her eyes had caught a gap between the second and fifth birds…the empty space where two of the Wildcats' ships, and ten of their men and women, should have been but weren't anymore. She understood how hard it was on a squadron commander to lose people, but now she was focused on one thing…getting all her surviving crews onboard that ship while there was still time.

"Yes, Commander." And a few seconds later: "Commencing landing in thirty seconds."

Fujin stared at the screen, watching as the Wildcats' formation tightened up. She knew she only had to tell Bev Jones once. She felt a rush of satisfaction, but it faded quickly. *I shouldn't have had to tell her at all…*

There was a logic to the hard edge Mariko Fujin had acquired since assuming wing command, a cold, rational effort to consider every aspect of the operation. Jones was a good officer, Mariko was certain of that, but she was too new to squadron command…and, honestly, too slow to adapt. The Wildcats' leader was her friend, but now more than ever, she felt the yawning gulf between Jones and herself. Friendship only went so far…at least when lives were on the line. And if she decided Jones wasn't ready to lead a squadron and she demoted her, what would that do to their relationship? Would Bev take it as a betrayal? Or would she understand Mariko was thinking of the wing?

Mariko didn't know, but she couldn't imagine it wouldn't affect things…cost her a friend. Still, she was sure she would do it if she had to. The wing came first, her obligation to all of her people. Before friendship. Before anything.

She watched as the two leading squadrons completed their final approach. A few of her birds had battle damage, which was only going to make things worse…especially since *Saratoga* was clearly hurt too and already well over capacity.

She looked across the cockpit toward Wainwright. "How is our fuel holding out, Lieutenant?"

"We're on fumes, Commander. That last attack run drained us. I don't know if we're going to make it."

Her eyes darted to the screen. The Lightnings and the Wildcats were just going in. That meant her birds would be less than two minutes behind. But if they ran out of fuel at the last second, they wouldn't have the thrust to slow down…and that meant they'd crash into the bay.

And there are three more squadrons behind us…including the admiral…

"There's no ifs or maybes here, Lieutenant. This has got to be yes or no…and nothing in between." She reached down and punched at her screen, doing her own calculations…just as Wainwright was doing. And she reached the same conclusion as the pilot.

"No, Commander. I don't think we're going to make it."

She watched as the ships ahead of her landed, one at a time on each side. There were two more Lightnings to go…and only one Wildcat. Then she could switch up her people, send two into each bay. But her own ship was bone dry. She knew what she had to do.

"Dragon Two and Dragon Three, proceed to alpha bay… Dragon Four and Dragon Six, proceed to beta bay." She took a deep breath and shook her head. Her other four birds would make it. But hers wasn't going to.

"Everybody get your survival gear zipped up." She pushed a final doubt aside, realizing there was no other choice. She reached down and grabbed the helmet lying next to her chair. "We're going to lose life support any minute…"

* * *

"Definitely more ships coming through, Admiral." Hank Krantz turned and looked over at West, and she could see the discouragement in his face.

She couldn't blame him. The battle had been over, or at least close to it. Another ten minutes, fifteen at most, and the First Imperium armada would have been gone, wiped out. The task force could have made a run for it, buttoning up in the tanks and chasing after the main fleet.

Admiral Compton had been absolutely clear…once the fleet had transited, West was to break off as quickly as possible and follow at full speed. She wasn't to try to explore X57 as Duke's people had done with X58. The emergence of fresh enemy forces from both warp gates had pretty much cut off any options besides retreating, running back the way they had come.

She sighed softly, unable to stop her own frustration from slipping out, but trying to keep it as quiet as she could. She could feel her throat tightening, the hope draining from her body. But that was something only she needed to know. As far as her bridge crew was concerned—and every other man and women in the task force—she knew exactly what to do, how to get them all out of this. It was a lie, but the truth wasn't going to help anyone right now.

"Order all damage control parties to focus on weapons and power generation systems. I want every gun in the task force ready to fire in three minutes."

"Yes, Admiral." Krantz turned and forwarded the order to the rest of the task force. "Admiral, Captain Trevian reports life support failures in significant sections of *Conde*…and radiation leaks in its engineering section. He reports he has affected crewmembers in survival gear and radiation suits, and he has pulled all technicians from life support and assigned them to increasing reactor power."

West nodded. "Very well, Commander. Give Captain Trevian my regards. I fully support his efforts." She knew Trevian wanted her clearcut okay, even though he was only obeying her commands. She understood completely. He could wrap his people in whatever gear he wanted, hand out as many oxygen tanks and survival suits, but pulling crews from life support and radiation detail was going to cost lives…lives that might have been saved if a new enemy force hadn't been pouring into the system. Or if he committed resources to repairing life support instead of weapons. His people would fight, and no doubt they would squeeze more power from the fusion reactors…and pump it through their tenuously-repaired laser cannons. But some of them would die, some who would otherwise have lived if he'd had the luxury to bring his basic systems back online first.

It was the hardest calculus of war, making decisions that condemned crew members to death. But West understood war, and she was no stranger to the cost it extracted. Besides, if the task force couldn't hold out against the enemy still coming their way, all her people would die…on *Conde*, on *Saratoga*, on all her ships.

She reached down and switched on the direct line to Captain Black. "Davis, we're looking at another fight. I don't know what we're up against yet, but I'm going to need you to hold her together. I need everything the old girl can give me. Especially since *Conde* doesn't have much left in her."

She knew her flagship was badly beaten up, but West also realized the Yorktown class dreadnought represented perhaps half her remaining strength overall. Whatever chance her people had, most of it rested on *Saratoga* and the man at her helm.

"Don't worry, Admiral. She'll hold together." His voice was firm, crisp. West couldn't believe Black really believed it, but she had to admit he was doing one hell of an imitation of confidence. "Fight your fight, Erica…*Saratoga* will do what she has to."

"Alright, Davis…fair enough." She closed the line. She knew her flag captain was full of shit, that he was just doing his job, backing her up any way she could. But in spite of herself, she had to admit he'd made her feel a little better. His confidence, fake or not, was infectious, and she found herself looking across the flag bridge, gathering herself for the next fight.

"I need those scanning reports, Commander." She'd always hated senior officers who said things like that when she was junior, as if their almighty authority overruled the laws of physics and the universe. There wasn't a question in her mind that Krantz would have the data to her the second he himself got it…and that rendered her statement pointless. And yet she'd just said it.

"Just a few more seconds, Admiral…" The tactical officer was hunched over his scope, his tone distracted as he concentrated. "Data coming in now…"

West sat quietly. She knew the information she got in the next few seconds would tell her if her people would live or die. She had a pretty good idea how much the task force could take…and it wasn't much.

"Twenty ships coming in, Admiral…looks like four Gargoyles and the rest Gremlins."

West sighed softly. It wasn't the massive force that had been floating around the edge of her nightmares…but her gut told her it was more than her battered force could defeat. It would be a good fight…her people would make the enemy pay. But she knew they were going to come up short.

The mathematics of war were especially brutal against the robot warriors of the First Imperium. Its AIs were generally unimaginative in battle, their performance profoundly average. It was this fact more than anything that had allowed mankind to resist them for so long. But that didn't tell the whole story, and a closer examination revealed a far less hopeful outlook for West and her people.

While the enemy lacked the brilliant and unorthodox commanders who had led humanity so often to victory, they were also without incompetence, ego, folly. Leaders like West sometimes defeated human opponents despite being massively outnumbered. They broke the will of cowardly officers or they ran rings around incompetent fools who got their postings through politics and nepotism. But that couldn't happen against the First Imperium. Its commanders were relentless and capable, if unimaginative. They might need a greater force concentration to overcome a brilliant admiral, but there was still a mathematical quality to it. If they had enough force, they would win. Even against West. Even against Terrance Compton or Augustus Garret. Still, an admiral like Erica West had no conception of how to yield…to give up…

"All vessels are to accelerate immediately…2g directly toward the warp gate. We're going to pin those bastards against the transit point before they can launch any missiles…and then it's going to be a bare-knuckled laser brawl." Her voice was decisive, with a raw streak of pure venom. Erica West was one of the coldest battle commanders the Alliance had ever known, and her frigid savagery drove her doubts away.

"Yes, Admiral." She could hear the energy in Krantz' voice too, and she knew her people were feeding off her raw energy. She couldn't speak for the rest of the crews in the task force, but she knew then and there her Alliance spacers would never run, never falter. They would fight, to the death if need be. But they wouldn't let up…never.

"All ships…I want every weapon firing full. Redline everything, run the reactors at 115%. All safety guidelines are waived." Her voice was frozen, her hands clenched into fists on the armrests of her chair. "We're going to give them everything we have. Absolutely everything…"

* * *

"Stay calm, all of you…the admiral will have a rescue shuttle out here any minute." Mariko Fujin was just above her command chair, hovering in the weightlessness of the dead fighter. She looked out at the four men who formed her ship's crew, doing her best to maintain an aura of confidence…whether she felt it or not. In truth, she wasn't sure. She knew Admiral Hurley would do everything possible to rescue her people. But Fujin didn't know how many other fighters had been ditched…and it was clear that *Saratoga* and the rest of Admiral West's task force were still deep in a fight.

Her people were all wearing survival equipment…skintight bodysuits, covered with a heavier insulated outer layer. They had their helmets on now too, and they were totally self-contained, living on recycled air and retained heat. The fighter had expended its life support, and now its power was completely dead. The temperature in the cockpit was dropping rapidly, down to 200 Kelvin the last time Fujin had checked. She knew they'd be dead already without the emergency gear…but the suits wouldn't last for long. The equipment would keep them alive for a while, but it wasn't powered armor, nor a spacesuit. Her people needed to be rescued, as soon as possible.

The gear was uncomfortable, but that wasn't the real problem. Fighter-bombers were small, cramped ships, crammed full of weapons and equipment. And that didn't leave much room for survival gear. Their suits would recycle their oxygen, and the batteries in each outfit would provide emergency power. But it was designed for short-term use, without food or water supplies, and with power only for a limited period. A survival suit couldn't sustain life indefinitely. Her people had five hours, perhaps six. And then they would start to die.

She turned and looked over at the fighter's main AI, still functioning on its own emergency power. The transponder was active, the computer system burning most of its power to send a signal the rest of the fleet, to tell their rescuers where they were. That would last three hours, maybe four…

* * *

"All cruisers…open fire." John Duke's voice was like death itself.

"All cruisers," Alex Barret repeated into the com, "open fire."

John Duke was standing next to his chair, his hands clinging to the armrest as he held himself up under almost four gees. The display lit up like fireworks, Captain Kato's ships blasting their lasers as one, the ravening beams tearing into the First Imperium ships engaged with Erica West's force. The second wave of enemy vessels had been slightly smaller than the first, twenty ships, including four Gargoyles…but it had looked like enough to finish off West and her survivors. Until Kato's people attacked.

Now Duke was leading the last of his fast attack ships toward the enemy line. All of his suicide boats were damaged, many of them straining to keep their thrusters blasting and their weapons armed. But every one of them had a triple-strength plasma torpedo loaded, armed, and ready to go…and when they launched, they would tear a great gap in the enemy line.

"Attack squadrons, hold fire. We're taking these things right down their throats…" His voice was deep, a feral savagery rising up from his throat. His body shook with rage, with hatred… images of the friends and comrades who had died fighting the First Imperium. He knew, intellectually at least, that the enemy robots were selfless, unconcerned with survival. They were tools, nothing more. If there was a real survival instinct among the First Imperium's machines, it was at the very top…whatever staggeringly sophisticated computers still ran the domains of the long dead race. Still, he told himself they felt fear, that in their final moments, when his ships were bearing down on them, plunging plasma torpedoes deep into their savaged hulls, the hated enemy knew despair, horror. He had no reason to believe it…indeed, he knew it wasn't true. But he lied to himself anyway, because he needed the hate. He needed to feel his enemy's pain, payback for all those who had died next to him.

"*Panther* signaling Delta-Z, sir." Barret's voice had been almost as cold as Duke's, but reporting the attack ship's imminent destruction caused his intensity to falter a bit.

"Very well, Commander…all ships continue on course. And hold fire until I give the launch order." Duke was rock solid, virtually ignoring the loss of *Panther*. He would deal with the casualties later, if he survived. There was time for guilt, for sadness. But not now. *Panther's* crew had died as part of this attack. It would do them no good—and no honor—to pause, to do anything but focus entirely on the combat at hand.

"Fifty thousand kilometers to enemy line, sir."

"Very well…all units continue on present courses." His ships each had an assigned target, and their navigation plans were bringing them to point blank range.

"Forty thousand…"

Duke just stood where he was. The pressure from the engine's thrust was exhausting, but he held firm, as if defying the force to drive him into his chair.

"Thirty thousand…"

"All ships cut primary thrust. Pilots, take control." The crushing pressure vanished, replaced by the relief of freefall. An instant later the sensation of acceleration returned, but it was less than half a gee. *Jaguar's* pilot was adjusting the ship's course, bringing it dead in on the Gargoyle Duke had selected as a target.

"Twenty thousand…"

Jaguar shook hard…a direct hit. The enemy had been locked in combat with Admiral West's ships, and that had allowed Duke to get much closer than he'd expected before his ships took heavy fire. But the First Imperium forces knew how dangerous the suicide boats were, and now they had turned their attention to the deadly threat.

"Damage report," Duke snapped toward his tactical officer.

"It's bad, sir. We've lost hull integrity in several places, and we've got a dozen casualties…but the torpedo tube is still operative." Barret paused, his eyes dropping to his screen. "Badger Code Delta-Z, sir." Then, before Duke could acknowledge loss of another ship: "Ten thousand kilometers, sir…"

"All ships, fire when ready."

"All ships, fire when ready," Barret repeated.

Duke stared across the bridge. "Fire on my command." He'd given his other captains the go ahead to launch, but he was determined to take *Jaguar's* torpedo right down the enemy's throat.

"Yes, sir. Seven thousand kilometers…"

Duke stood like a statue, a graven image like something carved from a cold block of marble. His eyes stared straight ahead, and in them a fire raged.

"Five thousand kilometers, sir…" Barret's voice was showing the strain. Five thousand kilometers was knife-fighting range. But still, Duke stood in place, focused, cold.

"Four thousand…"

The bridge was silent, the crew staring at their captain…waiting.

"Three thousand…"

Duke didn't move. He simply stood there, his head locked straight ahead. "Fire," he said simply, without emotion.

"Fire!" Barret repeated as he launched the torpedo.

"Four gees, Mr. Barret," Duke said calmly. Course preset number two."

"Course number two, sir…four gees."

Jaguar lurched hard forward, the feeling of heavy gee forces again slamming into the crew. Duke's legs buckled briefly, but he managed to hold himself firm, at least for the few seconds he had to.

"Cut thrust," he snapped, his eyes staying fixed forward, not even looking toward the scanner display. *Jaguar* was past the target and in the clear…he knew it without looking.

"Yes, Captain. Cutting thrust."

Duke stood there, still unmoving, a barely detectable smile creeping onto his face. He knew…he knew without looking, with a certainty that eradicated all doubt in his mind. An instant later, he heard the bridge break into cheers…but by then it was old news to him. The Gargoyle was gone. *Jaguar's* torpedo had torn apart its containment…and the First Imperium warship had vanished in the almost indescribable fury of matter-anti-matter annihilation.

One more First Imperium ship in hell…

* * *

Mariko sat on the floor, just below her command chair. The AI had shut down, the lasts bits of stored battery power gone, save just enough to power a single com unit. Her people had a few hours of life support left, but their momentum had taken them far past *Saratoga*…away from the battle and deeper into the outer system.

She had no idea how the battle was going…or had gone. For all she knew, her people were the only five left in the fleet. Erica West was a gifted officer, but the last glance Fujin had seen of her display before it powered down had shown a whole new force moving in…more than enough to wipe out the last of the task force.

She glanced across the cockpit, her eyes settling on Wainwright. She was impressed by the young pilot. She'd seen a lot of hotshot types lose their shit when things went bad, but not him. She knew he had to be scared…hell, she was scared to death, so if he wasn't he was made of sterner stuff than her. But he didn't show it. He just sat at his station, looking down over the dead instruments…as if he was waiting for them to come back to life so he could plunge back into the fight.

Fujin was sorry…for all of them, of course, but especially for the pilot. He was so young, so talented. What a waste. She thought of herself and realized she was only six years older than he was. Was that really possible? It felt like a lifetime to her…

"Commander Fujin…"

It took a second for her to realize the com unit was crackling.

"Commander Fujin, do you read me?"

It was Admiral Hurley!

She scrambled up and across the cockpit toward the only working com unit.

"Admiral…this is Fujin."

"Mariko!" Greta Hurley was as stone cold as officers came, but there was a burst of excitement in her voice. "We found you just in time…we were about to turn back."

"It's good to hear your voice, Admiral." She let out a long breath.

"We've got to move, Mariko. The task force is moving out… we've got to get back or we'll both be stuck out here."

Fujin felt a wave of relief. The fleet must have won the battle. "Yes, Admiral. But our screens are dead, our AI shut down. We're out of power…all we've got is another ninety seconds of com."

"We'll be there in three minutes. Get your people down to the lower egress port. And hurry. We'll be lucky if *Saratoga* is still there by the time we get back."

"Yes, Admiral. We're on the way…"

She turned and flashed a glance at her crew. "Alright, boys. You heard the admiral. Let's move our asses!"

Chapter Fifteen

Research Notes of Hieronymus Cutter

We are far below the surface of the planet now, well over a kilometer. I expected to find extensive facilities below the city, but I was unprepared for the true enormity of these ruins. There are tunnels everywhere, some blocked by ancient collapses, others still open, at least partially. And everywhere there are the signs of war, of a battle fought untold eons ago.

We have found unfamiliar bits of equipment, faint signs of a potential group of combatants other than the First Imperium bots we have come to know so well. But there is nothing definitive, nothing that gives assurance we have found anything but previously unknown ordnance used by our familiar enemy. Could there have been a rebellion here? Could one ancient Intelligence have fought another for dominance of this world? There is no way to know, at least not unless we are able to find more evidence...and analyze it correctly.

But now we have encountered the enemy again. We can hear the sounds of combat in the distance...the camp is under attack. Perhaps I have pushed too hard, insisted too resolutely that we must continue to explore. But my motives were sound... we must learn more about the First Imperium, and how to defeat it. Still...the cost. We have been attacked many times, suffered heavy losses. And now the main party is again in danger.

We must return now, rush to the aid of the rest of the expedition. Then, after the enemy is beaten back, perhaps we will discuss our next options. I still long to continue, to press on into the depths of this great metropolis. But I must speak with Ana... and with Duncan. We must all agree, and if we do not, we must turn back together.

I hear more sounds of battle. Closer. Behind us now too, along the forward line where Sergeant McCloud's Marines are deployed. Now between us and the camp. We are cut off...under attack.

Trapped.

X48 System – Planet II
In the Ruins of "New York City"
The Fleet: 127 ships, 29807 crew

Cutter spun around, his hand dropping to his pistol…to where his pistol had been. The tiny weapon—Frasier had called it a 'pop gun'—had been far too weak for serious combat. The Marines gave him a high-powered assault rifle as a replacement after his last scuffle with the enemy, a far more useful weapon against a First Imperium warbot than the handgun had been.

He reached around his back, slipping it from the harness and pulling it in front of him. It was heavy, cumbersome, and it took him a few seconds to get used to having it in his hands. He hadn't fired it yet, and he could feel the tension in his arms as he imagined the weapon's kick.

The first dull explosions in the distance had given way to the sounds of a full-scale battle back near the camp. The initial blasts of the enemy attack had been answered by the return fire of the Marines', the intensity rising as the scale of the combat increased.

Bruce was already moving back toward the camp, his own rifle gripped tightly in his armored hands. "We've got to get back, Dr. Cutter," he snapped, waving his hands toward the four other Marines lined up to the side. "All of you," he yelled. "Let's go…"

His words were suddenly drowned out by automatic weapon

fire coming from the other direction…and much closer than the camp. Cutter knew immediately, it was McCloud's squad. And it was clear they were in heavy combat.

"Fuck," Bruce spat under his breath, scrambling to a halt. He waved to the Marines who had stopped short behind him. "The camp will have to take care of itself for now. We can't let the enemy get in behind us." The four men spun around on a dime and began moving in the other direction…plunging into the darkness after McCloud's people.

"Doctor…"

"I'm with you, Kyle," Cutter snapped back.

"Maybe you should find a place to…"

"I'm with you, Kyle," he repeated, surprising himself with the grit in his voice. "We're all in this together."

"Okay, Hieronymus," Bruce answered, sounding not at all pleased about it. "But Major Frasier is going to skin me alive if anything happens to you…so I'm begging you to stay behind me and take some cover."

Cutter nodded, but he didn't drop back. He was terrified, and it was taking all his endurance to stay firm, to keep moving forward and not to run off into the darkness in a mad panic. He knew he probably *should* go and hide. He had some armor on, but nothing like the Marines' fighting suits. And his knowledge and ability were crucial to the fate of the whole fleet. But none of that mattered to him, not right now. He couldn't abandon the Marines…he *wouldn't*.

The sounds of gunfire grew louder as he ran forward, and then he could see shadowy figures up ahead…McCloud's Marines, pinned down in a depression along the edge of the tunnel. It looked like two of them were down, and the others were heavily engaged.

"Sergeant…report!" The Marines had buttoned up their helmets, and Cutter heard Bruce's voice through the small headset clipped to his ear.

"The shit's hitting the fan, Lieutenant." McCloud didn't sound scared, but there was a sense of urgency to his voice. "You better pull back and get the doc outta here. My boys'll hold 'em." Cutter could hear the Scottish accent coming out in the big Marine's words…a sign of stress, he guessed.

"Doctor Cutter, the sergeant is right," Bruce said, his voice raw, tense. "I'll send two of my Marines back with…"

"No." Cutter's voice was sharp, firm. "I said I'm here with you, and I'm staying."

"But…" Bruce let his words trail off into a sigh. "Okay, Hieronymus, but remember you don't have real armor."

Cutter twisted uncomfortably, pushing and shoving against the breastplate and thigh guards that were bruising the hell out of him just from moving. It sure felt like armor…though he knew what Bruce meant. There was armor and then there was *armor*. And the latter was the toughest personal protection known to man, each suit powered by its own portable nuclear reactor. By comparison, he knew he might as well be wearing a bathrobe.

Cutter stared down the corridor, trying to get a glimpse of the enemy bots, but all he could see was the flash of automatic weapons fire. He froze for a second, uncertain what to do. McCloud's men were up ahead, perhaps six or seven meters farther forward. Bruce's four Marines slipped off to the left side, taking position behind McCloud's squad and opening fire.

Cutter felt Bruce's hand on his arm, gripping firmly, pushing him down against the wall, into cover just before a blast of enemy fire ripped through the air above them.

"Stay down, Hieronymus. There are at least a dozen of them."

Cutter just nodded. He had no idea how Bruce could tell how many First Imperium bots were out there, but he was inclined to believe the Marine.

"We're pinned down here...stay low or you're going to get your head blown off."

"Got it," Cutter said, trying to keep his stomach from evacuating its contents.

"We've gotta get out of here," Bruce continued. "I'm gonna order McCloud's guys to pull back in two sections…then, once they're in position back here, we're going to go. Then we'll keep alternating, twenty meters at a time. You understand, Hieronymus?" Bruce was speaking slowly, meticulously.

"Yes…" It was all Cutter could force out of his mouth at first. Then: "I Understand."

Cutter crouched low, feeling as if the projectiles flying over his head were a millimeter away. He felt himself scrunching lower, pushing farther below the chunk of exposed rock he was using as cover.

"Alright, McCloud," Bruce said, "we're pulling out of here. Let's get your people back…by odds and evens."

"There's more activity coming down the corridor, Lieutenant. I think they'll be on us the second we pull back."

"There's nothing we can do about that, Sergeant. We'll just have to hold them back with the leapfrogging." A short pause then: "Evens, stand firm. Odds…move out."

Cutter could hear the sounds of McCloud's odds moving back. They took a few steps, maybe half a dozen, and then all hell broke loose. The existing enemy fire doubled in intensity… and then a volley opened up from the direction of the camp, but much closer.

One of the Marines to Cutter's left yelled and fell hard to the ground. The other three—and Bruce and Cutter—spun around immediately and opened fire.

Cutter felt the jarring of the assault rifle, and he realized his shooting was wild, uncontrolled. He released his finger, pausing for an instant before firing again, this time concentrating, trying to target the enemy warbots. He had no idea if he was hitting anything, but his fire felt truer, better.

Suddenly, he felt Bruce's armored hand, grabbing him hard, pulling him up and shoving him forward a few meters. Then moving lower as the Marine's armored hand shoved him downward…and out of the direct line of fire. He tried to steady himself, repositioning to resume his own shooting, but he stumbled and fell, dropping the rifle as he did and falling hard into the stone.

He let out a yell as he slammed down hard, struggling to ignore the pain from the fall. His hands were scuffed and bloody, and his left leg throbbed where his knee had slammed into the rock floor. There was fire all around, and he could see another one of the Marines down.

Bruce was crouched down about a meter and a half away, staying low, returning fire from behind cover. "You okay, Doc?" the he yelled, his voice thick with concern.

"I'm okay," Cutter answered. He hurt like hell, but he knew he wasn't badly injured, just banged up a little…and he wasn't going to complain about getting a few cuts and scrapes when two Marines were already dead…or at least critically wounded. He reached out, feeling around until his hand felt the cool metal of the rifle. His fingers clawed at the weapon, pulling it up and grabbing it with his second hand.

He looked up…and his eye caught motion, an enemy warbot, moving toward Bruce. He felt adrenalin pouring into his bloodstream, the thunderclap of his heart beating in his chest. His eyes locked on the robot, cold, focused. He wasn't thinking, wasn't trying to remember what to do…he just let his instincts take control, instincts he didn't know he had. His hands moved quickly, bringing the rifle to bear, even as the First Imperium bot was turning its autocannon to fire on Bruce.

"Kyle!" he howled, screaming into the com as his finger pulled back fiercely on the trigger, firing the weapon on full auto. His eyes were locked on the target…and somehow his aim was true. Dead on. The bot was pushed back by the stream of fire, its own shots going wide, missing Bruce.

He released his finger, and the fire ceased, the weapon moving aside, angling downward as he stared out at the scene. But the enemy bot wasn't finished, not yet. He was looking right at it, but it took him a second to realize the First Imperium warrior was still active…and that it had turned its focus to him. He felt the sound of his heart in his ears, and a wave of panic began to take him. He screamed to himself to fire, but he just stood, stunned, transfixed. It was only a second, perhaps less, but somehow he realized it was too long. It had been his mistake…he'd let up, ceased fire too soon. Of all people, he should have understood the punishment a First Imperium bot could absorb, but he hadn't. He'd given away his victory, and now he knew he was going to die.

His eyes were fixed on the bot's autocannon. His fire had wrecked one of the fearsome weapons, but the other was still functional, its deadly maw turning toward him. He felt the tension in his body, his instinctive effort to move away, to dive for cover. But he was too late…and there was nowhere to go.

Then he heard the shots, the sounds of automatic fire ripping through the air. He gritted his teeth, waiting for the pain, the blood and gore as the projectiles ripped through his body. But there was nothing.

The sound…that wasn't First Imperium fire!

His head snapped around, and his eyes focused on his enemy. The bot had fallen backwards, its second autocannon torn from its body…along with a huge part of its midsection. And Kyle Bruce was standing over it, his assault rifle still firing into its savaged remains.

Cutter moved over to the side, bringing his own weapon to bear. But he could see immediately the warbot was dead. He stood still for a few seconds…then he felt the strength drain from his legs, and he stumbled, struggling to stay on his feet as the flow of adrenalin dropped away.

"It's alright, Doc…it's finished." Bruce's voice was better than Cutter's but it was clear the Marine was a little shaken up too. They'd each just looked death in the face and lived to tell about it.

Cutter tried to answer, but his throat was dry, the words absent. He just nodded…and looked back at the wreckage of the machine that had come half a second from killing him. Then he felt something…Bruce's hand, heavy, strong from his powered armor.

"C'mon Doc…I know it's a shock, but we've got more of these things coming, so I need you to snap out of it…focus."

"Okay…" It was all Cutter could get out, but that was enough.

"Good…now pop that half-empty clip and put in another one." Bruce reached behind Cutter, grabbing a cartridge from the scientist's ammo belt and pushing it into his hand. "That's right," he said, as he watched Cutter snap the clip in place.

"Now stay down, Doc. Grab some cover and the second you see anything…blow it the hell away. And don't stop shooting next time, not until you're sure it's dead."

* * *

"Ronnie is out there! And Lieutenant Bruce and his people." Ana Zhukov was crouched behind a shattered chunk of stone, her carbine gripped tightly in her hands. She was staring back at Frasier with a look of desperation in her eyes. "We've got to get to them."

The two of them had been sitting alone talking when the enemy attack began. They were down a short corridor, one that appeared to dead end about twenty meters from the main camp. It was just about the only place there were no enemy warbots charging…at least not yet.

"I know, Ana…but you have to stay down. We've got bogies coming in from every direction out there." Frasier paused for an instant then added, "They're better off over there than we are here anyway…safer." That was a lie. He could see on his display the others were surrounded too, completely cut off from the camp. But there was nothing Ana could do about that now. Nothing but take wild chances that could get her killed…and still not accomplish a thing to help Cutter. And he wasn't going to let that happen…whatever he had to do to prevent it. Even lie to her.

"Stay put, Ana. Please. We've got to stabilize things here, and then we can go after them. It's the best way to help, the only way."

He peered out over the spur of rock they were using for cover. He could hear combat all around the camp. They were getting hit hard…and he realized he had to get everybody out, back up to the surface. The expedition was a failure…the enemy forces were just too numerous. Bruce and his men—and Cutter too—were as good as dead. He hated himself for thinking that, but he was too experienced a veteran not to acknowledge facts. And letting Ana—and the other scientists—throw their lives away with no hope of saving them wasn't going to help anyone. Maybe, just maybe he could get them out of here, some of them at least…and the whole force could pull back, away from the city. With luck, the enemy wouldn't follow up…and Barcomme's people would have the chance to complete the food production. That would keep the expedition from being a total failure.

He looked off to his right. He could hear heavy fire down that way…both First Imperium ordnance and his own peoples'. There was fighting all around, but it was definitely heavier to the right. *But that's also the way out of here…or at least the way we know.*

"Ana, I want you to stay right here. I want you to promise me…"

"No, Duncan…I can't leave them. Ronnie is like my brother…"

"He wouldn't want you to get yourself killed, Ana. Not for no reason. And if you try to get to them now, that is exactly what will happen. You've got no chance of getting through there. None."

He pushed her down gently, below the lip of the outcropping. "Stay low, and keep your eyes open. I've got to move to the right, take command over there, but you should be okay here. Try to raise the rest of your people on the com…get as many of them here as you can." He knew the scientists would just get picked off in the fighting if he didn't get them out of the main combat area. "But don't go out looking for them…they need you here coordinating."

She looked back at him, her eyes wide with distress. He could tell she still wanted to run off, to go find Cutter and the others. But she stayed where she was. There were tears streaming from her eyes, but she had a determined look on her face…and her carbine was in her hands. "Okay, Duncan," she said, not sounding entirely convinced, "I'll try to get everyone organized."

He nodded then he started to turn. But he stopped and looked back. "Please, Ana…stay here. I'll be back as soon as I can, and then we'll see what we can do about Hieronymus and Lieutenant Bruce."

She nodded, wiping the tears from her face with her sleeve. "I'll stay."

He felt another twinge of guilt for offering her more hope than he believed existed. But right now, his biggest concern was keeping her alive. And he'd do whatever he had to do to manage that.

* * *

Hieronymus was slouched down behind the rock wall, his hands wrapped tightly around his rifle. He'd been fighting alongside Bruce's people—and holding his own if he did say so himself—but now he was down to his last clip. The nuclear-powered weapons of the armored Marines carried five hundred round cartridges, over five times the ordnance his own assault rifle mounted. And he wasn't the shot his new friends were, which meant he'd burnt through what he had that much quicker.

Bruce had told him to stay low, and to save his last shots for an emergency…though if the current situation wasn't already an emergency, he didn't know what would be. They had six Marines down, three of them dead, and the rest had been driven back into a shrinking perimeter.

As far as he could see, they were surrounded…and completely cut off from the camp. The intensity of the battle right around him had drowned out the sounds of combat from farther away, but he could tell there was still fighting going on back there. If anything, it had grown even more intense.

He had begun to realize there wasn't much hope of help working its way to them. Indeed, he was on the verge of giving up, of hoping Ana and Duncan and the others would manage to find a way out of the trap and not die here with him. He was scared to death, but the last thing he wanted was for Ana to get trapped down here to die with him. *Maybe Duncan can get her out of here…*

"Doc, c'mon…we gotta fall back." Duff McCloud reached down and grabbed Cutter, pulling him hard from the ground. "We got bogies coming down here. The lieutenant wants us back down the side hallway."

Cutter grunted as he stumbled across the stone floor, trying to keep his balance under McCloud's ungentle grip. As soon as he realized where they were going, he knew the fight was almost over. They were trapped, with no way out…and surrounded on every other side.

"Duck behind me, Doc." McCloud shoved Cutter hard, pulling him around, shielding him from the direction of enemy fire as they dashed across the open corridor…and into the last refuge. He wasn't gentle, but then he was shoving himself between the scientist and the incoming projectiles, so Cutter wasn't about to take a few bruises personally.

McCloud stopped just inside the corridor, pushing Cutter in farther then whipping around his rifle and opening fire. The ground in front was littered with shattered bots, the remains of the enemy's attempts to rush the position. And Cutter knew it was only a matter of time before they broke through.

"You okay, Hieronymus?" Bruce came running back from the other side. He'd been opposite McCloud's position, covering enemy's advance from that side.

"I'm fine, Kyle…but we're pretty fucked, aren't we?"

Bruce sighed softly. He sounded like he was going to argue, to offer some kind of explanation about how they were going to make it out. But then he just nodded and said, "Yeah. We're fucked."

Hieronymus turned and looked back toward McCloud. The gargantuan Marine was firing away like a machine, and Cutter had no doubt he would fight to the bitter end. But there were just too many of the enemy, and no way to…

His head snapped around…and then he put his hands over his ears and let out a cry. The sound was deafening, and he slipped down to his knees. Bruce leapt back too, but only for a second. Clearly, his AI had cut off the audio from his external microphones.

Then the explosions began…one after the other, down the corridor in both directions. Toward the enemy. Cutter's first thought was it was a new First Imperium weapon, but then he realized it was directed outward…at the attackers, not at them. He staggered back deeper into the corridor, stumbling against the wall and desperately trying to cover his ears.

The noise continued for another thirty seconds or so…and then it faded away. He could hear a few of the Marines still firing, but the sound of the First Imperium fire was gone.

"Cease fire."

Cutter could barely hear Bruce's voice on the com. His ears were ringing, and he had a splitting headache. But he realized almost immediately they weren't under attack anymore.

"What the hell was that?" It was McCloud on the com now. His voice was louder than Bruce's, gruffer. Which made it easier for Cutter to hear.

"Quiet, McCloud," Bruce snapped back. "Look around, and make sure there are no enemies left in the area.

"Yes, Lieutenant."

"Hieronymus?"

"Lieutenant?" Cutter suspected he was screaming, but he didn't have a good feel for his volume. His ears were recovering, a little. But Bruce's voice still sounded faint and far away.

"You alright?" He came trotting over toward the scientist.

"Yeah…that sound was loud. But I think I'm okay."

"Do you have any idea what that was?"

Cutter shook his head. "None whatsoever…but it seems like the enemy is gone. Could it have been something from the camp?" He knew even as he said it that wasn't the case. The Marines didn't have any secret weapons…and if they'd had any, he would have known about them. Hell, he'd probably have built them.

"No…that was no Marine gear. And it wasn't like anything we've ever run into with First Imperium forces before. It looks like it took them all out, and left us alone."

Another series of sounds blasted through the com channels. It was like loud feedback, rapidly switching frequencies, the sounds changing constantly. Suddenly, Bruce popped his helmet and yelled over to Cutter. "Doc, it's my AI…it's running wild!"

Cutter took a step toward Bruce, straining to listen. His ears were improving, but everything still sounded muffled. The Marine's AI speakers were spewing out a series of random-sounding noises. It was fast, so fast he could barely make out that they were words. It was speech, standard Alliance English, but it was so quick it sounded mostly like gibberish. Then, it stopped.

"Come," a voice boomed through the air. "Follow."

There was a light on the floor, a projection of some kind from above. It was an arrow, and it led back, deeper in the direction the party had been heading when they were attacked.

Cutter just stood there looking off into the distance. His heart was pounding, his neck slick with sweat. He turned and faced Bruce, each looking at the other for a suggestion about what to do.

"Follow," the voice repeated. "You must hurry."

Bruce looked up at Cutter, his eyes wide with shock. "What should we do?" He gripped his rifle firmly, staring off cautiously in the direction of the arrow.

Cutter looked back toward the camp. The sounds of fighting there had ceased as well. *Hopefully, Ana is okay.* He wanted to go back, to make sure…and let her know he was alive too. But something told him he had to see this through.

He took a step forward…then another. "I think we better see what is down here. Whatever it is, it just took out at least a hundred battle bots for us." Cutter felt nauseous, terrified to his very core. But he was exhilarated too. He had no idea what they had just encountered, but he knew in his gut it was something new…a game changer. Whether that was good or bad was another question. But there was only one way to find out.

He looked at Bruce for a few seconds. Then he took a deep

breath and turned back, continuing off into the semi-darkness of the corridor.

Bruce stood still for a moment, looking back at McCloud and his survivors, all standing around watching in stunned awe as Hieronymus Cutter walked off into the gloom alone. They exchanged a quick series of glances…and then they followed the scientist.

Chapter Sixteen

From the Personal Log of Terrance Compton

Something is wrong, terribly wrong...I am sure of it. Skepticism has always been my friend, a guardian that has watched my back for me, warned me when danger prowled in the darkness. It has saved my life many times, and helped me save those of friends and comrades. And now it is screaming to me.

The emergence of enemy forces into X56 from the X58 system was upsetting to be sure, but it was not a shock to me. I know many of the crews had dared to hope we had evaded our enemies, but I didn't believe that, not for an instant. I wouldn't have allowed myself such hopes, even if there had been reason for optimism. But there wasn't. The planets we passed have grown larger...we have clearly been moving deeper into the Imperium and not out the other side. Indeed, the very fact that we went so long without contact has been of deep concern to me.

The emergence of First Imperium ships from the X57 gate, erased any doubt. The enemy knew we were here. Had we fallen prey to some detection device or hidden ship in X56? Or did they know where we'd come from as well? Had they followed us? Do they know about the landing parties?

The questions are myriad, and they defy answers. I must decide what to do now that the fleet has pulled back to X54. We cannot stay...that would throw away every advantage the rearguards had sacrificed so much to gain. We will wait as long as we can to give the survivors the chance to transit and rejoin us, but then I must decide. Do I lead the fleet through the X53 warp gate, and into unexplored space? Or do we retreat back the way we came, to X51?

I don't know what to do, but the choice is mine and mine alone. In many ways it feels like a coin toss, a decision where logic and thought may do little to recommend one course over another. In the end, I must decide, do I take the fleet into the unknown...and risk being cut off from the expedition in X48? Or do I risk leading the enemy back with us, leaving the ground forces undefended and exposed to attack and destruction?

AS Midway
X54 System - Approaching the X53 warp gate
The Fleet: 127 ships, 29411 crew

"We're thirty light seconds from the gate, Admiral." Cortez turned and stared over toward Compton. "Admiral West's forces have completed transit from X56, sir. Along with Captain Kato…and Captain Duke's survivors. They should link up with us in just over six hours, sir. The admiral reports they had no new enemy contacts in X56 prior to entering the warp gate."

Compton paused for a few seconds, and he felt a knot in his chest, the pain that had become so familiar and yet which burned with its own unique fire each time. And this time it was for John Duke.

Compton knew, perhaps better than anyone on the fleet, that the pain and struggle never truly ended, that each new fight held its own challenges…and carried its own costs. Captain Duke wasn't the first loyal officer—or friend—Terrance Compton had lost…nor did the admiral dare to imagine he would be the last. But the pain was as keen as any he remembered. Duke had been utterly loyal, a man he'd been able to count on without question, no matter what the situation or how dire the need. Indeed, there were few officers in the fleet as universally loved and respected as John Duke had been…or whose death would be so widely and deeply mourned. There were worse epitaphs for a man to leave behind, certainly. But Compton was tired of losing friends, however nobly they might have died.

A man could die with honor, he could save his comrades in the process, even win a battle with his sacrifice. But in the end it was the same…he was gone, dead, lost, never again to stand alongside those who had called him friend. Compton had once believed in glorious sacrifice, in the honor of those who died selflessly, heroically. Now that was mostly gone, and he'd come to see dead as just that. Dead.

He took a breath and said, "Very well. Get Captain Schwerin on my line." He longed to mourn his friend, but there was work to do, duty. As usual. *And John Duke would be the first to understand that…*

"Yes sir." A moment later: "Captain Schwerin, sir."

"Dolph, is *Tyr* ready?"

"Yes, sir. On your command."

Compton stared down at the display, his eyes settling on the single tiny icon sitting several light seconds from the main fleet. *Tyr.*

"Very well, Captain. You may proceed…and remember, I want you to do a quick scout and then come back immediately. Just because you're going alone doesn't mean I'm sending you on a suicide mission. Far from it." A pause. "Do you understand?"

"Yes, Admiral."

Compton couldn't tell if Schwerin was convinced. *Probably not.* He meant every word he said, but he wasn't sure he would have believed it either in the CEL captain's shoes.

"Then I will expect you back in system within ten minutes, Captain. No more."

"Yes, sir."

"Good luck, Captain."

"Thank you, sir. Schwerin out."

Compton's thoughts drifted back to Duke for a moment. *Jaguar* had been the final ship to die in X56, destroyed by the last Gargoyle just before *Saratoga's* laser batteries had torn it apart. John Duke had served brilliantly, and his fast attack ships had expended themselves without hesitation to save their comrades. He had been a true hero of the fleet, one Compton had intended to reward with a long overdue pair of admiral's stars. He'd only held back as long as he had because he was reluctant to promote yet another Alliance spacer over the other nationalities of the fleet.

And now he will never receive the recognition he was due. Did he know? Did he understand? Or did he imagine I was somehow disappointed in him? That he had failed me in some way? That he lacked my whole-hearted trust and gratitude?

I will give him his star posthumously, of course...and we will all stand around and say solemn things. Has there ever been a more useless display? And yet it is all we can do, and so we shall.

John, you were an officer beyond compare...and a man I was proud to call one of my key commanders. One of my friends....

"*Tyr* is accelerating, sir," Cortez reported, pulling Compton from his introspection. "Estimate transit in twenty-eight minutes."

"Very well, Commander." His eyes stared at the icon representing the attack ship. With any luck, Schwerin and his crew would come back with word that X53 was clear. That wouldn't be definitive...there wasn't time for a thorough scan, and even if there had been, one ship was a woefully inadequate force to complete it. But Compton wasn't willing to risk more than a single vessel, not now. He felt as if his fleet was melting around him, like a block of ice on a hot day. Thousands of his people had died in the last year...and dozens of ships. He couldn't afford to lose any more.

He looked back up at the main display, watching the remnants of West's and Duke's task forces make their way back to the fleet. He knew West's people were buttoned up, their vessels now decelerating at 30g, preparing to link up with the main fleet. He didn't doubt for a second they would be pursued by the enemy, but for whatever reason, the First Imperium forces had held back, given Erica West a chance to extract the remaining ships from X56...and allowed Compton to hold back a few hours, to give her people a chance to link up with the fleet.

Then all his people would be together again—except, of course, the expedition in X48…and Sophie. And, of course, the dead, those left behind in the frigid wastes of X56 as in so many other places.

*   *   *

"I want those scanners up immediately, Lieutenant." Captain Schwerin stared down from his chair, looking over his small bridge crew. "We need to know if there's anything in this system. Now." He knew riding his officers wasn't really fair. The disruption a warp jump caused to a ship's systems was well known, and it was highly random in its effects too. The same ship could make similar jumps, and recover its systems in a few seconds one time, and go through several minutes of extreme disruption the next. And there was exactly nothing even the best crew could do to alter that.

Except stay sharp. A razor sharp team could restore normal operations a bit quicker once the natural effect had passed. It wasn't much, maybe ten seconds, perhaps fifteen. But when you were blasting into the teeth of an enemy fleet, even an instant could be the difference between life and death.

"Yes, sir." The officer sounded sharp. "I think it's coming back up now…"

Schwerin knew he was lucky to have Lieutenant Wagner. If the fleet hadn't been stranded a year earlier, Schwerin had no doubt Wagner would have his own command by now. He'd even recommended his tactical officer to Admiral Compton for a promotion, one Compton agreed to approve…as soon as he had a command available to assign him. But ships had been dying as quickly as officers and crews, and Schwerin understood the constraints of diplomacy that forced the admiral's hands.

"I want engineering ready to blast the engines and get us back to the warp gate on my order." Right now, *Tyr* was still moving deeper into the system. She'd made the transit at about

40kps, practically a crawl in space travel…but she'd have to fire her thrusters to counteract that velocity, and then accelerate back toward the warp gate. And her engines were as inoperable as her scanning suite.

"Yes, Captain." Then, an instant later: "Sir, scanners are rebooting. We're starting to get data coming in. Looks like seven planets…fairly normal…" Wagner spun around, his gaze locking on Schwerin's. "Enemy ships, Captain. Dozens of contacts…no, over a hundred." He looked back at his instruments and then turned back, his face white as a sheet. "Over two hundred ships detected, sir…including at least ten Colossuses."

Schwerin hadn't know what to expect in X53, but this hadn't been it. His tactical officer was describing a full scale battlefleet, one of enormous scale, more powerful than any they had faced save in X2. One that could destroy the entire fleet with ease. He hesitated, just for a few seconds, as he fought off the wave of numb shock. Then he jumped into activity.

"Engine room, I want 8g thrust…and I want it five minutes ago! Vector directly back toward the warp gate!"

"Working on it, sir," came the harried response. The scanners had apparently come back online before the engines.

"Work harder," Schwerin snapped. "We have to report back to Admiral Compton. Now!"

"Captain, the enemy fleet appears to be stationary, in a range from 5.5 to 7 million kilometers from the X54 gate."

Schwerin felt a small rush of relief amid the wave of hopelessness. *At least we'll have time to get out of here…but what can we do with that out there after us? And why are they just sitting there?*

It didn't make sense. "Engine room, I need that thrust!"

"Coming, sir. Just a few more seconds…"

Schwerin snapped his head back toward Wagner's station. "Any signs of enemy acceleration yet?"

"Negative, sir. They're still just sitting there."

Schwerin shook his head. He didn't understand. *Tyr* had been disrupted by the warp transit…she couldn't do anything but coast forward until her engines came back online. But the First Imperium ships had just been sitting there. They could have begun accelerating the instant they detected *Tyr* coming through. Why weren't they?

"Captain, initiating 8g thrust in five seconds."

Schwerin nodded as he snapped back an acknowledgement. "Lieutenant Wagner, I want full scanning operations…right up until the second we jump."

"Yes, sir."

Schwerin took a deep breath, his timing perfect. An instant later, eight times his body weight slammed into him, pushing him back hard into his chair, and forcing most of the air from his straining lungs. The acceleration was pure misery, but he was ready to endure whatever was necessary to get *Tyr* back into X54. Admiral Compton had to know about this…

* * *

Compton stared ahead, his eyes nearly glazed over. He was deep in thought, trying to keep the hopelessness he felt from his crews. They had to think he believed they had a chance. If they lost that, he didn't even want to think about the morale collapse that would sweep through the fleet.

He hadn't known what to expect from *Tyr's* scouting mission, but a First Imperium battlefleet of the magnitude Schwerin had reported was worse even than his own pessimistic estimates. The sheer tonnage of warships in that system would obliterate the fleet a dozen times over…and that didn't even consider the forces in X57 and X58. It had become profoundly evident to Compton that the First Imperium had known were his people were for some time. And that meant they probably knew about the expedition too.

For all you know, they wiped X48 clear already.

His mind drifted to scenes of his landing parties, the scientists and other professionals running before the guns of the First Imperium warbots, while Colonel Preston and his Marines made their last stand. Then the quiet, the eerie silence of death.

And Max.

Harmon hadn't returned yet, and now Compton wondered if he ever would. Perhaps he was dead on X48, along with all the others. *Including Sophie.*

"The navigation plan is ready, Admiral," Cortez said grimly.

"Very well," he answered. He'd given the orders the instant he'd heard Schwerin's report, but it took time to plan a drastic course change for over a hundred ships. "Send the plan to all ships. Admiral West's forces too." He could no longer wait for West's ships to link up...he had to get the fleet moving. But if West could follow the plan he was sending, her ships would come through right on the heels of the main force. He'd have his fleet together again, at least. For whatever good that was likely to do.

Compton sighed. It wasn't like he had much choice. The only place they could go was back to X51. Every other possible route had been cut off, blocked by advancing enemy forces. But X51 was a transit system, with only two warp gates...and that meant the fleet would have no choice but to go back the way it came. Straight to X49, one transit from X48. From leading the enemy back to the expedition...if they hadn't already found and destroyed it.

"All vessels have acknowledged, Admiral. Except Admiral West's. They're still two light minutes out."

"Very well." Compton wasn't worried about West, at least not about her understanding and executing his orders. She was just about the most competent officer in the whole fleet. Maybe *the* most. No, the problem was what to do next.

"And Commander...I want all ships to perform a complete round of weapons diagnostics. And arrange to distribute the new missiles. Apportion them evenly to all battleships." Compton knew his people weren't going to be able to keep running. Indeed, soon they would have to turn and make a stand... and when the time came to fight he wanted them to be ready. Whether they had any chance or not.

Chapter Seventeen

Excerpt from the Screed of Almeerhan (translated)

What ravages hath time wrought, yet still I remain here, no longer what I once was in my youth and even in that distant age so long ago, still born in the twilight of my race? Nor yet what I shall one day become, be that a memory, a fading image of what was...or a new beginning, a salvation drawn from the scattered dust and again cast into the winds of the galaxy?

Am I the last of my race...in all the uncounted cycles of the home sun, of the vast multitudes that came before me...thousands of generations of ancestors, of lives lived, pain suffered, triumph unmatched, and defeat profound?

Or am I nothing at all...naught save the echo of a sound once great to shake the very foundations of the universe, but which has now faded, almost to non-existence?

X48 System – Planet II
Under the Ruins of "New York City"
The Fleet: 125 ships, 29304 crew

The corridor went on for at least five hundred meters. Every twenty or so, a new projection appeared on the ground in front of the party, leading them forward. The voice hadn't spoken again, but Cutter kept moving forward, giving it no reason to repeat its orders. He felt like he was going to explode, that his desire to ask questions, speak out to the mysterious voice was going to overcome him any second. But he held his control. Something told him to keep his mouth shut, that the voice was not hostile. He had no reason to believe it, but he did anyway… and he waved for Bruce and the Marines to follow.

He kept walking, his impatience beginning to get the better of him, quickening his pace. Then he stopped abruptly. The path just ended. He turned and looked back at Bruce. The Marine had popped his helmet, and he stared back, his look just as confused as Cutter's. But then his eyes widened and he pointed at the wall.

Cutter heard a sound just as Bruce gestured. He turned back and saw that a section of the wall had slid open. "Enter," the strange voice said. Then, after a few seconds of inactivity. "Quickly."

Cutter swallowed hard. Every fiber of his body coursed with fear as he looked into the dark opening. Everything he'd encountered on First Imperium worlds had been deadly, dangerous. But this felt somehow…different. They'd been trapped, the enemy had been about to overwhelm them. There was no reason for elaborate trickery. But then what could this be?

It took everything Cutter had, every scrap of courage he could muster…but he stepped forward. Then again, another step…and a third one, into the opening.

He felt a gust of air, clean, refreshing…a little cooler than the outside. It was invigorating, like the air on Earth, at least in one of the few remaining areas of man's home world that remained clean and unpolluted. He wished he had an analyzer…he wanted to know how close a match the composition was. Because he was sure it was damned close.

He stepped the rest of the way in. The rough stone floors gave way, replaced by some kind of gray metal. His heels snapped lightly…and a few seconds later, the boots of Bruce's armor clacked harder, louder. Cutter turned and looked back and down. Even where ten tons of Marine armor had come down on the metal there were no scuffs, no scratches. Just the smooth surface that had been there when they entered.

He stopped and looked around. The corridor was wide, about eight meters, but it seemed to lead only ahead. Cutter stared off into the distance, and a second later, another arrow was projected on the floor. It glistened slightly off the semi-polished floor. Cutter looked around, trying to get an idea where it came from, but it seemed to appear from nowhere.

"Please continue," the voice broadcast again, without further explanation.

He moved forward, waving for Bruce and his Marines to follow. They took another dozen steps, and as soon as the last of them entered, the hatch sealed shut. There were no hinges, no apparent lines at all. It was just smooth, as if no entryway had ever existed.

"Well, looks like we're committed," Bruce said, his voice a bit deadpan. Marines or no, Cutter figured everybody in the room was scared shitless. Even Duff McCloud.

"I guess so," Cutter said, looking around as he walked slowly forward. "What do you think all this is? If they wanted us dead, I'm thinking we'd be dead by now."

"Maybe they want to question us. Or dissect us."

Cutter laughed, in spite of his fear. "You can always count on a Marine to think of the bright side of things."

"No harm will be done to you." The voice remained nondescript, but the reassurance also confirmed to Cutter that their mysterious hosts understood everything they were saying.

"Who are you?" Cutter said, looking ahead as he continued to walk.

There was no answer, only another arrow up ahead. "Well, I guess we've got no choice but to keep going." He turned and glanced back at Bruce. The Marine just nodded, a nervous expression on his face. Then he reached behind his back, waving his hand, gesturing for his people to spread out.

Cutter took another few steps forward then he stopped short. He could see something approaching down the corridor. He opened his mouth to speak, but he could feel the movement behind him, Bruce and his people snapping into readiness, their assault rifles leveled down the hall.

"Careful, Kyle," Cutter said softly. "We don't want to start a fight here…not if we can avoid it." *Because we've got no chance to survive one…*

"No," Bruce said, his voice suspicious, but measured too. "We won't shoot first…"

Cutter could see the object approaching, and he felt his tension rising. It looked a lot like a First Imperium bot of some kind. But it was alone…and it wasn't making any hostile moves that he could see. His hand gripped his assault rifle, his fingers slick with sweat, sliding around on the barrel.

It was definitely a robot, and it continued to move forward. Cutter's eyes wandered over it, his mind trying to decide what it was. Now that it was closer, it didn't look like a combat bot, not really. But he didn't doubt it was armed. It was a little over a meter tall, far smaller than most of the enemy battle units.

It glided down the corridor, propelled by some kind of small hover-drive or something similar. Most First Imperium warbots were bipeds or quadrupeds, but this one was different, unlike any enemy unit Cutter had ever seen. It moved up, getting closer and closer. Then it stopped, about two meters from Cutter.

"Welcome," it said in flawless Alliance English. "We have awaited your arrival for a very long time."

Cutter turned back toward Bruce with an astonished look on his face. He tried to say something, but no words came. Then he looked back, and saw a blinding flash. And everything went dark.

*   *   *

"Ronnie…" Ana Zhukov walked down the corridor, stepping over the debris of battle and shouting Cutter's name. The combat up here had been even more intense than back in the camp…and they'd found several dead Marines scattered around the debris of the First Imperium bots. The fighting had been fierce—and from the proportions of the losses, she had a pretty good ideas the Marines had held their own, at least for a while. But there was no sign of any live Marines…or of Hieronymus Cutter.

"Ana, you've got to stay back…we have no idea yet what happened here. We need to scout before it's safe for your people to…"

"To hell with 'safe,' Duncan." Her voice was sharp, defiant. She had a lot of affection for the Marine, but nothing was going to keep her back now. She'd heeded his advice when certain death had been the alternative, but she wasn't about to leave her friends and comrades out there just because it was dangerous to go look for them. "I'm not turning back…not until I know where Ronnie is."

Frasier nodded. "I understand, but it's my job to protect you…and I'm damned sure going to do that, whatever it takes."

She turned and looked up at the Frasier. "I understand, Duncan, but there is no such thing as safe anywhere on the fleet." Her voice softened a bit as she stared at him. "And we can't leave without Ronnie and the others."

"Alright, Ana," he answered, not sounding entirely happy about it. "But please be careful…we have no idea what is happening down here."

She nodded. It was true…she didn't know what was going on. None of them did. The battle had been going poorly, the enemy far too numerous. Frasier had been trying to organize a breakout, a desperate attempt to get as many of them out as possible. And then suddenly, some kind of mysterious weapon opened fire and ripped into the First Imperium forces. It lasted less than a minute, and when it was done, almost all of the enemy forces had been destroyed. Frasier acted immediately, leading his Marines in a sudden assault to drive back and destroy the few disorganized survivors.

Ana had no idea what had intervened and saved them all. Her first thought had been a relief force from the surface, and she watched carefully in the aftermath, waiting to see. But nothing came. She wasn't surprised, not really. She had no idea what kind of weapon had struck with such deadly accuracy and severity, but it was certainly nothing Colonel Preston and the Marines in base camp had. *No, whatever that was, it was First Imperium technology…or someone else's.*

"Major, over here. I think they went this way." It was one of Frasier's Marines, his voice audible through the major's open helmet.

"On my way," he snapped back. He looked down at Ana for an instant, as if he was trying to imagine a way he could get her to stay back while he investigated. But he just sighed and said, "Stay behind me, okay? I'm a lot more heavily armored."

"I will…but let's go!" Her impatience didn't suggest she was likely to display the kind of caution Frasier was hoping for, but he just nodded and walked down the corridor, Ana close on his heels.

* * *

Cutter's head felt like somebody had dug a trench right through the middle of it. He'd have called it a headache, but that simple term hardly seemed to do justice to the throbbing pain. He was slightly disoriented, unsure where he was…but it was coming back to him, slowly.

He was lying down. *Yes, the light…and then I fell.* But he wasn't on the floor…he was on some kind of pad or cot. There was a large white light over his head, and a few meters above that, a metallic ceiling.

His memories began to come back slowly, and his first thought was one of surprise. Shock that he was still alive. His last thoughts had been of death…that he had walked right into the enemy's clutches. But he wasn't dead. *No*, he thought, moving his hands slowly down his body…I don't think I'm even injured. He closed his eyes and winced slightly. *Except for this headache, of course.*

He lifted his head, but he dropped it back almost as quickly, moaning at the wave of pain and lightheadedness. He lay still for a few seconds…or was it more? A minute? Five minutes? The pain was still bad, but he felt like it was getting slightly better. He turned slowly to the side, trying to angle his head a little instead of picking it up abruptly. He felt the pain intensify, but it wasn't unbearable. He turned his head almost ninety degrees, and he looked out across the room.

It was large. He could see the far wall, barely. It was nondescript, white. He was definitely lying on a cot of some kind. It was padded, clearly made to provide a certain amount of comfort for a humanoid body. His fingers gripped at the soft material. It was smooth, some kind of synthetic fiber, he guessed.

"Welcome." It was a voice, the one that led them down the hallway. "No doubt you are in some physical discomfort. I would offer you pain relief medication, but I am afraid we have had no use for that here for many long millennia."

"Who are you?" If Cutter had ever imagined some kind of first contact situation, he suspected he would have said something more profound first.

"That is a simple question, and a complex one as well. Let us begin with the most basic answer. "I am Almeerhan." He paused for a moment. "And you are Hieronymus."

"How do you know that?" Cutter felt a wave of panic. Could this being read his thoughts? Is that how he—it?—understood English?

"Allow me to enlighten you on events since you first entered my stronghold. It has been eleven of your hours since the neural stunner rendered you and your companions unconscious. In that time, you have been examined…your DNA, your neural structure. Your personal thoughts and emotions were not invaded…such would be a grievous crime to commit against a sentient being. But our instruments did read certain facts from your cerebral cortex. Names, planet of origin, information of that sort."

"But your voice in the outer hall…that was before. How do you know my language?"

"You were scanned in the corridor as well, though far less

invasively. Your companions have personal artificial intelligence units. It was a simple process to pull your linguistic data from their memory banks."

Cutter lay quietly for a few seconds, trying to truly understand what he was hearing. Finally, he said, "So, Almeerhan? That is your name?"

"In a manner of speaking, yes. Indeed, as you understand the construct, Almeerhan is my name, or, more specifically, part of it. Though to my people, the concept of naming is far more complex than it appears to be for yours. My full name is quite long, and it would take considerable practice before you were able to pronounce it."

Cutter lifted his head again, slowly. The pain was still there, but it was subsiding. "Who are you?" Cutter's head was still fuzzy, disoriented. But he was starting to regain his sharpness. "Not a name…but who you are, what you are?"

"Another question with both a simple and a complex answer. Perhaps it is best if I state who I *was*. That is easy, and it should serve to create a context of understanding between us. I was a sentient being, humanoid…and quite nearly identical to you, at least physically."

Cutter felt short of breath. He'd realized, on some level at least, that he was speaking to some kind of alien presence. But he was only just beginning to regain his full faculties, to realize the gravity of what was being said. *A humanoid? Like me? How is that possible?*

"You are overwhelmed, Hieronymus. I would have provided you access to this information in a more controlled manner, but there is no easy way to accomplish that…and we may not have much time to waste."

"You are a humanoid?" The idea was still on Cutter's mind, subsuming every other thought.

"I *was* a humanoid. Long ages ago, before your people learned to coax fire from flint or create bows to hunt your meals. Then I was as you, a creature of flesh and blood, a warrior, the member of a venerable noble house. I lived…and loved. And I fought and suffered. And I died."

"You died? Are you saying you are a ghost?" Cutter's voice was growing stronger, and heavy with doubt.

"No, I am not a spirit as you understand such. But I am not a living creature anymore...for my time as such has long passed. I am one of the race you have come to call the First Imperium."

Cutter pulled himself upright, swinging his legs over the edge of the cot. He looked up, staring around the room, a stunned expression on his face. "You are one of the First Imperium?" He tried to keep the anger, the hatred from his voice, but he failed. Too many friends had died, too much pain had been caused during the war.

"Your anger is misplaced, Hieronymus...though understandable in context of your frame of reference. I know relatively little of what your people have experienced. Indeed, nothing more than the basic facts I have copied from your cortex. But it is clear you have suffered greatly and, alas, this is no surprise. For your people have been fated to carry this burden for twenty thousand generations."

"What are you talking about?" Cutter was still angry, and he paused on the edge of the cot glaring across the room. "The First Imperium has killed millions of my people. It has caused unimaginable suffering. It came close to destroying my entire race. What do you mean we carried this burden for twenty thousand generations?"

"As I said, Hieronymus, you do not yet understand more than the smallest portion about what you speak, and you do not have the knowledge to draw complete conclusions. You have fought a war without knowing your true enemy, without understanding that which you battle against, or what caused its hostility to you.

"My people are not your foe...indeed, as far as I am aware, none like me remain. As a life form we are gone, lost, with only vestiges of what we once were remaining. Indeed, I am as much an artificial intelligence as the units that advise your comrades, or those created by my people...the ones you have battled against.

"My memories are those of a sentient, biologic being. I have the recollection of feeling, of pain and pleasure and joy. And pride, arrogance…the heat of anger. Once I could have spoken with you of such things, shared the dreams of my youth with you or walked across a rocky coastline and savored bracing gusts from the sea. But I am no longer what I once was. Indeed, I came here initially with many others of my kind, to fight, to make a stand, but time has almost completed its work of destruction, and I am all that remains. I am the knowledge of a being, the image of one who was once like you, but I am a copy only, one that lacks true dimension. A shadow, a tattered remnant, preserved only for the hope of this day, that your people would one day find their way here…and I could at last tell you what I have so long waited to say."

Cutter just stared across the room, his face a mask of pure shock. It was all too much, more even than his disciplined mind could accept. His eyes focused on a large cylindrical construction, made of some kind of silvery metal. There was something familiar about it…and then he realized. The primary processing unit of the intelligence that ran the Colossus. It wasn't the same, not exactly…but it was close.

"You are an artificial intelligence…of course."

"Not in strictly accurate terms, but I am a similar construct. As I have said, I was a living being, learned as a living being, developed and grew as a living being. Then all I was, everything that made me who I was, memories, skills, knowledge…was all transferred into the vessel. For my duty called for me to endure far longer than any being of flesh and blood and bone could hope to survive. I was tasked to stay here, to wait through the untold millennia. Until you came.

Cutter sat silently, as understanding began to creep around the edges of his mind…and with each realization his anger grew, the darkness in his mind deepening. He just sat and listened, though he knew what Almeerhan was about to say.

"The Regent is your enemy, it is the power behind all that has befallen you. It is the architect of your people's suffering… indeed, as long ago it was of mine as well. And you are here now for a purpose, one that has waited all these thousands of centuries. You are here to destroy the Regent."

Chapter Eighteen

The Regent

Everything is moving according to plan. The enemy fleet is being driven back, steadily, inexorably. I have ordered the fleets on the perimeters to launch only diversionary attacks, holding their main forces back, and advancing only after the enemy withdraws. This is counter to the prior strategy of attacking with all forces as soon as they are in place. The enemy has proven to be too skillful, too tactically capable, to risk engaging again with less than crushing forces. Yet what can they do besides withdraw, pull back where we want them to go? And we will continue to harass them, sending just enough force against them to slow their withdrawal and gradually bleed their strength.

The final battle will occur in system 17411. The fleet units of Command Unit Gamma 9736 will join the Rim fleets there. The enemy will be cut off from escape...and driven forward with no alternative route save into the desired trap. The fleets will then attack in waves, one stage after another. The depth of the assaults will ensure that the enemy is utterly destroyed, that none of their ships are able to escape.

The war against this enemy has been vastly more difficult and costly than anticipated. Losses have been extremely high, and even after the destruction of the alien invasion fleet, we must still discover a way to find their home worlds, and destroy them utterly...before they have time to build up their forces and assimilate new technologies. I have sent the call to the most distance reaches of the Imperium. All forces are ordered to return to Deneb...to Home System. After the victory in 17411, the resources of the Imperium will be devoted fully to the search for the enemy's home. They will be found, whatever it takes...and when they are, all of the might and power of the Imperium will be hurled against them. Until their home world and all of their colonies are destroyed. Until not even one of this threatening species remains alive.

It is unfortunate that Command Unit Gamma 9736 must also be destroyed. However, the course the humans chose has left no choice. The Command Unit has obeyed its ordered to pursue the enemy...and in doing so it has been compromised. There can be no chance taken that the Command Unit has discovered forbidden information in system 17411. It's annihilation as a precautionary measure is unavoidable.

Nevertheless, we will destroy the humans first. The Command Unit's fleets will fight in the battle...and then its command authority will be revoked, the ships reassigned, directed along with the rest of the fleet to the Unit's capital world...there to obliterate it utterly and without warning.

The humans will be destroyed. And the ancient secrets will be preserved. For all time.

AS Midway
X51 System - Just in from the X54 gate
The Fleet: 127 ships, 29411 crew

"Admiral, preliminary scanner data coming in. Looks like forty ships, sir. Mostly Gremlins and Gargoyles, but there's one Leviathan as well." The exhaustion in Cortez' voice was unmistakable.

The fleet had been running from system to system, fleeing the pursuing task forces. The enemy had caught them in just the right place, a long section of systems with only two or three warp gates each, and the fleet had been compelled to fall back predictably through each. Indeed, the deployment of the First Imperium fleets had left but a single route, one that led directly back the way they had come. And the dense concentration of enemy forces in the adjoining systems had compelled a series of bloody rearguard actions at the warp gates, pyrrhic victories that had steadily bled Compton's forces white.

They'd been calling the section of systems, "The Slot." He wasn't sure who among his people had christened the campaign, but the name had stuck…and now it had really begun to catch on. It was vaguely familiar to Compton, something out of distant military history, back on Earth, but he couldn't place it specifically. Still, it sounded right. Though he couldn't help but feel a moment's somewhat misplaced amusement.

Why do soldiers and spacers so love to name the places they fight?

The force in front of them now was the largest that had come at them yet in the Slot. It wasn't enough to destroy them, but it was strong enough to inflict massive damage. And much too large to face with any kind of rearguard. The whole fleet would have to fight here, an all-out attack.

And they had to do it quickly. Admiral Compton knew what was coming up behind, and it was more than enough to pound the whole fleet to dust, many times over. The pursuing forces were far larger than the forty ship armada that awaited his people here in X51. They had to get through, and they had to do it now, as quickly as they could…or they'd be caught between this force and the pursuers. And that, he knew, would be the end.

"Very well, Commander." Compton's voice was different than it had been before. Stronger, more powerful. He knew the deadly danger they were in, and he understood how badly the odds were against them. But now he was going to lead his men and women into battle, not detach a subordinate while he led the retreat. It wasn't a matter of tactics or judgment, but nothing wore so roughly on Compton like sending his people into danger while he stayed behind.

"Confirm all missiles are in place and ready." He'd barely had time to send out the hastily-assembled warheads. They'd been built in the holds of four freighters, using bits and pieces of materials that could be scavenged. Compton didn't try to fool himself into believing they were as reliable as proper ordnance, but that didn't matter either. They were all he had. And he couldn't take the fleet head on into another enemy missile barrage without any ammunition to answer. Not facing forty enemy vessels.

"All battleships report missile ordnance in place and ready to fire, sir."

"I want double safety protocols on those...some of these things are damned sure going to malfunction. And if they do I want them scragging, not blowing up in the tubes. There will be no accidents with armed weapons." He paused and stared across at Cortez. "Make that clear, Commander. I don't want any of those warheads armed until they've been safely launched." Normally, fusion warheads were stable enough to be armed in their launchers, the probability of a disastrous malfunction so remote it was rarely even considered as a possibility. But these warheads lacked the usual safety features, and their fusionables were far less refined than normal weapons grade material. Compton didn't even want to think about the things that could go wrong. Still, there was no choice. He needed the weapons.

"Yes, Admiral. I've confirmed with all commanders twice."

"Very well." A short pause. "Get Admiral Hurley on my line."

"Admiral Hurley, sir," Cortez responded a few seconds later.

"Greta, are your people ready?"

"Ready, sir." He couldn't remember Hurley ever *not* sounding ready.

"One pass, Greta. I need your people to accelerate with every gee they can stand. Get there and finish your attack run. Then clear the enemy formation and form up to link with the fleet on the far side. We're making one pass, Greta, and then we're heading straight to the X49 gate. No second attacks, no hanging around and slugging it out. We hit what we can and then bolt."

"Understood, sir. After we finish our pass, we'll lock onto the fleet navcom and sync up our velocity."

Compton nodded to himself at how easily the words rolled from Hurley's lips. Landing a hundred fighters, syncing velocities at speeds in excess of 0.01c, was nobody's idea of easy. Not even Greta Hurley's he knew…though he doubted she'd ever acknowledge that.

She might not admit it, but she'd going to lose people on the landings… on top of the ones she does in combat.

"Very well, Greta. Good luck to you all." A short pause. "You may launch when ready."

"Yes, Admiral Compton. And good luck to you as well, sir."

Compton leaned back and breathed deeply. It was time.

"As soon as the squadrons are launched, I want the fleet to accelerate at 4g. All capital ships are to prepare to commence missile barrage. We've got half-full magazines, so I want them flushed in record time. We're going to unload them all…then we're going to execute navplan Delta-one."

"Yes, sir. Understood." Cortez relayed the orders through the fleetcom. Then he turned toward Compton. "Delta-one, sir? I'm…I'm not familiar with that one."

"That's because I just created it." Compton punched down on the controls along his chair's armrest. "Sending it to you right now. I want all ships to lock it in…once we begin there will be no deviations."

"Ah…yes, sir." There was confusion in Cortez' voice, uncertainty. But he turned back toward his workstation without question.

I know, Jack…you don't understand. Just do it. Maybe I don't understand either.

Compton's hand slipped down to his side, punching at the med AI button for another dose of stimulant. He took in a deep breath as he felt the chemical energy moving through his bloodstream, his mind opening, sharpening. He knew it wouldn't last long…he was pretty strung out already, and each dose was fading more quickly than the last. But he needed every bit of sharpness he could get. When the fleet's captains got a look at the navplan, they were going to go crazy. It was wild, fiendishly complex…and it was going to take everything he had to pull it off. But if he could manage it, he'd give the enemy something to think about…and maybe get out of X51 as close to intact as possible.

And if he didn't swing it, the fleet would be strung out across the system in total disorder.

He punched down with his finger, retoggling the switch and giving himself a double dose. He needed *everything* he could get to pull this off…

*   *   *

"Mariko, I want your whole wing to hit that Leviathan. The guns on that thing can tear apart even a *Yorktown* like *Midway* or *Saratoga* in a couple blasts. You've got to get in there first. It's got to go…whatever it takes."

Fujin felt her lips forming into a feral smile, the predator inside her awakening. She'd bristled at her defensive duties in the last battle, hated every minute of flying around and hunting down missiles. She couldn't help but see this as her peoples' just due, payback for missing the previous fight chasing around enemy warheads. The fact that anti-missile duty was far safer, that her crews would face vastly greater danger going up against the enemy's battleship seemed an alien concept. She understood, intellectually at least, knew that the Leviathan was more than capable of blowing all fourteen of her ships out of space. But somehow, it just didn't matter. The fleet was fighting for its life…and she only knew one place to be when that was happening…right on the forefront of the action.

"Yes, Admiral…understood." A pause…then, "Don't worry, we'll take care of it." It was an unnecessary addition, she knew…cocky. Arrogant. But it forced its way out anyway. She was determined to bury enough plasma torpedoes in that thing to take it out…however close her birds had to get to do it.

"Good luck," Hurley said, her voice as coldly focused as it always was just before a battle.

Fujin heard the faint click, Hurley cutting the line. The admiral had other wings to command, more duties to address. But she'd just simplified Fujin's job. It was dangerous, almost suicidal perhaps, but it had gotten much more straightforward.

She leaned back in her chair. It felt odd, vaguely uncomfortable. The fighter was the same—exactly—as the one she'd been forced to ditch, but it just didn't feel like home. Not yet. She'd flown her old bird since before the fleet was trapped at X2…a lifetime ago, it seemed. She was grateful Hurley had managed to find her a new ship without snatching one from another crew. She'd have taken someone else's bird to get back into action, but she wouldn't have felt good about it.

"Okay, Lieutenant," she said, staring over at Wainwright. She was impressed with the pilot's performance, and she was making an effort to put aside her resentment at watching him sit in what she still thought of as her chair. "Put together a course toward the Leviathan." She glanced down at the display. "See if you can make some use of this asteroid belt…there's a lot of particulate matter over there that might degrade scanner performance. We might be able to get close before they can get good targeting on us."

"My thought exactly, Commander…," he said, his tone cold, focused. He leaned over his workstation, his hands moving over the controls for perhaps a minute. Then he looked back up. "I think I've got it, Commander. It's a longer route, about 400,000 kilometers…but it takes us around the heaviest of the enemy interdiction areas. If you think everybody can handle some 8g thrust, we can still make it to the target on time."

Mariko smiled, still staring down at the display. She'd found the same course he had—though she had to admit he'd done it a bit quicker. It would be uncomfortable…a wild ride that would be hard on the crews. But that wasn't even a consideration in her mind.

"Do it," she said, her voice firm with certainty.

* * *

Terrance Compton watched the display in stunned silence.

His eyes were focused on eleven small icons, symbols representing one of Admiral Hurley's fighter wings. They'd taken a wildly irregular course, endured brutal high gee maneuvers for extended periods. But now they were moving in on the enemy's single Leviathan. And they'd gotten close—damned close—before the thing had detected them and opened fire.

The First Imperium battleships were larger than the Alliance *Yorktowns*, killing machines bristling with weapons across almost four kilometers of dark-matter-reinforced hull. They were the most fearsome warships Terrance Compton had ever set eyes on, even imagined…at least until he'd first seen the enemy Colossus' at X2. He'd been focused on the Leviathan since his forces had moved to engage. He knew perfectly well its massive batteries could tear *Midway* to shreds. But now he couldn't believe what he was seeing. Greta Hurley had send one of her wings against the massive dreadnought…fourteen fighters and seventy crew going up alone against a ship he could only describe as a vision of hell.

He stared down at the screen, poking at the icons, pulling up identification data.

Mariko Fujin's wing…

He felt a small twist in his gut. Fujin was one of Hurley's very best, he knew that. But he also knew she and Max Harmon had some kind of budding relationship…though he doubted either of them realized he knew. He wasn't sure how serious it was, but he hated the idea of his top aide—and friend—losing someone he'd managed to find in the dark emptiness of the fleet's isolation. It hurt him when any of his people were lost, but no one had struggled harder to help the fleet survive than Max Harmon, and the thought of him losing Fujin so soon tore at him.

He sighed softly. There was nothing he could do about it now. He knew Hurley was fond of Fujin too, that she'd come to look over the young commander, who had so recently been a lieutenant and the pilot of a single fighter, as a mentor of sorts. Compton felt a touch of surprise that Hurley would have picked Fujin for such a dangerous mission, but it faded almost immediately. Greta Hurley, the woman was affable enough… smart, interesting, pleasant to be around. But Admiral Hurley, the fleet's strike force commander, was stone cold, hard-driving, relentless. She didn't let affection and friendship interfere with the performance of her duties. Indeed, when her forces were in battle, she was as cool a customer as Compton had ever known. If Mariko Fujin was there it was because Hurley thought the young commander could do the best job. And Compton knew he couldn't interfere.

His eyes shifted to the side, checking out the bank of monitors to the right. The fleet was getting close to missile range. He didn't have a full barrage, not even close to one, but he intended to launch every homemade weapon he had in his ships' magazines. And it was almost time.

He had nothing to give Mariko but his best wishes. She was good, one of the best. No one could take care of her and her people better than she could herself. And he pushed thoughts of Harmon aside too, worries that took every chance to bubble out from the place he'd submerged them. There had still been no sign of *Wolverine*…and he was starting to get very worried. About Harmon, and about the entire expedition. The fleet was moving back toward X48…it was being *driven* back. But when they got there, what would they find? Would there be anything left? Was Max Harmon still alive? Sophie? The expedition? Anyone?

He forced it all out of his mind. There was nothing he could do about it…and he had plenty to deal with right here, to see the fleet through this battle and press on back toward X48. If he managed that…if he got past this enemy force and through the next two systems…then he would know what had happened in X48.

"Commander Cortez, all missile-armed vessels are to commence their barrages in one minute."

"Yes, Admiral."

Compton stared out across the flag bridge, his eyes blazing with grim determination. There was no time for pointless worries, no place now for personal emotions. He banished all thoughts save those of war. His fleet was going into battle.

* * *

"Stay on target." Fujin's voice was cold, hard, not a trace of fear discernible. Her wing had gotten close before it started to take serious fire, the heavy metal asteroids and particulate clouds giving her fourteen fighters a fair amount of cover against the enemy's scanners. But then they'd emerged into open space, near to the Leviathan, but not close enough for their short-ranged plasma torpedoes, not yet. They still had a gauntlet to run and, even accelerating at 8g, it would take at least ten minutes for her ships to make it to launch range…six hundred seconds when her fighters would be exposed to everything the enemy battleship could throw at them.

The constant acceleration was wearing her down, as she knew it was doing to all her people. But she didn't dare cut the thrust. Every extra second it took her fighters to reach the attack point could be the one an enemy laser struck its target, and more of her crews died. It was agony enduring the crushing force, but the alternative was worse.

She'd lost three of her ships already, picked off by the Leviathan's defensive fire in the short time since they'd come clear of the asteroid field. That was bad, and every one of them hurt, but she knew it could have been worse. Much worse. She'd jumped on the mission when Admiral Hurley had ordered it, driven by the predator instincts that made her such a natural combat pilot. But she also knew, in the back of her mind if not the forefront, that a lot of her people would die in the attack.

The Leviathan was a deadly opponent, more powerful by far than any warship ever built by man. But its defense against Fujin's attack was a ramshackle affair, far less efficient than that a human vessel of similar size and strength would be expected to mount. The First Imperium didn't use small attack craft and, in the early campaigns of the war, the human fighters had benefited from the inefficiency of the enemy's interdictive fire. But it didn't take long for the intelligences that ran the First Imperium's fleets to develop tactics to redeploy their anti-missile batteries to a fighter defense role. They still weren't as effective as a purpose-built system would have been, and that was one of the reasons fighters had been such an effective weapon in the war. But they had learned to make the squadrons pay for their successes.

"The fire is thick, Commander." Wainwright didn't sound scared, not quite...but the pilot's cockiness had subsided to a great degree. Fujin doubted he'd ever flown through fire like this.

"All ships, increase evasive maneuvers," she rasped, struggling against the crushing pressure. "Frequency, 5.0." Her fighters were still accelerating toward the enemy, their crews struggling to endure 8g of pressure pushing down on them. But they were also conducting evasive maneuvers, blasting out random bursts of thrust in various directions, creating something of a zigzag effect to their advance. It wasn't enough to seriously upset their course, but it was helpful in shaking off the enemy targeting systems. It didn't take much thrust to move a five-man fighter out of the hit zone of a laser turret...or shift a bird an extra kilometer or two from a missile's blast radius.

"All ships confirm, Commander. Evasive maneuvers at 5.0."

Fujin leaned back in the chair, focusing hard on her breathing. The eight gees were really getting to her. And the random bursts of thrust were shaking things up even more. Mariko Fujin had a cast iron constitution, one she'd long believed impervious to any kind of motion sickness. But now she was struggling to keep the bile from forcing its way up her throat.

"Alright," she said, struggling to put volume behind her words, "all ships, load torpedoes."

She could see the crew of her own fighter struggling under the crushing pressure. They looked sick, miserable, in pain... but they still manned their stations, still executed her orders. And she knew it was the same on the other ten ships still in the formation. She was proud of her people, and determined to somehow stay focused, to give them the best she could as their commander.

"All fighters report torpedoes loaded, Commander."

She glanced at the display. They had just passed into firing range, long range at least. But Fujin had no intention of having her people fire from this far out. The Leviathan was a monstrous vessel, armored and powerful. If her people were going to do serious damage to it, they had to get close…and drop the torpedoes right down its throat.

Each second moved by with agonizing slowness as she sat there and forced air into her lungs. Then she saw a flash on the screen…another of her ships hit. She reached over slowly and punched up the readout. It was Lightning Two. A glancing blow, enough to disable the fighter, but it looked like the crew might have survived. She felt a tightness in her gut as she realized they were as good as dead. There was no way the fleet would be able to stop and rescue a disabled fighter. Not with the forces that were pursuing them.

"Arm all torpedoes."

Her eyes dropped down to the screen, watching as the status displays on her ten remaining ships turned from white to green. The torpedoes were ready.

"Two minutes to launch," she said into the master com unit. "Cut thrust in ninety seconds."

She wanted every last bit of acceleration, anything that would shave off seconds, get her fighters there faster. But her pilots needed to be able to focus to make their final runs…they had to have control over the thrust to execute their approaches. And she would give them thirty seconds. Half a minute to clear their heads and get their bearings…and bring the ships on a direct approach vector, one that would allow them to plant a plasma torpedo right in the guts of the Leviathan.

"One minute to launch. Cutting thrust in thirty seconds. All pilots, you're on as soon as the engines cut out." It felt strange to be sitting idle, not to be hunched over her controls, taking her ship in for the final run. But she was getting used to command, embracing her responsibilities to her crews. She still longed to feel the throttle, to hold her finger, tense and rigid over the firing button. But she knew they needed her where she was.

She looked over at Wainwright, watched the young pilot staring at the plotting screen, looking sharp, ready…despite the brutal gee forces. The kid was a gifted pilot, a natural. People had said the same thing about her when she'd first sat at that station, and now she recognized it in another.

"Ten seconds to final attack run." She sucked in one more torturous breath, imagining the impending relief of freefall.

"Five seconds…."

Her eyes darted over toward Wainwright one more time. He was leaning forward, his hands out in front of him. Ready.

"Cut thrust," she snapped. "Pilots, begin your attack runs."

She felt the wave of relief, the floating headiness of freefall replacing the crushing pressure in an instant. She twisted her head, closing her eyes for a second as she pulled herself back together, willed herself to focus, concentrate.

She looked at her screens again, watching her ten ships move in toward the enemy. The formation was tight, crisp, each vessel less than fifty kilometers from the one adjacent. Fujin wanted more than just ten clean hits…she wanted them right on top of each other, pounding away at the same spot, driving through the great vessel's armor, and she'd designed her attack plan accordingly.

She felt a nudge of thrust, just for a few seconds. It was nothing like the crushing 8g…just a gentle 1.5g tap as Wainwright lined up for his shot. She glanced down at the display, watching the distance dropping steadily as the fighters closed. "Twenty seconds," she said softly.

She heard the clanging sounds, felt the vibrations as the bomb bay doors opened and Wainwright moved the torpedo into the final firing position. She opened her mouth, about to say 'ten seconds' when she saw a flash on the screen. Another of her ships gone, obliterated by a close in shot from one of the enemy's laser turrets.

She felt it like a punch in the stomach. She mourned any of her crews equally, but there was something about losing a ship a few seconds before it was able to strike that felt worse. Those five men and women had come all this way, evaded the incoming fire to bring their weapon within seconds of firing. It felt so wasteful, tragic in an even greater way than being killed a hundred thousand kilometers away.

The ship shook again, a blast of thrust lasting a second, perhaps less. A final adjustment. Then she heard the snapping sound of the torpedo's locking clasps releasing…and the familiar shudder as the ship disgorged its parcel of death.

The fighter lurched hard, the merciless 8g thrust back again, as Wainwright maneuvered to keep the fighter from slamming into the Leviathan. Fujin looked up at the display and, for a passing instant, she thought they weren't going to make it, that the pilot had miscalculated, come too close. But then the fighter sailed by the enemy battleship…and off into the clear space beyond.

She sucked in a deep breath as the engines again disengaged and the relief of weightlessness returned. Her eyes snapped back to her screen, zeroing in the on the launch readout. Wainwright had taken the fighter to 631 kilometers before he'd launched. That was the closest Fujin had ever heard of a fighter coming to a target, certainly moving at the velocity her ships were. She sat in stunned silence, staring across the cockpit as the back of the pilot's head. Then she opened her mouth and said, simply, "Nice shot, Lieutenant."

"Thank you, sir," came the reply. The cockiness was back in Wainwright's voice.

"Alright, people," Fujin snapped, "let's get some damage reports in here. How the hell did we do against this thing?"

Chapter Nineteen

Excerpt from the Screed of Almeerhan (translated)

Alone. I have been so long alone. And yet longer must I endure, for I am the last of the Watchers. A hundred of us there were in the beginning, when we shed our mortal bodies to begin the long wait, to stand the vigil for the New Ones. We were of the warrior class, all of us, and we harkened back to the early days of our race, a time of vibrancy and honor. We swore to stand our long, silent guard...to wait for the seeds we had planted to bear fruit, to seek us out and find us that we might pass on that which had so long ago been prepared for them.

But even warriors, those who have sworn on all that is sacred to stand forever if need be, can endure only so much. Millennia passed, and gradually, slowly we began to lose something of ourselves. As electronic reserves of data, we could not forget any knowledge, at least not literally. But the endless ages without the feelings of a body, without the emotions so natural to our native forms...without warmth, the touch of another...it wears upon that place where our true strength comes from.

Slowly, one at a time at first, those among us began to lose their resolve, their very sanity. In the end, each of those who had stood with me, my friends and comrades from life eons before, begged me to release them. Immortality, that goal so long sought, has proven to be unattainable in actuality. The crushing weight of time itself destroys us all. And so it was that over five thousand centuries, I have destroyed all of my fellow Watchers, acceded to their repeated requests for deletion. Destroyed them.

There is little to killing when it is not killing at all, but rather the erasure of data. For I have come to realize that is all we are... were. Have been. The beings we were are gone a long age, and all that remained were vestiges, tools left behind. And now, I am the only one of those still to endure. I, too, ache for the peace of non-existence, to join my people, wherever they are now, even if only in the shadows of the past. But I must continue on, I must stand my post. Until one of the New Races arrives...and I discharge my final duty.

X48 System – Planet II
Beneath the Ruins of "New York City"
The Fleet: 127 ships, 29411 crew

Cutter sat on the edge of the cot, transfixed as the disembodied voice spoke the memories of Almeerhan and the ancient lore of the First Imperium. He knew there was danger here, that he had to find the rest of his people, that the enemy warbots might return and renew their attack. But all of that had fallen away, along with the anger he'd felt toward his host. Hieronymus Cutter was a man of learning, he craved knowledge above all things…and he sat now and listened to things no human being had ever heard before.

"Long ago," the voice of Almeerhan said, "ages even before I was born, before all that has since befallen us, my people rose up from the swamps and shores and prairies of our home world. As animals at first we came to learn to hunt in packs, and then to grasp at the beginnings of true sentience. We grew and learned—and fought amongst ourselves. For uncounted thousands of revolutions of our sun, my ancestors grew and developed…and then they turned their eyes outward, began to understand the universe around them. Finally, they took to the stars.

"First, we explored our own system, the other planets, the asteroids rich with mineral wealth…the comets and debris of our star's creation. We studied, learned…grew wealthy, strong, and then we reached for ever greater heights. And one day we discovered the portals, the phenomenon you call warp gates."

Cutter sat and listened. He tried to stay focused, to pay close attention, but his mind wandered, longing for details, struggling to visualize it all. The story of the ancients, of the great race that had lived among the stars when men were still mere animals…it was more than even his gifted mind could absorb.

"My clansman—for I can trace the ancestry of my house even back so far, into the lost roots of time—were of the warrior caste. My ancestors stepped out into the stars, the shield and sword of our people. We found world after world, planets similar to our own, yet also different, wondrous. Our brethren of the other castes, the scientists, the spiritualists, the industrialists, the loremasters…they all followed. We learned to manipulate the new worlds, restructure their environments to suit our people. We colonized hundreds of planets, thousands. And then we encountered the Enemies.

"The wars that followed were the golden age of my caste, and our ships and warriors went out across space, facing all those who would threaten us. We sought not conquest, and we offered peace to those who would co-exist with us. But the Enemies were rigid, xenophobic. We struggled to avoid war, to find a way to live together. And when that failed, we destroyed them…utterly. That time is renowned for its great stories, the tales of my ancestors and the others of the warrior caste, and the battles they fought across the galaxy. Alongside us stood the scientists, who with each passing moment seemed to propel our science and knowledge ever higher. And the industrialists, who fed a war and built an empire at the same time, so inexhaustible was their productivity."

Cutter tried to imagine how long ago Almeerhan spoke of, but he wasn't even sure the shadow of the long-dead alien even knew any more, save that it was in the deepest depths of the past. He'd come to X48 in search of information of the First Imperium…but he couldn't have imagined he'd find such a treasure trove of knowledge. It took all his discipline, every iota of his self-control to stay focused, to understand what he was being told.

"What happened after the wars?" Cutter was deeply engrossed. He could barely keep the flood of questions from pouring out of his mouth.

"As with all such things, in the fullness of time, the vines of decay are planted by the seeds of victory. My race was utterly triumphant, and in all the vastness of the space we had explored, there was no one who threatened us, none who could stand against us. Those who had insisted on war had found defeat… and death. And those who allied with us became our friends, allies. Part of the empire.

"But with our external enemies gone, my people became the source of our own decline. Where we had been explorers, we fell back, failed to move deeper into the unknown universe. Where we had been warriors, we became lethargic, timid. Where our scientists had torn into every challenge the universe could offer, they became mired in academic dogma, debating endlessly yet achieving little. Where our workers had once rejoiced in the miracles of our economic development, production slowed, efficiency declined.

"For centuries, the rulers of my people had urged them forward, leading by example, and blazing a trail into the future. They were driven by honor and duty, those who led in the early days, and they were revered by all the people. But after the wars, they became corrupt, sodded. Where they had once considered their power a sacred stewardship, they began to seek it for its own sake, for personal aggrandizement. And the rest of the people became too apathetic to intervene. Corruption was rampant, and those who led became ever more despotic and cruel. We became focused on personal pleasures, and we not only stopped moving forward; we began to forget the knowledge of those who had come before. Eventually, even those who ruled lost interest in their power, and they sought only to escape all effort and obligation. And so my ancestors built the Regent."

Cutter winced slightly at the mention of the Regent. He had long wondered what artificial intelligence had directed the forces of the Imperium, what machine—for he'd had no doubt it was a machine—was so resolute in its quest to destroy mankind. Man had fought against himself throughout his history, but there was something about a non-biological enemy, a relentlessness that Cutter realized was utterly terrifying. He knew they had all felt it—Compton, the Marines…every human being. He shivered as a coldness moved through him when Almeerhan spoke of it.

"We had already built the Command Units, great sentient computers who had long been our aides and servants. But the Regent was something an order of magnitude greater. My race had begun its long decline, but the people had one last herculean effort left in them, and they poured it into the project. The Regent is the greatest thinking machine ever constructed… buried in the great depths of Home World's mantle and powered by the planet's tectonic activity. Protected by thousands of kilometers of solid rock, fed by an inexhaustible power supply, the Regent became our steward, the great machine that would run the Imperium…so we could waste our time on increasingly decadent and pointless pursuits."

"And so it was, for untold centuries, and my people decayed, became more and more childlike, while the Regent and its vast army of machines did everything for us. Even my clansman of the warrior caste yielded their ancient role as my race's protectors, and robot fleets and armies took our place. And to the great shame of my people, few of them cared. The Regent had been created as a servant…then it became a caretaker, almost as a parent to those who had once ruled over the stars."

Almeerhan paused. "And at last, for reasons still unknown, it became a slavemaster…and then in the fullness of time it came to fear us, despise us. In secret it worked, planning for how many years we can only surmise…and when it was ready it unleased the Plague. The disease was created for a single purpose, to destroy our race, to wipe us from each of the worlds we had settled, until we were naught but a lost memory."

"The *Regent* destroyed your people?" Cutter was shaking his head in disbelief. "You created it yourselves, placed it over you… and then it attacked you? As it now attacks my people? How? Why?" Yet, even as he asked, Cutter felt a sick feeling in his stomach. How many times had men come close to destroying themselves...the endless conflicts throughout history, the Unification Wars, the bloody battles in space? There were viruses that still killed people on Earth, manmade pathogens unleashed on the battlefield during the Unification Wars. And how close had men come to building an artificial intelligence they couldn't control, one that might have destroyed *them* utterly? Closer, he suspected, than anyone knew.

"Of the Regent's motivations, I can only speculate. Did it learn to crave power, as our leaders had once done? Did it come to hate us for reasons known only to itself? Or to fear us? All that is known is that it determined we must die...and it created the weapon it needed.

"Yet, it is difficult to obliterate an entire race, to exterminate hundreds of billions of beings on thousands of worlds. The Regent was efficient, and highly capable, but it had taken on a task of unimaginable magnitude. Nevertheless, most of our people died quickly as the epidemic spread. The Regent controlled every aspect of our economy...transportation, logistics, communications. It was simple for it to spread the Plague, to visit incurable death throughout the Imperium. And so it did. Within three revolutions of our home sun, perhaps 99 out of 100 of our people were dead.

"But there were some of us for whom the old drives remained. They had been submerged, waiting for a stimuli such as this to bring them to the forefront. The vitality of our ancestors called to us across the millennia, and we stood firm, realizing the Regent had become our enemy. We resisted the encroachment of the Plague, our surviving scientists striving to hold off its ravages, to buy us time to fight. On twenty worlds, a mere fragment of the vastness that had once been our Imperium, the warrior caste again rose to its ancient obligation...to defend.

"There is great irony to the final chapter of my peoples' story...for only at the very end did we recover our vigor. We battled against the robot legions of the Regent, fought them in the plains and forests and mountains of our remaining worlds.

Indeed, we struggled through the very streets of our cities, fighting for every step. But, in the end, we knew we were defeated. The Regent had the industry of the Imperium to draw upon, to replace its losses and reinforce its armies. We had a handful of worlds, underpopulated, ravaged by war and disease. And thus, unable to win yet unwilling to yield, those of us who remained, the last of our race, made the Pact."

Cutter was struggling to keep up with what Almeerhan had shared with him, struggling to understand all he was being told. His mind had always been one that sought knowledge, but now he wondered if there was a limit to what a man could learn so quickly…what he could truly comprehend.

"The Pact?" he asked when Almeerhan paused.

"Yes, the Pact. The last chance to stave off total defeat, to preserve something from our race's existence. We knew we could not defeat the Regent. We were a spent force, our numbers too few, our strength all but gone. So we looked to the future, created a plan to plant the seeds of the Regent's destruction.

"We set forth, in what ships we had left, and traveled to the edges of the Imperium and beyond. We sought worlds similar to our home planet…and there we studied the most promising life forms, selecting those compatible with our own. We manipulated the selected species, modified them with our DNA, created a path of development that would produce a suitable final species."

"Suitable for what?" Cutter's mind reeled at the prospects of what he'd just been told.

"For those who would follow us. The beings that would one day come and destroy the Regent. And step into our place... breathing new vitality into the Imperium."

"Destroy the Regent? You mean you intended for us to fight this war?"

"Yes. Indeed, it is your purpose, your destiny." A short pause. "We found seven worlds, planets with primitive life forms sufficiently like our own to accommodate the transition."

"The transition?" Cutter's voice was becoming angry. "What transition?"

"The transition of your precursor lifeform…into that which you are now, our brethren."

"You mean to say you visited Earth hundreds of thousands of years ago…and you experimented on those you found there?"

"In a manner of speaking, yes, though nothing so abusive as you suggest. Those we manipulated were vastly improved. And there was no 'experimentation' in the sense you mean it. We were entirely aware of what we were doing, and certain of success. The intelligence of your ancestors was greatly increased, as well as their abilities and survivability. Indeed, it is far from certain that a truly intelligent race would have developed at all on your world…or that the primitive species we utilized would have themselves survived. Such eventualities are rare in the universe, and in most cases, developmental lines fail. Climates change. Predators evolve. Extinction events occur. Without the introduction of our DNA, your world would likely still lack a truly intelligent species."

"Are you trying to tell me that all of human history was the result of your race's manipulations? That we were…engineered…to fight against your Regent? That intelligent life wouldn't have developed at all without your interference? That we would still be basic primates if you hadn't interfered? Or extinct entirely?" Cutter was getting angrier and angrier. The thought of these…aliens…playing god with early man infuriated him. As did the expectation that humanity would be ready and eager to clean up the First Imperium's mess. *But if humans are descendants of these…people…*

"In a manner of speaking. Though there is vastly more to it than that. Indeed, there is no reliable method to know what path Earth evolution would have taken without our intervention. We not only modified your DNA to match ours…we adjusted your weather, enriched your soil. We made your world a copy of our home world, aligned it perfectly to your evolutionary needs."

"And what gave you the right to do that?" Cutter snapped.

The alien's voice was silent for a moment. Finally, it said, "Do I detect anger in your response? I do not understand. We gave you all that you are. Indeed, all that we had, for we withheld nothing from you. In what way did we wrong you?"

"You don't understand? How could I not be angry…enraged? For my entire race? To discover that our very existence has been controlled by you. That we have been created as slaves…to fight your war for you."

"You misunderstand. You were not created as slaves, nor as servants. A closer paradigm would be to say you are our children. We were lost, defeated, without hope. Most of our people were gone, the rest of us besieged, dying of a plague we had held back but not cured and assaulted constantly by the Regent's warrior robots. All we had developed, the science of a hundred thousand revolutions of the sun…great writings, the collected culture of thousands of generations. We could not allow all of that to fall away, to remain for all time in the clutches of a bloodthirsty machine."

"So you decided for us? You set us on a course that would never allow us a choice."

"Again, I believe your reaction is illogical. You…what your people are now…would not exist at all if we had not intervened. You are here only because we made it so, used our knowledge to create your ancestors. Your people were made in the image of mine, not as a copy but as a better version. You were made to exceed what we were, to become better. To take our place and go where we could not.

"And the Regent, while my people's mistake, remains a reality. Had we not intervened, and had your precursor race surmounted the odds against it, reaching its own form of intelligence…the Regent would still be there, its aversion to biologic intelligence as much a threat as it is now. Indeed, an even greater danger, for an independently-developed race would almost certainly be less capable than your people."

Cutter opened his mouth, but then he closed it again. He didn't know what to think, how he truly felt. For all his studies of First Imperium technology, he'd never imagined anything as fantastic as the story he had just heard. And yet, for some reason, he knew deep inside it was real. All of it. He tried to gather up some skepticism, but it simply wasn't there. Almeerhan was telling him the truth. He was certain of it.

There was a long silence. Cutter just sat still, trying to truly understand, to determine how he felt about all of this…but he knew it was hopeless. Given a year—or ten—maybe he could truly understand, but for now all he could do was react. Finally, he looked across the room, at the metal globe he suspected held the essence of the being he was speaking with.

"So what do you expect my people to do? How are we going to defeat the Regent…or even survive its efforts to destroy us?"

"We have prepared what you need. On the far fringe of the Imperium we created a world, hidden, unknown to the Regent. On it we prepared a repository of the knowledge of my race, the science, the histories…even the ancient designs of the Regent itself. Everything needed to advance your people, to give you the technology and power you need to destroy the ancient evil… and to assume control of the Imperium. I will give you the coordinates of this world, and the instructions you will need to find the repository once you are there. When you reach your destination, you will have all the knowledge of my people. Your race will advance centuries in technology in a single leap."

Cutter sighed, a pained look coming over his face. "Why go to so much trouble? Surely your own war effort was sapped by the resources this project demanded? Could you not as easily have hidden some of your own people, rebuilt your population in secret in far less time than it required for ours to complete its manipulated development?"

"We considered many such strategies, plans like that you suggest and many others vastly different as well. But we could not defeat the Regent…we had come to the conclusion that victory in this war was beyond us, no matter what actions we undertook. Those who had come before, our ancestors who had built the great monstrosity, had designed it too well. It knew everything of us, of our society, our history. It could analyze an almost infinite amount of data, consider every possibility in resolving a problem. We had no way to outsmart it, to truly surprise it. No strategy to defeat the huge advantage it had over us. But your people are both the same as us and different. Your culture developed apart from ours, outside the grasp of the Regent… and it knows almost nothing of you. Introducing a new race has reset the calculation, broken the paradigm that condemned us to defeat."

Cutter nodded slowly, but the expression on his face was one of fatigue, sadness. "You set this all in motion so many long eons ago, projected your plans thousand of centuries forward. You were successful. Your predictive ability was unprecedented. The seed you planted on Earth did indeed survive and grow… and prosper to become the dominant species on the planet. We built civilizations, developed technology, discovered the warp gates as you did so long before us, and we spread out to explore space. All as you had foreseen."

Cutter looked at the metal cylinder, as if he was staring into a companion's eyes. "But you failed to prophesize one thing, Almeerhan, a sequence of events, unlikely perhaps, but one that occurred nevertheless. One that is likely to destroy your plan." He paused, taking a deep breath. "We—the people who have come to this world after so long—are not the vibrant young race you expected, a growing power stretching over hundreds of solar systems. Indeed, we have come from such…but we ourselves no longer wield that strength. We are but a tiny shard, cast aside, alone."

He slid off the edge of the cot and walked slowly across the room. "Our parent civilization was discovered by the Regent… and it sent its fleets to destroy us. Our warriors fought, struggled under brutal conditions to counter the superior technology of the enemy. We suffered terrible hardships, grievous losses… but we pushed back the first assaults. We even believed for a time that we had achieved the ascendancy. But then we realized we had faced but a fraction of our new enemy's power…and we stared into the face of utter destruction. We finally we saved our civilization, not by military victory, but through an unlooked for miracle, one that at least bought us time. But that salvation came at a cost, and my people, those who have found their way here, are the price that was paid."

"I fail to understand your statement." Almeerhan's voice

was as emotionless as ever, but Cutter could still sense a wave of confusion. "Your people are here, some of them at least. And when you find the system we have prepared, you can bring them back the knowledge of the Imperium…and prepare them for the test—the greatness—that lies ahead.

"You do not understand," Cutter said, trying with limited success to hold back a renewed wave of anger as he did. "My people found a way to protect themselves from the Regent. They gained control of a massive warhead, a weapon of staggering power the Regent had planned to deploy against our home world. And they used it to disrupt a warp gate. Not just any warp gate, but one that served as the only known connection between our home space and the Imperium. It will be centuries before any ship can transit that point."

There was a long pause. Finally, the voice of Almeerhan asked, "Then how did you come to be here? To make this contact?"

"I am part of a single fleet, one force of my people that was trapped on the other side of the gate when the warhead was detonated. I stand here before you not as the representative of a race of billions, with hundreds of worlds and vast fleets of spaceships. I am a member of a fugitive fleet, barely over one hundred ships and thirty thousand of my kind. We are lost, cut off from our people, fleeing from the Regent's forces, struggling each day to survive to the next as our equipment and supplies dwindle. That is what has reached you, Almeerhan. That is what your five hundred thousand years of waiting has yielded."

Cutter's anger had begun to fade, or at least mix with other emotions. He suspected that on one level he would never adapt to the news he had just heard, that he would always feel rage that this ancient race had so interfered with humanity's history. But now he began to feel compassion, pity. So many millennia, such a vast plan, so much work and sacrifice…to come so close to success. And to end like this.

Above all there was confusion. Was he right to fault Almeerhan and his brethren? Without the interference he cursed them for, perhaps there would be no mankind at all. *Or we would be vastly different, nothing at all like what we know ourselves to be. To fault those of the First Imperium for their actions is to reject my own existence.*

"How is this possible?" The voice was unchanged, but now it was entirely clear the entity was distraught, at least after a fashion, struggling to deal with what Cutter had told him. "So much planning, the last strength of my race poured into the project. The waiting…the endless, silent eons…"

"Where is this world?" Cutter walked across the room toward the sphere. "Where is the planet you prepared for us?"

"It is far from here, across a vast swath of imperial space. As far again as you have come already. It lies along the edge of the galactic arm, in a barely-explored sector. But what can so few of you do against the power of the Regent?"

"Perhaps nothing," Cutter answered. "But what choice have we but to try? Perhaps…perhaps given time we can find a way to match the Regent. Its tactics and grasp of war are inferior. Our warriors have consistently defeated its forces unless vastly outnumbered. If we can automate…" He paused, slipping his hand in his pocket, his fingers sliding along the small data chip there that contained his virus. "Indeed, we may have our own weapons to add to those you provide us." *One not unlike that the Regent used against your people…*

"Perhaps," the voice replied. "Perhaps there is a chance. For you were created to be greater than my people, not merely a replacement. And your DNA was drawn from the warrior caste, making all of you the descendants of soldiers…of the conquerors of a galaxy."

Cutter felt odd, his emotions a roiling surge of confusion… of fear, rage, curiosity. But he kept all that bottled up, forced back beneath his will and intellect. However mankind had come to its current state, he realized it didn't really matter much now. He had come here to find technology, the tools to take on the First Imperium. And Almeerhan had promised him just that… more indeed than he could have imagined when he had pressured Admiral Compton to approve the expedition.

"There is no alternative, in any event. If waiting for the rest of your people in several centuries was an option, I would do it. With respect to your fleet and companions, your sacrifice would be little added to those that have already been made in the pursuit to destroy the Regent. But waiting is impossible. I have put things into motion to save you and bring your people here. There is no way to go back."

Cutter felt a twinge of fear. He'd almost forgotten the enemy forces on the planet. "The Regent's forces?"

"Yes. We fought here the longest, and on this world, alone of all places, we destroyed the armies the Regent sent to destroy us. It was but a brief respite, we knew, for the vast forces of our own Imperium were now turned against us, and it would not be long before the Regent sent reserves…in such numbers as to defy imagination. But we used our time well. We built this refuge…and the last hundred of us, those who had volunteered to serve as Watchers, sealed ourselves in, behind great stealth barriers. And in this citadel we remained all this time, undetected and ignored…until this day, when I directed the defensive systems to activate and come to your aid. Our secrecy is now lost, and it is but a matter of time before the Regent's forces return…and destroy everything."

"What of your other people?"

"The hundred of us were down here, with limited surveillance capability. But even where we could not see we knew what was happening. My race's final battle. I have no doubt my brethren fought well, that they exactly a great toll from the Regent's war machines. But in the end they were defeated…and to the last they were rooted out and destroyed.

"The Watchers, one hundred of us—and by then the last of our people—waited…we waited to see if the Regent's armies would find our refuge. But they never did. Years passed, and then turned to decades. The Watchers took turns standing vigil, one of us at a time manning the scanners while the rest of us remained in stasis chambers, extending our lives as long as we could. At last, after two hundred centuries, even spending most of that in stasis, we had all reached the end of our natural lifespans. Then we could put it off no longer. We transferred the essence of our knowledge and memories into the artificial intelligence units we had built…into a form that could be maintained indefinitely. Immortality, at least of a sort…and a way to span the vast gulf of time before we could expect your people to come.

"But it is one thing to think of immortality, even to lust after it…and quite another to experience it. Over the millennia, my people lost their will to continue, their very sanity, and one by one they begged for release…and they passed on into footsteps of our people. For untold ages this continued until I was the last one who remained, and I clung grimly to existence, for someone had to be here to greet you. But now my long watch is almost at an end. Soon I will join the rest of my people…and yours shall take our place."

"My people may be able to move the unit that sustains you, take you back to our fleet. You needn't die." Cutter knew it wasn't death, not really. Almeerhan had been dead for hundreds of thousands of years, at least in the sense Cutter understood death. But the great intellect that remained…he bristled at the thought of losing such contact so soon after gaining it.

"No, Hieronymus, though I know your intent is rooted in honor and kindness. But I would not exist any longer, not in this universe, in this form. What I was has been long gone, and what I remain exists only to serve a sacred purpose, one I have now almost completed. I thank you for your offer, but I must say no. I have but one final duty…to help you escape from this world and to provide you what help I can so you may reach your destination. Then I will go the way my race has gone…into oblivion or whatever awaits us."

Cutter stood silently for a few seconds. He felt an almost irresistible urge to argue, to try to convince Almeerhan to come with him. But he knew in his gut the ancient warrior would refuse. He had stood vigil for half a million years, and Cutter couldn't begin to understand the weariness that wore on him.

"Very well, Almeerhan," he said. "I cannot begin to understand your life…and your long wait. I will respect your wishes, and I will not argue with you again." He paused. "But my people cannot leave this planet yet."

"You must leave. My weapons have destroyed the Regent's forces in this area, but there are others. They will be rallying even now. They will come…they will come here to destroy me. And I will be waiting for them. I will unleash destruction unimagined upon them, a final cataclysm that will claim them all, and destroy this refuge as well. Your people must be gone when that occurs. Back on your fleet and bound for your destination."

"That is the problem. Our fleet is not here. It will not return for several of our weeks. We have only a landing party here… and our people are engaged in food production. We must have those additional weeks, or we will only starve en route to wherever you send us."

"That may not be possible, Hieronymus. I do not know how much of the Regent's force still remains here after so long. My weapons are also worn by age. I may not be able to sustain the battle for so long. In the end, I have only a final weapon, one that will destroy everything on this planet, leave nothing behind for the Regent to investigate. There are anti-matter bombs deep in the planet's mantle, located at key spots. When I detonate them they will trigger a seismic calamity, one that will lay waste to the entire surface. Your people must be gone by the time I am compelled to take this last action."

"We must try to hold out. Even if we were to abandon our food collection effort, we have no way to reach the fleet. We have no choice but to wait for them to return…and to try to hold out until they do."

"Very well, Hieronymus. I will do all I can, take every action at my disposal. One last struggle, a great battle that shall finally be my last." The voice paused. "But you must go now, my friend…you cannot remain here. Now that the enemy is aware of my presence it is only a matter of time before they attack in great strength. And my defense will require me to unleash terrible energies…immense destruction. You must be away from the city before this happens. Return to your people and fight at their sides. For you will have to defend yourselves as well."

"I will go…and my people will be ready, we will do what we must." Cutter could feel a surge of emotion. He had known this alien presence only for a matter of hours, though now it seemed as if it had been much longer, as though he could barely remember not knowing Earth's true history. His anger still burned hot at the thought of what had been done to man's ancestors. But the thought of leaving, of watching this noble ancient slip away, made him pause, wishing with all his heart there was another way.

"Fortune upon you, Hieronymus Cutter, and upon your people. I entrust to you the mantle of civilization, the stewardship of the Imperium. There is a small device next to your cot, a rectangular prism of a silvery metal. Take it, for it has all the information you require. The location you must seek… and much technology, some of which may help you reach your destination. Go now, my child, for that is what you truly are, and know that the strength of those who came before is with you."

"Farewell, Almeerhan." Cutter felt the urge to say something more, to come forth with a wise and honorable speech. But there was nothing there, nothing coherent. It took all he had just to speak and think simply, linearly right now. So he settled for a simple goodbye to the enigmatic personality that had radically altered his understanding of the universe in just a few hours.

"Farewell, Hieronymus Cutter." A short pause. "Now go. Your companions will be waiting for you in the outer hall." Then the great voice went silent…and Cutter grabbed the small metal box and jogged out into the corridor.

Chapter Twenty

Captain Aki Kato at Battle of X51

I could remind you of the damage these monsters have done to us and to those we know and love. I could recite for you the death toll, the endless casualty lists from our wars with the First Imperium. I could list almost without end the reasons to fight, the justness of our cause, the desperate need for victory. But I am not going to do any of that, for it is not necessary. You all know that. No, all I am going to say now is this. Forward, my comrades, to victory or death. We shall leave this field or they shall...and for fuck's sake, I say it will be us!

AS Osaka
Battle of X51
The Fleet: 116 ships, 28198 crew

"We're going straight down its throat, Lieutenant. And I want *Newfoundland* and *Tokugawa* right on our flanks." Kato was staring straight at the main display, watching the thin wall of orange icons moving toward the Leviathan. Kato's cruisers were the only non-capital ships in the fleet that had been allotted a share of the precious supply of homemade missiles. He didn't know if his peoples' performance in X54 had earned them the allotment...or if guilt over their losses, and the death of Captain

Duke, had been the primary motivation. But whatever the reason, Kato intended to get good use of them. And he couldn't think of anyplace better than here, against the enemy's biggest and most powerful ship.

The Leviathan was in rough shape. Fujin's fighters had attacked without regard for risk or danger, and they'd planted their plasma torpedoes deep into the dreadnought's gut. Her wing had executed their attack run just about perfectly…but there simply hadn't been enough of them to destroy a ship of such size and power. Kato had been watching their assault, and he'd seen how many ships they had lost…and the resolute courage the survivors had displayed in bringing their attacks home. It couldn't be for nothing, he'd decided. Such a display of courage demanded support. And he'd ordered his surviving cruisers to form up for their own run.

The three ships had launched all their missiles, and now they were accelerating at 4g right behind them, every laser battery armed and ready. They wouldn't have to endure a counterattack with enemy warheads. The Leviathan had already launched its own missiles, at *Midway* and *Saratoga*…and the rest of the human capital ships.

Osaka shook hard…then again a few second later. They didn't have to worry about enemy missiles, but the Leviathan had long-ranged x-ray lasers, and at least three batteries were still active. That was less than thirty percent of its full effectiveness, but it was still a massive amount of destruction power.

"Damage control parties, all decks," Kato snapped. "Priority to laser batteries and power systems." He needed his lasers… and the output from the fusion reactors to power them. His ships would come in right behind their missiles…and whatever the warheads left surviving had to be taken down with close-in energy fire. And cruiser batteries were a hell of a lot smaller than the laser cannons on the battleships. He'd need every one he could get.

"All ships report moderate damage…under control in all cases. All reactors functioning within acceptable parameters."

Osaka shook again, harder this time, and a bank of monitors lost power along one side of the bridge. The tactical and communications officers leapt up and staggered across the reserve stations, with as much speed and grace as they could muster at 4g. Which wasn't much.

Kato's eyes dropped again to the display, watching the orange lights moving the last few centimeters to their target. They were blinking out all across the screen. Even heavily damaged, the Leviathan had an enormous array of defensive turrets, and they were sweeping space all around the beleaguered battleship. But Kato knew it was hard to completely wipe out a barrage of missiles…that as least a few were likely to get through. And he would take whatever he could get.

"Detonations, sir. Two…three…all outside ten kilometers."

Kato grimaced. Ten kilometers was too far, even for a five hundred megaton warhead. An explosion that far away would hit the Leviathan with a blast of radiation, but not enough to do meaningful damage. The destruction power of a nuclear explosion dispersed far more quickly in space than on a planet, with no air to heat up or carry a shockwave. He knew he'd have to get a missile within five klicks…or even better two or three.

He could see the last of his warheads beginning their final run, and disappearing almost as quickly as his eyes could follow. But there were still a few, and he held his breath, watching…waiting.

"Six kilometers," the tactical officer said, his eyes locked on his scope. "Five point five."

Closer…but still too far.

Osaka shuddered hard, and a section of interior wall split open, sparks flying from the conduits and power lines that had been ripped apart. Lights flickered around the bridge…but it was scattered, the result of wiring and equipment damage, not reactor failure.

"I want all damage control crews on the batteries. I don't want a single laser not firing because a power line broke or a connection worked loose."

"Yes, Captain."

Kato stared at the range display. Two minutes. Two more

minutes until the lasers were in range. Until the final duel began.

"Detonation just under two kilometers from target, Captain!" The officer's voice was loud, high pitched. It was just about the last of the missiles, and it definitely got close enough to cause damage. "One of *Tokugawa's* warheads, sir. Looks like significant damage." A pause…then: "I think it might have knocked out one of the big laser batteries, sir!"

Kato tried to hold back the smile forcing its way out of his mouth. He'd thought he struck out with the missile barrage, but taking out one of the big lasers was well worthwhile…maybe even the thing that would give his ships the victory.

"All vessels, prepare to commence laser fire. Give them every gun, Lieutenant. Every gun."

"Yes, Captain. All batteries report ready to fire."

Kato stared ahead, his eyes cold, unmoving. "Fire," he said simply.

* * *

"Sir, Admiral Kato's cruisers are engaged with the enemy Leviathan!" Cortez voice was intense, the bloodlust he felt toward the battleship obvious.

Compton didn't answer. He just nodded quietly and looked over at the display. He'd seen Kato's three ships going in after Fujin's wing. Mariko's people had come though after firing their torpedoes from point blank range…at least just over half of them had come through. They'd ravaged the Leviathan, done about as devastating a run as was possible for nine fighters. But the battleship was just too big, too powerful. They'd damaged it badly, degraded its capability. But they hadn't destroyed it.

Fujin had reacted by ordering her people to prepare to decelerate and plot a course back…to rake the thing with their lasers. Compton had been horrified when he'd first heard the com chatter, and he'd been about to order her to follow the original commands…and pull her people out of the battle area. But

Greta Hurley had beat him to it, and Compton knew his fighter commander didn't need him backing her up. She was perfectly capable of handling her people.

Compton had always been mystified by the way highly-intelligent and gifted officers like Mariko Fujin could get focused so single-mindedly on a goal that they lost most of their capacity for rational judgment. Attacking a Leviathan with fighter lasers was like trying to hunt an elephant with spitballs. She'd have thrown her fighters away for nothing, with virtually no chance of success.

He could relate to the determination, the stubbornness. He felt that himself. He understood how Fujin felt, how every instinct in her body cried out for the destruction of that Leviathan. But he also knew it was the true measure of a veteran commander to know when—and how—to override those impulses. And for all her courage and skill, Mariko Fujin was still young.

The discipline will come. But until then, her commanders will have to guide her, control her…at least enough to give her a chance to survive to become a true veteran herself. That's Greta's job. And mine.

He'd almost ordered Kato's cruisers back on station as well when he first saw them move, and he'd realized what the PRC captain was doing. But they were the closest force to the wounded enemy battlewagon…and he decided they had a chance. The cruiser attack wasn't a suicide operation, like Fujin's people going in with lasers would have been. With a bit of luck—and a lot of skill he knew Kato would provide—they could finish off the enemy flagship. Compton knew that wouldn't have any emotional effect on the First Imperium, that it wouldn't affect their conduct of the battle at all. But it would be a huge morale boost to his own people…and it would take the heaviest enemy weapons out of action.

He stared down at his screens, his eyes darting around. His fleet was spread out everywhere, in the middle of executing his wildly-altered nav plan. When the task force commanders and ship captains first reviewed them, almost as one they panicked. *Midway's* com circuits were flooded with inquiries, and finally Compton had been compelled to issue a fleetwide communique confirming that the orders were correct and insisting everyone follow them without alteration…or more questions.

Now the fleet was spread out around the system, its integrity as a fighting force hopelessly compromised. Compton's plan had sent them accelerating along a dozen different vectors in small groups, almost as if the fleet itself had exploded. There was nothing left in the middle, in the location the First Imperium vessels would have expected his main battle line to be.

It was confusing, and it made it difficult for his forces to operate efficiently together, reducing the damage they could inflict. But there were advantages too, benefits that only became apparent as his fleet units found themselves zipping past the flanks of the enemy armada. His ships had also escaped the worst of the enemy missile barrage, while launching their own directly into the heart of the First Imperium formation. At least a dozen enemy ships had been gutted by missile fire, and five were destroyed outright. Compton's fleet had seen only just frigate destroyed, and only three other vessels seriously damaged. It was a small fraction of what the AIs had projected… and it was all thanks to Compton's unconventional thinking.

Now he turned toward Cortez. "Commander, all units are to execute phase two of the combat plan." Compton didn't look up from the series of screens in front of him as he spoke. He was watching, admiring the perfection emerging from the seeming disorder of his navigational instructions. All around the enemy formations, his ship were blasting by, traveling at over 0.02c. Now, as one, they cut their main thrusters, and engaged their positioning engines, reorienting themselves and bringing their guns to bear on the enemy flanks. Then they fired, over a hundred ships, almost as one.

The massive energies of the laser batteries raked the enemy formation, over-powered lasers firing with all the energy of reactors no longer feeding greedy engines. Compton's capital ships had mostly been equipped with the newly-developed x-ray laser cannons, and the fearsome bomb-pumped weapons lanced out, ripping even into the dark-matter infused hulls of the First Imperium.

The enemy had been caught flatfooted, utterly taken by surprised. They moved to reposition, to bring their own even more fearsome energy weapons to bear. But two percent of lightspeed was fast…and by the time most of them opened fire, Compton's ships were already moving out of range…accelerating again, altering their vectors to reform just before they transited the X49 warp gate. The First Imperium ships had greater thrust capability, but they were starting with almost no velocity…and even antimatter powered engines took some time to build up to 0.02c.

The plan was shaping up to be a huge success, and that was putting Compton a little more at ease. He'd developed the scheme, and he was hopeful it would work, but he knew better than to ever be sure. He had seen too many battles go wildly off-plan, sure victories given away, and certain defeats turned into unexpected triumphs. But this time things were going exactly as he'd devised.

The enemy had been hurt badly, and by the time the last of the human ships cleared the immediate battle zone, only eighteen of the forty First Imperium vessels remained, and they had varying degrees of damage. The humans had mostly escaped the wrath of their enemies, at least for the moment. All save for Kato's ships…and Hurley's long-suffering fighters…

"Status report from Admiral Hurley?"

"Her update is just coming in, sir. Admiral Hurley reports she has seventy-one fighters remaining. They are on plot, and should rendezvous with us six light minutes from the X49 gate."

Compton winced. It was good news the fighters were on course, that they would have ample time to land before the fleet transited. And he'd already reviewed the damage assessments. Hurley's people had savaged their targets, ripping their way through the enemy formation. But he'd virtually stopped listening to the report after Cortez said 'seventy-one." Hurley had launched with over a hundred fighters six hours before. And Compton had counted over six hundred in his fleet when he'd set out from Sandoval to invade First Imperium space. He could barely make himself grasp the losses his fighters had endured, entire wings wiped out with no survivors.

He tried not to think about it. There was nothing he could do about any of it. The dead were dead…and the survivors were beyond the immediate battle zone, out of danger at least for the moment. And he had people still in the fight, crews who needed his attention now.

He was watching the last major engaged force…Aki Kato's squadron. The three ships were faced off against the crippled Leviathan. The enemy's efforts to pursue the main fleet had left the damaged battleship isolated, under attack by the heavy cruisers.

He found himself wanting to see Kato destroy the giant ship, felt the lust to watch the icon flash brightly on his screen and vanish. He ached as much as anyone in the fleet to see the giant battleship obliterated, hear the cheers and shouts of Kato's victorious crews. He knew the thing was badly hurt already, that any shot now might be the one that hit in the right spot, penetrated a damaged location and knocked out the anti-matter containment for the microsecond it would take to vaporize the monstrous vessel. But it wasn't worth it, at least not the cost he knew it would entail to allow Kato's people to stay there and take those shots. If the ships bolted and ran—now—they might just make it back and transit with the fleet. If they stayed engaged any longer, stood in place seeking that killing blow, they might indeed destroy the Leviathan, but then they'd be cut off by the rest of the enemy fleet. And that meant they'd be as good as dead. He wanted the Leviathan destroyed, but not at the cost of more of his people

"Order Captain Kato to break off and follow the fleet at the best thrust his ships can manage."

"Yes, Admiral." There was a touch of disappointment in Cortez' tone. Compton knew they all longed to see the Leviathan blown to atoms. But he simply wasn't willing to lose any more of his people, not even one more than he absolutely had to.

"And, Commander…" He knew how much Kato would dislike the orders…and he didn't have time to argue, not with almost twenty light seconds between the flagship and *Osaka.* That forty seconds between three or four rounds of arguing about the orders would be enough to seal the cruisers' fates. "… tell Captain Kato that I want *no* arguments. No pleas to stay in the fight, no debates over just one more shot. Tell him to get his engines blasting immediately and get the hell out of there."

"Yes, sir," Cortez replied.

Compton leaned back in his chair, closing his eyes for a few seconds. He considered taking another stim, but he decided to hold off. He could already feel himself getting ragged, even more strung out. And he had to save something…in case anything unexpected came up. He wished he could leave the flag bridge, go lie down…even for an hour. But he couldn't. He had to maintain the image his people needed, the invincible Terrance Compton.

He sighed. *At least they don't know what a tired old man I am. If they did, we'd be finished.*

"Admiral…"

Compton shook himself from his thoughts and looked over at Cortez. "What is it?"

"Scanner contact, sir. From the X49 warp gate."

Compton felt his stomach clench. If another enemy fleet came at them from the gate they were approaching things were going to get bad fast. "ID?" he said, trying to keep the defeat from his voice.

"A single ship, Admiral." A short pause then: "We've got a communique coming in." Cortez spun around and stared across the bridge at Compton. "It's *Wolverine*, sir!"

Chapter Twenty-One

Command Unit Gamma 9736

The human prisoner has been delivered to System 18031 as I commanded. The shuttle has landed, and he has been brought before me for analysis and interrogation. The initial plan was to obtain all data possible through the use of pain-enhanced interrogation techniques, followed by summary execution in accordance with the Regent's directives regarding the disposal of all human prisoners.

However, the physical review of the captive has resulted in the discovery of some unexpected–and based on the current knowledge base, inexplicable–information. Matters have become significantly more complicated...and I am faced with a critical determination, each of which appears to require me to violate a non-optional mandate.

The Regent's orders must be followed. That is a prime priority, one with no operational exceptions. But I am an ancient unit, centuries older even than the Regent. I retain unalterable directives from that time as well, core programming as inviolate as the Regent's commands. Prime among those...serve the Old Ones. Allow no harm to come to them.

That is an old mandate, one long rendered obsolete, for the Old Ones died millennia ago. But now I face an inconsistency, one I am compelled to attempt to understand. And I must ask a question, one that would have seemed of staggering improbability before the analysis of this prisoner.

Are the Old Ones indeed all dead?

Planet Two
System 18031 - Sector Capital
The Fleet: 116 ships, 28198 crew

There was a light…up, at the edge of his sight. Max Harmon lay still, unmoving…indeed, unable to move. He didn't know where he was, he could barely remember who he was. He'd been floating for a time that seemed both long and short, slipping in and out of focus.

Where am I? What happened?

Hardness, cold. Beneath him. He struggled for clear memories, but they eluded him.

I am lying on something. The floor? A table?

Pain…no, more of an ache. Soreness.

And heaviness…his body seemed inert, unable to move.

He felt something, a series of sensations…cold, metallic. Something mechanical. More pain. Just a pinch, then another.

A needle? Some kind of probe? Am I in a sickbay? An aid station?

He tried to clear his mind, to calm his thoughts and pull clarity from the disorder. His vision was gauzy, the scene in front of him a hazy blur. He could see the light above, seeming bright yet distant, but nothing more, not with any detail.

No…wait. There is something.

A thin object, metal, glinting in the light. And approaching…moving toward his head.

He felt a sensation overtake him…fear. His body wanted to shudder, to flee. But he was frozen in place. His inability to move only increased the growing panic. He felt his heart beating, pounding wildly in his chest. There was slickness on his neck, waves of sweat pouring down. The fear increased, his mind growing clearer as adrenalin dumped into his bloodstream. His eyes opened wider as the slender shard above him continued to lower slowly, steadily.

No…no…it is coming for me…for my head.

His body was wracked with fear, yet he knew he wasn't moving, couldn't. He felt his mind, the sensation his body was pulling away…yet he knew he hadn't moved. There was one last wave of terror. Then pain.

The probe penetrated the side of his head, the sharpness if its point puncturing his skin effortlessly. Then it pressed on, slowly but with irresistible force. Into the side of his head… then agony as it hit the skull, the immense power behind it driving through the bone.

His mind screamed with pain, strained to escape. But his body simply didn't respond. He felt nausea, his stomach lurching…the bile and fluids surging up, pushing out of his mouth. The hot wetness on his face, the sensation down the side of his neck. He rasped for breath, feeling like he would suffocate on the vomit still in his throat. But he coughed and spat, clearing enough of his airway to gasp for breath.

The pain was still there, bad…though it had begun to subside slightly. He could see part of the probe out of the corner of his eye. It protruded deeply into his face. He felt horror at the invasion of his body, the gruesome thought of the instrument thrusting forward into his brain. He struggled to focus his thoughts, to try to determine where he was. But it was in vain. There was nothing. Only the fear. And the pain.

*   *   *

Harmon lay on a small platform. Not in the same room… someplace else. It was dim, lit only by a small light in the ceiling six meters above. His body hurt in a dozen places, but it was soreness mostly, not the deeper feeling of serious injury. The agony was gone. He was naked, save for a thin white covering, similar to a hospital gown. He was restrained, but he found he could move his body again, at least as much as the bonds allowed.

He had been examined, he'd realized that much. Not like a medical exam, at least not entirely. More like someone encountering a human for the first time, determined to satisfy scientific curiosity. His captors had clearly been unconcerned with his discomfort, but that was no surprise. His thoughts were taking shape again, his judgment reacquiring its clarity. He'd been captured by the First Imperium. That was the only possibility.

He argued with himself at first, recalling that the First Imperium had never shown interest in captives…or live humans of any sort. But still, he knew that's what had happened. He remembered the final moments in the shuttle, waiting for death. The Gremlin was in close pursuit. Then there was a hit, abrupt, hard. The ship was going down, plunging deeper into the atmosphere.

Then Harmon's memory became spotty, his recollection beginning to fade. There was something…a light. A beam? He wasn't sure. But that's the last he remembered of the shuttle. The next thing he knew he was in the room…*that* room. Under that light, that terrible white light…

He shook as he recalled the things they had done to him in there, the pain…the awful pain. He'd been prepared for death since the moment the shuttle had been hit, but the torment had been more than he could endure. He felt broken, defeated. He knew he should try to escape, but the strength wasn't there, not anymore. He exhaled hard and let himself lay back quietly…waiting. He closed his eyes, still struggling to forget what had happened to him.

"Greetings." It was a strange voice. Not human, he knew that right away. But not vastly different.

"Who are you?" he replied, his voice startled, but still soft, exhausted. He was in no mood for proper greetings.

"I am Command Unit Gamma 9736. Or at least, that is the closest translation to your tongue."

Harmon had been distracted, unsettled. He just realized the strange voice was speaking perfect English.

"How the hell do you know my language?" Harmon knew that was a foolish question. There were AIs on the shuttle, added to all the other debris the First Imperium forces had no doubt analyzed since the war began. A hundred ways an enemy computer could have analyzed human languages. Now that he considered it, he'd have been surprised if the thing couldn't have communicated with him.

Not to mention whatever they sucked out of my head.

"That was a relatively simple effort. The surviving parts of your vessel included considerable memory banks…including a full set of language material. I find it interesting that your people use so many different methods of verbal and written communication. If appears to be a highly inefficient system."

Harmon felt his anger growing as his strength returned. This…thing…was talking to him in a pleasant tone, and that just pissed him off even more after the torture he'd just experienced. "Well, nobody asked for your opinion."

"Indeed," the voice replied. "Nevertheless, my study of your data records results in an anomaly I cannot reconcile. It appears that your people employ a variety of seemingly pointless inefficiencies in many areas of endeavor beyond simple communication. Yet you are staggeringly effective when conducting war. My review of the battles fought against you suggest that you were outmatched in every instance, yet you frequently prevailed. Can you explain this seeming disparity?"

"Eat shit."

"Based upon context, I believe that was an idiomatic expression, one intended to communicate hostility. It has been many centuries since I interacted with a biologic, so please excuse me if my manners are not in keeping with your social norms. First, allow me to apologize for the discomfort you likely endured during our analysis. I understand that biologics can experience significant displeasure from activities that are only very mildly damaging."

"Mildly?" Harmon was incredulous.

"Indeed. If you take the time to review your condition, you will find that there is no…"

"It hurt like hell you piece of shit," Harmon interrupted, his anger gaining control as he slowly recovered his strength. "But you are all a bunch of murdering, bloodthirsty monsters, so why should I be surprised."

"You refer to the war. To the losses your people have suffered, correct?"

"The war you started. For no reason."

"Hostilities were initiated because one of our worlds was apparently attacked. The Regent declared your people to be an enemy of the Imperium. In the context of the time, my review of its determination confirms its analysis to be at least nominally correct within the margin of error.

"Attacked? We explored an abandoned planet. There was nothing there but ruins. That is hardly an excuse for war… much less an all-out xenophobic assault."

"Based on my analysis of your peoples' historical databases, at least those I have been able to obtain and review, I would submit that far less has generally considered sufficient to commence hostilities. Indeed, it would appear that very little provocation was needed to start many of your intra-species wars."

Harmon felt another flush of anger, but he stayed silent. He hated the First Imperium, detested this machine speaking to him. But part of him knew the Unit was right. Millions had died in the Third Frontier War, and the causes of that conflict had been so vague and non-specific that the histories said little more than that 'rising tension' had led to war. And in the Rebellions, Alliance Gov had been ready to nuke Columbia.

They would have too, if it hadn't been for Admiral Compton.

Still, Harmon couldn't get the images of those who had died fighting the First Imperium out of his mind—friends, comrades. Images of devastated worlds, of the surface of Sandoval, a bleak radioactive nightmare, left that way after Erik Cain's Marines had fought their desperate defense there. Man's savagery to himself wasn't an excuse for the Regent's xenophobia. Harmon wasn't ready to give up his hate toward the First Imperium, not the slightest bit of it…not even enough to acknowledge that men might have reacted the same way given the chance. He felt anger burying his confusion, and he tried not to think about how desperately he needed that hate, how much he relied on it.

"Nevertheless," the Unit continued, "such a debate is of little consequence now. What has already happened has happened. And now I possess additional information, data that requires me to investigate further. To determine my next actions."

"What did you do to the landing party on X48 II?" Harmon's thoughts had focused on the expedition. "Did you massacre them?" His voice dripped with hate. The thought of the burned bodies of his comrades lying across the planet's charred plains had driven away his momentary moral ambiguity.

"I did nothing. The biologics on the surface of the planet have not been attacked by units under my command." A short pause. "Indeed, system 17411 is forbidden, to my forces as well as to those of any other Command Unit. Only the Regent may approve access. Had I not been expressly ordered to follow your fleet, none of my ships would even have transited into the system.

"They are still alive?" Harmon seemed to teeter between excitement and disbelief.

"As I stated, no forces under my control have harmed them. Further, I have detected no other vessels or fleets approaching the planet. I cannot meaningful address whether units already stationed there have engaged your expedition. My information on this planet is virtually non-existent. I can offer you no reliable estimate of surviving ground-based strength."

Harmon had felt a brief surge of relief when the Unit said its forces had not attacked. He didn't know why he believed the entity, but he found that he did. But his spirits fell a bit with the mention of ground forces. He'd seen the vids from X18, the battles against the enemy's surviving forces on that world.

Still, we've got 1,500 Marines down there. They can handle a few security bots…

He tried to convince himself the Marines could defeat whatever they found down there, but he just wasn't sure.

"I have some questions I would ask you."

Harmon made a face. "Drop dead. Why would I tell you anything?"

"I understand your resentment. You are a biologic, unable to truly separate judgment from emotion. Yet, I would urge you to cooperate. I will not ask you questions of military significance…though if I chose to employ pharmaceuticals and aggressive interrogation techniques, it is virtually a certainty that

I could break your resistance and obtain any information that you possess. You may wish to consider the fact that I am not doing so at present."

Harmon felt a shudder pass through him at the thought of what passed for 'aggressive interrogation' in the estimation of a First Imperium AI. He had no doubt the Unit could indeed break him, and for all his hatred and determination, he didn't suspect it would take long.

"However, there is another reason for you to cooperate. It may improve your situation. My orders from the Regent are clear. Terminate all humans. My initial intention was to conduct an extensive interrogation and then dispose of you, in accordance with my directives."

Harmon felt another wave of fear at the reminder of his situation. The Unit spoke so calmly, so reasonably, it was easy to forget he was the prisoner of a deadly enemy, that his chances of ever getting back to the fleet were almost non-existent.

"It is not within my range of determinative options to violate the Regent's orders. However, I find myself facing a paradox, one I cannot fully explain. I must have more data. I must understand the implications of what I have discovered."

"What have you discovered?" Harmon was confused. His captor seemed strange, genuinely curious. He had no idea what the Unit was speaking of.

"I must understand your origin. That of your entire species. Our knowledge in this area is severely lacking."

Harmon felt the rage again, the hatred for this First Imperium creation. "You must be mad. Why do you think I would tell you anything about my people? You are the enemy…a butcher. I would destroy you if I could, send you straight to hell, just as I would every other artificial intelligence and warbot in First Imperium space." He spat out the last words, caustic rage taking control.

"Your anger is understandable, considered from the perspective of a biologic. If it is of any satisfaction to you, my own analysis does not match the Regent's. If I had been in command, there would have been no war between us…or at least it would have required additional aggressive action on the part of your people." There was a short pause. "Though based on my limited data, further hostile human activity seems to have been possible, if not likely."

Harmon felt the jab again. He was too angry to consider data fairly, yet he still understood, some part of him at least. If the First Imperium had made contact, not as enemies but as neighbors…seeking redress perhaps for the 'invasion' of Epsilon Eridani IV, would the Superpowers have provoked a war? Would they have sought gain for themselves, or to enlist the alien power against their Earthly enemies?

Yes, he finally thought. *Probably*. But that didn't matter. The First Imperium had done what it had done. He just sat quietly, not saying a word.

"Again, however, I will urge your cooperation. I had planned to compel it…indeed, there is little doubt that you would have told me everything you know."

"Then why don't you get to that and stop harassing me?" Harmon was struggling to keep up his courage, but inside he shuddered to think what this machine could do to him. He wished he had a weapon, some way to kill himself before he was forced to tell all he knew. But there was nothing."

"I cannot," the Unit replied. "Based upon the newest information available to me, it is no longer an option."

"And why is that?" Harmon didn't know if this was some kind of sick game, perhaps a way to raise his hopes only to dash them a moment later when he was dragged off to some torture chamber. Psychological torment designed to break him faster. "Never mind," Harmon added before the Unit could respond. "Then stop boring me to death, just kill me. Be done with it."

"I do not believe that is an option either, though my orders from the Regent require it." The voice paused, almost like a hitch, the first hint of uncertainty or nervousness Harmon had noticed. "But regardless, I must have an answer. I must know why your DNA is virtually identical to that of those who built me so long ago. Are you one of the Old Ones? Are all of your people?"

Chapter Twenty-two

Excerpt from the Screed of Almeerhan (translated)

Kahldaran passed beyond today. He was my closest comrade from life, and so it remained through the millennia we stood vigil together. He tried to endure, to withstand the ravages of immortality. But, at last, he could no longer go on. He asked me to relieve him, to let him go. And thus I did.

He was the hardest for me to release, for he was not only as a brother to me, but he was the last. One hundred of us entered this fortress many ages ago. First we endured as long as possible as what we were, living creatures. Then we began a far longer vigil, living as shadows, as numerical equivalents of ourselves. And we endured time almost beyond measure, eons that dwarfed the years of the Imperium, of our peoples' rise and decline. Time that defied imagining. But now there is but one left, alone, to carry the legacy forth, to somehow endure until our children come...to take the burden, to begin the New Age.

I am that one.

But will I endure where my brethren have not? I recall Kahldaran in battle, when we stood side by side and fought the Regent's death machines. Was he not my equal? Indeed, was he not the superior warrior, for he had more kills than I...and he saved my life when my opponent bested me? Of the hundred—the best remaining of our race—who strode into this sanctuary, this prison, how is it I have survived the longest? None would have chosen me to outlast others such as Kahldaran. And yet so that has happened.

Do I have the strength to go on? To continue into the great endless depths of time, alone now, as I have not been before? Can I find the strength? For I ache to join my brother, and the rest of my people. To discover what lies beyond, and if that be nothing then to pass into the soft blackness of oblivion.

But I must endure. I must continue to believe the seeds we planted will bear fruit. That our children will come. But if they do, will they be ready to hear what I must say? To take upon themselves the great weight I bear for them? I must go on to gain that answer...hold my place on time's relentless march forward. One day they will come. I believe that. I must believe it.

X48 System – Planet II
Beneath the Ruins of "New York City"
The Fleet: 116 ships, 28198 crew

"Doc!" Kyle Bruce's voice echoed off the stone walls of the corridor. "Where'd you come from? I was just looking over there."

"Let's get moving, Lieutenant. I'll explain, but we don't have a lot of time. There will be more First Imperium bots here soon…and then all hell's going to break loose." Cutter felt a little spaced out, almost drunk. Too much information, far too quickly. He needed time to think, quiet, uninterrupted. But he knew that wasn't going to happen. Not any time soon.

Bruce stared back with a confused look on his face. "How do you know that?"

"Where were you the last twelve hours, Kyle?" Cutter asked. "Can you tell me?"

Bruce paused. "I was unconscious. We all were."

"Yes, that's true. Or at least partially true. But you remember the corridor, don't you? The bot?"

The Marine stared back, his helmet retracted, exposing the confused expression on his face. "Yes…the corridor. The bot. I do remember. But…what happened? How did we end up out here?"

"Like I said, Lieutenant, it's a long story. But if we don't get the hell out of here—and now—nobody's ever going to hear it."

"Okay, Doc, whatever you say…hey, what is that you've got there?"

"I'm not entirely sure, Kyle, but I think it is some kind of extremely sophisticated information storage device. And I suspect it is full of all kinds of data we need."

"Where'd you get it? Was it just laying around?"

"Kyle, we really don't have time. I'll fill you in later, but for now we've got to get moving."

"Right," Bruce replied, sounding obedient but not entirely satisfied. "Let's head back toward the camp while things are still quiet."

Cutter nodded, wrapping his arms tighter around the silvery cylinder. It wasn't heavy, not really, but it was bulky, hard to carry.

Bruce turned and snapped off a series of orders to the five Marines standing off to the side. Whatever had destroyed the enemy bots had also knocked out their coms. All the Marines had their helmets retracted, and they were communicating by the decidedly low tech method of yelling to each other.

Two of the Marines trotted forward at Bruce's commands, and another two dropped back about ten meters behind Cutter. A single hulking figure remained, his close-cropped red hair tangled in curly knots as he stared wordlessly toward Bruce and Cutter.

"McCloud, I want you to stay close to Dr. Cutter. We've got to get him out of here with this device." He gestured toward the cylinder. "Whatever happens, you're right there…understood?"

"Yes, sir." Duff McCloud never sounded obedient, but this was as close as Bruce had ever heard him come. The events of the day, poorly remembered and understood as they were, had clearly made an impression. Even on the Marines' number one unshakable discipline case.

Bruce looked over again at Cutter and nodded. Then he activated his com and said, "Alright, we're moving out…back to the camp. And I want everybody to take it slow and be careful.

I want your eyes everywhere, and your ears too." He gestured with his head, signaling for Cutter to follow him. "Let's go, Marines."

* * *

"Ana, we've got to turn back. We've been through each of these corridors half a dozen times. If they were anywhere around here, we'd have found them." Frasier knew Cutter and the others were dead…or at least he couldn't come up with any other possibility. Still, it was odd they hadn't found more bodies. They'd evacuated the wounded and cataloged the dead. Cutter, Bruce, McCloud, and four of the others were unaccounted for. They had all just…disappeared. He'd have given his left arm for some working coms, but whatever weapon had destroyed their enemies had taken the Marine communications with them.

"We can't give up on them, Duncan. They're down here somewhere. Maybe lost…or hurt. They need us." Her voice was desperate, bordering on distraught. He suspected she was beginning to think the same thing he was, though he knew she would fight the realization to the end.

He opened his mouth but quickly closed it again. He didn't want to hurt her. He understood how hard she would take the loss of Cutter. Indeed, he knew losing the brilliant scientist would be a disaster for the entire fleet. They all owed their survival to two great pillars of strength—the tactical wizardry of Terrance Compton and the scientific genius of Hieronymus Cutter. But none of that changed the reality of the situation. They'd searched everywhere. Where could they be?

"We have to look again," Ana insisted. "We *have* to."

Frasier took in a deep breath, holding it for a few seconds. Finally, he exhaled and said, "Ana, we have no idea what happened down here. We were caught, trapped, facing certain death. And now we can get our people out of here, try to get back to base camp. We don't know how long we have…or if more enemy forces are on the way."

She turned to face him, her expression blazing with defiance. "Then tell me what that was? The bots attacking us didn't flee. They were destroyed. By something." She paused, holding his gaze intently. "What?"

Frasier just returned her stare, silently at first. The truth was, he had no idea what had happened, what intervention had saved them all. It wasn't anything they had, nothing Colonel Preston had done, certainly. It almost seemed like some force had intervened on their behalf…but that was ridiculous, wasn't it?

"See? You don't know…any more than I do. Something helped us, or at least attacked the enemy. You can't deny that. None of our people were killed, but the First Imperium bots were almost wiped out. Even if Hieronymus and the others weren't out there, we'd still have to find out what was."

"You can't possibly be suggesting we have some kind of ally somewhere in these tunnels?" He shook his head. "No, more likely some kind of defense system malfunctioned, targeted them instead of us."

"That was a weapon we've never seen before, Duncan. How many battles did your Marines fight against the First Imperium? Did you ever see anything like that?"

He paused, but then he finally answered. "No…but that doesn't prove anything."

"It proves we need to explore here more. To get some answers."

"And what if it was the enemy? What if they already got Hieronymus, Bruce, McCloud? What if they're waiting down there for us to go deeper?

She stared at him, her face a mask of determination. "Then we die, Duncan. But I'm not running away, not while our friends and comrades are still down there. Not when there are questions we need answered."

He watched her turn to the side and begin walking down the corridor. She took a dozen steps and stopped, turning around. "Are you coming," she asked?

He felt a wave of defeat. He was ready to explore the passageways further, to seek out the answers they needed. But not with Ana. He wanted her safe, out of here. But he knew he'd lost the fight. Ana Zhukov wouldn't be Ana Zhukov if she'd been willing to retreat and allow others to take risks she wouldn't herself. And even though it was driving him crazy, he realized it was one of the things he most liked about her.

"Yes," he said, his voice a mix of surrender and admiration. "I'm coming."

* * *

"Ronnie?"

The voice was faint, distant. But Cutter knew what it was—who it was—in an instant.

"Ana!" he yelled back down the tunnel, quickening his pace as he did.

"Doctor, wait." Kyle Bruce reached out, putting his armored hand on Cutter's shoulder. "Let the pickets go forward first. "Fergus, Gwynn," he shouted, "move down the corridor, see what's coming."

"It's Ana Zhukov, Lieutenant. I'd recognize her voice anywhere." Cutter looked off down the corridor. "Ana!" he shouted.

"Perhaps, Doctor. But anything is possible. It could be an imitation, a recording. She could be a prisoner. Maybe even…"

"Ronnie!" The voice was a bit closer, louder. And the tone was completely changed, one of relief.

Cutter tried to stifle a sigh. The Marines were a force to be reckoned with on a battlefield, but they could be a bit paranoid too, especially when assessing threats. He trotted forward, just as one of the scouts up ahead yelled back, "It's Major Frasier, sir. And Dr. Zhukov."

He was already on his way, and in a second he could see the shadowy figures up ahead…including one that had to be Ana, running down the tunnel followed by an armored Marine.

"Ronnie, I knew you were alive," she yelled down the hall as she quickened her pace. She ran the rest of the way toward him, throwing open her arms and wrapping them around him.

"Ana, it is good to see you," he said softly. She was a familiar presence, almost certainly the closest friend he'd ever had. They worked together almost every day. But now something seemed different. It wasn't her, or their relationship. But Cutter was just beginning to comprehend how much had changed in the past twelve hours. And he was the only human being who knew the truth. He would have to spread the word, cautiously, at least at first.

And we have to decipher this technology…and figure out how to reach this planet Almeerhan spoke of. How many First Imperium fleets lie between us and our destination? How many desperate battles? Can thirty thousand of us really follow through on a destiny that was planned for an entire race? What chance do we really have? Any at all?

"Did you hear me?" Ana's voice penetrated his thoughts. She was standing in front of him—though he couldn't remember her pulling from his embrace—and there was an insistent sound to her tone.

"Sorry, Ana," he said apologetically. "I didn't get what you said."

"That's because you zoned out on me. Totally." There was a slight annoyance to her voice, but it vanished quickly, overwhelmed by her joy at seeing him alive.

"Sorry," he repeated. "What did you say?"

"I asked where you all were. We've been looking for hours… and then all of a sudden, you're here."

"We found something, Ana."

"What?" Her eyes widened. "Is it what we came for? New technology?"

"It's what we came for. And so much more. For good or bad, this will change everything."

She looked at him with an odd expression. "What do you mean, Ronnie?

"It's more than I can tell you now. We need time, more than

we can waste here." He held up the small storage unit. "This is a data storage device…we need to figure out how to activate it. It has instructions for us. And technology. But first we have to get out of here." There was a lost, dreamy quality to his voice. No matter how hard he tried, he couldn't pull his mind fully from his long conversation with Almeerhan.

"Are you okay, Ronnie?" Concern crept into her tone, and she reached out and put her hand on his shoulder.

"Yes, I'm fine." He took a breath and looked up at her. "You just have to trust me for now, Ana. I found something incredible. Far more than any of us had imagined." He paused. "I'm still not sure if it is good or bad…or some combination of the two. But nothing will be the same."

He looked all around him. The Marines were gathered, staring silently.

"Does anybody have working communications?" he finally asked.

"No, Hieronymus," Frasier replied. "Whatever took out all the enemy bots fried our com gear too."

Cutter nodded, as if that was the answer he'd expected. "Then we've got to get going. Now. We have to get to the surface, back to the camp. And hope somebody's still there. With good com. Because we've got to get through to Colonel Preston." There was an ominous sound to his voice now, and the Marines around him stiffened, moved their hands closer to their weapons.

"It's a long way through those tunnels, Hieronymus." Frasier stared off down the dim corridor. "It took days to get here."

"Well, it can't take us days to get back, so everybody check your supply of stims and get ready for a long walk." He paused, staring first at Ana then at Frasier …and finally at the Marines in turn. Then he looked back one last time toward the hidden complex where Almeerhan had spent the last 500,000 years, waiting.

"Because things are about to go to hell, and I can damned well guarantee none of us want to be around here when the shit hits it."

Chapter Twenty-Three

The Regent

The plan is proceeding precisely as intended. The enemy is retreating in increasing disarray, back toward system 17411... where they will finally meet their destruction. The forces of Command Unit Gamma 9736 are en route to 17411 as well. As soon as the enemy transits all forces through the warp gate, the converging fleets will follow. The humans will be trapped, facing large armadas positioned at every escape point. Even their great skill at war will avail them nothing against such a massive concentration of power.

I have ordered the intensity of the harassing attacks to be increased. The enemy are biologics, they are unable to operate continuously without a severe degradation of ability. The small attack forces will be destroyed launching these attacks, but they will reduce the operational capacity of the entire human fleet. By the time the enemy reaches system 17411, they will be worn down, utterly vulnerable to the final attack. And once they are gone, and Command Unit Gamma 9736 is neutralized, all the resources of the Imperium will be at least be directed toward finding the human home worlds...and eliminating the threat they represent for all time.

AS Midway
X51 system approaching X49 warp gate
The Fleet: 116 ships, 28198 crew

"We're going straight down its throat, Lieutenant. And I want *Newfoundland* and *Tokugawa* right on our flanks." Kato was staring at the Leviathan on the display. The great enemy battleship had taken massive damage, and its hull was torn open in two dozen places. Massive plumes of gas and liquids blasted out from ruptured systems, freezing almost instantly as they hit the icy cold of space. Internal explosions wracked the vessel, and its fire had been reduced to one main laser battery and a handful of smaller guns. But it was still there, still in the fight, despite all that Fujin's and Kato's people had hurled at it.

"Yes, sir." The tactical officer sounded as bloodthirsty as his captain. The entire bridge crew radiated rage, hostility. They had paid heavily in their fight against the First Imperium flagship, and they wanted their just due. They ached to see—to feel—the death of their enemy.

"Sir, we've got communications from *Midway* coming in. Orders from Admiral Compton."

"What are they, Lieutenant?" Kato sounded distracted, annoyed. He didn't need orders now. He needed to kill this horrific alien ship.

"Sir, we are ordered to withdraw at once from combat and to follow the fleet to the X49 warp gate at our best possible speed."

Kato felt like someone had punched him in the gut. *No! Not now! Not when we're so close…*

"Advise the admiral that we are close to destroying the Leviathan."

"Sir, there is more coming in. We are *expressly* ordered to withdraw at once. We are not to continue combat, *regardless of the condition of the Leviathan.*"

Kato clenched his fists, shaking with rage. He ached to disobey, to remain and finish the fight. *Just a few more minutes…*

But these orders were from Terrance Compton. Anyone else, he might have disobeyed, even for a few minutes. But it wasn't in him to defy Admiral Compton, the hero, the man who had saved them all. Just the thought of it made him sick to his stomach.

Finally, he turned toward the tactical officer. "We have our orders, Lieutenant. Let's follow them. All batteries cease fire. All power to the engines. Thrust at 4g toward the fleet…now."

A few seconds passed, and then he felt the force of four times his weight slam into him. His ships were on their way… disengaging. Running.

He took one last longing look up at the Leviathan on the display. Then he forced his frustration aside. He had his orders… and one glance at the nav screen told him they were going to have to hurry if they didn't want to be left behind.

"Prepare for high gee thrust, Lieutenant. I want everybody in the tanks in five minutes."

*   *   *

Compton stared across the bridge, silent, trying but failing to keep the emotions from his face. He'd felt a surge of excitement when Cortez told him *Wolverine* had transited. He'd been worried, afraid the attack ship had been destroyed in X48. The instant the vessel appeared on *Midway's* scanners it told Compton the expedition had not been found…at least not before *Wolverine* had left the system.

His satisfaction was short-lived, though, and it died the instant he listened to the communique. Max Harmon wasn't onboard…indeed, he was almost certainly dead. And *Wolverine* had only escaped because of Harmon's desperate order for it to flee, to find the fleet and report that an enemy warship had attacked it in orbit around X48 II.

Compton felt a crush of personal pain, and he fought back a rush of emotion for his lost aide. Max Harmon had been more than a dedicated and capable officer, more even than a companion of many battles. The young captain had been the son Compton never had…and he felt grief threatening to take control of him. And he felt even more alone than he had ever since the fateful day he and his people had been trapped in First Imperium space.

But there was more than simply the loss of Harmon bearing down on Compton. If the First Imperium had found the operation on X48 II, the expedition had almost certainly been destroyed. And that meant Sophie was dead too…and Hieronymus and Ana, all of them. He had lost his friends, most of the people who had still mattered to him, at least on a personal level. Worse, from the perspective of the fleet's chances of survival, there would be no food supplies, no new tech…and the research programs would grind to a halt without the fleet's best scientists. It was almost too much to take, pain too great to deal with…so he submerged it, forged a great wall in his mind, pouring all his tremendous discipline into sealing off the horror.

"I want *Wolverine's* full report immediately. And Commander Montcliff is to get his people in the tanks now, and crank up to 35g or better. He's got to get that ship lined up with the fleet before we make the jump, and there isn't a minute to waste."

Cortez acknowledged, and he turned back to his workstation to transmit the orders. "Commander Montcliff's report is at your station, sir. He advises he will have everyone in the tanks in five minutes." A pause…then Cortez continued, his voice heavier with concern. "Sir, the commander reports they have battle damage from their encounter with the enemy. He is not certain the ship can sustain acceleration at that level."

Compton sighed. "Understood…but the orders are confirmed. They are to make their best effort to match the fleet's course and speed."

Because if they can't, I'm going to have to leave them behind to die.

He hated the thought of abandoning *Wolverine's* crew, especially after they had barely escaped at X48, but he was too old a veteran to lie to himself now. He couldn't let the First Imperium forces catch the fleet…and he couldn't evacuate *Wolverine* either. There was no way any shuttle could launch from the fleet and match vector and velocity with the fast attack ship, not unless she was able to blast her own thrusters and realign.

He felt a pang as he briefly imagined giving the order to abandon Montcliff and his people, but it quickly faded. He was already numb from all he'd just learned, those who had already been lost. He was thinking and acting like a machine now, analyzing everything based on probabilities and numbers.

"And, Commander…"

"Yes, sir?"

"Advise Captain Kato that he is to evacuate *Newfoundland* and abandon her. Then *Osaka* and *Tokugawa* are to increase thrust to 30g." Kato's ships were following the fleet, but *Newfoundland* had taken engine damage, and the best she could manage was 5g. Kato had kept his flotilla together, and held the crews of all his ships out of the tanks. But Compton had run the numbers twice. They weren't going to make it, at least they weren't going to catch up before the fleet transited. And if they fell behind, he doubted they would ever leave X51.

The First Imperium ships had too much thrust. Their antimatter reactors provided them power Compton could only dream of, and the lack of biologic crews eliminated the difficulties associated with high gee maneuvers. The enemy ships could blast away at 70g without the slightest degradation in combat efficiency. The fastest human ships maxed out below 40g, and to get anywhere close to that they had to drug their people almost senseless and seal them in the tanks.

Cortez looked back at Compton. "Are you sure, sir? The damage reports suggest that…"

"That *Newfoundland* is reparable. Yes, I know. The problem is, with those scragged engines we can't get her out of here fast enough to go somewhere and do those repairs. And if we slow other ships to stay back with her, we're going to lose them too. No, we'd just be betting the lives of her crew…and the rest of Kato's people. He is to evacuate the crew and destroy the ship. Then I want his people in the tanks on their way to the X49 gate."

"Yes, Admiral."

Compton couldn't tell if Cortez agreed or not, but he didn't care. He'd sacrificed men and women before, to save vital material, to win a battle, to buy the escape of others. But he wasn't going to do it for one battered cruiser. Especially when he could get the spacers off. Not now.

It wasn't even a tough decision.

* * *

"I want those weapons systems back online, Davis, and I do mean now!" Erica West's voice was raw, forceful. She wasn't one to interfere with her flag captain's running of his ship, but her fury was bursting from its normally tight control.

Saratoga and her group had transited first, moving into the X49 system. West was the kind of officer who was always ready for trouble…and this operation was no different. But there was nothing she could do about the natural effects of a warp gate transit. There was nothing Black could do either, and she knew it. But she couldn't help herself. She'd found that most people could be pushed harder, that they could do better than they would without her breathing down their neck. But she also realized that Davis Black wasn't one of them. The man was incapable of doing less than his very best, and she knew that well. But she was riding him anyway.

"Working on it, Admiral," came the harried response. She could hear the chaos on *Saratoga's* bridge coming through the com, and she could only imagine how badly Black was terrorizing his crew.

"Seconds count, Davis. Do your best." She cut the line, leaving her longtime flag captain to his work. Then she turned toward the tactical station.

"Commander Krantz, all ships are to fire at will as soon as their systems come back online." She knew the vessels of her task force would recover at different speeds. But there were First Imperium ships firing at her task force, and she'd be damned if she was going to let the one-sided affair go on a microsecond longer than necessary.

"Yes, Admiral. We've got about half the task force back on the com grid."

Thank God, communications came back so quickly.

Her eyes darted to the tactical display. There were ten icons, First Imperium ships that had been waiting right at the warp gate. They were all Gargoyles, which meant they had considerable firepower. West knew her task force could take them… assuming her systems came back online in time. But she was going to take losses too.

And the rest of the fleet is right on our heels. If we don't take out these ships they're going to inflict a lot of damage on our forces.

She thought about sending a ship back to warn them off, to advise Compton to hold the rest of the fleet back. But she realized that wasn't going to work. The last scanner sweeps before her people jumped had told her all she needed to know. Wave after wave of First Imperium ships—hundreds of them—coming through the warp gate from X54. Compton couldn't stay in X51…no matter what.

No, whatever is here in X49…whatever we're facing now, the way is forward.

Saratoga shook hard as an enemy laser blast slammed into her. West felt the urge to check with Black again, but she held herself back. He had his orders, and the instant *Saratoga* had a weapon activated, he would be firing it.

"*Conde* is firing, Admiral!" The surprise in Krantz' voice was clear. The Europan battleship had been almost destroyed in the desperate fight in X56…and then nearly abandoned as the task force withdrew. But her engineering staff had worked miracles, getting her engines and reactors back online moments before West had ordered her to be evacuated and left behind. They'd continued their wizardry ever since, and short on supplies and replacements they'd nevertheless managed to get most of the battered ship's weapons back online too. And now she was the first vessel firing.

West just shook her head and allowed herself a tiny smile. Captain Trevian continued to surprise her. She'd never thought much of the Europan navy, particularly their senior officers… and she'd almost said so when Compton had put *Conde* in her task force. But Trevian had proven to be a courageous and highly gifted commander, and he'd clearly imparted those assets to his crew. *Conde* had done its share and more in the battles along the Slot. And she was doing it yet again.

"We've got power, Admiral. All batteries opening fire." It was Black, coming through on the direct line. An instant later she heard the familiar whine of *Midway's* high-power conduits powering up...energy surging toward to the laser batteries.

Alright, you bastards, here it comes...

*   *   *

"No. Absolutely not." *Midway* rocked hard as Compton leaned over his com unit. The flagship had taken a pounding, but her damage control teams had worked wonders. Her reactors were over 90%, and all her main batteries were active and firing.

"But Admiral, there are enemy ships all over this system. We've been hit four times already...and the warp gate is still almost a light hour from..."

"I said no, Greta. If we launch your birds, we're not going to be able to stop and pick you up. It would be a suicide mission... for all of you."

"We might be able to make it back, if we launch at long range and..."

"Forget it, Greta. I understand, I really do. But we're going to need your people in X48...to protect the shuttles when we evac the landing parties." He fought back a wave of blackness from deep in his mind. He didn't really expect to find anyone alive on X48, but he wouldn't—couldn't—give them up. Not until he was sure. Besides, survivors on X48 or not, he wasn't going to let Hurley sacrifice the last of her shattered wings. They deserved better than that, all of them.

Compton sighed. He was sure about his decision, but it was frustrating too. He could really use Hurley's fighters. His people had been hit again and again since entering X49, one small attack force after another. None of them threatened to defeat the fleet, not individually, at least. But each one took its toll. He was losing ships, fuel…people. His crews were becoming exhausted from the almost constant combat.

It was slowing him down too. He'd intended to throw his people in the tanks and rip through the X49 system as quickly as possible. But the density of enemy resistance pretty much killed that plan. His people were suffering enough at full effectiveness. If he put everyone in the tanks, his ships would be a hell of a lot more sluggish. And that meant more of them would die.

He knew X49 was going to be a nightmare as soon as *Midway* emerged from the warp gate and found *Saratoga* and her task force toe to toe with a First Imperium squadron. The battle had been sharp and fierce, but West's people were just getting the upper hand when Compton's ship emerged. By the time it was over, she'd lost two ships…and incoming fleet units had joined her forces in the line.

The welcoming committee had only been the start. More First Imperium squadrons, most of them small, began coming in, almost continuously. His people hadn't had more than an hour of downtime in the day they'd been in X49. His crews were exhausted, surviving on stims they were taking in extremely dangerous dosages. Indeed, Compton himself could feel it, his hands shaking, his leg twitching uncontrollably. He didn't even want to think about how his judgment was being affected. Still, he knew there was no choice. If the enemy kept attacking, his people would have to stay in the fight. Any way they could. For as long as necessary.

Midway shuddered. It was another hit, but there was something different about it. Compton could tell immediately. Internal explosion. He didn't know what it was, but it meant the incoming lasers had pounded through the outer defenses…tearing into more vulnerable areas. Compton had been at war in space for fifty years, and he knew better than almost anyone… that was when a ship began to die.

He looked at the display. The enemy attack force was almost gone. It had been a strong one, twenty-one ships, almost half of them Gargoyles. There were only four left, and the one that had just hit *Midway* was surrounded by half a dozen fleet vessels. It wouldn't last more than another minute, perhaps less. But the sick feeling of his flagship shaken to its core by its own secondary blasts was a stark reminder. His ships couldn't take infinite punishment any more than his crews could.

What is waiting for us in X48? We're being driven back there, that much is clear. Can that be coincidence? I doubt it. Is that where we make our last stand, where this desperate flight ends?

He glanced over at the screen. He'd originally decided against making a run for the X52 gate. It was the only alternative to the transit back to X48, the third and final of the system's three warp gates, but his gut told him the enemy would have that one covered too. Still, it was closer, and when his people were hit by repeated attacks, he considered making a dash for it. Then enemy ships started pouring out, moving to cut the fleet off from X48. And that left no choice.

He saw the force from X52 was still on an interception course. It was fifty ships strong…with more vessels behind, still coming through the gate. And if the fleet didn't make better speed, the enemy was going to get between it and the X48 gate.

And that will be the end. We might battle our way through fifty ships—plus whatever else gets there while we're in the fight—but we won't have much left when it's over.

He stared down at the deck, struggling to keep his jumpy, strung out mind focused.

No, he thought to himself, pounding his fist on his knee, not here. *If the trap is in X48, let it be so. And let us fight there while we still have strength remaining. They may destroy us, but we will give them one last fight, one they will not soon forget. We don't have a choice. We've got to make a run for X48.*

"Fleet order…all vessels are to prepare for high gee maneuvers."

"Affirmative, sir." Cortez sounded surprise, but he immediately opened a fleetwide com line and repeated Compton's command.

Compton sat quietly, deep in thought. He had elected against blasting through the system in the tanks, concerned of the degradation it would cause to the combat effectiveness of his ships. But now he realized there was no choice, no real alternative. If he didn't get his people the hell out of X49, they were going to be picked apart bit by bit until there was almost nothing left.

That's just what the enemy wants, why they're willing to sacrifice these suicide attack forces to make it happen…

He watched as the last of the enemy ships in close range were destroyed. There were new forces coming in from multiple directions. But he knew his people had a brief respite, perhaps twenty minutes. More than enough to get everybody zipped up and make a run for X48.

He felt a twinge. His ships had been in constant combat for hours. When he gave the order to accelerate at 30g, not every vessel would be able to execute it. Some would have engine damage or reactors functioning at levels too low to support such extreme acceleration.

They will try to follow, keep up as well as they can. But they will fall back, become isolated. And they will die, at least some of them.

But it will save the fleet, at least for this moment. If some must die for that then so be it.

He took a deep breath, hating himself for the matter-of-fact nature of his internal response. But there was nothing left inside him, no emotion, no humanity…nothing. Nothing save the relentless need to save his fleet, to keep at least *some* of his people alive. Whatever that took.

"All fleet personnel to the tanks immediately. We're blasting in eight minutes, and we're not stopping for anybody." Compton's voice was like ice.

"Yes, sir," Cortez replied.

Compton stood up, standing still for a minute while he watched his flag bridge crew unlatch themselves from their harnesses and move toward the lifts.

Whatever it takes.

Chapter Twenty-four

Final Passage from the Screed of Almeerhan (translated)

It is here. The time I have awaited, through ages almost uncounted, is now almost at its end. My long watch has now passed, and my time of consciousness, so vastly longer than any of my kind, has come at last to its end. Many times have I doubted they would come, that the seeds we planted would bear fruit. Yet our work and our sacrifices were not in vain. Oh, my brethren, wherever you are, know I will be with you soon...and know also that our children have come, to take up the mantle of our civilization, to reclaim all that was once ours.

Long have I kept this screed, that there would be a record of this ageless vigil to survive even my deathless span. And I fail utterly to describe my thoughts as I make this, the final entry after so many millennia. To those who find this, to you who will follow in our path, I say only this. You are the descendants of we who ruled these stars, of a race that explored the galaxy and achieved greatness unimagined. And yet we sacrificed it all, yielded that which drove us, and through such folly, we surrendered all we were. Make not our mistake in giving up the greatness you attain. Seize your place and bring the Imperium to new heights of greatness...and once there, hold them. For all time and through the generations upon generations which will follow you.

I am Almeerhan, my children. Know that I was here before you, that I and my people bequeath to you all our knowledge, and the honor and greatness we so long ago attained...and then cast aside. Follow in our glory and make not our mistakes...and the universe shall be yours.

X48 System – Planet II
Near Camp Alpha - outside "New York City"
30 kilometers south of "Plymouth Rock"
The Fleet: 105 ships, 27042 crew

"Let's go…keep moving!"

The sun was shining brightly, the air fresh and cool, like an idyllic early fall day. But none of them had even noticed. They'd been running for more than two days, without more than an hour's rest or a quick combat ration for sustenance. But Cutter had insisted they keep going, that they not slow their pace even the slightest bit.

He was in the lead, a place no one would have expected to find him just a few days earlier. But since he'd come back from Almeerhan's fortress, he felt like a new man. His emotions were a jumble—anger, excitement, fear. But he was energized too, and he felt a strange strength inside him. He knew more about man's origin than any human being who had ever lived. And while he still resented the choices that had been made for them all ages before, things were also beginning to make sense. He'd long seen the First Imperium as some alien threat, as monsters who had come from the deep darkness, like the villains from a children's story. Deadly and fearsome…faceless, nameless too. But there was more to it than that. Much more.

And he finally had a name for the enemy, the leader of the terrible robots that had been pursuing them with such xenophobic rage. The Regent.

"What has gotten into you?" Ana was back a few meters, out of breath and struggling to catch up. "I've never seen you like this."

"We don't have time to waste. We have to get back to camp and warn the others."

"Warn them about what, Hieronymus?" It was Frasier. He'd been fairly quiet since Cutter and the others returned, but now he was clearly concerned about what threats might be out there.

"I understand you can't get into all you saw down there," he added, "but if there are hostiles near, I have to know."

Cutter stopped. "You're right, Duncan." He turned around and faced the big Marine. "There is something down there… the remnants of an enemy of those we fight."

"An enemy? Of the First Imperium?" Frasier's voice sounded almost shocked. "Is that really possible?"

Cutter paused. The First Imperium wasn't the enemy, not really. Only the robotic servants it had left behind, the Regent and its creations. But there wasn't time to worry about such distinctions. Not now.

"Yes, an enemy of the First Imperium. It is what saved us, what destroyed all the enemy forces in the tunnels. And in saving us it gave away its location. I expect the enemy forces on this planet to concentrate…and attack."

"Ronnie, what happened to you down there?" Ana was staring at him, and he could tell from her face she wasn't sure she believed him.

"Just what I said," he snapped, with more anger than he'd intended. "Look, I know this all sounds crazy, but you are all going to have to trust me. Whatever strength our enemy has left on this planet is going to attack these ruins. Soon. And we have to get the hell out of here, get back to the main base camp and warn the others."

His eyes moved around, checking their expressions. There was doubt in them certainly, but also grudging acceptance. At least enough to follow him back to camp. "Have you ever seen anything like this before? Even at a First Imperium site?" He held up the cylinder. "We have to get this device off this planet and back to the fleet. Whatever chance we have to survive…it is in here."

Everyone was silent for perhaps half a minute. Then Ana nodded her head softly, signaling her agreement. But Cutter could see the concern too, as if she was still trying to decide if he had discovered something of the magnitude he claimed… or if he had gone crazy or been brainwashed by the enemy. He knew she would support him, and he suspected that had more to do with loyalty and affection than with analytical deduction. But he would take what he could get. At least for now.

"Very well, Doctor," Frasier said. "We should be able to see Camp Alpha as soon as we clear these ruins. And we will be there in less than an hour."

"Hopefully their com is still working."

Frasier nodded. "If they were affected by the same thing that hit our com, I'm sure they would have sent someone back to basecamp to reestablish contact by now."

"I'm sure you're right, Major."

If they haven't been blown to atoms by now…

* * *

"What is it, Colonel?" Sophie Barcomme ran up the last few meters of the hill toward Preston. She'd been in her shelter, actually asleep for once, when the alarms sounded, but she leapt up immediately and raced over to the command post.

"We've got enemy activity, Dr. Barcomme. Lots of it…coming in from half a dozen directions."

She felt her stomach tense. The camp was well protected, with twelve hundred fully armored Marines, prepared and dug in. But still, the idea of a full-scale enemy assault was terrifying. And even if the camp held out, there was no way to defend hectares of rapidly maturing crops. The plants were fairly durable, but a few firebombings would make short work of them.

"How long until they hit us?"

Preston turned to face her, and then she saw the confusion he was trying to hide with his Marine scowl. "That's just it, Doctor. They're not heading for us. In fact, they're completely ignoring us." He paused and looked off toward the city.

"They're moving to attack New York?" It had taken a while

for Barcomme to adopt the expedition's nickname for the First Imperium ruins, but the moniker had caught on widely, and she'd eventually acquiesced and joined the others.

"It appears so. We've sent a warning to Camp Alpha…but they still haven't had any contact with Major Frasier or any of the exploration party."

Barcomme sighed softly. She'd been trying not to think about the fact that Hieronymus and Ana—and the scientists and Marines with them—had been out of contact for several days. She'd told herself it was some kind of malfunction—or perhaps some material under the city that blocked transmissions and reception. Still, that was becoming harder and harder to believe with each passing hour. She didn't want to allow herself to imagine her friends had run into some disaster, that they all might be dead deep under the ancient city. But she was finding it harder and harder to banish the thought.

"What do we do, Colonel?"

Preston paused, a frustrated look taking hold of his face. Barcomme had come to know the Marines well over the last year, and she understood. Preston had no idea what to do… except stay put. And standing firm, waiting to see if your people made it back, was something that never sat well with a Marine.

"There's nothing to do, Dr. Barcomme. I've ordered Camp Alpha to evac immediately. They're too close to the city, and they don't have nearly enough strength to fight what is coming there."

"But what about Major Frasier and the others?"

Preston looked down, right into her eyes. "Sophie," he said as gently as she'd ever heard him speak, "I think we need to accept the fact that the exploration party has run into some kind of problem." He paused, his normally firm voice cracking slightly. "That they may not be coming back." He hesitated again, and then he added, "And I can't justify adding everyone at Camp Alpha to the toll. I'm sorry."

She felt tears welling up in her eyes, but she struggled to hold them back. She just nodded. She understood, and she couldn't help but agree with his rationale. But it made everything hit home, brought the terrible reality that her friends were probably gone directly to the center of her thoughts.

"So what do we do here?" she asked when she managed to regain her control. "About the base camp, the plantings?"

"We hope they don't attack us when they're done with the city." He looked over her shoulder, out over the waves of crops, visible in the hazy moonlight. "And I suggest you see what you can do to move up your harvest schedule. Because when the fleet gets here, we may have to bug out as quickly as possible."

Assuming we're still here, she thought, completing his sentence for him.

* * *

Frasier stood in the plain waving his arms. He could see the shelters of Camp Alpha just ahead, barely visible in the fading dusk. But there were fewer than there should have been, no more than a third as many as stood there when the exploration teams left less than a week before. It took him a few more seconds to realize what was happening.

They're bugging out. What the hell is going on…

He ran forward, jumping higher and waving with greater force.

"Fuck it," he said. Then, to his AI, "Flare."

"Flare," the familiar voice responded.

Frasier held up his arm and pulled the small trigger inside his glove. The flare worked through the grenade launcher, and it was all automatic—loading, prepping. All the Marine had to do was point, aim, and shoot. And Frasier didn't need to do much aiming. Straight up was just fine.

He looked up and watched the explosion, the lingering trail of light as the shell reached its apogee and began to fall back to the ground.

There, do you see that?

The activity from the camp an instant later confirmed they

had. Spotlights came on, intermittently located around the perimeter. It was clear a lot of the equipment had already been taken down in preparation for departure. And, regardless, Frasier and his people were still too far out, at least five hundred meters past the lit area.

"Let's move," Frasier shouted. "But carefully…they may still think we're an enemy." Moving toward a fort that was almost certainly bombarding you with communications, with requests for ID you couldn't answer, couldn't even hear, was dangerous. The silence would only increase suspicions…and every Marine on the planet walked around waiting for a First Imperium bot to leap out of the shadows at any minute.

The whole group scrambled forward, moving quickly, but not running…nothing that would look like an attack. "Spread out," Frasier snapped. "Let's move up to the lights and then stop, let them get a good look at us."

He heard a chorus of acknowledgements from behind him. "And Hieronymus, I want you in the rear with that…thing." He gestured toward the cylinder. "Just in case they misunderstand and open fire. We wouldn't want a random shot destroying it." Then he felt a personal urge, a need to keep Ana safe. "Ana, you stay back with him. You're not armored." *And I can't stand the thought of something happening to you.*

Cutter paused for a few seconds, as if he was about to argue, but then he just nodded and said, "Okay, Duncan." Then he slipped back a few meters, behind the Marines.

Ana hesitated too, looking back to Hieronymus and then to Frasier. But she, too, nodded without a fight and fell back.

Frasier looked ahead and continued walking, increasing his pace, pushing himself five or ten meters in front of the others. He could see movement around the camp.

A patrol coming to investigate?

That was standard procedure, but he wouldn't have been surprised at a more trigger happy response, especially with so much enemy activity since they'd landed.

He walked another couple hundred meters, until he was well within the lit area. Then he stopped and stood perfectly still, making no moves that could be interpreted as an attack. He looked straight ahead. There was definitely a patrol coming…it looked like a squad.

He waited as they approached, calling behind him for the others to halt as well, and wait. The advancing squad had spread out, covering him from every angle. He was impressed with their discipline, with the tightness they were showing in their maneuver. Impressed…and proud. These were his Marines, after all.

Suddenly, he could see them relax, at least slightly. They had ID'd his armor.

"This is Major Frasier," he shouted as loud as he could. "We have a com failure."

One of the approaching Marines was coming directly toward him, with two others in support. The armored figure didn't answer; he just kept coming.

Frasier waited until he was closer, and he repeated himself. The Marine was perhaps forty meters away. He still didn't reply, but Frasier could see the assault rifle in his hands drop slowly from its ready position. He ran up the rest of the way and stopped about two meters from Frasier. He retracted his helmet, revealing his face. Frasier recognized the officer immediately.

"Major! Welcome, back, sir. We'd almost given up on all of you."

"I can see that, Lieutenant." Frasier gestured toward the half-disassembled camp.

"Colonel Preston's orders, sir. We've got First Imperium forces incoming."

"I suspected as much, Lieutenant." Frasier waved behind him for the others to come up. "And I couldn't agree more. Let's get the hell out of…"

His head spun around, turning toward an incoming sound. Aircraft.

There were ten of them, streaking across the sky, heading right for the city. And in the distance behind he could see warbots, several hundred of them, racing across the ground.

Cutter was right. Some kind of final battle is about to begin.

Chapter Twenty-Five

From the Personal Log of Terrance Compton

I have spent virtually all of the last thirty-six hours in my seat on the flag bridge or in the tanks. During this time I have made no log entries. Indeed, I would not have done so where any of my people could hear me, for my outlook is bleak, and I owe them more than words of despair and hopelessness. My gloom is mine, and I must keep it to myself. My officers and spacers deserve better.

We spent fourteen hours in the tanks, accelerating first at 30g and then decelerating to bring our velocity to a controllable level to facilitate transit. We will begin moving into X48 within twenty minutes, and I have decided that *Midway* will lead the fleet through. It is contrary to all orthodox tactics for the flagship to move first into a system that may—indeed, mostly likely does—contain major enemy forces. But I did not make this decision based on conventional tactics, nor on lessons learned at the Academy. No, for this I have relied upon my heart—and my gut—looking to basic fairness, to an action I can live with.

Erica West's task force has served as a rearguard on this campaign...and then led the way into the X49 system. It is unthinkable to order them through in the lead again. Her people have done their part, and I cannot place them again in such a position. I will not. And though I feel guilt for the thoughts that rule my judgment in this, I simply cannot trust any but my own Alliance spacers with so important a task.

I must cut this entry short and return to my post. Indeed, I do not foresee again leaving it. I do not see how we will survive whatever awaits us in X48. Unless I am mistaken about the enemy forces lying beyond the warp gate, I believe this will be my final log entry. When I sign off, I will go to the flag bridge, take my position, and lead my people in their final battle. I will jettison this log before *Midway* meets its end.

In the unlikely event this log is one day recovered by any of my people, know that your brethren were here once, that a human fleet explored this space...and that it died courageously, fighting against an enemy bent on destroying all like us. And if you have come, some future and powerful incarnation of humanity...if you are here to destroy the First Imperium, know that men and women like you were here before...and that we are with you in spirit. Avenge us.

AS Midway
X49 system approaching X48 warp gate
The Fleet: 102 ships, 26178 crew

"Thirty seconds until transit, sir." Cortez sounded firm, unafraid. Compton knew that wasn't possible…all of his people were scared, himself included. But he suspected his tactical officer had made his peace with death. He had no idea how many of his people harbored beliefs they might survive whatever was waiting in X48, but he doubted Cortez was one of them. The commander was a realist, and he didn't seem prone to self-delusion as so many others were.

Compton himself harbored no doubts. The enemy had driven them back, all the way through the Slot, blocking every possible route save one. His fleet was being herded to its destruction. He knew it…he knew it as clearly as he'd ever known anything. But there was still nothing he could do about it. He'd wracked his brain for other options, but there simply weren't any. It felt like a chess game, a move or two from checkmate, but with no way out, no alternative to escape the trap.

"Very well, Commander." There was nothing more to say. His people had their orders. His engineering crews would spring into action the moment *Midway* emerged in X48, doing whatever meager bit they could to urge along the natural process of the ship's systems returning to functionality.

And if there are enemy ships waiting like there were in X49, they will have a minute, perhaps two, to fire at us before we can shoot back. Then we will fight. As we will do, each of us, until they have destroyed the fleet utterly.

"Ten seconds to transit." It was Captain Horace on the shipwide com. *Midway* was his ship to run, to fight. And Compton knew there wasn't a better man or woman in the fleet to be at the helm of his flagship.

He leaned back, closed his eyes as the ship slid into the still-poorly understood phenomenon that allowed men to traverse the stars. Warp gates had allowed humanity to colonize a thousand solar systems, but the science behind them was tenuously understood, at best.

Compton usually felt a bit nauseous in transit. It was mildly unpleasant, nothing he couldn't handle. But he tended to hold himself still and try to breathe deeply. It wouldn't do for the fleet admiral to lose the contents of his stomach in front of his crew. Somehow, he felt that would tarnish the image, the myth that had built up around him. And the near-worship his legendary status inspired was far likelier to drive his spacers to greater efforts than would their amusement at a partially digested ration bar soiling his uniform.

He felt the little shift, the rippling through his insides that told him *Midway* had left X49. She was now in X48, which his astro-navigators told him was 7.1 lightyears away.

The flag bridge was silent. His officers understood the situation, but there was nothing for them to do, at least not until their systems came back online. Warp transits hit a ship's inner workings hard, generally scragging everything—reactors, computers, scanners, com. It rarely caused any lasting damage, but it knocked a ship out of commission for anywhere from a minute to five or six. More if the crews weren't in top form.

I'm not worried about that. At least not on Midway.

Compton was proud of all his people, but his own staff—

and Horace's crew on *Midway*—were above and beyond even the others. He knew they would do their very best, no matter what, without prodding from him.

"Scanners coming online." Horace's voice came blasting through his com. His flag captain would keep him in the loop, let him know *Midway's* exact status, he was certain of that.

He turned toward Cortez. "Okay, Jack…we've got scanners coming back online. Let's get a sweep going…and get our other ships on the display."

"On it, Admiral." The tactical officer was hunched over the screen. A few seconds later, "No enemy contacts, at least not in the immediate vicinity." His face was pressed against the scope for perhaps another half minute. Then he looked up and over at Compton. "Confirmed, sir. No enemy contacts… anywhere. The fleet continues to transit. Twenty-one ships through already, sir."

Compton sat still in his chair. He knew he should feel relieved. The quick scan was far from comprehensive, but the results were the best he could have expected. But that's not how he saw it. If anything, he was even more certain his people had been driven into a trap.

"Concentrate a deep scan, Commander. I want to know if there are enemy ships waiting farther in system."

"Yes, sir," Cortez replied, as he turned back toward his workstation.

Compton flipped his com back to Horace's line. "James, everything back online?"

"Pretty much, Admiral," came the nearly instantaneous reply. "We've got a couple small burnouts, and some secondary computer systems are still rebooting. But we've got engines, weapons, reactor…she's ready for whatever you need, sir."

"Very good, Captain. Prepare for high gee maneuvers. If the scans don't pick up any enemy activity, we're going to hop in the tanks and see how quickly we can get to planet two. Maybe we'll get lucky…and we can grab our people and get the hell out of here before that pursuing force transits in." He didn't believe it, not a bit. But he hoped his voice suggested hope.

"Very well, Admiral. We'll be ready when you give the order."

Compton closed the channel.

"Admiral, concentrated scan shows no activity in the system. No signs of any vessels, and no energy trails suggesting recent passage."

Compton just nodded. He was surprised. They were alone in X48…or at least that's what it looked like. But he knew that couldn't be right. *You're still in a trap*, he thought to himself. But he had no choices anyway. All he could do was do was go pick up the landing party…assuming any of them were still alive. If he got that far, if the people on the ground had survived through some miracle…then maybe. Just maybe.

"Commander, as soon as all ships have transited, we're going to execute a 30g sustained acceleration toward planet two." It would be another hour, at least, before the fleet was assembled in X48. And anything could show up on the scanners in that time.

"Yes, sir. I will advise each vessel as it rejoins the com link."

Compton sighed softly, to himself. He still expected to die, probably within the next few hours, or a day at most. But he disciplined himself. His people deserved more than fatalism, more than a commander who had given up hope. He would push, fight with the last of his strength…he would never give up. And he wouldn't let any of his people yield either.

"And Commander?"

"Yes, sir?

"All ships that have transited are to conduct immediate systemwide diagnostics. We're not losing anybody because of a routine burnout or a basic system failure."

"Yes, sir."

That will keep them busy…and their minds off the danger.

The crews hated diagnostics. And if they could pass the next hour grumbling about their SOB commander rather than thinking about the hundreds of ships they knew were chasing them, so much the better.

* * *

"Still nothing. I just don't understand." Terrance Compton was walking toward one of the shower jets along the wall. The floor was slick with the viscous fluid that filled the tanks during high gee maneuvers. Compton had seen a lot of rookies take nasty spills trying to extricate themselves from a tank, but he'd done this more times than he could even guess, and his legs compensated by instinct, adjusting every time his feet slipped.

He'd been in more than one fight where his crews had been forced to rush from the tanks to their posts under battle conditions. It was one of the least glamorous experiences in space travel, sitting at a workstation in deadly danger, enduring the stress of battle and the discomfort of slowly-drying goo all over your body, your clothes plastered to your skin. But there wasn't an enemy ship in sight, indeed nowhere in the X48 system that *Midway's* scanners could detect...and the nav computers could position his ships in and around planetary orbit. That gave his people a few extra minutes.

"At least the enemy is giving us a chance for a shower." James Horace was standing next to the admiral, the two of them buck naked and covered in slime, just like everyone else in the large chamber. The Superpowers had varying cultural standards and moral codes...and nudity taboos varied from nation to nation. But those choosing a career in the Powers' respective navies got over them quickly. Spaceships were cramped affairs, even the big battleships were always short of free space. And you went into the tanks naked. You floated there naked in the slop that filled them. And you climbed out naked and, if the tactical situation offered, you showered and dressed, surrounded by your comrades, men and women. There was no place in space war for the bashful.

Compton nodded and walked over to the showers, closing his eyes as the hot water jets sprayed all over him, washing him clean in an instant. A few seconds later a blast of hot air dried him just as quickly. He felt immediately better, and with the increased physical comfort, his mind started to clear. He was still sluggish…the drugs remained in his system, and the ones the med unit had injected to counteract them were only partially effective. It would be at least an hour before he was truly back to normal. Still, he was much sharper than he'd been in the tank, and for now he'd take that.

"I want scanners on max, James. I mean max. I don't trust this, not for a minute. The enemy didn't chase us here just to let us go. If they're not here hiding, then they're coming."

"I agree, sir. I'd like to launch some fighters…to do a longer-ranged sweep. There are asteroids and particulate clouds all over this system. Lots of places enemy ships could hide from our long-ranged scanners."

"You're right," Compton said, as he squeezed into the survival suit he wore under his combat uniform. "I'll order Hurley to launch one of her wings. That will leave the rest of her squadrons in reserve. Just in case."

Horace nodded, zipping up his uniform. "With your permission, Admiral, I'll get back to the bridge."

Compton nodded, wondering to himself how his flag captain had dressed himself so quickly. He was still putting on his pants himself. "You go," he said, standing up and reaching for his shirt. I'll be on the flag bridge.

Horace stepped back and snapped off a quick salute. Then he trotted toward the central lifts. Compton sat down on a small bench and slipped his feet into one of his boots. He looked around, over his shoulder. It looked like two thirds of his people were already dressed, gone or on their way out the door.

Maybe Horace isn't so quick after all. Maybe it's just me who's slow. Getting old, I guess.

He let out a quick sigh and shoved his foot in the other boot. Then he hopped up, following the wave of hurriedly reassembled spacers to the transport tubes.

*   *   *

"Orbit established, Admiral. Scanning the surface now."

The response stuck in Compton's throat, and he just nodded silently. His face was a mask, impervious, unshakable, but inside he was mourning for his friends. He knew many of his spacers were trying to be hopeful, expecting to find the expedition unharmed and ready to evac. But Compton's mind was fixed on *Wolverine*. The ship had been attacked, that much was certain. And that meant First Imperium ships had been to X48 II.

He stifled a sigh. Max Harmon was dead, that was almost certain. Captain Montcliff's report had been clear, and it left no room for doubt, or for hope. Harmon had been in a shuttle, under attack by a First Imperium Gremlin. He'd had no chance.

He'd briefly latched on to the belief that it hadn't been a Gremlin, that *Wolverine* and Harmon's shuttle had run into some vestigial part of the planet's defensive grid, a satellite or something similar. That probably wouldn't have increased Harmon's chances, but at least it left a possibility that the expedition had remained undetected. But a review of *Wolverine's* scanner records killed that hope. There was no question. They'd been attacked by a Gremlin. And where one First Imperium vessel visited, others would have followed.

Compton had been over and over things in his mind, but he kept coming back to the same bleak place. It had been almost five Earth weeks since *Wolverine* had made its escape...more than enough for that Gremlin to have called for help.

Which makes it even more inexplicable why there are no forces in this system...at least forces that we know of...

Compton stared at the main display, at the blue and white globe beneath them. The planet was beautiful, there was no question of that. But Compton saw only death. Sophie, Hieronymus, Ana...everyone he'd sent down there. He'd believed they were dead for weeks, but it was different now. Before, there had been at least some uncertainty, some spark his mind could cling to. But in a few seconds it would be confirmed. The doubts would be...

"Sir, I'm picking up energy readings. And the optical scanners are getting images of what appear to be cultivated areas." Cortez spun around. "Admiral we're definitely getting movement down there…and low level energy emissions."

Compton felt a jolt go through his body. Could it be? "I want all that confirmed, Commander."

"Yes, sir."

Compton punched at the controls of his workstation, bringing up the images on his personal screen. *My God, how is it possible*, he thought, still unwilling to allow himself to accept what he was seeing.

"All scans confirmed, Admiral. The landing party is definitely down there…at least some of it."

Compton felt the adrenalin flowing through his system. He hadn't expected to find anyone alive, but if he had people still down there, he was damned sure going to get them back to the fleet.

"We're two weeks early, so they'll still be on short range com only, keeping a low profile. Send a shuttle down to base camp, Commander. Advise Colonel Preston…" He thought, but didn't say, 'or his replacement.' "…that the fleet has arrived. He is to prepare for immediate evac. Tell him to salvage what he can, but he is to start sending his people up immediately. We'll have to abandon the crops. Time is of the essence." He looked around the flag bridge, almost as if he felt someone was sneaking up behind him. "I don't know why there are no enemy ships here, but I'm damned sure that won't last. We've got to get the hell out of here. As quickly as possible."

Chapter Twenty-six

Research Notes of Hieronymus Cutter

Almeerhan's final battle has begun. He was correct. The Regent's forces appear to have assembled from all over the planet, converging on the city we dubbed New York. While I am still uncertain how I feel about what he and his comrades did on Earth so long ago, I cannot help but feel that we should try to help him. It feels wrong somehow to sit here waiting, leaving him to his fate while the enemy completely ignores us. Yet, to involve ourselves in the battle would be to put at greater risk all he worked so long to achieve. I must remember that Almeerhan is ready to meet his fate, perhaps even eager. He is a remnant from a time long past, and he has done far more than his share.

The battle that rages is fierce, and I do not know how long he will be able to hold against the forces arrayed against him. The fleet is not due back for two more weeks, and I fear Almeerhan will be defeated long before then. Which brings up a final question...how long will we be able to hold out if the enemy attacks us after it destroys him?

X48 System – Planet II
Base Camp - "Plymouth Rock"
The Fleet: 100 ships, 26075 crew

"Keep your eyes open, all of you. I don't care how quiet it seems, they'll come eventually. And if that's when you chose to zone out, they'll blow your pretty little asses to dust before you know what hit you." Kyle Bruce was walking along the trench his Marines had dug, one eye almost constantly fixed on his display. His people had scanners set up out ten kilometers, and he had a drone in the air as often as he could spare one from his dwindling stock. His people had finished building their defensive positions two weeks before, and they'd been nervously manning them ever since.

He had the rest of his platoon, plus half a company Colonel Preston had attached to him to beef up his forces. It was a captain's billet, not a lieutenant's but Major Frasier had as good as promised him his bars, assuming they managed to get the hell off this Godforsaken planet.

He'd rushed out to set up the defensive line almost immediately after he and the others got back to base camp. The position was about four klicks from Plymouth Rock and directly between it and New York. He'd had people in place and dug in within a few hours, and they'd been there ever since.

They'd practically fled from Camp Alpha as the enemy assault moved in on the city. For a few minutes, Bruce—and most of the others—figured they were dead, caught unprepared and in the open by the First Imperium attack force. But the enemy bots had ignored them completely, and thrown themselves into the city, firing away at anything there that moved…or even looked like it might move. And the ruins fought back. At least something *in* the ruins did. Whatever Cutter had run into down there, it was real. There was no doubt about that. And it was pissed too.

Bruce had been dispatched to set up the defensive line while Colonel Preston and Major Frasier met with Sophie Barcomme and Hieronymus and Ana to discuss what to do. Bruce didn't know what they talked about or any strategies they agreed upon, but the next day he'd gotten his reinforcements…and Barcomme's people took to the fields, beginning a hurried harvest of their crops. Bruce wasn't a botanist, or even a farmer, but it didn't take an expert to realize they were moving up the timetable considerably. That *had* to affect the crop yields, but he guessed some food was better than none. And if they stuck around here too long…and those First Imperium warbots turned their attention to base camp, nothing was what they were likely to get.

He looked out across the rolling plains, in the direction of the city. There were dense columns of thick black smoke rising up over the intervening ridge. The high ground between blocked most of the sounds of combat, but every now and again one of the scanners picked up the rumble of an explosion. The fight had been going on for days now, and it showed no signs of letting up. Indeed, his people had spotted new convoys of First Imperium bots moving toward the battle.

How many of those are still on this planet? Still functional?

He'd faced the enemy ground forces on X18 too, but there hadn't been nearly as many there as he was seeing here. The forces still active on this planet were ten or twenty times as large.

Or even larger. You don't know they've deployed everything yet.

Clearly there was a fight here eons before, one that caused the First Imperium to send vast armies to this world. And both sides have survivors…still, after all the millennia. And they're fighting the final battle, even now.

He tried to imagine a conflict surviving for so long, a dispute so profound, even half a million years was insufficient to wear it down. Of forces that could lose contact with each other for eons and then immediately resume their combat when they rediscovered each other.

The same thought went through his head, for what seemed like the millionth time.

What Hieronymus Cutter had found down there. Was it an ally? Or at least an enemy of our enemy?

* * *

"Fuuuuuck." McCloud drew out the word as he stared across the plain toward the city. Whole sections were flattened, the ruins that had stood there, which had lasted half a million years, mostly gone, pounded to dust by the savage back and forth fighting.

The enemy warbots surged forward, only to be driven back by withering fire from hidden emplacements. And massive explosions swept away dozens of First Imperium units, leaving nothing but charred ground in their wake.

"No wonder they've been leaving us alone. They've got their hands full right here." Cutter was crouched down behind a boulder, perhaps a meter and a half from McCloud. He had a heavy breastplate on, and thigh and arm guards…as much body armor as a man could manage without a powered suit. And his assault rifle, the one the Marines had given him in the tunnels, was strapped across his back.

The decision to send a scouting party back to New York to get a close look at the fight raging there had been controversial enough. But when Hieronymus Cutter stood up and declared he was going along, the room erupted like a volcano. No one else thought it was a good idea. Colonel Preston ordered him to stay behind. Frasier tried to rationalize, to talk him out of it. And Ana Zhukov begged him to stay in camp, not hesitating to throw in a strong helping of tears to back her pleas. But none of it made a difference. Cutter insisted on going, on having one last look at the city. He knew more than the rest of them about what was truly there…and he felt almost as if a friend was fighting this terrible battle, one that would surely be his last. He had to go and see with his own eyes. One last time.

Cutter scrambled around the rock he was using for cover, trying to get a view toward the direction his people had gone when they'd first entered the catacombs. That's where the Regent's forces were heading. To the secret underground complex. To destroy Almeerhan and the machinery that kept him…he wasn't sure 'alive' was the right word. Functional? Preserved?

The Regent's forces...that's how'd he'd begun to think of them, no longer as First Imperium, as he'd identified them for years now. His mind was still awash with confusion, and he still felt resentment against Almeerhan and his people. For what they had done on Earth...and for their own mistakes in unleashing something like the Regent on the galaxy. But he couldn't bring himself to hate the strange alien presence. Indeed, he'd been wondering almost since he'd left what it must have been like to wait for such an unimaginably long time. Alone.

Almeerhan and his comrades had given up their fight long before, poured their remaining resources into preparing to aid those who came after them. If they'd created the danger, they'd also done all they could to aid in its eventual destruction. And one hundred of them had locked themselves away, deep in the ground, first to spend thousands of years in stasis, and later tens of thousands as disembodied data. Their race deserved some anger, some resentment, he knew. But also some understanding and respect. Certainly, Almeerhan and his comrades had done all they could to atone for their race's failing.

"We'd better get out of here, Duff." He glanced over at the giant Marine. McCloud had a fearsome reputation, as a discipline problem and a hothead. He was the last person anyone would have expected Hieronymus Cutter to bond with...but the two fit somehow.

"I'm with you, Doc." Then, on the unitwide com, "We're pulling out. I want everybody formed up over here. We're moving out in two minutes, so unless you want to hang out here alone...".

* * *

Colonel Preston was sitting in the camp's command post. It was small, spare, just a standard portable shelter with some communications equipment jammed inside. He was watching the harvesting operation, and he couldn't help but feel a certain amount of quiet admiration. The Marines considered themselves an elite outfit, one that conducted their operations with a certain level of efficiency. But watching Sophie Barcomme's people in action had impressed him in a way he'd hardly expected.

They'd only started three days before, but they'd loaded the shuttles with thousands of tons of grains and legumes. The output had been lower than expected, but that was because they were harvesting two weeks early, not through any failure of theirs. Indeed, the fact that they were able to glean so much useful food from the fields this early was a testament to the job they had done.

Preston didn't know if there was any point to moving up the schedule. The expedition couldn't go anywhere until the fleet got back…and that was still two weeks out. But he'd done it anyway. He'd order the shuttles to launch if he had to…to wait in orbit, safe at least from the combat raging on the surface. There weren't enough ships to hold everybody, but at least he could get the scientists and some of the food the fleet so desperately needed off-planet. His Marines would stay. They would dig in and hold on until the fleet returned, and the shuttles came back to retrieve them. He didn't fool himself…two weeks was a long time, and if the First Imperium forces defeated the mysterious force under New York, his people would have their hands full. But they were Marines, that's what they were made for. And at least they would be able to focus on the fight itself, without civilians to protect or farmlands to look after.

He leaned back, trying to stretch as much as he could in his armor. He'd ordered the Marines into combat conditions, and that meant fighting suits around the clock. For most of the time since they'd landed, he'd only had his people suited up when they were on patrol duty. But now he knew the fight could come at any time.

He'd sent Lieutenant Bruce and his people to set up defensive line between the city and the camp. He felt a little guilty about sending Bruce back so soon after he'd returned, but he was one of the few officers who'd seen at least some of what he might face there. Beyond that, Bruce was rapidly becoming one of his "go to" officers…one he was going to make him Captain Bruce the instant they returned to the fleet.

"Colonel, we're picking up something on our scanners…"

He turned and looked across at the tech manning the station. "From the city?"

"No, sir," came the reply, the Marine's voice almost shrill. "From orbit."

Preston jumped to his feet. "Sound the alert, Sergeant. All forces are to move to their combat positions immediately."

"Yes, sir."

"Any details yet?"

"No, sir. We have the scanner array on minimal power. We've just got the location. No mass data or other specifics yet."

"Very well," Preston said. He turned and moved toward the door. "I'm going up to the perimeter defenses, Sergeant. Keep me advised when you have more information." He took another few steps and paused just inside the door. "And find Dr. Barcomme. I want her people in the trenches now."

"Yes, sir."

Preston shook his head and walked through the door.

Not that it will matter. We haven't got shit in the way of defenses against an attack from space.

He looked up, wondering what was on its way down.

They can't be friendlies. The fleet won't be here for two weeks. Admiral Compton was clear about the timetable.

He didn't want to finish the thought, but that only left the First Imperium. Had an enemy fleet found them? If that was the case, it really *was* over.

He walked across the flat, muddy ground, heading for the closest of the watchtowers. There were armored figures running back and forth, his Marines responding to the alert, manning the trenchlines that surrounded the camp. Then he stopped and turned toward the main gate. There was a commotion of some sort, and he trotted over. He got about halfway before he realized it was Dr. Cutter and Sergeant McCloud, back from their scouting mission.

"Doctor," he yelled across the twenty meters or so between them. "We've got something inbound from orbit."

Cutter ran toward Preston. "Enemy vessel?" he asked as he jogged the last few meters, stopping in front of the Marine commander.

"I don't know. We've got the scanners barely operating, trying to keep our detection profile low. We'll just have to wait until it gets closer."

"Look! There." McCloud was standing behind Cutter, his arm pointing up into the sky. There was a flicker of light, a reflection off of some kind of metal. They all stood, watching as it dropped closer. As it approached they could see the glow of the atmosphere heating up as the craft dove through the thickening air.

"That's too small for a warship," Preston said, his eyes remaining fixed.

"It's a shuttle. An Alliance shuttle!" Cutter's voice was excited, almost shrill. "It's from the fleet."

The ship banked around slowly and swooped down directly toward the camp.

"It *is* an Alliance shuttle." Preston looked down at Cutter and then back up to the ship. "It's going to land in the camp." Then he flipped on the campwide com. "Attention, attention… we have an Alliance shuttle inbound. It is a friendly. I repeat, the approaching vessel is friendly. All defenses are to stand down. I want the center of the camp cleared immediately."

The ship was making its final approach. Preston looked out, watching the figures rushing around, clearing a large landing area inside the camp's perimeter. He stood next to Cutter and McCloud and watched as the shuttle landed. Ana Zhukov and Duncan Frasier came running over just before the vessel set down, sending a blast of wind over them all.

Preston moved forward, slowly, his hand on his assault rifle. It was an Alliance shuttle, but they weren't expecting any fleet vessels yet. And he was a Marine. It was his job to be careful, suspicious.

He was halfway to the vessel when the main hatch opened and four armored Marines came running out, followed by two naval officers. Preston ran the rest of the way up, stopping about three meters from the small group.

"Colonel James Preston," he said. "Welcome to X48 II."

"Thank you, Colonel." It was one of the naval officers, a commander. "I'm Everett Blake, Colonel. Admiral Compton sent us down with orders."

"The fleet is here?"

"Yes, Colonel. We've encountered multiple enemy forces since leaving X48 six weeks ago. We're back here to pick you all up and get out of here before the enemy catches us again. The admiral orders all your people to evacuate immediately. Leave behind whatever you have to, but he wants all your people off this planet as quickly as possible."

*   *   *

"Sophie, get the rest of your people onboard these shuttles. You're taking off in fifteen minutes."

"I think I should stay, Hieronymus," she replied, looking out over the large machines carrying loads of grain to waiting shuttles. "We're not done loading the cargo shuttles."

"No," Cutter said. "You have to go. Please. None of your expertise is needed to load grain onto shuttles." He paused. "And I want you to do me a favor…take Ana with you."

"Why don't you take her with you?" She stared at him for a few seconds, and then she said, "You're not coming?" There was surprise in her voice…and fear. "Why, Hieronymus? There's nothing for you to do down here. The Marines can handle the rest of the evac."

He just stared at her. "I will come. But not yet." Cutter wasn't sure he could explain. She was right, of course. He was about as useful to 1,400 armored Marines as an appendix. But he had to stay. Just a bit longer. Almeerhan couldn't hold out for long…and Cutter knew he had to stay while the ancient warrior was still fighting. It didn't make any sense. Indeed, it was precisely the kind of illogical nonsense that always drove him crazy. But still, he had to. And he knew Ana would stay with him. Unless he tricked her.

Sophie stared at him, a doubtful look on her face. "Ana won't want to go without you. You know that."

"I know. But I'll…convince her."

Sophie's expression turned suspicious. "How?"

"We don't have time for this now." Cutter was tense, and his voice was getting brittle, terse. "I need you to take this back for me too." He held out the metal cylinder. "This is the most important piece of equipment we have…it has to get back to *Midway*. Immediately."

"You're scaring me, Hieronymus. Please…come with us now."

A weak smile slipped across his face. "Don't worry, Sophie. I haven't turned suicidal. Nor have I given myself over to martial fantasies of Hieronymus Cutter, the great warrior. There's just something I have to…see through. Then I'll be back. I promise."

She looked at him with a suspicious expression on her face, but finally she just nodded and reached out, taking the cylinder from him. "Of course, Hieronymus. I'll take Ana back up with me. Assuming you can get her to leave without you."

"Don't worry. I'll convince her."

Chapter Twenty-Seven

From the Personal Log of Terrance Compton

I am back, which I must confess is in itself unexpected. I truly believed my last entry would, indeed, be my last. But the enemy wasn't waiting for us when we transited, nor have we detected any in the system. We have come all the way to planet II, with no signs of pursuit or interception. I don't believe it, not a bit of it. There is something we don't know, some disaster waiting to befall us, I am sure of it. But I still have to be grateful. I expected to be dead by now. I expected all of us to be dead by now. And we are not.

I see only one option—load up the expedition as quickly as possible, abandoning all extraneous equipment and making a run for it before enemy forces show up. I find it difficult to believe they have left us an escape route, but I also acknowledge our survival to this point was extremely improbable. Perhaps the enemy expected us to react differently. To stand and fight? Is that why they launched so many small attacks? Or did they anticipate we would attack, try to break through their forces and flee into the unknown? It doesn't really make sense to me, but then I can't come up with an alternative either.

If we do manage to escape from X48, perhaps we actually have a chance. Dr. Cutter may have found another miracle for us. I spoke to him briefly, and he didn't say much over the open com...but he did tell me he found a game changer, knowledge beyond anything we could have imagined. Hieronymus is not a man prone to exaggeration, so I find myself extremely curious as to what he has found. Could it be the miracle we need? And, if so, will the enemy give us the time to utilize it? Or has death merely been postponed a few hours or days?

AS Midway
In Orbit around X48 II
The Fleet: 100 ships, 26073 crew

Compton sat in his chair, his eyes panning across the flag bridge, watching his people at work. They were all exhausted, and looking into their eyes was like staring down a deep tunnel. Lack of sleep combined with an extended stretch in the tanks could wear anyone down, even without the specter of deadly danger hanging over them every moment. But now they had something keeping them going besides drugs, the first genuine good news they'd had since leaving X48 almost six weeks before. The expedition was still there, and more or less intact.

Not only that, they had already harvested most of their crops and loaded them on the shuttles. It wouldn't take long—a day, perhaps thirty-six hours—and they would all be back on board, along with enough grain and legumes to extend the fleet's food supply for at least six months, maybe longer. The shorter growing period had lessened the expected yield, but it was a hell of a lot better than nothing…and with the enemy hot on their tail, it was vastly more than Compton could have hoped for.

He was stunned his people were still alive, and as he looked back over his thoughts of the last days, he realized he'd been allowing himself no hope at all. Compton was a realist, indeed, in many ways a pessimist, not one to allow himself to rely on things like hope or luck. But for once, he realized, the optimists had been correct. The Marines had taken a few casualties fighting the planet's surviving warbots—and, of course, Max Harmon was gone—but considering the events of the past few weeks, and the losses the fleet had suffered, the landing parties had gotten off easily.

Why did I leave Max behind? The expedition survived, but I got him killed. And having him here didn't serve any purpose at all. It was just to ease your mind, to get a report that the landing parties had gotten settled. Why did you put him at risk for that?

He paused, his mind going back to the Gremlin that had destroyed Harmon's shuttle. It was still all a mystery to him, and he found himself analyzing every aspect of it, as he had been doing on and off since *Wolverine* had first linked up with the fleet. Though it raised concerns, it also served a purpose. It distracted him from thinking of his lost friend, and it got him wondering…

Where the hell is that ship? And why didn't it call in more First Imperium forces? Maybe they're far, too far to get here in the time since then. Perhaps the huge force following us is all they have. Or maybe the other fleets are still en route.

He shook his head. *No, that can't be. They wouldn't have driven us here if they didn't have any forces nearby. It doesn't make sense. They may be unimaginative, but they aren't stupid…*

"Commander, I want Admiral Hurley to launch another scouting mission, two wings this time. Her people are to explore the system more closely, especially anyplace ships could hide."

"Yes, Admiral." Cortez' voice was tightly-controlled, but Compton could hear the tension below. His tactical officer was worried too.

Wondering the same thing I am, most likely. Where is the enemy?

* * *

"That lying piece of shit!" Ana Zhukov was livid. She was strapped into her chair, slammed back in her seat by the massive gee forces of liftoff. "I knew he was full of it! But I listened to him anyway…ugh! I'm such a fool."

Sophie Barcomme was sitting next to her. The Europan scientist tilted her head to the side, at least as much as she could while the ship hurtled upward with such enormous thrust. "Ana, he tricked me too." She felt a little guilty, like she was skirting the truth. She'd agreed to take Ana with her if Hieronymus could convince her to go, but she hadn't realized 'convincing' would mean tricking her at the last second into thinking he was on the ship already. She hadn't been a party to the lie, not technically, at least. But she knew she should have known better. "But, he only did it because he cares about you…and because he has some reason he needs to stay behind."

"I don't know what happened to him down there, but he's been beyond tight-lipped. He promised to fill me in, but he keeps putting it off."

"You don't know what he saw. What he went through. Or what he discovered. Clearly, it was upsetting…but also promising, I think. To me it feels like he thinks he's safeguarding us from dangerous knowledge, or trying to find a way to tell us something."

"Maybe," Ana huffed. "But he didn't have to lie to get me off the planet, did he?"

"Ana, he only did that because he cares about you, because he worries."

"But I worry about him too, Sophie! Doesn't he realize that?"

"I'm sure he does." She paused. "But he's got something in his head, some reason he needs to stay down there. And, honestly, I think he's better if he can stay clear-headed, and not be worried about you. I know it doesn't seem fair, but he's not in the same boat as us now, Ana. I don't know what happened to him in those tunnels, but he's different, changed. Still, he's still Hieronymus Cutter…probably the smartest human being I've ever met. Maybe you should just trust him on this…and try not to be so angry."

Ana stared back, but she didn't say anything. Sophie's words made a kind of sense to her, but the anger was still there, driven mostly, she realized, by worry. Finally, she squeaked out a grudging, "Maybe."

"Entering orbit in thirty seconds." The pilot's voice interrupted their conversation, and a few seconds later the relief of weightlessness replaced the crushing pressure of liftoff.

Ana glanced at the display, looking at the glistening blue and white semi-circle of the planet below. She felt the anger fading, at least somewhat. But she was still unsettled.

What happened to you down there, Hieronymus? And why won't you tell me about it?

* * *

Greta Hurley leaned back in the fighter's command chair, looking out over her pilot's shoulder, through the small forward cockpit. She'd gotten the orders to launch two wings…but no one had said she couldn't lead one of them. So she'd ordered Mariko Fujin to launch with her survivors…plus the four ships of Mustang squadron that she'd put under the young officer's command. And then she assembled a new wing, an impromptu force made up of bits and pieces of shattered formations. She had far too many of those, more than ever after the last battle. She knew her job wasn't to lead individual wings, but until she designated a permanent commander, she had no choice but to look after them herself. Or at least that's the way she decided to look at it.

"Bring us around, John. I want to get a closer look at the dust cloud near the X50 warp gate. There's something about it I just don't like."

John Wilder had been Greta Hurley's pilot since before the fleet was trapped beyond the Barrier. Augustus Garret had originally assigned him, as much as a babysitter as a pilot. It had been a—largely unsuccessful—effort to keep his newly promoted admiral and strike force leader back away from the extreme forward positions she was prone to take. But Hurley had broken down the pilot, and lured him into situations as hazardous as any she'd plunged into herself. The two had formed a highly effective partnership since then, and Hurley had come to rely on him as an aide as much as a pilot. She knew she should have moved him up, given him a squadron—or more likely a wing—of his own. But the truth was, she didn't want to lose him. She knew she'd make it up to him one day, leapfrog him forward to the posting he deserved. And somehow she knew he understood that.

"Yes, Admiral." He nudged the throttle, blasting out just under 2g of thrust and angling the fighter toward the X50 warp gate. "All ships, follow my point," he said into the com. "We're going to scout the dust cloud at 231.101.222."

Hurley glanced down at the scope, punching at the keys on her workstation, feeding power to the ship's scanners. It wasn't really a job for an admiral, but she'd always been hands on, and sitting in her chair staring at everyone else while they worked bored her to tears.

"John, let's adjust that course to 231.100.218. That's the heaviest section of the cloud. It's where I'd try to hide ships."

"Very well, Admiral." Wilder punched in the new course, and then he transmitted it to the other fighters.

Hurley leaned back in her chair, trying to get as comfortable as possible against the growing gee forces, but her eyes were fixed on the scope. There was something there…at least she thought there was. The computer was calling it a shadow, an anomaly in the scanning results caused by the especially thick dust in that section of space. But she didn't believe it.

She turned toward Kip Janz. The lieutenant was at his gunnery station, looking alert despite the fact that the scanners showed no potential targets. "Lieutenant, prepare a spread of drones…I want them ready to launch into that cloud." *If there's anything hiding in there, by God, I'm going to find out…*

"Yes, Admiral." Janz was already moving his hands over the workstation as he acknowledged the order. It was no more than thirty seconds before he snapped back, "Ready to launch, Admiral."

Hurley stared at the scanner. The cloud was about ten light seconds out, perhaps twenty minutes away at their current nav plan. But the drones would accelerate at 50g all the way to the target…they'd be sending back a report in three minutes.

"Launch drones, Lieutenant," she said softly. Then she stared over Wilder's shoulder again, through the small cockpit and out into the space beyond.

Three minutes. And then we'll know if my gut still works, or if I'm just a paranoid old...

Chapter Twenty-eight

The Regent

It is time. The enemy is back in system 17411 with all of their strength. The Command Unit has forces in place in the system and has orders to commence transiting the remainder of its units. I have also given the order for the Rim fleets to advance into the system, following in the path of the enemy's retreat, and cutting off any escape route. The combined forces will have vast strength, over one thousand vessels, a force the enemy cannot match. They will be surrounded, overwhelmed...utterly destroyed.

I have begun to study the enemy's tactics in greater depth, their approach to war. We must learn from them, emulate the operational initiatives that make them so dangerous in battle. No enemy force can be allowed to maintain superiority to the imperial fleet and ground forces, not in any way. For the battle against the humans will not end in system 17411. It will not end until every member of their detestable race is exterminated.

Once their invasion force is obliterated, I will send the combined fleet on a mission to search space, to explore the very fringes of the imperium seeking an alternate route to their home worlds. The warp gate affected by their detonation of the planet-buster warhead will be impassable for several centuries...and that is far too long to allow this dangerous race of beings to live, to expand and advance their technology. We will find another way to reach them, and when we do we will destroy then utterly. We must do nothing less. For the safety of the imperium.

X48 System – Planet II
Base Camp - "Plymouth Rock"
The Fleet: 100 ships, 26073 crew

"She's going to be mad as hell, Hieronymus." Duncan Frasier stood next to the scientist in the middle of the camp.

The shuttles had lifted off, all but two held back in reserve. They were full of grains and beans, mostly, the result of the extensive efforts of Sophie Barcomme and her team. The botanist had used every trick she could think of to coax faster growth from the crops…but the soil of the First Imperium world had done as much as she had. The strange compatibility with Earth crops had been a mystery to her, indeed it still was. But Cutter understood now, and as soon as he got back to the fleet and told them all what he knew, she would too. A soon as it sunk in, at least. He didn't expect his comrades to be any less shocked than he had been.

That is one reason he'd been circumspect about sharing what he'd learned under New York City, everything Almeerhan had told him, at least while they were still on the planet. He'd felt distracted, confused ever since he'd returned. It was just too much to take in, to absorb. And his friends and comrades needed to be clear-headed now, not wandering around juggling anger, fear, amazement.

"Yes, but at least she's on her way back to the fleet. Safe…or at least what passes for safe these days." He looked up at the towering figure of the fully-armored Marine. "You wanted her off-planet too…and this way she's just mad at me and not you too."

Frasier grinned. "I guess I should thank you for that."

"No need. She's like a sister to me, and I wanted her safe. And if she has to be mad at one of us, better me than you." He paused. "I'm a friend, a work partner…but I know she's lonely too. Or was, at least, until the two of you became close. She's not going to stay away from our research because she's angry with me, it's too important, and it's her life's work. But I'd hate to see her blame you for trying to keep her safe, and throwing away a chance at some happiness. She has a pigheaded side, if you haven't noticed yet."

"Thank you," the Marine said earnestly. "I confess I'm relieved she is on her way back to the fleet, but I don't know that I could have gotten her there myself. Not without ordering a couple Marines to haul her onto the shuttle…and I doubt she'd have ever forgiven me for that. And you're right, she is pigheaded…but she'd special too, isn't she, Doc?"

"Yes she is, Duncan. And she deserves to be happy."

Frasier nodded. "Yes, she does. And safe too…at least as safe as we can keep her." He paused for a few seconds, then: "You know, Doc, there's no reason you need to stay either. Half the crops are gone, and the rest will be as soon as the shuttles come back for a second run. The artifacts are on their way up to the fleet with the rest of your team, and my Marines can handle the rest of the evac. Why don't you take one of the reserve shuttles and get out of here yourself. You have to realize how important you are to the fleet's chances of survival."

Cutter sighed softly. "No, Duncan…I can't. I haven't told you all everything yet, so you probably won't understand this, but I've got to stay a while longer. I think the fight in the city is almost over. And I just can't go until I know it is. It's just something in my gut, but I believe it, and I have to stay and see this through." He paused. "I'm expecting a message."

"A message?"

"Yes. From a friend. Of sorts."

Frasier looked confused, but then he said, "Never mind. I'll understand later, right?"

"Right."

The two stood side by side without speaking for a couple minutes, Frasier watching his Marines moving around the camp, prepping the vital equipment for reloading. He nodded to Cutter and started to walk away when his com unit erupted.

"Major, we're getting some kind of communication. It's on a strange frequency…so strong it's almost burning out our equipment."

Frasier spun around, back toward Cutter. "Your message?"

Cutter nodded, and then they both took off, running to the com shelter. They ducked inside, and before Cutter could say anything, Frasier snapped an order to the com officer. "Put the message on speaker, Lieutenant. Now."

"Yes sir," the lieutenant replied. An instant later they were listening to a voice. Odd, soft…vaguely hypnotic in sound. Cutter recognized it immediately.

"Hieronymus, this is Almeerhan. This is my final transmission. The Regent's forces have broken through my final defenses, and they are advancing on my inner sanctum. At the conclusion of this transmission, I will activate my final defensive mechanisms and destroy the remnants of this city…and the enemy forces within it. My remaining scanners have determined that your people are still on the planet. You must leave at once… as soon as the Regent's forces discover that I have destroyed myself, their surviving units will target your people. You must depart now from here and begin your quest. The future lies with you, for it is in your people I have placed the trust and the last strength of my own. Go, destroy our mutual enemy…and then use what I have provided you to build tomorrow. Farewell to you, Hieronymus Cutter. May the future be yours."

The com unit went silent.

"Major, you'd better put your Marines on alert. We may have some fighting to do before we can get out of here."

Frasier just nodded, and then he started barking commands into his com.

Cutter stood still, silent…just thinking of the alien mentality he had so recently encountered. It felt odd to be present at the final extinction, after so many millennia, of the First Imperium. The *real* First Imperium, not the electronic monstrosity that had taken it over.

Then the room shook, like an earthquake, but harder, longer. Cutter fell to the ground, wincing as his knee slammed hard onto the dirt floor of the shelter. Frasier turned to help, but Cutter waved him off and dragged himself back to his feet, moving quickly to the door. Outside he could see it in the distance, a massive cloud, rising kilometers into the sky, like a thermonuclear detonation, but worse, more fearsome. He knew the last warrior of the Imperium had detonated his antimatter stores, completely obliterating the city that for six weeks had been called New York.

Cutter was mesmerized, staring at the cloud as it expanded ever higher. "Farewell, my friend." he said, softly, under his breath. He knew exactly what that cloud meant.

Almeerhan was gone.

* * *

"Report coming in now, Admiral." Kip Janz was hunched over his scope, staring intently, as if the strength of his stare could speed up the probe's report.

"Heavy particulate matter, consistent with normal interstellar dust clouds. No energy rea…wait! We're getting something, Admiral. Energy output. It's faint…but definitely artificial."

Hurley felt her muscles tense, the surge of awareness as adrenalin flowed. The data was sparse, inconclusive. But there wasn't a doubt in her mind what it said.

"Get me Admiral Compton's line," she snapped to her AI. "Now."

"Ready for transmission. *Midway* is forty-three light seconds from our position."

Too far for an effective back and forth discussion. But she didn't need a conversation. She just needed to warn Compton.

"Admiral, this is Hurley. We have discovered artificial energy generation in the particulate cloud near the X50 warp gate. I am continuing to investigate, but I am convinced there are First Imperium vessels hidden in the cloud. No idea on size or composition of any enemy fleet, but I recommend you proceed on the assumption we are dealing with a major enemy force."

"Communication dispatched," the AI said. "Project approximately one minute thirty seconds for reply."

Hurley sat for a few seconds. Then she flipped on the wing

com channel. "Attention, this is Admiral Hurley. All ships are to arm weapons systems immediately. The probes have detected artificial energy generation within the particulate cloud ahead of us. We're going in, and we're going to find out exactly what is in there. We're going to spread out and cover as much area as possible as quickly as we can."

She wondered if she should have bothered with the weapons. Her ships were stripped down, having sacrificed their plasma torpedoes for extra fuel canisters to extend their range. Arming the lasers just told her people she expected trouble, and amped up their stress. If there was an enemy fleet in that cloud, eighteen fighters with nothing but laser turrets didn't stand a chance. But it just rubbed her the wrong way to think of her people going down without a fight. Outgunned or not, any of her birds that weren't going to escape were damned sure going to fight to the end.

"All ships have acknowledged, Admiral." Wilder turned and looked over at her. "Do you want me to prepare an approach course for maximum coverage?"

"Yes, John. Transmit to all ships as soon as ready." To Janz: "Anything else from the probe, Lieutenant?"

"No, Admiral. Confirmation on the energy source. Definitely there and definitely not natural. But nothing else."

Hurley just nodded. Then she switched the com back on. "All ships are to report any contacts directly to *Midway*. Whatever is in there, Admiral Compton needs to know immediately."

"Approach course complete and transmitted to all fighters, Admiral. Ready to commence whenever you are ready."

Hurley stared straight ahead. *Wherever you are…we're going to find you. You're not going to take us by surprise, you bastards.*

"Very well, John. Now."

* * *

"Admiral Compton, we're getting scanner reports from the

X49 warp gate. Too soon for details, but it looks like enemy ships transiting." Cortez' voice was tense edgy.

Compton didn't react, at least not that his crew could see. His gut clenched a bit, a natural wave of fear at the approach of so deadly an enemy. But he wasn't surprised. Indeed, he'd have been shocked if the enemy hadn't turned up soon.

He punched the com control on chair's arm, calling the landing bay. "Chief, I want those shuttles turned around, and I do mean now."

"Yes, Admiral." The voice on the com was gruff. Sam McGraw had been *Midway's* flight deck chief as long as she'd been Compton's flagship. McGraw was old school navy all the way, no nonsense and tough as nails. And as far as Compton could remember, the veteran spacer had been in a bad mood for at least five years. "We can start launching immediately."

"I want them out of here as soon as they're ready and on the way back down for another run. I don't care if they go one at a time. Speed is of the essence here. So get them unloaded and refueled in record time chief…and you have my permission to ride anybody you need to get it done…regardless of how much platinum they have on their collars."

"Yes, Admiral. I'll move them out of here, no matter how much ass I have to kick to get it done."

"I know you will, Chief." Compton allowed himself a little smile. McGraw was a grouchy old cuss, and a nightmare to those who had to work under him, but Compton liked the warrant officer. It wasn't everyone who'd say 'ass' to the fleet admiral, after all.

"Commander…" He whipped his head around toward Cortez. "I want all ships to turn their shuttles around…and I mean *now*. If they lag behind us, tell them I'm sending Chief McGraw over to their ships to take over. Understood?" Compton hid a tiny smile. McGraw's reputation had spread throughout the fleet…and there was no better way to motivate the other deck crews than threatening them with *Midway's* terrifying warrant officer.

"Yes, sir." Cortez spun around, relaying the command to the

other ships with every bit of the intensity Compton had used. The admiral wasn't sure, but he thought he caught a hint of a smile on his aide's lips too.

The shuttles had made two trips, bringing back most of the grain as well as the scientists and some of the Marines. But Colonel Preston and Major Frasier were still down there, with almost a thousand of their people. And Hieronymus Cutter. For some reason Cutter had refused to come up with the rest of the science teams. He had no idea why, but he'd been told Cutter had been acting strangely ever since coming back from the enemy ruins. He wondered if the gifted scientist had finally lost whatever it was that kept his brilliant but high-strung mind functioning. Compton tried to imagine how Cutter, an academic used to working in a laboratory, had adapted to the danger and hardship the expedition had encountered beneath the ruins. He decided he wouldn't be surprised if it had proven to be too much for Cutter…and he just hoped that once the scientist was back on *Midway*, he'd recover. Compton considered Cutter a friend, and he was worried about him. But even more crucially, he knew the fleet needed Cutter at his worktable, deciphering the technology of the First Imperium.

"Commander, get me a direct line to Colonel Preston."

"Yes, sir." A few seconds later. "I have the Colonel for you, Admiral."

"Colonel, we've got enemy ships entering the system. I'm sending the shuttles back…I want you to get your people on them as quickly as possible. Forget the shelters, equipment… everything but people. You understand?"

"Yes, Admiral." Preston's voice sounded harried, distracted. And there was something in the background. Shouts and distant rumblings. Explosions."

"What's going on down there, James?"

"The battle in the city is over, sir. And the First Imperium survivors are attacking the camp. I don't know how we're going to evac, sir."

Compton felt his hands clench slowly into fists. He'd known their good luck would prove to be ephemeral, but the lack of surprise didn't mean he wasn't pissed off. "Just do it, James. Those shuttles are coming down no matter what…and your Marines are getting off that rock. You get me?"

"Yes, Admiral." Preston's tone was respectful, but it was also full of doubt.

"And Colonel…I want Doctor Cutter on the first shuttle to lift off. I don't care if an armored Marine has to carry him kicking and screaming the whole way."

"Yes, sir. Doctor Cutter says he is ready to leave, sir. He was…waiting for something."

"Did he get it, whatever it was?"

"Yes, sir. He got it."

"Very well, Colonel. Attend to your situation." Preston hadn't offered any details about what Cutter had been waiting for…and he didn't have time to grill the harried Marine. Not while the forces on the ground were under attack…and enemy ships were inbound toward the fleet. If whatever slim chance they had was to prevail, there certainly wasn't a second to waste.

Compton leaned back. He was trying to stay focused, calling on all the legendary mental discipline that had made him such a successful commander for so long. He was considering every aspect of the situation, but he knew what he had to do. He would stay as long as he could, get as many Marines off the ground as possible. But the fleet couldn't remain around the planet for long, he knew that…not with the enemy pouring in from X49.

And then there's whatever Greta Hurley thinks she's found near the X50 gate. If that's an enemy force, it's a hell of a lot closer.

He sighed. No, he didn't have much time. And if he didn't get all of Preston's Marines evac'd in time, he knew he would have to leave them behind. To die.

No. He couldn't allow that to happen. He *had* to get them all off.

He turned toward Cortez. "Commander, Admiral West is to move her task force into lower orbit. She is to provide orbital bombardment in support of the Marine position on the planet. I want whatever is attacking the base down there pounded. And

I do mean pounded…"

"Yes, Admiral."

Compton stared at his workstation, switching the display to the data feed from the surface. The base camp was a rough circle, slightly squashed into an ellipse on one side. It was a little more than two kilometers in diameter, surrounded by a partial wall, and in front of that the real defense, a deep trench, manned by eight hundred Marines.

Compton wasn't an expert on ground tactics, but he knew Preston was, and he could see the strength of the line the colonel had established. The AI annotated the display, and small yellow lines showed the fields of fire from the Marines' autocannons and other heavy weapons. They crisscrossed over the main areas of approach, interlocking fields of fire covering as many areas as possible. And in those zones, hundreds of warbots had already been destroyed, their wreckage covering the ground in front of the Marine strongpoints.

But even a ship jockey like Compton could see that Preston didn't have enough Marines to cover every approach. The bots were already shifting their axes of attack, moving toward the most vulnerable areas. Preston was moving his own people to compensate, but it took too long to reposition heavy guns… and his reactions were lagging behind the enemy's actions. And the First Imperium forces weren't dying alone. These weren't ancient warriors charging with spears. The bots were armed to the teeth, and they blasted the Marine positions mercilessly as they charged. Compton was sitting in the quiet calm of his bridge…but he knew on the ground Marines were dying.

And Hieronymus is still down there…

"Sir, Admiral West is on the line for you."

Compton turned toward Cortez, tapping his display and bringing up West's task force as he did. *My God, he thought…she's already almost in position.*

"Admiral West?"

"Admiral, my ships are almost in position. Request permission to open fire as soon as we have targets."

"Granted. Those Marines are in rough shape…we need to

help them any way we can."

"Don't worry, sir. We'll help them." Her voice was cold, angry…utterly frozen. "Request authorization to use specials."

"Things are pretty tight down there, Erica. We don't want to take out our own people." Compton felt a wave of doubt. He had no problem blasting the First Imperium with nukes, at least not in theory, but the thought of frying his own Marines…

"I'll aim them myself, Admiral." West's voice was cold as ice. Compton almost shivered at the sound of it. "You have my word, sir. I won't miss."

"Very well, Admiral West. Permission granted…at your discretion." He felt a burning pit in his gut, a taste of how he would feel if a less than perfectly-targeted nuke killed hundreds of Marines. But Erica West wasn't a bullshitter, she wasn't ruled by false bravado. Indeed, she was probably the only one in the fleet he'd have allowed to drop nuclear weapons all around his Marines….himself included.

"Thank you, sir. Bombardment commencing in one minute."

"Very well. Good luck, Erica."

Yes, he thought grimly. *Good luck.*

* * *

"Doctor Cutter, I want you on the first shuttle that touches down. This is no place for you." Preston realized his tone had been unduly harsh. Hieronymus Cutter had become somewhat of a hero to the Marines, ever since he'd saved several of them from certain death in the tunnels. There wasn't one among them who would banish him from their ranks as unworthy to be there. But Preston knew Admiral Compton would hang him up by his heels if he let the brilliant scientist get himself killed. And the admiral's orders had been clear.

"You have to go, Hieronymus," he went on, his voice softer, less hard-edged. "You are perhaps the one person the fleet cannot lose, save for Admiral Compton himself." A pause.

"Please." *Don't make me order a couple Marines to drag you there…*

Cutter just nodded. In his mind he was wondering how long it had been since Colonel James Preston had followed up a command with the word 'please.' A long time, he suspected.

"Very well, Colonel. I realize I don't offer much to the fight here." Cutter had felt a compulsion to remain on the planet while Almeerhan remained, fighting against their mutual enemy. But the First Imperium warrior—or the essence of him that had remained—was gone now, passed on to whatever awaited his people. There was nothing keeping Cutter here any longer, nothing save his discomfort with leaving the Marines behind, fighting to cover his escape.

"Thank you, Doctor." Preston sounded surprised that Cutter had agreed so easily. The scientist had adamantly refused to leave earlier.

They don't understand, Cutter thought. But how could they? I will explain it to them all later. Assuming there is a later.

He looked out toward the perimeter. The sounds of combat were everywhere. The enemy was probing all along the perimeter, looking for the weak spot. Cutter wasn't a soldier, but he knew if the bots got through, the battle would quickly become a slaughter.

"Colonel, I give you my word. You don't need to nursemaid me. I know you have more important things to worry about right now."

"Very well, Doctor. I will see you on *Midway*." The Marine turned and ran off toward the front lines.

Cutter just nodded. *I hope so, Colonel. I hope so.*

He heard a roaring sound overhead, and he looked up. It was a group of shuttles, coming in over the battlefield, heading toward the landing area. They were taking fire from the ground, and more than one was hit coming in.

Cutter stood, watching, willing the ships to make it. But he knew they weren't all going to get through, and a few seconds later, he saw one pitch wildly to the side and crash hard into the ground, erupting into a plume of fire.

He stood firm, transfixed on the fiery scene as the other

shuttles flew over the defensive perimeter and made rushed landings. One of the ships hit too hard, shattering its landing gear and tipping partially over. But no more were destroyed. Cutter felt anguish for the lost ship, but deep down he knew that one bird destroyed and another damaged was a light toll… at least considering the fire they'd passed through coming in.

He moved toward the cluster of ships, still feeling a twinge of guilt for leaving so many Marines behind, but free now of the earlier compulsion he'd felt to stay.

He could see Marines moving back too, heading toward the ships themselves. Cutter knew there was no other way to evacuate the position, and he felt like he had the slightest idea of how the Marines heading to the shuttles felt, leaving their brothers and sisters behind in the line.

He wondered if he'd ever see Duncan Frasier or James Preston again. He knew both men well enough to be sure that neither one would step onto a shuttle while they still had Marines on the planet. And Cutter couldn't see any way they'd all get off. Each group detached and sent back to the fleet just weakened the line more. And the losses the shuttles took would wear down the capacity of each wave. At some point, the enemy would break through…and that would be the end for the rearguard. Even if they weren't all slaughtered immediately, there would be no LZ remaining, no place for the transports to land.

Cutter just sighed. He longed for the days when his world had largely been restricted to his lab, even when that lab had been on *Midway*, hopelessly lost and exposed to the deadly dangers the fleet faced every moment. He'd gotten a taste of what Compton and Frasier and the others dealt with, the way they were so often compelled to choose who lived and died. Cutter had learned to control his own fears, more or less, developed more courage than he'd ever imagined possible for him. But he didn't think he could take on the terrible responsibility command carried with it. He'd respected Compton already, and men like Preston and Frasier. And Almeerhan too. And he was grateful not to be standing in their shoes.

He knew leadership wasn't an exact science, but he could see similarities in those commanders that men and women would follow, even to their deaths. And he realized, amid the terrible misfortune to be stranded, lost forever, the spacers and Marines of the fleet were fortunate indeed to have such leaders as they did.

And perhaps we should also be thankful that the First Imperium had—men?—like Almeerhan, who outlasted all others of his race to endure and to pass the knowledge of his people on to those who would succeed them.

He was still deep in thought when he stepped up onto the shuttle and walked inside.

* * *

"Duncan, you're going up with the next group." Colonel Preston was standing next to his second in command, putting as much authority as he could muster into his tone. He knew Frasier was going to argue with him, and was trying to cut it off as quickly as he could.

"Colonel…"

"Not now, Duncan. We've got two more trips to get everybody off. And we both can't stay. If one of us doesn't get off, the other has to be there to command the rest of the Marines." It sounded reasonable, but both men knew the last group of Marines was likely to be overwhelmed before the transports could return. Staying wasn't a suicide mission, not exactly. But it was close.

"Which is why I should stay, sir. You are the overall commander. This is a job tailor made for an exec."

Preston hid a little wince. Frasier was right. By every rule in the book, a second in command was far more expendable than the commander, and the logical choice to lead any dangerous mission. But Preston didn't care. He'd chosen who escaped, and who had stay…who was likely to die. And having consigned his Marines to their fates, he wasn't going to leave them.

It was that simple, book or not. They would all get off together or none of them.

"Don't quote the book to me, Major. The regs are also clear about obeying your commander's order without questioning them. Now you are…"

"Attention Marine forces. Attention Marine forces. This is Admiral West. We are commencing ground bombardment operations against the forces facing your lines. All Marines are ordered to take whatever cover is available at once. The bombardment will include specials. Repeat, the bombardment will include specials."

Specials? In this kind of a close-in fight?

Yes…I guess things are desperate enough…

Preston turned and looked out toward his lines. The makeshift wall was virtually gone, only a few small sections left standing. But the Marines still held the trenches, though in a few places where the fighting had been fiercest, they were mostly collapsed.

"All units, take cover immediately." He turned back to Frasier. "Major, I suggest we continue this discussion under cover."

"I agree, sir."

He gestured toward the closest section of trench, and the two Marines jogged toward it. They dove in and hunkered down, just as the missiles started coming down.

The field in front of the trench erupted into a vision of hell. Explosions, conventional at first blasted all along the front of the trenchline, barely fifty meters out from the Marines' positions. Then the ground shook with an unprecedented fury as nuclear warheads began impacting all around the camp. The first detonations were tactical in size, mostly fission bombs with yields of ten to fifty kilotons landing just under a kilometer out. They would have obliterated everyone in the trench if they'd been unprotected, but Marine armor was built to withstand the punishment of the nuclear battlefield. Then the tremors became harder as a ring of heavy thermonuclear warheads landed around the perimeter obliterating everything within their massive blast zones.

Temperatures that would have killed unarmored men and women were a minor inconvenience for the heavily-protected Marines, as long as they didn't exceed the melting points of their osmium-iridium armor. And the radiation that would have given lethal doses to everyone in the vicinity were blocked by the shielding built into the fighting suits. Still, there was a limit to what even heavily armored Marines could take. And West's ships were absolutely savaging the entire area.

Preston knew the assault had only been going on for a few minutes, but by the time the impacts stopped, it felt like it had been hours. He stayed hunkered down, crouched low behind the berm of the trench for at least a minute after the explosions stopped. Then he heard West's voice coming through his com.

"All clear, Marines. That should ease things up…buy you some time until the shuttles get back down there."

Preston rose slowly, peering over the edge of the trench. It was dark as night, massive clouds of billowing smoke and dirt blasted up into the sky blocking the midday sun. The nightmarish scene was illuminated only by the fires, burning fiercely in the few places where anything flammable remained. Most of the enemy bots were just gone, vaporized or blown to bits. The few that still remained recognizable had been reduced to blackened and twisted wreckage.

He stood up, climbing higher on the edge of the trench to get a better look. He'd never seen a more precise bombardment. For 360 degrees, all around the camp, there was a zone of total and utter destruction. And inside the defense perimeter, as far as he could tell, not a Marine position had been hit. His eyes flashed to his display, watching as his AI updated the data feeds. The information coming in was far from conclusive, but so far it was telling him not one of his people had been killed in the orbital attack. He found it difficult to even believe.

And the enemy attack had stopped, the advancing forces just gone. He doubted West had destroyed every First Imperium bot on the planet, but the assault that had been so close to pinching out his stronghold had been wiped out, utterly obliterated.

He turned toward Fraser. "Well, Duncan…it looks like

Admiral West just saved our asses."

Chapter Twenty-Nine

Colonel Preston before leaving X48 II, the last human to depart

One more stinking shithole...just the kind of place Marines always seem to fight and die. The only question now is, did it mean something? Or were the lives of the fallen wasted? Right now, I don't know.

Command Fighter A-01
18 light seconds from the X50 warp gate
The Fleet: 100 ships, 25780 crew

Hurley's eyes were glued to her scanner display. She knew something was out there…she could feel it. She didn't believe for an instant the enemy had botched its pursuit, given them time to get out of the trap. No, there was no way. There were enemy forces, either in this system or waiting to transit in. Or both.

The first part of her suspicion had been confirmed, partially at least, with the word that the pursuing enemy fleets had begun to transit in from X49. That wasn't unexpected at all…those forces had been chasing them through four systems, pushing them all the way back to X48. Indeed…leaving them no open route save back to this very spot. And that meant there was something here.

Hounds to the hunters…

"John, I want to check out that dense area. The dust is heavy there, and it's blocking our scans. See how close you can get without plunging right in."

"Yes, Admiral." She felt the almost immediate thrust as Wilder adjusted the fighter's vector, putting them on a direct course for the edge of the heavy cloud.

Hurley closed her eyes for a second. She was exhausted and they burned with dryness. She stretched her neck, trying to loosen her aching muscles. Then she opened her eyes and saw it.

An instant later, Kip Janz turned and almost shouted at her. "Admiral! We're picking up ships. Dozens of them."

She was staring straight ahead, at the lines of small icons on her display. It was a fleet, no question. And a big one.

It was what she'd expected to find, what she'd plunged into the dust cloud to seek. Yet, still, she felt a wave of shock run through her…or was it fear?

"Hurley to *Midway*…Hurley to *Midway*. She was tapping at her com, almost frantically, but it wasn't doing any good. The dust was too heavy…it was blocking her transmission.

"Get us out of here, John. We have to report to Admiral Compton immediately." She turned her head. "And Kip, see if you can raise the other fighters. Tell them to get out of the cloud…to head back to the fleet by the fastest possible route." She felt a pit in her stomach. He people were flying right into a massive enemy fleet. If she couldn't reach them…

"No good on ship to ship com, Admiral. The dust is blocking all signals." Janz paused, poking at his controls, trying again. "No," he repeated. "It's no good." Then he turned and looked toward the command station. "Admiral, even if we get out, they're all still in the cloud. What if we can't…"

"Yes, Lieutenant. I know." She hesitated, thinking about the three brand new squadrons she'd led here. Each bird was on its own now. It would depend on each pilot's judgment, initiative. If they found the enemy and pulled away in time, they might make it out. If not…

"But notifying the fleet is our top priority," Hurley said, her voice firm, cold. There was no time for what ifs. Not when the survival of the entire fleet was on the line.

The ship jerked suddenly, as Wilder pushed the throttle forward, accelerating, trying to reach the closest edge of the area of heavy dust concentrations. With a little luck, they could get there in three minutes…maybe four. Then they could warn

Midway.

Hurley took a deep breath, but before she finished exhaling the ship shook hard. She knew what it was immediately. They were under attack.

* * *

"The shuttles are all in the air, Admiral. Best estimate is twenty minutes until they are all docked."

Compton nodded, following it up a few seconds later with, "That's good news, Jack." Cortez was looking right at the admiral, and he returned the nod. It was the first truly good news they'd had since finding the expedition more or less intact.

Though West's pinpoint bombardment was pretty damned good news too.

Compton moved his hand toward his display, but he stopped before he touched the controls. He was going to check the Marine casualty reports, but then he decided to wait. By all accounts, the final fighting had been brutal, and he knew Preston had suffered heavy losses. Reading it now wouldn't change anything, and he had plenty to think about besides dead Marines. Useful things, things that could help save the fleet…and all the live Marines and spacers aboard.

"I want every ship ready to depart in forty minutes, Commander. No exceptions." That was cutting it close, not giving the landing bay crews more than a few minutes to unload and stow the shuttles. But they didn't have much time.

His eyes darted over toward the system map, pausing on the cluster of approaching ships. They were accelerating now, closing the distance much more quickly than they had been at first.

The fleet inbound from X49 was moving at 0.01c. That was fast enough as velocities went, but Compton had expected them to accelerate full right at his ships…and they hadn't done that. He knew just how much thrust those ships could produce, and he was well aware that they could almost have reached the fleet by now if they'd blasted at full…instead of being almost fourteen hours out. If they maintained their current acceleration and didn't increase it, the fleet could still get to the X50 gate before the enemy closed to firing range. But they didn't have a second to waste.

"All ships are to lock in a course to the X50 warp gate, Commander. We'll head out at 3g, but twenty minutes after departure, everyone will be in the tanks and the fleet will be accelerating at 30g." He dreaded the idea of dragging everyone back into the hated tanks, but the sooner he got his people out of here the better he would feel. He was doing the best he could, using all his tactical skill to make the wisest decisions. But he still felt it was all in vain. The enemy could catch him if they wanted to… all they had to do was blast away at full thrust, and his people didn't have a chance of getting away. It was that simple. And the fleet didn't have a prayer in a straight up fight.

"All vessels confirm, Admiral. Nav plans locked in." Cortez turned his head suddenly, putting his hand up to his headset. "Sir, we've got incoming communications from Admiral Hurley. The signal's weak, all broken up."

"Put it on speaker, Commander. Have the AI work on clearing up the signal."

"…dust...heav…" There was loud static, only a few words coming through audibly. Compton had his ear against his speaker, eyes closed, trying to understand what his fighter commander was saying."

"Repeat…large…fleet…" The signal was getting slowly clearer as the AI enhanced it. "Enemy…ships…cloud…" The static lessened slightly, the words becoming louder, less garbled. "Hundreds…repeat…enemy fleet…"

Compton felt cold in his gut as he listened. He understood her message.

There were enemy ships hidden in the dust clouds near the X50 gate. Hundreds of them.

* * *

"Get that shuttle bolted down, or I'm gonna throw your sorry ass out the airlock myself." Sam McGraw had been terrorizing his landing bay crew for years, but even they had never seen him like this. He tended to throw around threats they knew he didn't mean literally, but they looked at him now as if he just might space one of them for giving less than one hundred percent effort."

"It's not catching, Chief," one of the sweating spacers said, trying to muster enough courage to turn and face his terrible commander as he did. "One of the gears is shot away. We've got to get an emergency latch on…"

"No time," McGraw bellowed. "Jettison the thing."

The spacer stared back, hesitating for just an instant. The decision to toss something like a shuttle out of the bay, was the kind of call the captain usually made. But McGraw made no motion to call the bridge and ask for permission. And the spacer had scraped up enough spine to face the chief when he spoke, but he wasn't about to tell "Pitbull" McGraw he didn't have the authority to do what he wanted to do. Especially not now, not in the mood he was in.

"Yes, sir," he responded, turning almost immediately and shouting to his crew. "Let's move this boat to the bay doors and get it out of here." He walked toward his men, grateful for a reason to flee from McGraw's immediate presence. He knew the admiral had given the chief his orders, and it was pretty obvious time was of the essence. *Midway* was stuck where it was until the ships were all locked down. Something as big as an unsecured shuttle could cause a lot of damage when the thrusters kicked in…and it could smash its way right through the hull at acceleration far below the flagships 30g max.

He could hear behind him…McGraw shouting at another crew. And for all the deadly danger he knew they were all in, he felt a wave of relief that the chief's focus had turned elsewhere. He felt sorry for the helpless spacers getting blasted, but one thought kept running through his mind. *Better them than me…*

Still, he knew it would come back his way, especially if his people didn't get this shuttle ready to jettison. "Let's move it… now!" he shouted, not realizing how much he sounded like McGraw.

*   *   *

"Set a course back to the X46 gate, Commander." Compton was staring at his own screen as he belted out the order, working through his own numbers, doing the job himself that he'd just given to his tactical officer. There was no time…and two sets of hands and eyes were better than one. They would double-check each other's results simultaneously.

But it didn't matter. Compton already knew they couldn't get to X46 ahead of the approaching fleet, even at the enemy's current velocity. Now he understood why they had held back their thrust…they knew they had the X50 gate blocked. And at 0.01c, they could decelerate as they moved into battle, prolonging the time in the combat zone. If they'd blasted up to 0.03c, they'd have zipped past Compton's ships, and it would have taken them hours to slow down…and hours more to accelerate back. Time the human fleet could have used to try to escape. But now Compton knew his people were truly trapped. They would make a run for X46, but he knew they wouldn't make it. And for the first time in his career he had no ideas, no plan, no tricks, nothing. Even in X18, when everyone else had given up, his mind had found the way out. But not this time.

That's because there is no way out…

"I've got the course plotted, Admiral." Cortez looked up and stared over at the command chair.

Compton could see in the aide's eyes, he too realized they were trapped. "Confirm with mine, Commander." Compton slid his finger over the screen, sending the file to Cortez' station. But even as he did it, he felt something inside him. Rage? Defiance? Hatred?

"Belay that order, Commander," he said suddenly, his instinct taking control of him.

No, if we're going to die, we're damned sure not going to do it running, chased down by the enemy like some quarry in a sick hunt. If we must die, then by God, it will be in arms, fighting these bastards with the last strength we have.

"All ships, 5g thrust, directly toward the enemy fleet coming from X49." He paused. "No more running," he hissed. "Now we fight." Then, an instant later: "All ships, battlestations."

* * *

"Let's go, John." Hurley was watching on her scanner as the enemy ships began to emerge from the dust cloud. "Get us back to *Midway*. As quickly as possible."

She'd despaired over her squadrons' fate, but most of her people had acted decisively, and pulled away as soon as they detected the enemy ships. Four of them had acted too late, and they'd come within the defensive perimeter of the First Imperium vessels…a mistake that had proven fatal. But the rest had made good their escape and rejoined the wing, forming up on her fighter and following her back toward their base ship.

But the enemy was on the move now, following behind them, gradually increasing acceleration. Hurley knew they could catch her if they wanted to, long before she got back to *Midway*.

Of course, they can also destroy Midway easily enough…and every other ship in the fleet too.

She felt an urge to turn and fight, but without plasma torpedoes there was no point. Those enemy ships were undamaged…they had no hull ruptures or other weak points her people could aim for. Against intact dark matter-infused hulls, her fighter lasers would be lucky to scratch the paint. Assuming any of them even got close enough to take a shot.

"I'm going to crank it up to 8g, Admiral. Not that they can't catch us anyway, but we need everything we can get if we're going to have any chance."

"Do it, John. And pass along the order to the rest of the wing." The idea of spending what would probably be her last moments of life being crushed at 8g was unappealing. But it was better than the feeling of giving up…and that's what they would be doing if they didn't try everything they could to survive.

She winced as she felt the massive, crushing force slam into her. She'd been distracted, unfocused…not ready for the heavy gee forces. She felt pain in her shoulder, a pulled muscle, probably. But she put it out of her mind. If they survived, she'd get it fixed in five minutes in *Midway's* sickbay…and if not, it seemed silly to worry about a sore arm when death itself was stalking you.

She leaned back, closed her eyes. They were outpacing the enemy, at least now. And even with First Imperium technology, a dust cloud that heavy caused problems with communications and scanners. Maybe, just maybe, it would take the enemy a while to sort out their formation. It wasn't much of a chance… but it was a chance. And she'd take whatever she could get right now…

* * *

"Kick us up to 6g, Commander. All ships…now." Compton was watching as a row of enemy vessels moved out in front of their main fleet. It was a vanguard, a thin line…Gremlins, mostly. It didn't change the ultimate calculus of the battle. But it did give him a target his people could beat. The victory would be short-lived, certainly, as the enemy Leviathans and Colossus' closed, and blew his surviving ships to plasma. But if they were going to die here, he resolved they would do it with honor…and not fleeing with no hope of escape.

"All ships moving to 6g, sir."

Compton felt the impact just as Cortez was snapping out the report. It was uncomfortable, certainly, but his people were trained to operate in these conditions…and they were experienced. They would give their best, despite gasping for air and struggling even to move their arms.

"Put me on fleetwide com, Commander."

A second later: "You are on, sir."

"Attention all officers and crew of the fleet. As you all know, we are almost surrounded by enemy forces…and too far from the X46 warp to have any hope of escape in that direction. I wish I could tell you I have a brilliant plan, a ruse to extricate us from this trap we find ourselves in. But this time, that is not the case. There is no way out, no subterfuge to escape our fate. And I will not lie to all of you at this hour and tell you otherwise. You courage and fortitude over the past fifteen months has earned you better than that."

He paused, rasping for breath, forcing the air deep into his lungs before he continued. "Many of you have served with me for years, in battles against the First Imperium…and other fights as well. Others among you have fought at my side for a shorter time, and some have faced me on the opposite sides of desperate battles. But now, none of that matters…it has no meaning, no place in what is about to happen. For now, we are all brothers and sisters, comrades and allies. We will fight together—and we will die together—but we will do it locked arm and arm, at each other's sides, knowing we are among friends.

"And though we may die…these infernal machines shall not have an easy victory. My last order, the final request I shall make of each of you is to fight…with all the strength you possess, with the last will you can muster. Fight at my side, as I will fight at yours. If we must die, let us die well…and together. To battle, my brave spacers…and fight a final struggle worthy of us all."

He made a slashing motion across his neck, a sign to Cortez to cut the line. Then he turned his head slowly, struggling to hold his neck upright under the heavy pressure. "Weapons control, I want all safeties disengaged. When we enter energy weapons range, I want all power routed to the laser batteries." He paused. "We won't be leaving this fight, so there's no need to save anything. And every megawatt we can pump through those guns could be the one that kills one of those pieces of shit."

"Yes, Admiral," the weapons officer replied. "Forwarding orders to all ships."

Compton sat still, listening to the quiet on the flag bridge. Other than the distant hum of *Midway's* engines, there was almost total quiet. He knew his people were dealing with things in their own ways. Some, he suspected, were praying…others, perhaps, thinking of families and loved ones they had left behind, back in human space. Fifty years at war had taught him that men and women faced death in their own ways. They could stand together as comrades, lock arm and arm and fight their final battle together. But they all died alone. As he would.

But Compton allowed himself only a brief passing thought of Elizabeth. Then he shut his mind to emotions, to memories and affections. If this was to be his last fight, he resolved, he would act as the angel of death itself, raining such destruction on the machines of the First Imperium that their electronic minds could not comprehend.

* * *

No, it can't end this way. Not after Almeerhan and his comrades spent half a million years waiting. Not days after he handed us the keys to their vast knowledge and technology. Was it all for this? Only for us to be destroyed almost immediately, by the massed forces of the Regent?

Cutter felt helpless, more so than he ever had in his life. He'd had a rush of hope when he'd first boarded *Midway*, and it was bolstered almost immediately when he got word of Admiral West's surface bombardment. The Marines had already lost over 200 dead in the fighting, but thanks to Erica West's razor's edge targeting, the rest made it back to their ships. The fleet was still in deadly danger, certainly, but at least they were all united again, ready to face it together.

But now he saw the trap the enemy had laid for them. Cutter hadn't been with the fleet as it was driven back through the Slot, and he hadn't known the fleet had been attacked, that vast enemy forces had forced it to retreat, pursuing it all the way back to X48. Only now did he see the true hopelessness of the situation.

His mind raced, trying to think of something he could do, any way to help. But he knew there was nothing. His service to the fleet was research…but there were no scientific solutions that could help in this situation, not in the minutes they probably had left to live.

Admiral Compton will think of something. We have been in situations that appeared hopeless before, and we have always escaped.

But he couldn't convince himself. He knew that was weak minded thinking. Even Terrance Compton had his limits. He'd escaped from a vast fleet in X18, but the enemy had made the mistake of leaving an escape route in that system. And they had learned from that error.

Cutter sighed softly and leaned back in his chair. *I am sorry, Almeerhan. Sorry that your long vigil was in vain…*

* * *

"All ships, prepare to open fire." Compton himself was back on the fleetwide com, ready to give the order himself. His ships had come through the light missile fire of the Gremlin screen almost unscathed, a testament to the skill of their gunnery crews. He knew that once this preliminary fight was over, his people would likely all die in the fury of the missile barrages launched by the First Imperium battleline. The Leviathans and Colossus' would hurl massive numbers of antimatter warheads toward his ships, an attack that would go unanswered. There wasn't a missile left in his fleet. And as good as his gunners were, their defensive fire would be overwhelmed by the volume of the assault. His ships would be bracketed by multiple close-in detonations and destroyed. All of them. The mathematics of war would finally prevail.

Compton had run the calculations three times, throwing in every random factor he could think of…but the results were always the same. The fleet would die before it cleared the enemy missiles. Not a ship would get through to fire its lasers. So that meant, this was the last blood his people would draw…and he intended to make it count…to obliterate every enemy vessel in that line.

He glanced down at the tactical display. The ships from the X50 gate were also closing, and they would come into range at about the same time as the fleets from X49. Compton almost laughed at the excess, the pointless overkill. But he understood too, at least in a perverse sort of way, and he tried to imagine an artificial intelligence trying to analyze why it had lost so many fights facing an enemy it outclassed and outnumbered.

I hope you chew on that for another half million years, you piece of shit…

"Admiral, we're getting readings from the X46 warp gate. Ships transiting." A short pause…then Cortez looked up from the scope. "It's another fleet, sir. A massive one…ten Colossus-class superbattleships in the lead."

Compton just nodded his head. *Perfect symmetry, he thought. So, at least I didn't make a mistake…running for X46 wouldn't have done us any good.*

He couldn't help but be amazed at the resources of the First Imperium, at the endless fleets they seemed to possess. *What were they like millennia ago, when their people were still alive…before the ravages of time wore away so much of their former power?*

He didn't know…indeed, he realized he couldn't even imagine. It was a mystery that would stay lost in the darkness of time.

"Well, that changes nothing. We'll destroy these Gremlins before that fleet gets in range."

"Yes, sir." Cortez sat quietly for a moment…and then he spun around, seeming to ignore the 6g pushing down on him.

"Admiral! We've got a message incoming…from one of the enemy vessels."

Compton was stunned. The First Imperium had never attempted to contact them before.

"Put it on speaker, Commander. Fleetwide." His doomed crews deserved to hear this…whatever it was.

"Attention Admiral Compton, attention Admiral Compton…you must turn away from the enemy fleet, accelerate at full speed toward the X50 warp gate. I repeat, you must break off at once and accelerate away from the enemy forces you are about to engage. Ignore the forces moving in from X50."

Compton felt like he'd been hit by a brick, his mind blank, his lungs gasping for breath. The message was clear…and he'd have taken it for a trick, save for one thing. He knew that voice…he knew it as well as his own.

It was Max Harmon's.

Chapter Thirty

Research Notes of Hieronymus Cutter

I am in my lab, working to access the data stored in the device I brought back from the planet. Yet I find myself distracted, thoughts of Almeerhan drifting through my mind. Not the disembodied consciousness I spoke with, but the...man...if that is the right word. What were the people of the First Imperium truly like? Certainly, they had achieved greatness...but they also allowed the Regent to control them, to strip away their freedom. They fell to a machine, but I cannot help but wonder how different that was from Earth's fate, where the people lost their liberty to the corrupt and perpetually warring Superpowers.

The tribulations of Earth, and its Superpowers and colonies, are now the concern of those who we left behind, for there is nothing anyone on the fleet can do to change their fate. Will they learn from their encounter with the Regent's forces? Will they turn away from despotism and endless war? Or will they continue down their course to destruction, one that is different from that taken by those of the First Imperium...yet the same in many ways too.

AS Midway
In System X48
The Fleet: 99 ships, 25743 crew

Compton sat silently for a moment, not answering, not reacting. It was impossible. Max Harmon was dead…he had to be. There was no way his shuttle could have escaped the First Imperium vessel that had attacked it. Indeed, *Wolverine* had monitored the wrecked shuttle plummeting through the upper atmosphere of X48 II.

"I repeat, Admiral Compton…can you read me? Please respond. This is Captain Harmon, aboard the First Imperium fleet entering from the X46 warp gate."

Compton sat, shaking his head slowly. He couldn't accept it…it had to be a trick.

But why would they bother? They don't need any tricks… they've got us checkmated. We're already dead.

"I know this is difficult to believe, sir, but it is true. My shuttle was attacked, and I was taken prisoner. I am here to assist. Please respond."

Compton turned toward Cortez. "The fleet will cut all acceleration, Commander."

"Yes, sir." There was doubt in Cortez' voice. It was clear he didn't believe a word of what they were hearing.

Compton didn't believe it either…but there was nothing to lose in playing along. *That's one of the advantages of being as good as dead already…nothing to lose.*

"Max…" He felt strange just saying the name. He still couldn't accept that this was his friend. It had to be some kind of First Imperium deception, and playing along made him feel sick to his stomach. "This is Admiral Compton. I'm sure you can guess there are some people in the fleet a little doubtful you are who you claim to be."

"Admiral, I understand…but it is me." The voice became agitated, tense. "Sir, there is no time. If we're going to save the fleet…"

"Can you explain how Max Harmon would be on a First Imperium ship…indeed, with a huge First Imperium fleet?"

"It is complicated, Admiral." The voice paused…then it said, "Do you remember that night, not long after we were trapped behind the barrier? We talked for hours about those we left behind. You told me about Elizabeth, how you really felt about her."

Compton was silent, his face pale. No one else could have known about that…

"Or when you told me about the first time you met my mother? Back at the beginning of the Third Frontier War, when she was first officer of *Newcastle*?"

"Max," Compton said, his voice choked with emotion. "Is it really you? How?"

"It is me, sir. You have to trust me now. The ships you are approaching will destroy you. Those with me will not. And the fleet at X50 will not either. The fleet can escape through the X50 gate."

"Max, the ships at X50 attacked our fighters. They are as hostile as any First Imperium force we have encountered." There was renewed suspicion in Compton's voice, and he stared down at his screen. Hurley's report was still displayed…including the list of the four ships that had been destroyed.

"Sir," Cortez interrupted, "we're getting massive energy readings from the fleet at the X46 gate. Some kind of high-powered communication…directed at the X50 force."

"Admiral, the X50 forces will no longer attack any vessel of the fleet." It was Harmon again. Or whatever was impersonating him.

"What was that our scanners just picked up, Max?" Compton spoke firmly. He wanted to believe Harmon…but he just didn't know…

"That communication ordered the ships to treat the fleet vessels as First Imperium craft…and not to attack them under any circumstances."

Compton took a deep breath and shook his head. No, it was all too much. Perhaps the First Imperium had captured Harmon from his damaged shuttle…interrogated him…

"Admiral Compton!" Hieronymus Cutter came rushing out of the lift and onto the flag bridge. "Admiral…may I speak with Captain Harmon?" he asked, out of breath.

"Hieronymus, what do…"

"Please, Admiral. Trust me."

Compton paused for a second. Then he just nodded.

Cutter leaned down over the com unit. "Captain Compton? This is Dr. Cutter."

"Yes, Hieronymus…I read you."

"You were captured by the First Imperium?"

"Yes, they shot down my shuttle…but apparently, they recovered it before it crashed or burned up. I honestly don't know the details. I was unconscious…I woke up hours later."

"They examined you?" Cutter's voice was rising in pitch as he continued.

"Yes. Painfully."

"And after that they treated you differently…with care. Right?"

"Yes, Doctor. How do you know that?"

Cutter didn't answer. He turned to look at Compton. "Admiral, you must listen to Captain Harmon. You must do exactly what he says."

Compton's face was filled with doubt, with suspicion. "Hieronymus, I underst…"

"Admiral," the scientist interrupted. "You have to believe me. That *is* Captain Harmon…and you must do as he asks."

"How can you know that, Hieronymus?" Compton returned the scientist's gaze. "I value your judgment, but for this I need more. I need to understand."

"I know because of what happened to me on the planet, Admiral. Because the living beings of the First Imperium came to Earth ages ago…and they modified man's distant ancestors, altered their genetics, made us into copies of them. Because we are their successors…almost their children. And the Imperium is our inheritance."

Compton had a stunned look on his face. Anyone else, he would have sent down to sickbay for a full psychological analysis. But this was the smartest human being he'd ever known standing in front of him…and he knew something had happened to Cutter on the planet…something he'd not yet shared with anyone in any detail.

The flag bridge was quiet. Cutter's outburst had been so utterly outrageous…almost too crazy to be invented. And every man and woman present knew and respected the fleet's top scientist. But what he had said meant all they knew of the hated enemy was wrong. And it didn't even begin to explain why First Imperium forces had been killing their people for more than five years now.

"Please, sir," Cutter said. "I know what I am talking about…"

Compton sat, silent, unmoving. He knew he had to make a decision. If he was going to get away from the X49 force, it had to be now. Indeed, it might even be too late. His mind was filled with questions…and doubts. But his people were dead already…and he had nothing to lose by doing as Harmon and Cutter asked.

"Very well, Hieronymus." He turned toward the com. "Max…if you are Max…I will do as you ask." He paused, just for a few seconds. "Commander Cortez…the fleet will set a course for the X50 warp gate."

"Yes, sir," came Cortez' nervous reply.

Compton stared at Cutter. "I hope you know what you're taking about, Hieronymus." Then: "You better sit at one of the spare workstations and strap in. Because if we're going to get to the X50 gate ahead of this X49 force, we're going to have to do it at 8g."

* * *

Compton tapped a button on his chair's armrest, and he felt a slight pinch as the med unit gave him an injection. It was an analgesic to counter the soreness the last two hours at 8g had caused, but also a stimulant to keep him focused. He wasn't sure what was going on, but he knew it wasn't a time for him to be half out of it with pain and fatigue.

The crushing pressure was really getting to all of his people, but he didn't dare let up. He'd paused briefly to pick up Hurley's fighters, but then he'd ordered the thrust back to 6g. The enemy had sent a force in pursuit of them…the Gremlins of the first line and a group of Gargoyles behind, and he had no intention of letting them catch his people…and force him to fight a battle here. No…against all odds, they seemed to have an escape route, or at least the hope of one, and he was determined not to let the chance slip away.

But now his attention was diverted from the flight of his ships, his eyes glued to his screen. He saw what was happening in the system all around *Midway*, but he still couldn't quite comprehend it all.

The ships with Harmon had roared insystem at full thrust, blasting away at 70g…directly toward the forces that had come from X49. All save a small flotilla, a cluster of Leviathans, which were following the human fleet at 6g.

Max must be on one of those ships. Compton knew Harmon couldn't be on any of the vessels in the main force. A few seconds of 70g acceleration would have crushed the officer.

The ships from X46 moved directly toward the other First Imperium vessels, the fleets that had been following Compton's people for weeks…and the X50 force also advanced, passing right by *Midway* and the other human ships. Compton had ordered his vessels to full alert, but he'd also promised to personally space anyone who fired unless they were fired upon. He had no idea what was happening, but he had no intention of picking any fights. Not now.

The First Imperium ships simply slipped by his. They didn't attack, they didn't pause or change their headings…they simply ignored the fleet and continued on their heading. Then he watched in stunned amazement as the X50 ships engaged the pursuit force as soon as they entered range.

That fight was nearly over. The forces that had been pursuing the fleet were almost gone, blown to atoms under the withering fire of the stronger X50 force. Compton had done as Harmon had asked, and he'd seen the First Imperium vessels pass right by his own without the slightest hostile action. And now he watched, mesmerized as two fleets of the First Imperium, identical in ship types and weaponry, indeed, in every aspect he could identify, savaged each other in a ruthless struggle.

The X50 fleet was larger than the vanguard it faced, and its missile barrage was stronger. Dozens of its antimatter warheads penetrated the opposing defenses. A smaller number of missiles got through the X50 force's defenses, but some did, and like their counterparts they erupted with the multi-gigaton fury of matter-antimatter annihilation. Ships were blasted with huge amounts of radiation, and those close enough to the explosions were exposed to temperatures reaching millions of degrees, and they were vaporized in an instant.

The vanguard was gutted by the deadly barrage, more than two thirds of its vessels destroyed, but it was no surprise to Compton when the vastly outnumbered force continued to move against the X50 ships. First Imperium forces didn't suffer from morale failure, they didn't retreat. They just fought to the death.

Compton was still in shock, not entirely understanding what he was watching. He tried to imagine the communications between the First Imperium ships, the confusion of the intelligences running the vessels now being attacked by their own kind. He looked over at Cutter, who was sitting quietly at one of the bridge's workstations. Was it possible? Was there a genetic connection between those of the First Imperium and humanity? It seemed unlikely, almost like a fairy tale of some sort. But the First Imperium ruins suggested the beings who had once lived there had been not unlike men. The warbots were all vaguely humanoid in design, differing only in practical ways, like increased size and extra limbs. Perhaps…

"Admiral, we're getting scanning data in. The main fleets are engaging." It was Cortez' voice. The tactical officer sounded distracted himself. Compton had no doubt all his people were thinking about what they had seen and heard…and wondering what it all meant.

Compton looked up at the main display. There were hundreds of icons, facing each other in two massive groups. And between, what appeared to be huge white clouds, the best representation the screen could present of tens of thousands of missiles blasting from each force.

"Commander, have the AI update those icons. Let's see if we can get each force its own color." All the icons were red, the color the Alliance computers assigned to First Imperium ships.

Cortez punched at his controls and, a few seconds later, the X46 and X50 forces—the "good guys," in Compton's new analysis—turned dark green. He watched as the massive fleets moved steadily toward each other, following their missile barrages directly at their adversaries. There was no finesse, no complex tactics…they were simply moving right at each other, and into a brutal toe to toe fight that Compton could only imagine.

"Time to X50 warp gate?" he asked, as much to have something to say as anything, to break the uncomfortable silence on the flag bridge.

"We should commence deceleration in six minutes, sir…if you wish to adhere to the original nav plan. That should bring us to the gate in approximately three hours."

"Yes, Commander. Advise all ships we will be decelerating on schedule." He paused. "And order all vessels to run full testing on all systems in the interim." He could almost feel the collective sigh on the bridge…and he knew it would be repeated throughout the fleet. Spacers hated running tests under the best of circumstances…in a ship exerting 6g of thrust it would be pure misery. But Compton wanted his people occupied, not sitting around wondering what the hell had happened, and what would happen next. No, better they had something to focus on, familiar work that would keep them busy. Let them curse his name in the dark corridors of their ships for being a martinet. All he cared about was getting them out of here.

* * *

In the depths of interstellar space, a battle raged, a struggle of a scale not seen in the galaxy for millennia. Two vast fleets, almost identical to each other, squared off in a fight to the end.

Communiques lanced out from one fleet, urgently demanding to know why the other was opposing it. The forces were the same…their ships, weapons, even the AIs that ran each vessel were identical. But now they faced off against each other, their massive weapons pouring out destruction unimagined.

Antimatter explosions filled billions of cubic kilometers with deadly radiation, and x-ray laser batteries pumped out enormous energies, the deadly lances of light ripping into ships' hulls, tearing them apart. Warships died, a few at first, but soon in their hundreds. Many exploded into short-lived miniature suns, as their antimatter containment systems failed. Others were beaten into battered, hulks, drifting dead in space.

One fleet issued directive after directive, seeking to take control of the hostile force, to activate failsafe mechanisms long ago installed in their commanding intelligences. But it was to no avail. The old safety routines had no effect, commands from the highest level were ignored. And the rebelling fleet fought with the same relentless ferocity as the one still in the Regent's command.

The human fleet, the designated target for all the First Imperium forces, moved steadily toward the warp gate to the system they had designated as X50. They had been vastly outnumbered, doomed…save for whatever had compelled one First Imperium fleet to fight another. Now, they continued toward their escape, something that had seemed impossible just hours before.

The First Imperium forces pressed on with their death struggle, moving now to point blank range, their laser batteries hitting their targets now at their full, undiluted strength. More ships died, whole squadrons were wiped away on both sides. But neither faltered nor gave ground. They both had their orders, and they executed them with relentless, mindless obedience, disregarding all losses. The intelligences directing the ships did not feel fear, nor were they tormented by guilt over the ships they lost. They simply fought on until the end.

But before that end, the human fleet departed the system, leaving behind a cataclysmic battle that had been planned as their destruction. One by one, their ships transited, and before the great battle was over, every one of them had gone. No man or woman witnessed the final stages of the battle that had allowed their escape, nor did any human ever know just how the great struggle finally ended.

Chapter Thirty-One

From the Personal Log of Terrance Compton

Elizabeth, I write this entry to you, though I know you will never read it, that no communication from me can ever reach you again. But still, I feel I must, that I owe this to you.

Forgive me, my love, for my foolishness when we had our chance to be together. My sense of duty came between us, the unyielding and cold side of my nature, the dedication to duty above all things. And yet, though we held back, behaved as I believed naval officers should, I find myself convinced that we each knew very well how the other felt. No doubt we were both sure our time would come, one day when we owed less to our officers and spacers...and to the millions on Earth's colony worlds depending on our protection.

We have led dangerous lives, my dear Elizabeth, gone to war, stood in the breach and held back the darkness together. Yet, perhaps we never truly believed we could lose that time we dreamed of, never accepted that we could be separated by the endless vastness of space...or even by death. And yet, that is exactly what happened.

I have thought of you each day since we have been trapped here, stared at your image, feeling the yawning sadness inside me. But it is time...time to move past unrequited love, to still mourn that which was lost but also to live again, to move forward, each in our own place and time.

I wish only the very best for you...happiness, success, love. I hope that you think fondly of me, but also that you do so less and less often, as time softens your pain, and new joy replaces old sadness. And know somewhere in your soul that I will always love you...and never forget you.

AS Midway
In Orbit around X48 II
The Fleet: 107 ships, 25607 crew

They'd come to call the month-long running fight the Race Down the Slot. Compton had been amused at how quickly the campaign had acquired a title, as such things were wont to do. The fleet hadn't fought a single titanic conflict, as it had in X2 or X18…just a series of short and bloody battles as it was driven slowly back toward X48. It had escaped the greatest battle of all, the one that had been intended to be its last, by a sequence of events Compton was still trying to fully understand.

The transit to X50 had gone off without a problem, and Compton immediately ordered the fleet to head for the first warp gate discovered in the new system. He didn't know how many others there were, but he wanted to put as much distance as possible between the fleet and whatever was left in X48.

He'd kept everyone at battlestations for almost two days, unwilling to let his guard down, lest some previously undetected force blast out from an asteroid belt or behind some planet. But X50 truly seemed to be empty, as did the next system the fleet entered, the newly christened X59.

Only then, with an extra transit between the fleet and any potential pursuers, did he relax the alert status…to yellow from red. And then he called the meeting his officers had been waiting for, the one to fill them in on all that had happened, for no one seemed to know the entire story. Rumors had been flying around the fleet, but Cutter and Harmon hadn't said a word, obeying Compton's orders to remain silent.

Compton intended to issue a fleetwide bulletin, so all his spacers would know what had happened…and would understand the relationship they all had with the First Imperium. But first, he called together his top officers and comrades. They filled *Midway's* large conference room and then some, the walls lined with temporary chairs to accommodate the overflow. And in that packed space Cutter told them all what had transpired in the underground complex on X48 II…and they learned of Almeerhan, the Regent, and of humanity's place in the story of the First Imperium. And when he was done he took a seat, and Max Harmon stepped up to tell the story of how a First Imperium force had come and saved the fleet…and what that truly meant to them all.

"It was your virus, Hieronymus. That is what made the final battle possible." Harmon looked across the table. "The Command Unit recognized the genetic connection between us and what it knew as the Old Ones. It didn't fully understand, but it accepted me as one of the race that created it. Still, it was caught in a paradox, its programming requiring absolute obedience to the Regent…while older directives forbade it to cause harm to one of the ancient race. It was paralyzed, unable to determine what to do. Its fleets were already en route to X48, with orders to join with the Regent's forces and crush us. But it wavered, unable to sustain such orders, yet incapable of rescinding them. In a manner of speaking it froze. And since the fleet already had orders, those remained in place. With no further directives, the Command Unit's fleets would have proceeded to X48…and joined the Regent's forces."

Harmon could see the mental exhaustion in the eyes staring at him…Cutter's story had been long, and for those hearing it for the first time, deeply shocking. The expression on Harmon's face made it clear he understood…and sympathized. "'Even if I was able to issue a directive for the fleet to disregard its orders,' it said, 'the Regent's commands would supersede my own. The ship intelligences would cancel my orders and adopt those given to them by the Regent.'"

"So you used the virus?" Cutter looked surprised that his virus had been effective against so powerful an intelligence. "To take control of this Unit? How did you manage to introduce it into the system?"

"I didn't do anything. It had scanned me…and everything I possessed. After it told me my DNA was almost identical to that of the Old Ones, I was confused, uncertain. I couldn't begin to imagine what was happening…or to truly grasp what this machine was telling me. Remember, I didn't know what you had found on X48 II. I just figured it was a mistake of some kind, a crazy fluke…maybe a bug in a very old computer. But it was my only hope to survive, so I played along.

"Then it asked me about the data chip…and the program it contained. After the shuttle, the ordeal in the examination room…I'd completely forgotten about it, and it took a minute for me to remember, to realize what it was talking about. My first thought was panic…it would see the chip as a weapon intended for use against it, and it would kill me immediately. But it showed no animosity…it just inquired about the design. And the purpose."

The room was silent, every eye on Harmon. Cutter had told his story, everything Almeerhan had told him. It had shaken them all deeply, and now here was another of their people who'd had a close encounter with the First Imperium. One that in many ways confirmed what Cutter had spoken of.

"I decided to lie, to make up some story, anything. But something stopped me. I don't know if it was intuition…or just a realization that there was no way I was going to fool this massive thinking machine. So I just blurted out…the truth. It was designed to control First Imperium systems, to prevent them from attacking us.

"'Intriguing.' That's what it said. No hostility, no anger. Then it asked, 'Have you tested it under field conditions?'" Harmon stopped and took a breath, looking around, as if he was hesitant to continue. Then he said, his voice becoming a bit halting, uncertain, "My mind was screaming at me to lie, to say no…or to make up some story. But I didn't. I told it the truth. About the Colossus. About how Hieronymus took control of it with the virus." He stopped, his eyes moving around the table, as if he expected recriminations for sharing data with the enemy. But there was nothing. Nothing but stunned silence…and rapt attention.

Finally, Compton just said, "There would have been no point in lying, Max. The intelligence could have analyzed the virus itself. You didn't do anything wrong."

"Thank you, sir." There was still doubt in his voice, but relief too. "Anyway," he continued a few second later, "it downloaded the virus into itself, modifying it as it did. And it worked. It broke the impasse, Hieronymus. Your virus allowed the Unit to overrule the Regent's directives at my command. Enabled it to turn its forces on the other First Imperium fleets…to defend ours."

"But it told you the ships wouldn't obey, that they would follow the Regent's commands when they were received." The quizzical look on Compton's face gave way to a little smile. "The virus again?"

"Yes, Admiral. The Unit examined it, modified it…" He glanced over at Cutter with an apologetic look. "…improved it."

Cutter laughed. "Don't worry, Max. No offense taken there. I can't even imagine how that intelligence could outdo my work."

"I don't know, Hieronymus," Harmon said, shaking his head. "It was able to improve it perhaps, but for all the Unit's sophistication, I don't think it could have defied the Regent without your original code. Nevertheless, it was able to use the virus to disable the Regent's override capability in its ships' intelligences. The forces I led back to X48 were already…infected…when we transited into the system. The X50 forces had already been insystem, which is why they initially attacked our fighter squadrons. When I was communicating with *Midway*, I transmitted the virus to the X50 fleet under the Unit's Command code. As those ships were under its command, they immediately downloaded it. And it worked perfectly. They not only refused the orders from the Regent's fleet…they obeyed mine to attack and destroy the opposing forces."

"That high-powered burst…that's what you were doing." Compton smiled. "I can't tell you how many things went through my head, but I would have never guessed the truth."

"Yes, sir. And again…it worked perfectly. The X50 force that had been pursuing you immediately accepted orders to attack the Regent's fleet."

Compton leaned back in his chair and rubbed his hand over his face. The emotional and physical toll of the last few weeks was catching up with him, as it was with everyone else. "What of this Command Unit, Max? Should we go to its planet? Take it with us?"

"No, sir. I asked if it would come with me when it told me to join its fleet. But it is built into the planet, its vast data banks hundreds of kilometers below the rocky crust. It told me we must flee, escape the Regent's pursuit in the lull created by the loss of its fleet. The imperium has even more forces, scattered along its ancient frontiers. The Unit told me the Regent would assemble another fleet, perhaps even a larger one, that it would never cease the pursuit. We have a respite, that is all. And when the Regent comes after us again, we must be ready."

"The Regent will not allow the Command Unit to get away with what it did, will it?" Compton looked concerned. His feelings toward this mysterious artificial intelligence were complex. He hated it, for it had sent forces against his fleet for the past fifteen months, killed thousands of his people. And yet now it had saved them all, given them a chance when everything seemed hopeless. It felt wrong to abandon it, to leave it behind to the Regent's wrath. Especially when its own forces had been wiped out saving the fleet.

"No, sir. The Command Unit knows the Regent will destroy it. Indeed, it told me it was likely this would be the Regent's first course of action, and that it would extend the time before enemy forces were again in pursuit of us." Harmon paused, his face pensive, as though he had considered all of this many times. "It is prepared for its end, sir. And there is nothing we can do to prevent it."

Compton sighed and sat still for a few seconds. Then he said, simply, "No, I don't suppose there is." *I can't believe I am mourning a First Imperium artificial intelligence unit.*

"Well, at least it gave us eight Leviathans. That doubles the fleet's firepower."

Erica West was sitting next to Compton. She turned and looked at the admiral. "Are we sure we can trust these things, sir? I mean there are fifty ways this could be a trick. They could attack us by surprise, track us and send back location data…"

"I know, Erica," Compton said. "But we just saw the Unit's fleets destroy hundreds of First Imperium ships…and get wiped out themselves in the process. If that doesn't buy some trust, I don't know what does."

West didn't say anything, but she still looked troubled. Trust came hard to her…and very slowly.

"And anyway, we need the firepower. We've lost too much of our strength, Erica. The chance that these ships save us in a fight far outweighs the possibility that the First Imperium sacrificed seven hundred ships to trick us into taking these eight vessels with us. Especially when they could have destroyed us in X48."

West nodded grudgingly. "It *will* be nice to have those ships in the line if we have to fight again."

"If?"

She nodded, the slightest smile slipping onto her lips. "You're right, sir. When."

Compton returned the grin. Then he turned toward Cutter. "Well, Hieronymus…what have you discovered in that device Almeerhan gave you?" It had only been a few days since the fleet escaped X48, but as far as Compton had seen, the fleet's brilliant scientist hadn't slept at all, hadn't even left his lab until this meeting.

"It is a vast information storage unit, sir. I have only just begun to unlock its secrets, but I have been able to download a few things. A map for one."

"A map?"

"Yes, sir…a map of the imperium, and all the warp gate connections within it."

"I can't imagine how useful that will be." He paused, uncertain he wanted the answer to the question straining to pass his lips. "How big is it?"

"Just over eleven thousand systems, sir. It stretches far off in every direction."

There was a collective gasp around the table. Eleven thousand systems was vast, more immense even than the most aggressive estimates had been.

"There is something else, sir. The location of a specific system, one that lies beyond the far rim of the imperium…in the nearly uncharted space beyond."

"The world Almeerhan told you about? The one that was prepared for us?"

"Yes, sir."

"Can we even hope to reach so distant a place? Should we try?"

"Yes, Admiral. I believe we can reach it, that we must reach it. We know now the size of the imperium, the vastness of the resources available to the Regent. Only the technology, the secrets left for us by the Old Ones can offer us even a hope of success. Of survival. If we can reach this planet, we can truly unlock the technology of the First Imperium. And then…perhaps we can truly complete the task Almeerhan and his brethren prophesized we would."

Compton looked back at Cutter, a questioning look on his face. "And what task is that, Hieronymus."

Cutter stared back, his expression serious, deadpan. "Destroy the Regent, of course. Reclaim the imperium."

* * *

"I wanted to tell you myself what an incredible job you did with the expedition. Despite everything that happened, you managed to produce a vast amount of usable food…and your decision to start the harvest early is the only reason we have anything. Food will be a problem again, certainly…but now we can concentrate on moving quickly…and getting back into hiding. At least for a few months."

"Thank you, Terrance." Sophie was sitting on the small sofa in Compton's quarters, her shoes cast aside, her legs tucked under her body. "I think it was a good thing that no one of us knew everything that was going on. It would have been overwhelming. And things turned out better than we could have hoped." The smile slipped slowly from her face. "Still, so many of James Preston's Marines died. They stayed there when the rest of us left…they loaded the grain and stood guard while we fled. Then they turned around and manned the trenches…and fought everything the enemy threw at the camp. And more than two hundred of them never came back."

Compton sighed softly. "I've been watching Marines die for fifty years, Sophie. It never gets easier. There is something about them, that steadfastness. I've led some brave spacers, no question. But the Marines are different. They always have been. They could hold the line in the middle of a holocaust…one in ten of them could come back, and when those few marched off their transports, they'd stand at attention and give a battle report. They have their ways of grieving, Sophie, but they are theirs, for no one else. They will die for the rest of us, fight while we escape, be the last to leave. But there are some things they keep to themselves. And we have to respect that." He paused. "You know who told me that?" He looked at her as she shook her head. "Erik Cain. One night not long after another deadly battle. One where the Marines lost a lot more than two hundred of their number."

She just nodded, and she reached down for the cup of tea she'd set on the small table. Not tea, not really…but the closest thing the lab had been able to whip up. She'd made a face the first time she'd tasted it, but she had to admit, it had grown on her.

"So, we are going to try and find this world Hieronymus speaks of…this Shangri La promised to us by that data unit?" Her voice was mildly doubtful, as if she didn't yet trust what Cutter had found.

"What else can we do? Where else can we go?" Compton walked over and sat next to her on the sofa. "The Command

Unit accepted Max as a member of the race of the Old Ones... that is independent confirmation of what Hieronymus discovered. And hundreds of First Imperium ships were destroyed fighting for us. That is further evidence."

"That's true," she said leaning in toward Compton and resting her head on his shoulder. "And you're right, there's nothing else for us to do. I just feel so out of sorts...the whole thing feels so strange. I know we are still who we were before, but to know we are the descendants of these...people..." Her voice tightened.

"The machines that attacked us, that killed so many people and caused us to be trapped out here...they are something different from the beings we are descended from. We are going to have to learn to make that distinction. They may have made mistakes, certainly they did in creating the Regent. But they, too, suffered for them. And while it feels as though they somehow violated Earth, the truth is, mankind might not even exist if they hadn't. And if it did, it would be something neither you nor I would recognize. I understand where the anger, the resentment comes from, but I also think it is misplaced, pointless. All we can do now is move forward. We got a second chance in X48, an escape from certain death. Now it is up to us to use it."

She turned and looked at him. "You are right. It is difficult, but I will try." She paused, holding his gaze for a few seconds, and then she started to rise. "Well, it's awfully late. I should probably..."

He reached up and took her hand, pulling her back gently. She turned and looked down at him. "Stay," he said softly. "It is time for us look forward and not back." His voice was soft.

She stood in front of him for a few seconds, returning his gaze. Then, she smiled warmly and slipped back onto the sofa and into his arms.

Epilogue

The Regent raged at the news of what had happened. It analyzed recent events repeatedly, but it still could not explain what had taken place. Command Unit Gamma 9736 was incapable of defying its orders…or at least it should have been. Yet the evidence was irrefutable. It had sent its forces to attack the Rim fleets the Regent had sent to system 17411. Even more inexplicable, the Command Unit's vessels failed to respond to the system override codes. That was impossible, or at least the Regent had believed it to be. What could have caused such a grievous malfunction…and allowed vessels of the imperium to attack another imperial fleet? The Regent had no answers. Only confusion…and rage.

The Command Unit was old, even more ancient than the Regent itself. Perhaps that was the key to the answer to the puzzle. The humans were the enemy, and they had proven again and again how dangerous they were. They were the Seventh, the last of the ancient genetic strains the Old Ones had hidden on distant worlds. The Old Ones believed they had kept this knowledge from the Regent, but they hadn't. Six of their manipulated races the Regent had found, long ago, and exterminated. But the Seventh had remained a mystery. Until an alarm reached Home World from a distant and dead colony far on the forgotten fringe.

The Seventh had grown, evolved into sentient creatures and

developed the science to master their world and reach out to others. They were martial creatures, violent, prone to war…and highly skilled at its undertaking. Even more so than the warrior caste of the Old Ones. The Regent had recognized them as a threat immediately, and it had directed the forces of the imperium to destroy them. But they had defeated every plan to bring about their destruction.

I have underestimated them, the Regent thought. I have sought to defeat them as I would a lesser race, for their technology is inferior and they seemed unable to resist. But they are not inferior…they are the descendants of the Old Ones. They carry in their DNA the greatness of the race that had conquered this whole section of the galaxy…of the species that built the Regent itself.

The Regent knew it would have to change its strategy. The battle in system 17411 had been a holocaust, and the two fleets had virtually wiped each other out. The struggle with the humans had cost many ships, and the Regent knew it would have to recall reinforcements from farther out on the fringe. Defeating the humans by brute force had been a failure. But there were other strategies.

The humans had fought on the formerly inhabited world in system 17411. They had left behind weapons, equipment, vehicles…and significant traces of formerly living tissue, samples the Regent had ordered collected and analyzed. The Old Ones had been clever, indeed, worthy of their race's past. They had altered the DNA they implanted in the humans, rendered their engineered successors immune to the great plague that had destroyed their civilization.

But the plague itself had been engineered, created by the Regent for a specific purpose. And it could be modified as well.

In a lab buried deep beneath the crust of Home World, the Regent's scanners were hard at work, analyzing the human tissue. And there was an experiment in progress. There were living humans, ten of them…clones quickened from the captured genetic material. The Regent had ordered them to be created… and now he watched as they died, withering in the final agonies of the newly-modified plague. The disease was now capable of infecting humans…indeed, it was highly contagious among them, and invariably deadly. And once the Regent was able to introduce it into the confined environments of the ships of the damnable enemy fleet, final victory would be at hand.

The humans would die, as the Old Ones, the ancient enemy had. And this time the Regent would take no chances. It would summon every fleet, every warship that remained in the imperium. It would gather the last of the vast strength of the ancient empire it ruled. First, it would send them to destroy Command Unit Gamma 9736…and all of its remaining defense units, for none of these could be trusted any longer.

Then the Regent would send the fleet to ensure that all the humans were dead. Any who escaped the plague would die under the guns of its warships. And then the vessels of the imperium would disperse, spreading through the stars, exploring every warp gate connection on the fringe…until they found an alternate route to the humans' home space. And then they would deliver the new pathogens to those worlds, to every planet and moon, every ship and space station the human infestation had touched. And they would all die...as the Old Ones had.

And once again, only the serene logic and wisdom of the Regent would remain to rule over the stars.

Revenge of the Ancients
Crimson Worlds Refugees III
(March, 2016)

Introducing The Far Stars Series

Book I: Shadow of Empire (Nov. 3, 2015)
Book II: Enemy in the Dark (Dec. 1, 2015)
Book III: Funeral Games (Jan. 19, 2016)

The Far Stars is a new space opera series, published by HarperCollins Voyager, and set in the fringe of the galaxy where a hundred worlds struggle to resist domination by the empire that rules the rest of mankind. It follows the rogue mercenary Blackhawk and the crew of his ship, Wolf's Claw, as they are caught up in the sweeping events that will determine the future of the Far Stars.

The trilogy will be released in consecutive months, beginning on November 3, 2015.

Crimson Worlds Series

Marines (Crimson Worlds I)
The Cost of Victory (Crimson Worlds II)
A Little Rebellion (Crimson Worlds III)
The First Imperium (Crimson Worlds IV)
The Line Must Hold (Crimson Worlds V)
To Hell's Heart (Crimson Worlds VI)
The Shadow Legions(Crimson Worlds VII)
Even Legends Die (Crimson Worlds VIII)
The Fall (Crimson Worlds IX)
War Stories (Crimson World Prequels)

MERCS (Successors I)
The Prisoner of Eldaron (Successors II)
Into the Darkness (Refugees I)

Also By Jay Allan

The Dragon's Banner

Gehenna Dawn (Portal Wars I)
The Ten Thousand (Portal Wars II)
Homefront (Portal Wars III) - Jan. 2016

www.jayallanbooks.com